Praise for The Feud

...Heiberger establishes a classically gothic premise in a fabulous locale, which sits "nestled in rolling hills and ridges at the junction of two rural roads." ... a worthy supernatural whodunit. A macabre thriller with a message of tolerance and respect for nature. - Kirkus Reviews

... There are new twists at every few pages and the author's spacing of the horror elements in the book is quite apt. ... The author's treatment of other themes in the book like synergy with nature, superstitions, religious differences and courage is quite good. ... I rate the book 4 out of 4 for its riveting storyline and superb characterization. - onlinebookclub.org

The story gripped me tightly with the first sentence and wouldn't let go until it deliciously unwound... - Reader review on Amazon

The story flows, the emotions jump from word to word... as the reader you long for more, desire this story to never end. - Reader review on Amazon

I would recommend this book to anyone who loves a good mystery. - Reader review on Amazon

Frank Heiberger has done it again.. - Reader review on Amazon

This is a work of fiction. Any resemblance of any characters or places herein to actual people or places is purely coincidental.

All rights reserved.
Copyright © 2014, 2015 by Frank Heiberger.
This book may not be reproduced in whole or in part either electronically or physically by any means what-so-ever without permission.

ISBN-13: 978-1502814289
ISBN-10: 1502814285

Also by Frank Heiberger
Available through CreateSpace and Amazon
Entangled
Mr. Smith?
The Seventh Seal

Find the latest titles, obtain signed copies, and read excerpts at
www.authorfrankheiberger.com.

The Feud

Frank Heiberger

To the lovely Melissa Moore for her unwavering support and invaluable input on witchcraft.

Author's Note

The idea for this story came to me in a flash while I was driving. Within ten minutes ninety-percent of the story was in my head and wanting out. I spent an entire morning scribbling and typing up notes and partial dialog to get the bulk of it out.

It was one of those moments that astound you even as the person creating the story. There is no explaining where ideas come from, how they come to you or what triggers them. Suddenly you have one and you have to deal with it. Some, like this one, take control of you and demand telling.

I did a lot of reading and consulted with practicing witches to get their religion correct. As with any story, though, you often need to take some literary license to maintain the story. Any fault found in my depictions was not meant in malice. Please forgive any that exist within these pages. I have nothing but love and respect for all of the witches that I know.

Chapter 1
Getting Myself Into It

At first, I put it off to optical illusions, phosphenes, or form constants caused by fatigue and going from the light to dark, something with an underlying medical cause. It was the same thing every evening as I left the cellar workroom and shut off the stairwell lights. My eyes, adjusting to less light and tired from a long day's work, saw shadowy images. Malevolence stalked me from the gloom. I put it off to my imagination simply seeing things in the dark.

I'm a writer, you see. For sure, it was always non-fiction. I wrote research pieces and books about heraldry and other historical work. At the time, I was researching the lineage of a family that had commissioned me to transcribe their history. But deep within all writers is a story that always wants to come out. Some manage it. Most don't. I'd always been an imaginative and sensitive woman. It was even more natural for me.

Moreover, my inner tale had always been a ghost story. All of those heraldry books and histories, all of those characters from the past that I could see in my mind's eye as I wrote about them. It was a natural concept for me. So, when I would leave the records storeroom, I always imagined their presence and that I was catching glimpses of them as darker shadows moving within the natural shadows of the dingy, mostly unused cellar. And I felt the malice they held toward me and any mortal person coming within their realm.

The sensation would linger as I left at the end of the day, making my spine tingle. They were always there, at the edge of the darkness, ready to take their long, unsatisfied wrath out on me. But light pushed them back. They came to the edge of it, leaping forward into the new darkness as I switched off the basement hall light, then again to the top of the stairs as I switched off that light after ascending.

They could go no further. They were bound to the cellar. In the rest of the old manse, I was safe from them and their murderous intent. For some reason, I simply knew they wished for harm to come to me. Some nights, it was all I could do to keep myself from running up the steps and leaving the lights on as I fled the old building.

But I controlled myself and used the unprotected bulbs only when I needed them to pass through the hall and up the stairs. The wiring in the worn structure was fragile at best, still being knob and tube, as they called it, cloth and rubber insulated copper wire from the end of the nineteenth century tacked to exposed beams and running loosely up through the ancient lathe and plaster walls.

The old mansion had sat untouched and all but abandoned for decades because of it, and the legend that it was haunted, which only helped my active imagination. It had once been the mayor's residence, a perk of the office from earlier times and older ways. However, when the laws had demanded it be brought up to code, it had been retired from active public use for lack of funds in the town's coffers. The only upgrades ever done had been a single modern electric line to run the heater and air conditioning equipment required to preserve these records temporarily.

They had needed somewhere to put the old records, when the City Hall was renovated. The basement of the mayor's unused manor had been an obvious choice for the duration. Then, the City Hall renovations dragged on as tax income dropped and contractors demanded more than they had originally estimated. Years went by and the temporary solution was never undone. When all was said and done, they decided the archives were safe where they were and the new computers needed the finally renovated space.

When a fire at the church had necessitated moving parish records during repairs, the city leased some of the basement space. A few more improvements were made, such as sealing the old, stone walls and running better ductwork to keep away the dust and dampness. Temporary had been upgraded to indefinite. And it had no planned end. Selling the mansion was no longer necessary with the rent from the church and it was also impossible to find a buyer when one could build a replica for less than reconstruction would run.

But isn't that the way things always seem to work out, when a government sets something up as a temporary measure? The quick fix finds a way of becoming a permanent solution, even if not the best one. Perhaps despite not being the best one.

I had everything I needed in one place, though, city records and church records both. With my laptop, I was tied into the net and even this little town's newspaper had gone digital, including uploading the old microfiche images as PDFs. I could read back issues all the way to the end of the nineteenth century. It was really a great setup.

Everything was good, so long as I kept the lights on whenever I was not in the records room. I don't know what kept those spirits I felt in the darkness out of that room, perhaps the presence of the church records. Some of them had been consecrated, I thought. I wasn't sure. I only knew I was safe in that room.

Suffice to say it seemed like a wonderful job for a stormy, cool October in the Heartland. I did my research by day, logging and outlining what I needed into the computer, sometimes going for an interview with family members and local historians, and then headed back to my cozy room in the old B & B to do the rough drafting while I sipped some wine and noshed on cheese and olives, my weakness. It was heavenly.

So I'm sure you've already guessed that such wasn't the case at all; that what I'm describing was just the veneer which was about to peel away.

But let me not get ahead of myself. Let me tell this more as a story than as a stream of consciousness narrative.

August that year was boiling hot in the shade and the humidity dogged you twenty-four hours a day. There was no drying off after a shower. There was no drying off in front of your air conditioner. There was no drying off at all. The humidity was just too insistent. It clung to you everywhere throughout the day and night.

My old window unit AC was rattling ominously as I came in to my third floor, walkup apartment, myself half wheezing from the climb in the trapped, superheated air of the stairwell. Sweat oozed from every pore and my shoes stuck to my feet. My blouse was glued to my back. My hair hung in a limp, damp ponytail. This was one of the few times I knew I would be skipping my run. Hell, I wasn't even going to take a walk in this.

I propped my laptop up and switched it on in the full blast flow from the air conditioner. The old unit clanked and paused, but rattled on. I didn't know how long it was going to last. If it went, I wasn't sure what I would do. The place would quickly become too hot for the computer, much less for me, and a deadline was looming.

I sipped ice water and waited for the laptop to finish booting, praying my stuff would hold on just through the summer. I had a fair final payment coming from the history I was compiling on the old river merchants who were long forgotten by most people. The state had commissioned me to put together something nostalgically romantic to use in their tourism campaign. It wasn't much more than a thick chapter. However, it had been hard to research and the state had been relatively understanding in covering my expenses.

The fee was going to be enough to get me through the fall, but I was going to need to pick up some assignments from the local papers and magazines. Especially since my regular editor had rejected my last book proposal, thanks to cut backs in the down economy. People still read in bad times, of course, perhaps more. That didn't mean publishers weren't immune to the cutback fever, or that they wouldn't still be leery of projects that would be expensive to research. And, in bad times, everyone became a writer and flooded the houses with so much stuff that even good ideas weren't given the second look they deserved. I wasn't going to make it through the winter without something more.

I went straight to emails and saw that I had one marked urgent from my publisher. The subject line was *Duvall Family History - $$$*. That was enough to make me curious and begin fantasizing about a new air conditioner and bigger laptop. It was an email he had forwarded to me from a Robert Duvall-Richards of Willow Creek, Missouri. He had seen some of my past histories and liked my writing style. He was wondering if I would be interested in writing the history of their family, something his grandmother had always talked about, but never done.

My publisher had talked to the guy, but learned they only wanted a few copies printed. It wasn't anything they could make money on, but that was no reason I shouldn't look into it on a commission basis. In the industry, we call those vanity books. There's absolutely no chance of a commercial market for them, but the person or family wants their story memorialized forever in print and pays you to do that for them.

I felt a huge wave of relief come over me. I had gone from praying everything would work out to seeing a comfortable, even prosperous closeout of the year. Forget a new window unit. Now, I was thinking a new place to live, where the paint on the walls wasn't older than me and with central heat and air. I was excited even before calling the man. My imagination was suddenly running at full speed, with my hopes keeping pace, perhaps even yelling to catch up.

First, I calmed myself. I still needed to make the deal and sign the contract. That all had to happen yet. Measuring my breathing and my pace, I moved far enough from the air conditioner to be able to hear my phone call, but close enough to feel like I was still cooling off. So far, I think I had gotten myself down to the surface temperature on Venus.

I dialed the business number and a secretary answered.

Her drawl was thick when she said, "Hold on, please."

A few minutes later he answered, "Good afternoon, Miss Hills. Your publisher told me you were the person to write our story."

It was a dangerous voice. I could hear the smoothness in it and sense the uncompromising confidence behind it. Over the phone, my first impression of Mr. Robert Duvall-Richards was the big fish in a small pond type celebrity. I knew he was from an old moneyed family in a town where status mattered.

"That's very flattering, Mr. Richards," I replied.

"But you can call me India."

"And you can call me Robert," he returned as though it was some favor.

"Tell me what you're looking for," I prompted.

"It will be something of an eventual birthday present for my grandmother," he told me. "She's been talking about having a book written about our family for ages, even made a few notes for it. Our family has had an interesting run here in Willow Creek."

"So a complete history going back to the first Richards that arrived? How far back would we be going?" That affected the cost of a book for all the added research.

"Into the mid-1800s," he answered. "And it will be mostly Duvalls. My father married into the family and my mother hyphenated her name."

"There are no more Duvalls?" I wondered.

"No," he answered with a hint of wistfulness. "I'm the last of the line, which makes it time to write the book."

That sentiment did not play well in my mind. Surely he meant to perpetuate their line. But I let it go. It was too personal to get into on an initial phone consultation. Instead, I explained the process of writing a vanity book to him without using that industry term. I specifically pointed out that all I did was the research and writing, and that I would point him to some self-publishing resources for hard copies. You'd be surprised at how many people expected me to hand them a finished book. I made it clear a finished product was up to him to arrange. I would write it and he would pay me a fee for that alone. The fee I asked for was $18,000, what one normally gets for a celebrity bio these days. I was hoping to settle on $15,000, but no less than $12,000.

I was almost floored when he accepted the requested fee with only a few questions of what costs were included, and I accepted the job, starting at the beginning of October, when he returned from a business trip to the Orient.

I felt saved, and wary. I was looking a gift horse in the mouth, but I had always been made nervous when things went too well. Why I had that issue, who knows. It's not like I'd been taught by anyone. My parents had been realists. They had cautioned me never to rely on *magical thinking*. Why I should have taken that to the level of pessimism is still beyond me. I was just untrusting of Fate back then. She had never liked me. And she had surprises in store for me, once again, as you might imagine.

Willow Creek turned out to be a nice little town, if you trusted their website. It sat nestled in rolling hills and ridges at the junction of two rural roads, just gray lines if anything at all on an atlas. The Marais des Cygnes river flowed through it on its way to joining the Osage River, meandering along the northern edge of the Ozark Mountains. The main industry had changed over the years. Farming had always been a part of the mix. There had also been coal and lumber in the early years, and carpets and woolens after that. Currently, it was mostly corn and wheat and some leather processing. Logging still figured in, but to a lesser extent.

One of the largest industries turned out to be an importer of cheap goods from the Orient: Duvall Trading, owned and operated by my new employer. The family was rich and had been for generations. Mayors, judges, lawyers, doctors; you name it, the family had held those posts at one time or another. At thirty-five, Robert Duvall-Richards was the President of the Chamber of Commerce and a major Captain of Industry. Yes, the website actually used that old phrase. The family appeared to be still getting richer. Henry Richards, the father, had died a decade earlier of a heart attack at the age of fifty.

What caught my eye, though, was a different death in the local news from a week before. A woman working in the tannery had been killed in a freak accident. Somehow her hair had come loose from the net she wore and had gotten tangled up in machinery that rolls a large drum. Her head had literally been pulled off. Little more was said of it, which struck me as odd. It was such a hideous way to die. In a small, supposedly sleepy, town how could it not be a big deal?

Were such accidents always swept under the carpet? Or ignored? I could see where that would be, if the tannery was an artery for the town's life's blood. I wasn't naïve. If it meant the town survived economically, then the risks were taken. Money and paychecks make Utilitarians of us all.

Including me, or I would have turned and left after meeting Richards.

The estate was neither a sprawling ranch nor a replica of an English country manor. It was a typical suburban-looking structure, if thrice the size of any I'd seen before. There had to be forty or fifty rooms in it, I figured at first sight. A good, full minute passed as I drove down the entry lane from the county road to the turnaround before the columned front doors. Other than its size, it did not seem that pretentious in design or ornamentation. Or maybe it was just diminished by the gray skies and persistent drizzle falling in a constant hush on the trees just beginning to hint of autumnal colors.

A housekeeper met me at the door and showed me into a music room. I'll call it that because a full-sized, deep black grand piano stood at the far end along with a harp and cases for violins and larger instruments. This was probably where they held their cocktail parties.

Dust had been banished from the furniture and apparently every corner of the room. The hardwood floor sparkled and the piano glowed. The brass at the fireplace gleamed so warmly it seemed to heat the room without any flames. The room was kept in perfect shape. It was meant to impress the people they kept waiting, like me.

And then, Richards entered the room with a trotting pair of gorgeous Weimaraners and I swallowed the smirk I felt rise at Fate's first surprise. Richards was a handsome, confident man with a façade of humility though his eyes couldn't hold back the shine that vanity gave them. I suspected he was the best looking man in this little town, although he would have had a lot of competition in any big city. Naturally, he was considered to be a good catch and surely took advantage of it with the local ladies. In short, he was the kind of man I normally had disastrous relationships with.

I held my breath, willed my hand to be still and firm as I shook his, and probably missed my first and best chance at running.

"We're so excited to have you here," he told me as he directed me into a seat. The maid was waiting expectantly a few paces away and Richards indicated to her without motion as he asked, "Some refreshment, perhaps? Would you prefer cold or warm after your drive?"

The chill of fall was in the back of Mother Nature's mind that day. You knew it was coming soon, but the warmth of Indian summer lingered despite the light rain.

"I'll have cold, thank you," I chose and the smiling woman went off for iced tea. She seemed really eager to please the new guest, which was embarrassing. I'm just me, not someone famous or anything.

"I'm happy to be doing this book for your family," I said. Which was the truth; I liked getting paid. The first half of the fee was already in my bank account and my lodgings at the Bed and Breakfast were being directly paid by the family, as well. I had checked in before coming over to the estate. I can only describe it as quaintly posh, like VIP accommodations in the Victorian era, but with a mini-fridge and modern plumbing.

If you're getting the notion that I was a little on edge, I can tell you, you're right. I was. Like I said, when things are going well and looking good, I start peeking over my shoulder for the man coming to take it all away or at least make a muddle of things. Money in the bank, a simple family history, sweet lodgings; and then the man himself comes in as the first wrinkle. Yes, I was on edge. Because I'd learned just how certainly things are never simple.

"My grandmother will be along shortly," he told me, sitting on the sofa with one ankle up on the other knee. The dogs settled elegantly by the fireplace. "She plays bridge with her lady friends on Mondays. I never developed a liking for the game. It still surprises me to think that people still play it. I guess when you're in your eighties, though, an Xbox is not a good option."

He smiled, pleased to have a new audience for this joke. I smiled in return. If I had been more relaxed, perhaps it might have been humorous. Regardless, I tried some of my own irreverence.

"Are you sure they aren't secretly playing World of Warcraft?" I asked with a sly grin.

He smirked and I'll be damned if it wasn't sexy and made me wish I'd stayed mute. "I wouldn't put it past her," he said.

"Leads an interesting life, then?" I asked, going into interview mode. That was what I was here to write about, after all.

He gave a different smirk, considering the question. "I would imagine she has from some of the stories she tells," he said. "But, of course, she hasn't told me everything."

"No, I suppose she wouldn't," I replied.

The maid reappeared with a tray bearing two pitchers, dripping with condensation, and several tall, clear glasses. One pitcher held iced tea of rich red brown with perfect lemon slices floating in it. The other was the pale yellow of lemonade. Just the sight of it made me thirstier and I went for that without a second thought. For a moment, my mind went back to that hot, steamy August day we had first spoken.

And then, Grandma came in wearing a designer suit she must have gotten while traveling. I couldn't see a store making it in this borough by trying to sell such high end merchandise. Every small town has its place where the elite meet to socialize and be envied by the rest of the town. Monday Bridge was held in a corner of the country club's restaurant over after lunch coffee.

The smile on her face was cordial, if not entirely enthusiastic. She had her doubts about having someone poking into the family history, I saw. No wonder she had only thought about having the book written, but never done anything about it.

Like there were families that didn't have secrets and skeletons in the closet. It didn't matter to me. I wasn't here to write an exposé, just an embellished family tree in my elegant prose. Hey, not my words. Praise from my publisher, I'll have you know. I was going to have to get their matriarch here to see that and relax. I expected it would take a few meetings. I wasn't going to push her.

I stood up to shake her hand and stayed standing until she had taken a seat between me in an armchair and next to her grandson on the settee. It was entirely a position of power, and one I sensed the grandson only tolerated out of thin respect. Like I said, I'm familiar with his type. He was not pleased with taking a second seat, but family decorum required it.

I wanted to say something along the lines of thanking her for giving me the opportunity to write their history, or that I was really looking forward to it. My tongue was stilled by the scrutiny in her eyes. Platitudes did not go well when you were being judged critically.

"Thank you for having me," I said instead.

"You're glad to be here, I suppose," she replied, appraising my reaction.

"Of course," I told her. "It's good to be working."

"You enjoy your work?"

"Very much," I told her.

"And you do very well at it?"

"Not very well," I said. "But I've never had to do anything else."

Which was mainly because I'd banked my inheritance after Mom died and had been using it to make ends meet until car repairs had taken the last of it over the winter. I wasn't much making it on my writing income alone. Not just yet anyway. But this book for them was going to get me over the hump, I hoped.

"My grandson seems to think quite highly of your work."

"That's very flattering," I replied, although he had mostly just accepted the word of my publisher.

"Sounds like him." She gave his knee a squeeze and let out a sharp chuckle with a warm smile. Then, she patted his leg, as though this was an old, inside joke of theirs. Her next words were ones I'd heard so often, it was one of those phrases you wished you had a nickel for every time you heard it. "India Hills is such an unusual name. It sounds more like a place than a person."

"I know," I replied. "But at least it's memorable."

"It is at that," she agreed. "How long do you figure the work will take?"

"A few months to half a year," I told her. "It depends on how easy or not it is to organize all of the material and for you and everyone to tell me the story. I've done a little research already and your local newspaper is well-organized. That will be tremendously helpful. What I need to see yet are the archives for the historical records."

"Those are kept very well at the old mayor's mansion," Richards spoke up. "You will have the run of the place. I'll take you over there tomorrow."

"I'll meet you there so I have my car," I told him. I was not about to be escorted like a new employee at orientation. He saw the sense in it and nodded.

"The writing will go through the holidays, then?" Alice Duvall asked for clarification. I guessed she was estimating the expenses.

"I wouldn't be here for all of it," I said. "I will be doing a lot of researching and interviewing and transcribing to start. Once the outline and some rough drafting are done, I'll finish it up back in St. Louis."

"So what does a family history look like?" Mrs. Duvall asked, apparently satisfied with my answer.

"I brought a few examples of prior work," I told her and dug into my bag for the CD. She looked unsurely at it.

"I was never comfortable reading things on a computer," she said almost disdainfully.

"Yeah, it's not like curling up with good, old hard copy," I agreed. "But when you only print ten or twelve copies of something and all for the family, an Adobe copy is all I get."

"Adobe?"

"It's a software program," Richards told her and reached past her for the CD. "I'll print them for you, Nana."

"Thank you, Robert," she said and returned to me. "So, how do you go about writing a family history?"

"The family lineage can be traced easily enough through church and town hall records, and significant events will be chronicled in some detail in the local paper. For the most part, though, it's done through interviews, what people remember, what mementoes they may keep... things like that. I find that people recall different parts of their family's past. I piece it all together to come up with as clear and complete an account as I can."

"Who do you interview?"

"Family and friends," I said. "Sometimes local historians." Her eyebrows couldn't help twitching at that. "All through the process, as I build the history, we refine it together and fill in any holes or gaps that might still be there."

"You'll show it to us?" she asked, which was what she really wanted to know.

"Absolutely," I told her. "You're the inside source, Mrs. Duvall. I'll be working with you a lot. In fact, you may even wonder who's writing this book, me or you."

"But the final say is yours," she wanted to know.

"By that stage, we'll have gone over it so much together, it will be impossible to know who made the final call," I answered. "It's your book, your history. Focus on story. If we do this right, it will be lively and fun. Definitely, I do not want to write a simple documentary. A group of high school seniors could do that."

Which, ironically, was actually how I got my start with a summer job working for a history professor that needed factual accounts of local lore. The research was such a challenge and such a new world, and opening doors to new sources of information was a huge thrill to me. Even more exhilarating was finding a way to make it come alive with words from my own mind. There's a sense of power in knowing you can delight, even move others with just the words from your mind. I'd found my calling and had been writing for the twelve years since.

"That's not entirely what I expected," Mrs. Duvall remarked.

This always gave me a big smile and now was no different. "Well, it's the way I work. And when we're done, I'll give you some contacts at different publishing houses that do small runs for you to choose. These days, with computers and laser printers, popping off even one book is not that expensive. Though I imagine you'll get a few dozen for everyone to have a copy, including the library."

"We'll see about that when the time comes," Mrs. Duvall said. "When will we begin?"

"Tomorrow," I told her. "I'd like to get settled in this evening and then spend tomorrow morning familiarizing myself with the archives. After that, we'll start with some general interviews, starting with you, if that's okay."

"That will be fine," she said. "I have an appointment right after lunch, so perhaps tomorrow afternoon around 2:30 or 3:00."

"Here?"

"Yes. And we can look at the albums and some of

the old records we have here."

"Perfect," I said. I wasn't sure that would be entirely comfortable, but letting her hover over me for a few days wasn't going to hurt. "I'll be here."

"Very good," she said and rose, so we all did, including, amusingly, the dogs. "And now, if you'll excuse me, I need to rest and refresh myself for this evening's dinner with the mayor. They want money for something or other again, so I want to be rested and sharp." She gave a conspiratorial grin and wink and I smiled without comment. "Very nice meeting you. And tomorrow we get to work."

"Yes, indeed."

She left us without looking the least bit in need of resting and refreshing herself. I remained on my feet. All that was left to determine was when to meet Richards at the old mayor's mansion. I wanted a bath and dinner and to learn a little about the property, perhaps take a walk, or a run, by if it was close to my lodgings.

"When should I be there tomorrow?" I asked.

"Would eight be good?"

"A little early," I told him. I was determined not to spend any more time with him than necessary. "Are there hours for the mansion?"

"Regular business hours are nine to five," he answered. "But you're being granted special permission to come and go as you please. I'm getting a key from the mayor tonight."

That would make things easier, I thought. No waiting until the next day to verify dates and what-not I learned in interviews. Perfect.

"Nine o'clock, then," I told him. "See you then." And I stuck out my hand to shake his, which he did, but not in an entirely business-like manner. He couldn't keep himself from going for the charm. It was too much a part of him.

He walked me to the front door and, of course, set a

hand on my shoulder in a friendly gesture as I went out. It angered me a little, but I let it go as it was just him. And that was probably when I missed my second good chance to run.

The inn keepers were David and Marianne Wells, a retired couple who hadn't wanted to move from Willow Creek, but who had always traveled and loved meeting new people. So, when the income became fixed and travel a rare option, they opened up the empty nest and brought the traveling public to them, what little came this way. I fell for them instantly.

The Willow's Wells, as they called the place, was totally Victorian; wood clapboards in a somehow ruddy gray, gingerbread trim, spired tip to a turret that housed the wide, spiraling stairs, and a deep, wrap-around porch with swings and rockers. We sat there on that first afternoon, as the rain paused and let a few warm rays of sunshine through, and drank steaming Jasmine tea, Marianne's favorite.

"Well, dear," she said at one point, "I'm sure you don't know what you're getting yourself into."

"Now, Marianne," her husband began in mild reproach, but she waved him silent.

"She has the right to know," was her reasoning. "Know?" I asked. What in the world could I be getting myself into in this sleepy little town? Was there really a meth lab in that old mansion or something? "Know what?"

Marianne Wells leaned forward from the swing and gave me a serious stare. "That mansion is haunted."

"Haunted?" I think I kept any laughter out of my voice to keep from insulting my hosts. It wasn't something you take seriously when you hear it. I had a writer's belief in ghosts, as I've already mentioned. However, being told I was going to be in a place that was actually and truly haunted was not something I could accept as true. Ghosts were existent to me as fictional concepts. In the real world, I didn't much believe it. But Marianne did, so I politely listened.

"The male ghosts of the Duvall family," she told me. "All of the men for the last century or so. Robert is the only male descendant left and he knows it's his fate. I'll bet anything he's hoping you'll find the key to release him."

"I see," I said by way of giving myself time to think. There was no sense to be seen yet. "All of the male Duvalls become ghosts in the old mayor's mansion?"

"Yes," said Marianne. "Back when it all started, the mayor was a Duvall. The Duvalls have always been one of *the* families in this town, as you probably know. And now, whenever the men pass on, their souls remain trapped in the mansion."

"Why would that be?"

"The witches did it."

At which I involuntarily blinked and gave a brief shake of my head. My mind simply paused for a few seconds. From the plausibility of ghosts to the improbability of witchcraft; Marianne Wells, I was thinking, had spent way too much time in this little town, despite her world travels.

"Now, Marianne," David spoke up. "You can't expect an educated woman like Ms. Hills, a big city woman, to believe in witches and ghosts. Hell, I grew up here and I don't think it's anything to talk of. Those ladies are just a little wacky, is all."

"Well, David Wells, you've seen the evidence yourself," she said. "You just don't want to believe it. But I do. And I'm going to tell Ms. Hills, a fine, open-minded young woman, all about it."

I tried to suppress a smile. This had the ring of an old argument that went on and on and over and over. How many guests had she told and he'd rolled his eyes at her story was anybody's guess. There was no animosity in the argument. It was apparent they'd been together way too long to get angry at each other anymore. This was just a part of their routine now and I found it somewhat entertaining.

"Anyway," she returned to the tale. "The story is that the Duvalls of the time did something to slight the witches, and in return the witches cast a spell that bound their souls to the cellar of the mayor's old mansion. And it's going to stay that way until a male member of the family atones for what happened to them."

"Oh that ain't the case at all," said David. "We had that Thomas Duvall, when he was the judge back in the fifties, toss all of those claims against them, when people still believed in that bunk and thought they were being made ill by their spells." He turned to face me and added, "Turned out to be the chemicals they were using in the tannery back then. They were being dumped into the river and making everyone sick. People blamed the witches, when it was really the Berkmans, the folks that own the tannery. Thomas made them clean up their act, so to speak, and folks eventually got better. He cleared the witches. If that ain't atoning, I don't know what is."

"Well, they're stuck here until something happens," Marianne replied. "I don't know what it is for sure. Atoning was just one speculation." She gave her husband a sideways glance of one-ups-man-ship. "That's just the way it is. The mansion is haunted and they aren't happy spirits, and we have an active, secretive coven of witches."

"Secretive?" he asked. "Their store is out on the county road just north of town."

"You never know what a witch wants," Marianne cautioned. "Never. And you probably never want to find out."

David looked at me and spoke as though in an aside to the audience. "What they want is to make a living and believe their own beliefs. They's said as much hundreds of times."

"That's what they *say*," Marianne noted. The witches were secretive and conspiratorial against the rest of us. They may not have been meaning to do harm, but they certainly weren't aspiring to altruism. So she believed and nothing was going to shake her from that viewpoint. "You'd be doing yourself a favor to stay well away from them women."

"I probably won't need to have anything to do with them," I replied to placate her, although part of my mind was already framing how to approach this issue with Richards. This was a part of their history and so the job required me to ask. I just didn't know if it was a sore point with the family or not. It didn't seem like anything that would be. Witches and ghosts? Come on. Who's going to take that seriously in the twenty-first century?

But you never knew with people and families.

I'd once made the observation that there was nothing blue in someone's house. You would have thought I'd declared I was Satan himself come to defile the women and eat the children from the way they reacted. How was I to know the person believed the color blue was bad luck? I'd never heard of color phobias before. Have you? Google it. Cyanophobia is the fear of the color blue. Xanthophobia is the fear of the color yellow. Wild stuff.

So you never knew. You just never could.

"Well you just be careful in that old place," Marianne admonished in all seriousness. "Whether you want to believe it or not, they are there and they aren't happy."

"Well, I expect I'll only be there during the day," I replied to put her mind at ease. I couldn't generate even the slightest apprehension over something like ghosts. "By the time it's night, I'll be back here writing up what I learned during the day."

"Honey, ghosts are around all the time, not just at night," she warned me and I confess the tone of her voice and stern light in her eyes gave me an instant of fear, but it passed as quickly as it came.

"Well, I can't see why they'd bother me," I told her. "If anything, I'd be on their side, since the family hired me."

Marianne didn't seem much certain of that, although she did purse her mouth and give the thought some consideration. "I hope so," was all she could say about it.

"If they're so bad," I wondered, "why hasn't anyone tried to get rid of them or get the witches to release them?"

"The witches claim it wasn't them," Marianne explained. "They say they had nothing to do with it and couldn't have done so if they wanted. Said they wouldn't know how."

Not sure of what I'd heard, I asked, "I'm sorry?"

"They ain't *those* kinds of witches," David said, which was only more confusing.

"They're earth witches or green witches," Marianne clarified. "Or so they say."

"What's that?" I asked, really getting lost now. There were different kinds of witches? "Something like the difference between green belts and black belts in karate?"

"No. It's a different kind of magic, they claim," she answered. "They say their magic is only nurturing and healing."

"So, what causes the ghosts to be there then?"

"It's just stories," David told me. "People like to believe in them. And no one has ever tried to get rid of them for two reasons. One, there's nothing to get rid of. And two, it brings in some tourism money. There's another paranormal researcher over there right now. Some professor from the university in Ames."

"Really?" This was curious. A scientist looking for proof? This was actually starting to feel like a very colorful side note to the book.

"Kind of an odd name," David said. "Something

Willis."

"Sandoval Willis," Marianne noted. "Kind of an odd person, too. But I guess that's what you'd expect. He's staying down at the River Lodge, another Bed and Breakfast down in Nevada. Don't know why he didn't want to stay here in town."

"Enough of this, though," David finally declared. "Ms. Hills, you're welcome to join us for supper tonight. We have a nice roast in the oven."

"Thank you! I'd love that." I meant that, too. Despite Mrs. Wells' choice of initial conversations, I truly liked them and wanted to spend some time getting to know them better. Learning a town and adding its story would give a lot of color to the Duvall history. But mostly, I just liked them. "I need to go for a run to work out the kinks from the long drive. How much time do I have?"

"Oh, hour and a half, I guess," he said, looking to his wife for confirmation.

"I can keep a roast warm and moist for hours," she said. "How much time do you want?"

"An hour and a half will be plenty," I told them, especially as dusk was approaching and the night promised to be heavy and soon.

Maps of small towns are usually to be found in their local phone books. Willow Creek was no different and it was almost too simple to learn. If you ever got lost, you found one of three streets that always led you to the river. From there it was always only a short distance to the town center, from where it was easy to find your way back to anywhere. And since the town was built in the hills that climbed gently up from the river basin, as long as you were going down instead of up the slopes, you were headed for the center of town.

The old mayor's mansion was about a mile from the Willow's Wells. I was barely warmed up when I found it, alone almost in the middle of Creek Street as the lots on either side had been left empty. The weak and widely-spaced streetlights weren't of much use in the deepening twilight. I had to train my eyes on the darkest spots to accustom them to the gloom to see much of anything. It hardly seemed worth the effort to have the lights; I was so used to the brighter ones of the city.

The lawn seemed tended and the flower beds and shrubs looked neat, although a stray weed poked from the evergreens and the grass was scraggily and pocked with dandelions in places. It was maintained, but not with any sense of priority. The house itself was something out of a movie. In the twilight, with storms brewing in the west and thunder threatening from the distance, I could understand why people believed it was haunted. It had all the trappings; gables, Victorian era trimmings, the short iron rails of a widow's walk along the roof, loose shingles and worn clapboards. It was perfectly stately and in advanced disrepair.

It made for a classic haunted house and I wondered why the city hadn't taken advantage of that. It would have made for the perfect attraction; given it was only weeks until Halloween. It was a perfect money maker and it was surprising the city wasn't using it.

But then I recalled what I'd read on the internet. How it was closed rather than brought up to code and had basically become unsafe to some extent. The reports had been sketchy on details, simply saying it had been closed to tours a few years back. To see it now in the darkness, I got a clearer feeling for the reports. I got a feeling that maybe it wasn't going to be all that safe for my own purposes, much less trying to make a haunted house of it.

Yet, the spooky ambience was fantastic. It was inspiring in a way and I decided then to keep a diary of the job separately from my history of the Duvalls. That was going to make for an interesting story of its own, perhaps give me a chance to do some writing of a more creative nature. Practice for when I finally wrote my novel, perhaps even the basis for it.

Little did I know at the time, as you're probably already thinking.

Chapter 2
The Mansion in the Morning

In the daylight of the next morning, the structure lost its creepiness. Especially after a soaking from a thunderstorm the night before, its paint-starved clapboards and warped porch planks made it more run down and shabby than scary. There were more dandelions than grass in several places under the old oak trees and more weeds amongst the flowers than had been visible in the dark.

I could clearly see the depressions forming in the sagging roof that the twilight had concealed. The left end of the veranda angled toward the ground. The place was in danger of collapsing at a minimum, I thought, and one wrong step anywhere would see you going through the porch floor and, perhaps, the floors in many of the rooms.

The town's indefinite solution to their records storage problem was going to have a definite end in the very near future. They must have known that and been operating on wishful thinking that it was going to be later rather than sooner. Because no one who could have moved the records anywhere else would have left them there. Surely, there was an old building somewhere sound enough and just as cheap to lease as to keep this place standing. I almost felt afraid to go into it.

Apparently, I was the only one. As Richards, in a perfectly fashionable and seamlessly tailored pin striped blue suit waited for me in the open front door. I went up and he ushered me into the musty front parlor, where we were met by three very important men. Two of them were easy to identify. The sheriff was a heavy set man wearing a brown uniform and typical trooper style hat. His nasty-looking sidearm jutted out from a belt at his hip as obviously and ridiculously as did the extra thirty or so pounds around his middle. I instantly got the impression he had the job as a crony of Richards or the mayor.

The second easily-identified man was the local minister, obvious by the gold cross hanging from his neck. It was not as large as one might have expected, but I got the feeling he was trying not to look so pretentious and was just as corruptible as the rest of them. It was embarrassing that I got such a negative impression on first sight, but I did. And I had no reason to feel that way.

The third man was tall and relatively good looking, dressed in a simple gray suit. In the company of these other men, I made the assumption he was the mayor, because that completed the triumvirate come to meet me, or rather come to have a look at the invited invader and decide for themselves about her.

Of course, I don't normally meet people with such a negative attitude about them. Particularly people I have no knowledge of or any reason to think poorly of. But when I first saw these men that morning, those thoughts swirled through my head. I couldn't have told you why that was at the time.

I put on my professional smile and shook hands with them in turn as Richards introduced them: Mayor John Baker, Pastor Joe Cogdon of Willow Creek Baptist Church and Sheriff Gus Levinson.

As I committed their names to memory, the desire to come up with snide ways of recalling them rose within me. I ignored it, but felt bad at having the uncalled for urge. They were being pleasant to me, even cordial, and Mayor Baker was definitely welcoming. However, I couldn't shake the suspicious attitude that had come over me.

The mayor laid down some ground rules for me about the mansion. "As you can see, it's not in the best of condition, so please be careful if you walk about it.

Especially upstairs, I'd walk very gingerly and carefully, if I were you. You have the run of the place and taking photos is okay. Although, I'd recommend you stick mostly to the records room downstairs."

"I expect I will spend most of my time there," I replied. It wasn't an admonition or a warning, but it felt like a rather strict recommendation.

"The alarm code is 3434. If you're the last to leave at night, please set it," the mayor continued, then indicated a skinny, elderly gentleman in overalls who stood aside from them. "Sam here, is the caretaker and usually leaves at five. I imagine you may stay somewhat later than that on occasion. The alarm is not so much to protect the building from theft as it is to protect us from being sued by a burglar falling through the floor somewhere."

Which was true enough, I thought, although I didn't have a response.

The sheriff spoke up in a deep voice full of southern accent. "I wouldn't be staying too late, though, if I were you. And make sure you park right out front under the light. Stay in the well-lit areas. I'm not sure how you'll react to this, but the reason we're saying these things is because a woman was murdered down by the riverbank last night."

And that snapped me back to normal. The negative thoughts fled from the shock of his words. "What? When?"

Was it while I was out running? Alone?

"We aren't sure exactly yet when it happened," Sheriff Levinson told me. "The woman was last seen alive around six o'clock." Which *was* when I was out running. "So, if you are going to be here late, I'd feel better if you'd call us and have one of the deputies be here when you go out to your car. If you walk, we'll escort you back to the Wells' place."

"I appreciate that, Sheriff," I told him genuinely. "How did it happen?"

"She was out gathering waterside plants for herbal medicines," he answered. "Someone came along and decapitated her. We're waiting on the coroner's tests to find out if he did anything else to her first, if you know what I mean."

"Decapitated?" I felt cold and a little weak. The warm, comfort food breakfast the Wells' had provided was suddenly a rock in my queasy stomach. Decapitated. The sick bastard had cut her head off. I couldn't think of a more horrible way to die, than one in which you knew you had been killed and had no hope before death actually found you. How long did your head live after being cut off? Five minutes was it? I know there were accounts of people winking after being executed on the guillotine. So I knew you remained conscious for some time. It was awful to contemplate. Richards' hands on my shoulders brought me back to the moment. I had closed my eyes thinking about it. They must have thought I was getting dizzy.

"I'm sorry, my dear," Pastor Cogdon was saying. "Perhaps we shouldn't have dropped it on you like that. But we felt you should know."

"Yes, thank you," I replied. "I'm okay. It's just a horrifying thought to have your head cut off. I mean, you don't die right away."

"Yes, most dreadful," said Pastor Joe in a very quaint way.

"But you get the point," the sheriff added. "I'm sorry that was rough, but I wanted to be sure I drove it in. Don't be running around alone late at night. I understand you like to go jogging, so please keep it to daylight or find someone to go with you."

"I've got a fitness room at the house," Richards offered, as though his thirty room place was a simple house. "You're welcome to it any time. We have a new treadmill I think would work for you."

"Thanks," I said, although I ran for relaxation of my mind as much as for exercise. I couldn't see myself doing that with him around, probably joining me during my workout. I wasn't about to share my personal time with him. The wall was going to stay up.

"So despite that sour note," Mayor Baker said with a wry smile, "welcome to Willow Creek and good luck with your work. We hope you'll enjoy staying with us for a while."

"Thank you. I'm sure I will," I said, but I was suddenly filled with curiosity about the woman. "Who was she? Why was she gathering plants by the river?"

"One of the witches," the sheriff replied. "They use wild plants in their potions and soaps and all."

"Wiccans," the mayor corrected him. "Witches has a bad sound to it. They prefer to be called Wiccans, so that's what we will call them."

The perfect politician; politically correct to the end, even about people he obviously disapproved of. But they had a business, David Wells had said. That meant tax revenue or at least money coming into the local economy. Willow Creek definitely needed that.

"We'll leave you to your work now," Mayor Baker said. "Feel free to call on any of us if you should need help with anything."

"Thank you. I will," I replied and the three of them shook my hand and filed out, leaving me with Richards and Sam, the aging caretaker.

"The basement is this way," Richards said and strode ahead to lead the way. I would have been happy to have had Sam show me around, but Richards was already through the open door and walking down the stairs.

I followed with Sam in my wake to the cavernous feeling cellar. Not because it was large, but because it was all old stone with a hard-packed floor. The hallway going right and left gave you the sensation of being in a mine tunnel; rock walls, dirt underfoot and a ceiling held up by rough beams and boards overhead. An iron door was in the stone wall in front of me. The hallways turned toward the back at each side, isolating a central room.

Richards led to the right, where a very new-looking, aluminum door to a room along the outside walls sat in a solid frame in the stone bulwarks at the corner of the hall.

The portal opened inward to the most out of place, clean room it could have. It was like entering a secret headquarters buried in a mountain somewhere. The floor was polished tile. The plastered walls were painted bright white. An acoustical tile ceiling hung seven feet up. The air was fresh and cool. I could feel the slightest of breezes as it circulated. It was almost as though we should have gone through decontamination and donned clean suits before entering. The rest of the place was coming apart, but this room was immaculate.

"The genealogy records are all over here," Richards said as he gave me a brief tour of the room. It had once been two rooms, the wine cellar and the cold storage room where blocks of ice taken from the river were used to keep food cold late into the hot summers. A new opening through the old stone wall joined them. It was, as I said at the beginning, a sweet setup. Almost everything I was going to need was right here in one place and I was likely to have it to myself almost, if not all, of the time.

"Okay then," I said to get him out of my hair. "Best leave me to it so I can get started."

"Right," he replied, clearly hoping he could have been of more help and continually impressive. "See you later at the house then."

"Two-thirty," I replied, the time I was to meet with Alice Duvall to begin reviewing their private files.

He shook my hand, taking a little too long to do so again, and headed out after giving me one of his best smiles. And damn me for having some reaction to it. This was not good. It just wasn't.

Sam started to leave the room, but I waved him over. I wanted to get a tour of the mansion, too, and see what he could tell me about the town and the people. I had a suspicion that he was in a position to have heard and seen a lot over the years. And I wasn't getting that hostile sense about him that I had on meeting the others.

"Hi Sam," I said offering my hand for him to shake. "India Hills."

"Sam Bassett," he replied, shaking back. "That's a distinctive name."

"Sounds more like a place than a person, I know," I repeated myself. "How long have you been taking care of this place?"

"About thirty years now," he answered. "Used to be three of us at one time, when they gave tours and had events here. Once the state pulled their funding because of its condition, they cut it back to just me. But it won't be long before there's no need for me either. The place can't stand much longer."

"Is it that bad?"

"Creaks the devil all day and night in stormy weather," he said. "And in the winter with a load of snow on the roof..." He waved a hand at the air to say the groaning was beyond worse. "I don't like even being in here then. Figure I'll just retire, when it finally comes down."

"Aren't there plans to move the records then?"

He snorted a laugh. "You must not know a lot about politicians. Of course not. They'll wait for the roof to cave in and then rush and find someplace, and it will be a location belonging to someone connected to them because they can get away with setting that up in an emergency, but not as a process that needs bidding and voting on."

"And that temporary solution will become indefinite and permanent," I concluded. I wasn't that naïve. I was just trying to engage him in conversation before asking too many questions.

He smiled. "So you do get it?"

I nodded. "What can you tell me about the place?"

"About the haunting, you mean?"

"I mean, in general," I replied. It was clear he had an opinion. "Do you believe it's haunted?"

"I know it's haunted," he answered with no doubt at all. "They move my mops and things from time to time."

"Excuse me," came out of my mouth before my brain caught up to it. A pang of panic hit me at sounding condescending.

"That's something ghosts do," he said. "I talked to folks at the universities when it started happening. At first, we thought it was the other guys playing pranks on each other. Then, we got to realize that it wasn't and we looked for answers. That new researcher's got his cameras watching the areas where it happens a lot. Said some spirits like to mess with you."

"Mess with you?"

"Jokesters in life, jokesters in death," he said. "People's bodies die, but their essence remains the same is what we're told."

"I've never heard that."

"Neither had we," Sam replied with a grin. "Learned a lot about ghosts over the years. Mostly that no one is really sure what they are. People here see shadows and what not. I think it's more the way the lights move through the trees outside playing through the windows. I've never seen anything I can't explain. Except my mops and all getting moved to the other side of the room. I even took pictures on a digital camera so I could see where I left stuff, in case I was just forgetting. But nope, the stuff was really moved."

"That's wild." I didn't know what else to say and it surely was.

"Yeah, but they ain't never bothered me none," Sam said. "They play little jokes on me, but leave me alone otherwise."

"I was told they were angry."

"Perhaps," Sam said. "Like I told you, they don't bug me. Guess it's because I look after their place."

"But they bug other people?"

"They make you feel things, is what I'm told," Sam replied.

"Like what?"

He shrugged. "Anxiety. Anger. Paranoia. Things like that."

Things like making you immediately negative on

meeting people, I wondered. No, that was foolish. Wasn't it?

"Not in here, though," Sam said. "When this place was built and the church brought their records in, the bishop came in and blessed the room. So they can't come in here."

That might explain why I wasn't hostile toward Sam when I had the chance to introduce myself. But again, come on. That was silly thinking.

"Is it safe to wander about the house?" I asked. "I mean, physically."

"Sure," he answered. "For the most part. It's the roof that's in really bad shape. But if the floor feels spongy, I'd just as soon you didn't walk on that part of it."

"Rest assured I won't," I promised sincerely. That was all I'd need; getting myself stuck between two floors with my legs dangling from the ceiling in one and the rest of me squirming to get free above. With my luck, it would be a Friday night and I'd be trapped until Sam came to work on Monday morning.

Told you I was imaginative. My mind was always seeing nutty stuff like that.

"Mind giving me a tour?" I asked and Sam agreed readily with a smile.

"Going to be nice to have someone else around for a while," he said.

"They tell you why I'm here?" I wondered.

"No. Just that you'd be a month or so."

"I'm writing the Duvall family history," I told him. No one had said it was a secret, and my upcoming interviews with people would certainly get the word out.

"Is that so?" Sam replied.

"Yes. Have anything you can tell me? Don't worry, if it's bad. I know how to phrase things."

He gave a short laugh. "All I know is they's one of the richest families around here and have been for a very long time."

"And the patriarchs are the ghosts in this building?"

He gave me a sideways glance. "You already heard about that, huh? Well, yeah, that's what people say. How they know is a good question."

"That is a good question," I suddenly realized. "How do they know? Do you know that?"

"I heard it was because one of the widows went mad and used to come here to talk with her dead husband all the time. She was some sort of medium, people said. I don't know about that. I think she was just off her rocker because he died so young."

"I heard Robert Richards' father died at fifty."

"They all die young. Robert's father lived about the longest of any of them. Started a rumor that the curse had been lifted."

"Do you believe there's a curse on them?" I asked.

He shrugged. "What else would you call having the male spirits condemned to spending eternity in this building?"

"Good point," I conceded. "Do you think it was the witches? I guess I should say Wiccans."

He shook his head. "Not if the old ones was anything like the ones we got now," he told me with certainty. "I use their teas for my stomach and back aches often. There isn't a bad bone in the lot of them."

"You heard that one of them was murdered last night?"

"Not until the sheriff said something this morning." He shook his head. "It's a shame. They's all nice people. Not a bad bone among them. Don't believe in causing trouble."

"Well that's at odds with the story, then."

"Because the story ain't true," Sam told me. "There's something in this basement and maybe it's the Duvall men. Maybe it isn't. Maybe it's an old mayor that never wanted to give up power or is stuck here as his purgatory for the things a politician does. I don't know. So long as all it ever does is move my brooms, I don't really care who it is."

And that made me laugh, and push away the malevolence that was trying to creep back into me as we had ascended the stairs.

"Okay, so this was the main room where they held the receptions and the parties," he began telling me as he led me on a tour of what turned out to be a colorful old building, despite its creepy atmosphere.

Chapter 3
Getting to Work

The rest of the day passed much as I had expected. The first task was to begin tracing the family line back as far as the church records would take me, which seemed like it would be a couple of centuries at least. Birth certificates and county records were good for the twentieth century. But earlier than that, the church was usually the better source, particularly in areas where midwives were common. The church would have been the only place the birth was documented, usually as part of the baptismal record.

This would take days. It kept me busy until about one p.m. that first afternoon, when the Wells' hearty breakfast finally wore off. It's really quite amazing how many calories can be burned by mental energy. My stomach growled as I set out in search of a reasonable local lunch place Sam had suggested, before keeping my appointment with Alice Duvall.

It was a very sweet setup with my lodgings covered and getting paid what I'd initially asked for in hopes of actually getting two-thirds of it. Things were looking better. A nicer apartment was still in my plans for when I got back home to St. Louis. I couldn't consider myself out of the woods financially just yet. My car was old. My computer was even older. A lot of my clothes and furniture were getting to a worn out stage. It would still only take one bad year to ruin me completely and with rejection letters from three more publishers for my latest book proposal, that bad year was still looming over me like the

Sword of Damocles. Google that, if you don't know the reference.

Even with the good pay and most of my expenses covered, I still felt the need to stretch my funds as far as I could. Clearly, I still wasn't in a position to be in charge of my own fate. Not just yet.

The heavens opened up again as I arrived at the Duvall-Richards mansion a little early. This time, the rain came down in absolute sheets and I waited it out in my car for several minutes until the maid came out to get me under an umbrella big enough to go over a bistro table. Still, the lower six inches of my slacks got soaked from the spray in our short dash to the house.

"Thanks," I said and then realized embarrassingly I didn't remember her name or if Richards had even mentioned it.

"Agnes," she said. A last name was not important, I sensed in her tone. The rich and powerful only needed to know your first name to feign deference in using it.

"Thanks, Agnes," I said. "I haven't seen it rain like that in ages."

"We have here, Miss Hills," she said. "All too much. The river's already partially sandbagged. Mr. Richards is overseeing the delivery of several thousand more in case this keeps up."

It may sound odd in these drought years, but a few years back these western Missouri towns had seen a lot of flooding. You might have thought it had been a one-time event, but it wasn't. They sandbagged before it got bad this time.

"Sounds like you could use a few small levees," I remarked.

"They're trying," Agnes said. "Environmental impact and costs and all that have them bickering and horse-trading in the capitol."

I grunted my opinion. Wasn't that always the way? In the meantime, short another major disaster, nothing changed other than how the locals got things done.

"Mrs. Duvall is in the library," Agnes told me. "I'll show you in."

It was an actual library. A room three times the size of my living room at home with built-in bookshelves lining all of the walls and jammed with hard bound books of all kinds and ages. It was the collection of generations of educated people and avid readers. Their value alone undoubtedly dwarfed what they were paying me.

Alice Duvall sat at a large folding table that had been brought in for the purpose of working on the book. It had to have been, because it was totally out of place in the center of the room and the chairs were pushed too close to the shelves. I saw the indentations in the burgundy Oriental rug from where the chairs usually sat. Banker's storage boxes sat on the table and under it. The family's private records. A lot of them. The dogs, lying at either side of the table, seemed to be guarding them.

"There you are, dear," Mrs. Duvall greeted me warmly. "You haven't washed away in the storm."

"Does it always rain this hard here?"

"It never used to," she told me. "But with this global warming thing or whatever it is making the climate change, it's been brutal for years now."

"Agnes said Robert was arranging for more sandbags."

"Yes. He's on the County Emergency Board. With this recent series of storms, they've been sandbagging the lower areas and already need to add more. The river hit flood stage in those low areas twice already. Thank God they had the sandbags down ahead of time."

"Why don't you leave them down, if it's that constant?" I asked, scratching the head of the nearest dog as he greeted me.

"Can't," Mrs. Duvall told me. "The environmentalists are already screaming about upsetting the natural flooding of the land, but mostly the sacks rot out and break and the bags become useless. So you have to pick them up and put the sand into new ones every year."

"Sounds expensive."

"Jobs for some people, though," she said, and I thought that was what I should have thought first, not that it was expensive. One for Alice Duvall, none for me, I thought to humor myself. "How about a tour of the house first before we get down to work?" she offered.

"Sure," I said. I wanted one for background and getting a better feel of how the family lived. So the offer saved me the trouble of asking.

Her open and friendly manner was also taking me a little off guard. I didn't sense anything false in it. It was as though she had slept on it and come to the decision that it was going to be rather fun and damn it, she had been wanting and talking about it doing it for years. So what had she been reluctant about yesterday? That was the sense I was getting.

It was as grand a place as was to be expected. Much of the furniture was antique; family owned for generations. The rest of it must have come at prices I didn't want to imagine. I wouldn't say I got a sense that they lived opulently. But their idea of comfort was levels above mine and most everyone I knew. None of this made me uncomfortable or surprised me. I was familiar with families of their status from many past jobs.

The dogs' names, by the way, were silly; Ben and Jerry. It seemed Richards had a thing for ice cream. He arrived about the time we were finished admiring the original oil paintings and other artwork in the downstairs hallway. He came in through the kitchen from the attached garage, his raincoat as dry and clean as the day he bought it. He hadn't been out in the weather for even a split second. He hung the coat in the back as he called to us that he had one last call to make and then he'd be free, before he disappeared into a room off the kitchen.

"Home office?" I asked.

Mrs. Duvall nodded. "His private sanctuary," she told me and immediately led me to it.

Richards was already finishing the call, absently

petting a happy-looking Jerry. I caught the drift that he had been following up on something that had already been taken care of.

I was somewhat prepared for the room, but not entirely. I knew the family business dealt with importing Oriental goods. Yet, the juxtaposition of the Orient with the Victorian era furniture, parlor palms, ivy and ferns was at the edge of overwhelming. There was so much of it all but falling over the next bit. Massive, mahogany bookshelves were crammed with classic tomes and littered with cork sculptures and ceramic figurines. A deep, red oriental rug covered the deeply polished hardwood floor and was permanently indented by the legs of the heavy wooden desk and two armchairs in front of it. I wondered if those chairs were ever used or merely moved for vacuuming.

The most striking feature was the wax figure in the corner, all decked out in period armor and sporting a long, Mongol-esque mustache. That was quite the crowning touch, I thought, until I took a closer look and realized this was no simple costume piece. There was an old mark on the side, as though the wearer had taken a hit.

"That's my Chinese Captain's suit of armor," Richards proudly announced as he hung up. "I bought it many years ago on one of my best trips. The armor is made up of thousands of over-lapping leather hemispheres that were lacquered over and over until they were hard as a rock, yet still lightweight. The sword, however, was a different matter."

The figure was holding a sword with both hands atop the pummel and the point down into a depression in the stand. It glistened brightly and the edges gave off no reflection. It was razor sharp.

"It took me years to get that the weapon," he told me. "Years of asking, begging, and making the right payments. I finally got it this last trip. It's only been there for two weeks now, but it makes all the difference in the presentation. It was just a costume before. Now, it's a suit of armor worthy of an officer."

"What dynasty is it from?"

"Han. During the building of the Great Wall. Its original owner had to be quite pleased with it," he said. "They told me the mark along the side was from a spear, most likely, that would have gutted him if not for the armor. They offered to restore it, but I wanted to keep the original history of it."

"I would," I truthfully replied. But then, I'm an historian. So of course I would.

"And still sharp as ever," he stepped over and dragged a piece of paper along the weapon's edge. The sheet's own weight was enough for the blade to slice it. "The Japanese Samurai swords weren't the only finely made ones of the era."

There couldn't have been too many of these ancient ones left in such good shape, I thought. Its value had to be astronomical. However, I controlled my curiosity and didn't ask. He was trying to impress me again and querying would have been giving him an opening.

"Nice," I acknowledged and that was as far as I was going with it. Especially because it was impressive. It was useless and extravagant, but it was the real thing. From an historian's perspective, I liked that. From a personal perspective, I admired when people held out for the best and for what they wanted. I know I'm belaboring the point, but I didn't want to start liking things about him. I was already starting to fail at keeping my distance, though.

"Well, let's get to work, shall we," Mrs. Duvall said, as eager to put a good face on and get going on the book as she was to stop her grandson's bragging to me. At least, that was the sense I got. I may not have been too clear on her intentions as yet.

Back in the library, we began unpacking the boxes, pulling out photo albums, old letters, newspaper clippings, and enough loose photos to choke an elephant. The ones she didn't immediately recognize, she recalled or figured out within moments of reading the notations on the back.

Almost every picture had some notation on it. The family had an obsession in that regard. They had been diligent in documenting their past, when it had been their present. It was making my job easy.

I lost track of the hours that Mrs. Duvall and I spent in organizing the photos and the stories that went along with them into a very rough outline. It would be days before we finished that part, with me scanning snapshots and transcribing their notes into a log that became the flesh on the bones of the outline.

Richards commented, at one point that first afternoon, on my being left handed as a sign of creativity. I think he really believed that and thought he was showing how clever or how educated he was. It didn't matter. I was into the work now and my focus was beyond his skill to interrupt. He left us alone most of the time, working on something in his kitsch and book packed office, only poking his head in now and then.

I think Mrs. Duvall got into it, too. She was quite startled when Agnes announced that dinner was ready and we saw that dusk had not only come but gone on into night. She laughed at herself and just said we'd finish up the last of it over our after-dinner coffee. There was no question I was going to be staying, or that such would be the norm, when we were working at the house.

"I am a superstitious, old woman, to be sure," she chuckled at herself over a final aperitif of brandy, before the coffee was served. Dinner had been good, roast with yellow potatoes, sugar snap peas in the pods, and a spring greens salad. Agnes was an experienced cook who ate the same meal as we had eaten, only, she did so in the kitchen. That was a perk one could get jealous of.

"I do talk to my husband and the others at the cemetery," Mrs. Duvall told me. I had earlier learned there was a large family plot at a far corner of the property. "I talk to my mother and all of our relatives buried there. Sometimes I go to the church yard where others of us are interred. I know it seems silly, but somehow I feel that they really are there, listening to me. Sometimes I think they answer me, but I can't quite hear them."

"Maybe they make their answers known in other ways," I suggested. The brandy was burning my tongue deliciously. Being full of warm food and sipping spirits after a long and productive day was having a sedative effect. The aroma of the fresh coffee was counteracting it in a comforting way. This was a perk I could get used to.

"Perhaps," she said. "But it's comforting, nevertheless, and writing this book feels like it will keep them alive and with us longer."

I simply smiled and nodded. She had been thinking about it and this was the reason she'd wanted the book written; to keep her memories and family close to her. Perhaps she feared Alzheimer's. Perhaps she just feared there was too much to remember, or that Richards didn't care to recall. Perhaps she feared that when she died, the family history would go with her instead of into the book. And, she'd overcome her fears of a stranger learning their past and putting it on paper.

This was looking like an easy job, even if it might take a while to complete. Wisely, I kept my mouth shut about the male spirits being bound to the old mayor's mansion. Mrs. Duvall believed they were in the family plot or the church graveyard. That was fine by me. Even after Sam's stories of moving brooms, I wasn't a believer. Besides, like I said, who was I to say it wasn't one of the old mayors?

Ghosts. Bound souls. Black magic. Green witchcraft.

Really?

I sipped some more of the golden liquid fire and inhaled the rich aroma of the coffee. The realities of life were good. Who needed old wives tales?

Thunder rattled the windows and startled everyone. Even Ben and Jerry jumped up as though ready to flee or defend the house. Heavy rain had been slashing down off and on all evening. Mrs. Duvall and Richards glanced worriedly at the window. Their estate was along the river on the eastern end of the town. They were on high enough ground and their land rose higher still eastward to a curve in the river. They were in no danger. But they were as flood weary as the rest of the county.

"Did the new bags arrive?" Mrs. Duvall asked her grandson.

"Yes," he told her. "That's what I was checking on when I got home. The men were already putting them down. I placed a call to get ten thousand more ready. We may have to close Randall Road."

"Randall Road?" I asked as Mrs. Duvall frowned.

"The lowest of the marinas is at the end of it," Richards told me. "It's always the first area to flood. Our only choice is to wall it off with sandbags."

"Why doesn't the owner move further up?"

"There weren't any problems when it was built," he said. "The marina has been there since the twenties, I think. The piers float and can be winched back. He did rebuild the office higher up and has a short wall around it. But you can't put a permanent wall on the road. So, we have to bag it off when it gets bad."

"The Wells told me about something called Union Bluff."

"It's the eastern tip of our property," Richards told me. "It's called Union Bluff because federals seized and occupied it during the Civil War to keep the Confederates from using the river. There wasn't much more than a skirmish over it, so Willow Creek was spared any real damage. It's mostly just woods and tangles now, natural forest again. We don't need it for anything, so we leave it be."

Lord help me. He was conscious of the environment, too. Or at least that one part of it. A token measure to show his concern. Not like he was trying to save the world. Right? Or maybe I was forcing myself to be too judgmental. Maybe wine with dinner and brandy afterwards wasn't such a good thing for someone like me who rarely drank.

It would be almost ten by the time I arrived back at the Willows Wells, woozy and smelling a little of the fire they'd lit in the library fireplace. There were a couple of other cars in the lot beside the house. Marianne had told me some more guests were arriving that day; folks in for a wedding that weekend. Most likely, I'd see nothing of them other than at breakfast. Somewhere in the back of the house, I heard a television playing what sounded like a sitcom. The Wells occupied rooms at the back.

I went up the heavily-carpeted stairs and to my room at the front. The others were at the back. I saw lights coming from under the doors and heard televisions and some talking, all mumbles to me in the hallway. In my quiet room, I heard nothing from them. I opened the two front windows a few inches for the air and unpacked my gear as the semi-cool breeze that smelled of clean rain pushed at the lace curtains.

Fatigue was heavy on me. My shoulders slumped and my eyes were beginning to burn. My legs felt like lead. I wanted to consolidate my notes. I wanted to take a warm bath and breathe in the storm-freshened air. Most of all, I wanted to crawl into bed and sleep for weeks.

The coffee. It was wearing off and the post-caffeine crash had come. I gave in to it. I changed into the shorts and tank top I slept in and tugged back the uncooperative covers. I noticed then that the old phone on the nightstand was blinking with a message.

I picked it up and heard a young woman's pleasant voice introducing herself. Melissa Ferrier was one of the witches out north of town, further into the hills. She had heard about the book and thought it was a great idea and wondered if we could meet. Not to discuss the Duvalls, but to talk in general about historical books and other lore.

At that point, I was too tired and too mellow to find anything wrong in that idea. Maybe if I had, things might have worked out differently. But then again, probably not. The hand of Fate was operating by then, possibly guiding me. I would call Melissa back in the morning. The pillow was impatiently waiting.

I dreamed of rivers running deep and fast with clear rain water and a young girl guiding me over the rocks to cross it, while stern Chinese guards with impossible mustaches and glinting swords scrutinized our every step. They didn't want us going up to the high ground. It belonged to people that had other plans for it.

Chapter 4
Settling Down to Work

I woke up to a dry mouth, clogged sinuses and a slight chill in the room. The days were nice, but it was October and the storm had cooled the night down. I was going to have to keep the windows shut when I slept, which I hated. I sleep better with fresh, moving air in the room, even using a small fan pointed away from me in the winter sometimes. Maybe the Wells' would have a little one I could borrow.

Heat was rising from the radiators thankfully. I closed up and ran a very hot bath to let the steam warm that room while I pulled on jeans and a robe and went to the kitchen for a big mug of coffee.

Marianne Wells was happily humming as she prepared breakfast, but she did a double take at my appearance.

"Oh dear, I hope you didn't have a bad night's sleep," she said.

"No, I slept fine," I told her. "This is just my special morning beauty."

Which brought out her laugh and a bigger smile. "Well, here's the biggest mug we have," she told me and handed over a soup bowl sized, black, latte cup. "If the coffee isn't strong enough, you just say so and I'll make it like Starbucks does. Make the hair on your scalp tingle all day."

I grinned, thanked her, and returned to my still chilly room. The edge hadn't even been taken off of it yet. I grabbed my clothes for the day and took them into the bathroom, which was steamy behind its shut door. The hot bath and the coffee would do the trick. A little under an hour later, I was my usual energetic self, pulling my still damp hair back into a pony tail and joining the wedding guests at the big dining table for another hot, stick-to-your-ribs type breakfast. As long as Richards was paying for it, I was going to make sure I got his money's worth.

After telling the wedding guests about life as a writer, at their questioning, I headed up to my room for my equipment. On slipping my phone into my purse, I remembered the call from Ferrier. I didn't really feel it was a good idea to talk to them, given the stories about the feud or whatever with the Duvalls. It was fairy tales to me, but might not have been to them.

But I called her anyway. What was the harm in just meeting her and talking a little bit? Her voice mail picked up and I told her I was free for lunch and gave her the name of the place I'd been to the day before. I didn't know any other places yet. Eventually, Melissa would show me all the nice places in the area. But that day, I only knew of the one. I also gave her my cell number.

Then, I spent the morning in a blissful state of research and writing in the basement of the old mansion. The rest of the place still felt creepy, especially when I explored it at dusk or after nightfall. But that musty smelling records room with the intermittent sunshine glowing through the frosted glass half windows above the foundation; that room was peaceful, almost like a slice of heaven.

Okay. So I enjoy what I do. I don't see anything weird in that.

Lunch found me sipping coffee and waiting for my grilled cheese to come up while staring out the window at a sky that couldn't make up its mind between real overcast and patchy sun. I had a feeling overcast was going to win out and judging by some of the looks on the locals looking up at the clouds, they felt the same and were bothered by it. Never mind that rain here would flow away and flood further south. It was enough to make them nervous. Unless, of course, I didn't understand how where it flooded related to where it rained. I was kind of thinking maybe they knew better, when Ferrier walked in.

It was obviously her. There was something of an all-natural, modern, hippy aura about her. She was a little younger than me with short, dark hair that she wore in a loose, shaggy sort of bob. Her oversized blouse and long jeans were a size or two too large for her, making her look a bit ragged and unkempt. But when she came through the door and reached back to keep it from slamming, her clothing stretched back and I saw the figure that she was hiding.

I'm not a petty woman. I don't secretly rage over those females with better figures than the one I was struggling to keep. Needless to say, we all want to look better. We all get a little jealous and envious of movie stars and models, wishing we looked like that. That's just human nature. I felt a little snide at noting she was better looking than me, both in her figure and her face. But I swallowed my envy and stood up to greet her.

Her hand, when we shook, was neither soft nor calloused. But she clearly worked with them. What completely killed the bit of spite over her looks, though, was her smile. You know when a person is genuinely glad to meet you for you and not for any purpose or desire of their own. I got that sense from Melissa instantly and knew I had found a friend.

"Thanks for meeting me," she said, sliding into the window booth across from me.

"No, thank you," I replied. "Meeting people is one of the best things about my job."

She smiled again. "Your job sounds fascinating. How did you get into it?"

And so I told her about the professor and the research project and all of the books and articles and what-not that had come since, and where I hoped to go with it. Her questions spurred me on for the next hour as I told her half of my history. She was good at getting you to talk and she listened with her heart, as well as her mind.

Finally, I caught myself and said, "I thought you wanted to talk about your family and your..." I was lost for the correct term. Somehow I knew coven was absolutely the wrong word. In my mind it had connotations of evil.

"Religion," she supplied, perhaps not seeing where I had been heading. "Witchcraft is a religion like many others with our own beliefs and practices."

"I want to hear about it," I said truthfully. "Now I understand that you are green witches. Is that correct?"

"Yes. Do you know what that means?"

"No. Not a clue," I answered with a grin. "You'll have to tell me."

"In a nutshell, we try to be in touch with the world and with ourselves," Melissa said. "Our spell work and rituals are meant to go hand-in-hand with nature to improve our lives and those we care about, to make a better place of where we are, and to thank the world for aiding us."

"The world is a living thing," I understood.

"Yes. Very much," she replied. "There is energy and intelligence in everything, that is, if you see it the right way. One thing you should know is you never cast spells that will harm people, especially another practitioner. For that energy will come back at you three-fold, once from the person you aimed it on and once more each from the Lord and the Lady."

"Lord and Lady?"

"The deities of the world and the cosmos," she told me. "If you really want to learn, then this is not the place. My grandmother's place is where you should come."

"Your grandmother runs the shop I've heard of?"

"Yes. The Gentle Wiccan's Herborium."

I smiled at the name. "I like that. Seems to me you wouldn't get much business around here though."

"Very little," she told me. "We are twenty-first

century witches, though. We do a great business over the internet."

Which caused me to chuckle and she laughed with me at the seeming contradiction.

"We changed the name of the store back in the sixties," she told me. "People seemed to respond better to it and accept the term Wiccans over witches."

"So, that's why you prefer to be called Wiccans," I said. She smiled as if at an old joke.

"It doesn't matter to us," she said. "There's nothing wrong with the term witch as far as we're concerned. It was purely a marketing thing to change the name, but it made people assume we were embarrassed to be called witches."

I smiled at my own naivety. Of course, the mayor had sought to be politically correct. "What was it called before?"

"The Willows Witch Supply," she told me.

"I can see where that would have been limiting," I noted. "Herborium would appeal to a wider customer base."

"That's a good point," she said. "But you should understand that Wicca is a neo-pagan faith that came about in the thirties. We're blood born witches from back into the eighteenth century."

"I do recall reading something about that now," I said. If memory served, some English fellow had coined the term and organized the religion.

"What else have you heard about us?" she inquired.

"You mean the story about the curse on the Duvall men?" I replied. It was easy being open with her. "I didn't put much stock in it."

"You should know something," Melissa said seriously. She set her fingers lightly on the backs of my hands, seizing my attention. "There is a curse on the Duvall men, but we did not lay it."

A dread began to fill me. It wasn't over her telling me there was an actual curse. The dismay was over the fact she believed it. I thought I could be friends with her, but it seemed she was leaning toward the lunatic side of things. I love my job, but it got lonely being somewhere strange a lot. "We would not have done so even if it were within our realm to do so. We don't believe in that. Why I am telling you this is because you are working where those spirits dwell. You should protect yourself. I have a crystal necklace you can have."

"Thanks, no," I said. "I'm sorry, but I don't believe in that stuff."

"That is no protection," she told me.

"I think I'll be all right," I told her. Though, I'd confess my active mind was already saying to me, 'If you're okay, then why do you feel creeped out everywhere but the blessed room?'

"I won't force you," Melissa said and moved back from having leaned toward me. "Remember that I am here, as are we all, if you should find your mind gets changed."

"Thanks," I told her. "I *will* come out to the store. Maybe this Sunday. I don't work on Sundays."

"That would be good," she said, smiling. "I will leave you to your work. I've taken too much of your time as it is."

"Hardly," came out without thinking. "I haven't been so chatty in ages. I probably used up a lot of your time."

"I enjoyed it."

"So did I. Thanks."

"I think we could be good friends," she said and I smiled.

"I think so, too," I admitted.

She took my hands in hers and then leaned forward with a suddenly intent look. She peered into my eyes as hers seemed to deepen, like pools of liquid onyx. I felt odd, embarrassed. I twitched and wanted to turn my head, but didn't. I had begun to trust her, despite the oddness she had just shown.

"You need to let life be what it is more," she told me. "You fight with it too much."

How one can feel despair yet uplifted at the same time is a mystery. But I felt it then. She'd hit my core and left me dazed. Life was a struggle then, had been for years. Only, I'd never thought I was fighting against it. I felt I was trying to deal with it. That wasn't what I thought at hearing her words, though. In that moment, I didn't think anything. All I knew was something inside me knew she was right, and the rest of me was confused.

Then, she patted my hands as she got up from the bench. "I will see you Sunday then, unless you find time to come out earlier."

"Yes," was all I said.

"Please do be careful," she added.

"I will. I promise."

"Good. See you Sunday."

"I'll be out in the morning," I told her.

With a wave and another of her easy smiles she went out. The sun was making a valiant attempt at burning away the clouds and warmed my face through the plate glass. I watched Melissa walk down the street as far as the angle let me. She had a feminine walk. No amount of baggy clothes could disguise that.

I understood the oversized clothes then. She was indeed hiding within them. This was a small town and Melissa Ferrier was undoubtedly one of the prettiest, sexiest women in it. She was Richards' counterpart; the best female catch in the county. But, she wasn't one of them and wanted nothing to do with the country males, or so it struck me then. She was holding out for something more; someone more. So she hid what would have drawn much unwanted attention to her.

I was no longer envious of her better looks. I was sorry for her situation. St. Louis was where she needed to be. Or Kansas City. Maybe even a place as big as Chicago or New York. Whichever, Willow Creek was not the place for her. I had already planned on spending every other weekend back home. I decided to bring her with me. I looked forward to it.

That had been Wednesday. I was falling into the routine I expected: researching in the morning, working with Alice Duvall or interviewing historians and other family members in the afternoon, compiling notes and writing in the evening. When it wasn't raining, I got a run in as dawn became early morning. Never when it was dark. I hadn't forgotten the Sheriff's warning.

I ran into the professor the next day, Thursday, when I had gone back to check on something after interviewing a cousin on Richards' father's side. Willis was doing something with his electronic gear as I was leaving.

"You must be Miss Hills," echoed a sudden voice from down the hall toward the back, half scaring me out of my wits. "Oh, I'm sorry. I didn't mean to startle you."

He had a vaguely European accent and deep set eyes. In a large room with his voice raised, it would probably be booming. In that small space, it was deep and startling enough. He was coming toward me with a smile breaking in a face of advanced, but undeterminable age.

"I didn't realize you were here," I replied and shook the offered hand. It was calloused and warm. For a professor, he was still a man that used his hands a lot.

"Just replacing the memory cards and batteries in my equipment," he told me. "It takes an incredibly long time to catch any sort of paranormal activity."

"Nothing like the movies."

"No, nothing like," he said. "People would be asking for their money back"

"Have you found anything?" I asked, meaning in general.

"Do you mean here?" he asked. "No, not as yet."

"I meant before."

"Some things, yes," he told me. "It is hard to prove these things scientifically. There are many good, logical reasons for why things happen. My equipment is designed to measure those influences so I can rule them out if something happens."

"I see," I replied, understanding vaguely. It sounded

like a good idea. I had no idea what he might have been measuring or what those influences could be. I wasn't sure if I was curious enough to ask at the moment. Or maybe his oddness was putting me off. He seemed okay, yet a little weird.

"You would be surprised if I found something here?" he wondered.

"I've heard the stories about the Duvall men being confined here," I non-answered.

He smiled and gave a small laugh. "Yes. Imprisoned by the witches. A very interesting story."

"You don't believe it?" I asked. "Couldn't that be a reason?"

"Not if you truly understand what the witches are," he told me. "And if you believe that magic is real."

"You don't?"

He shrugged. "I believe there are many things and many forces or energies that we have not yet come to understand. Nevertheless, I am a man of science. Magic, if you want to call it that, is a theory. My research is to prove that something other than what we know really exists, then perhaps try to explain it."

"Sounds like a tall order."

He pursed his lips and nodded in agreement, but resigned to accepting it as a fact of his life. "Perhaps I will be like Madame Curie and find what we suspected was always there, even if quite by accident."

"You'll let me know, if you find anything here?"

"Of course," he told me. "If I can find any evidence that they exist here. You will let me know, if you experience anything odd. Yes?"

"Of course," I said. For whatever reason, though, I felt reluctant to follow through on that promise. I never told him about the odd feelings I got in the building.

"Thank you," he said. "Well, I won't keep you any longer. I know you must have things to do and I should finish my work here."

"Good night," I said and shook his hand before

heading up to the wan light of the early evening. As I stepped from the building, I never had such a sense of not being wanted somewhere in my life. It was as though the spirits of all those Duvall men had wanted me gone and had been willing me to leave.

    I drove quickly to the Wells' so I would have a little time to freshen up. Richards was treating me to a break, as he called it, from our working dinners at his home. Alice Duvall had an event at the local Rotary or something like that. I was still trying to grasp how many organizations she was an active member of. That left Richards taking me to dinner at one of the nicer, out of the way places further east along the Little Osage and nearer the resort areas. I would have been happy with a quiet evening in my room nibbling some cheese and olives and sipping some red wine. It was the one culinary vice I treated myself to from time to time and it would have been nice. Especially since I'd eaten at least twice as much for dinner during the week as I normally did. My bank account was not the only thing that was getting a little fatter on this job. My ass was gaining on it.

    I'd have to say that Richards had been on his best behavior during the week and I was wondering if I hadn't been too quick to judge. My friends would have said, 'Yeah, you were breaking down and warming up to him; just like you always do with his type.' And they would probably have been right. But, you know, it was one of those seemed-like-a-good-idea-at-the-time sort of things.

    The restaurant was a large cabin or lodge, very quiet inside with several smaller rooms to keep the noise down. We were given a table near the window that overlooked the dark, western edge of one of the lakes in the Lake of the Ozarks chain. I never did get its name. But there wasn't much to see beyond the windows as it was full night and the warmly lit room reflected off the thick glass. A wood fireplace burned steadily toward the center of the building and lent its heady aroma and gentle heat to where we sat.

The place smelled also of steak and coffee and the lineage of its patrons. There were elite places to stay and eat in the Ozarks. This was one of them and it had its own, unique aura. Or perhaps I simply wasn't used to such places. I felt almost as out of place here as I had earlier felt unwanted at the mansion.

It was clear why Richards had told me to dress up. I wished I'd done a better job than a black cocktail dress and low heels. I did have a nicer outfit, of course. Who leaves home for a couple of months without bringing something? I just hadn't wanted to wear it for him.

I really knew I was out of my league when the waiter brought the menus. There were no prices.

"Order what you want," Richards told me. "You deserve a bit of a treat with how hard you've been working this week. I can't believe how much you've gotten done so far."

"We've got a lot more to do yet," I pointed out.

"True," he said, then lowered the menu to look at me with a grin. "But there's no reason not to treat ourselves for getting off to a good start."

That made me smile, because it was silly and true at the same time. I looked at the priceless menu, read the extravagant-sounding dishes, and starting thinking about two runs a day. The wood fired brook trout captured my imagination and the waiter seemed very pleased with my choice. It was fresh that day, he told me, so happy he could serve it at its best. Of course, I'd already had a nice glass of Chardonnay so it could have been that imagination of mine adding thoughts to his words.

Dinner was fantastic. At some point, a storm began brewing in the south and we watched the lightening in the clouds beyond the lake. No one seemed the least bit worried about flooding tonight. Perhaps the river levels had subsided enough over the last two days of dry weather. Or maybe this was a place where you just didn't let such things enter into your thinking.

Richards told me about the family business, which I

justified in my mind as we were still working. I listened and took it in, not bothering with notes or a recorder. The family had started in coal and textiles, and shifted focus over the years as markets and goods changed. They had been fortunate in their choices of directions and always managed to do well. Currently, importing inexpensive household goods and decorative items was doing very well for Willow Creek, and keeping a number of the townsfolk employed, which helped support the other businesses.

He spent a lot of time in China and Japan and had made a lot of good contacts and friends over there. The antique sword was something of a gift, by way of simply letting him buy and export it. It had been used by an officer back in the days of Genghis Khan. Perhaps there was blood on it; likely there was. But that was its history. Now it was Richards' prized possession.

"To get back to what I was saying," he remarked and returned to the subject of the family business. "I took it over about ten years ago, when my father was killed in a car wreck. It was hit by a large chunk of granite, the falling rocks the signs warn you about. Sent him skidding out of control and over the edge into the river. Sounds horrible, but the coroner told us he had hit his head on the door frame or the steering wheel and was knocked unconscious almost instantly. He hardly knew what happened."

"Still," I said. "Such a bad way to go. It must have been hard to take."

He nodded and I regretted the personal question. "It was. Mom took it worse, of course."

"I would expect."

"She was somewhat sick of Willow Creek," he told me. "And she was so broken hearted that she simply left; went east to South Carolina. We have a summer home near the shore. She went to live there, but passed in her sleep one night a few years later. No one knows why for sure. A stroke is our best guess."

My hackles were back up. Was he really trying to

endear himself to me with his parents' deaths? What a typically slimy thing of his kind to do. Was nothing sacred?

"What about your parents?" he wondered innocently.

My mind shifted. Was this the logical turn in the conversation we'd started? Was I just being too guarded? Terrified of letting myself be manipulated again?

"Gone," I told him. "Dad died of an aneurism and Mom from cancer."

"I'm sorry," he said and really did sound it. "How long has it been?"

"They were older," I explained. I was the baby of the family; that oops baby that pops out much later than you would have expected. "It's been fifteen years."

"They died when you were in your teens," he quickly computed. "That sucks. That really does."

It had. I was the one girl whose father wasn't there to beam over how she looked in her prom dress. Neither of them were there to swell proudly, when I graduated from college. As much as teens and parents fought, it was rough growing up with no one to ask for advice. Fate had left me on my own for the last nine years and I had a real bone to pick with her. Especially for doing nothing but throwing these self-absorbed, alpha males in front of me.

"I'm sorry," he said and I saw in his eyes that he was. The change in my demeanor had been that obvious. "I shouldn't have asked. I'm sorry. I guess I've ruined the evening now, haven't I?"

I tried on a smile. No point opening those old wounds, I thought, as the hurt rose in my chest and made my heart feel like bursting. But then again, I'd grown good at controlling my rage. I had worked myself into a decent, if still tenuous, position in life. I was doing okay. I was going to be doing better. Yeah, I had a grudge against Fate. But I was beating that bitch and making my way in the world.

Melissa's admonition to stop fighting life so much

came back to me. I saw her liquid onyx eyes staring into mine again and the anger subsided.

"It's all right," I told him. "You just never really stop missing your parents, once they're gone."

He nodded with a wistful look and said, "Amen to that, sister. Amen to that."

"So... tell me more about the business empire," I said to get us back on track and my mind on something else.

The evening finished on a more businesslike note. Richards told me all about how he had made some lucky decisions and where he envisioned going with the company in the future. He didn't sound like a man from a family where all the men died young and were imprisoned in the dank cellar of a decaying building.

There was a second glass of wine and a small brandy after dinner with some insanely sumptuous chocolate dish. My memories of the meal are a little skewed from the drinks. But, it was divine. The fact that there were no prices went along with the fact that there was no check at the end. Apparently, you had to be a member and they just charged your account.

I was sleepy when Richards dropped me off in front of the B & B. It was the closest to the covered porch and the rain from south of the lakes had found its way to Willow Creek. If he had expected or hoped for a kiss or a hug or anything of the like, he didn't act like it, because he told me I'd better make a run for it, while the rain was a bit light.

"See you tomorrow then," I said as I clambered out. "Thanks for dinner."

"You're welcome," he said. "And by the way, I didn't say anything earlier because it was still sort of a working dinner, but you looked quite lovely tonight."

The bastard! Not for waiting until I was about to run in out of the rain to say anything, but because it made me feel good. Business relationship or not, a person still liked to be complimented, and you couldn't hate someone for saying you looked nice. He waited until I waved from the open front door and then drove off.

I wanted to scream. What the hell? Couldn't I control myself? I was there to write a book, not get involved. Why did I feel it was drifting inexorably to the latter? My head was clear, but the rest of me was following a familiar path. Was I ever going to get it under control?

In bed, I started crying. I really wished my mom had been there to talk to.

I woke up a stronger person the next morning, resolved not to be such a whiny bitch. In retrospect, it was clear that something was up with me, as they say. I promise not to bore you by belaboring the point any more. It was just that the fear of losing everything was still fresh. I had been on the verge of running out of money over the winter because work had been drying up in the economy. That had only been averted by this job for the Duvall's, but it would only take Alice Duvall changing her mind to put me right back where I had been. I was on an emotional roller coaster without realizing it.

On Friday of my first week, I had a few more hours' research at the mansion, finishing up the family tree, and tomorrow I would spend the rest of the day roughing out the outline of the book. I would drop that off in printed form for Mrs. Duvall and Richards to ponder and take some time to myself to explore this part of my state a little more; relax a bit and meet the witches. I was looking forward to that and to seeing my new friend, Melissa, again.

Thankfully, the day went calmly as planned and I recovered my shaky emotions. The only disturbing part of that entire day came as I finished work. It was the first night I finished up still in the mansion after dark. So it was the first night I thought I caught a movement in the shadows of the storeroom at the end of the stone hallway.

"Sam?" I called. "Professor Willis?" There was no answer, of course, other than the sound of pure silence.

My imagination sensed a man hiding just out of sight in that distant doorway. My sensible self shook the feeling off and I headed back to my cozy room. I gave a very rough update by phone to the Duvall's and begged off Friday dinner with them for needing to get some rest.

Saturday was just as peaceful and productive and by late afternoon, I had dropped off a very rough outline of where I saw the book going. I was going to beg off dinner again, but somewhere along the line I had let it slip that I adored a good pork tenderloin, and Agnes had been hours preparing one. How could you turn that down? We talked some more about the structure of the book and I stuffed myself silly. The woman needed to be running a cooking school, not working for Richards.

A few hours later, uncomfortably full and sleepy, I was sipping wine and reading about western Missouri and its lore, while curled up in bed. It was as much for my own knowledge as it was background for the book. I slept like a baby that night, content in a week well spent and a good amount of work done.

Sunday came a little warmer and clearer than the last few days. I took a short, early run up and down the winding, hilly roads of the town and sated myself with a plate of Marianne Wells' buttermilk biscuits with honey and strong coffee. After that, I grabbed my camera and other gear and drove north along the county road in search of the Gentle Wiccans' Herborium.

As I might have imagined, it was a classic two story frame house, as wide as it was long and featuring a full-length covered porch along the front. It was pure country, paint-starved wood graying elegantly in the sun where the old white wash had worn away. Flowers of all sorts hung in baskets or stood in pots along the porch, but were showing signs of dying back for the coming winter as the first few chilly mornings of fall had come recently. Wicker and oak furniture lined the back and wind chimes added a tinkling, cheerful cacophony.

I parked my deep blue Civic in the gravel lot,

partially overgrown with weeds, coming to a stop at a hitching post used for barriers the length of the lot. There were two other cars, a white Scion and a green Cavalier, around the side of the building on what had been a gravel driveway decades ago, but was now a mere rocky and spotty area of the wild growing lawn on the east side of the south facing building. It smelled of autumn rising from the damp earth and flowing from the red and yellow tinged forest that surrounded me. The slow wind through the trees made them sound as though they were shushing me and the entire world to be calm and quiet. A couple of sleepy cats stretched in the sun, blinked at me, and then proceeded to ignore me. I liked the place even before I stepped inside.

 Warmth was my first impression after the cool morning air, followed by a completely wild, but pleasing, mix of aromas. It was a cramped space full of candles and bins of loose herbs and teas. Candle holders, metal and ceramic bowls, feathers and pastel-colored bottles of oils and extracts filled the shelves and displays. There were also simple decorative items and tea pots; the sorts of things you'd expect to find in a country store. A few more cats were inside, sunning themselves on the window ledges or checking on the merchandise.

 An older women of sixty or perhaps seventy, but still so fit it was hard to say, was busy at a nearby work table, packaging leaves and crystals in mason jars and plastic bags, and then into a straw lined box for shipping out somewhere, I assumed. Melissa had said they did most of their business over the internet. I saw a short stack of orders on the table that the woman was obviously filling. But it was not such to demand her full attention as she noticed me within seconds of walking in.

 When she looked up, I saw she was still a handsome woman, whose eyes reminded me of Melissa. At first, she had the expression of the shop keeper ready to help a customer, but then a light of recognition came on and she displayed a happier, more personal smile.

"You must be Miss Hills," she reckoned. "Melissa told me you might come by. She's upstairs brewing us some tea. I'm Francine Brindley, her maternal grandmother."

She came around the table to greet me and I shook her extended hand. Much like the professor's, her hands were soft while still bearing the calluses of use. But unlike him, Francine Brindley was warm and inviting and I instantly liked her a hell of a lot more.

"That sounds good," I said regarding the tea and turned to the sound of foot falls coming quickly down a central staircase.

Melissa came bounding down the steps in a properly wispy summer dress of pale blue and wearing a band of white flowers around her head. Today, she looked like the beautiful, young hippy that she was and it made me happy to see it. She quickly wove her way through the shelves to greet me with a big hug, which I returned gladly. Odd how you can just take to someone, isn't it? It suddenly seemed like I hadn't seen her in ages, rather than five days, and that we'd been friends for years. How much of that was part of my roller coaster emotions and how much was because we hit it off was hard to say. Whichever, I was feeling like I had a new best friend.

We sat and sipped Melissa's sweet and spicy herbal tea by the work table, while Francine continued her task. FedEx would be coming to pick up her twenty orders early in the morning. While a friendly cat, named Arthur, sat and purred in my lap, they told me of the history of the witches in the area.

Once there had been many families of witches in the Willow Creek area. For a while, the largest concentration of witches had been in these woods north of town. So many in fact that the ridge, now known as Union Bluff, was once referred to as Coven Ridge, because it was where they performed their group rites and still celebrated the Sabbats.

Its original name was Greater Ridge, before the Civil

War, because of its commanding position over the bend in the river. However, that changed with time, as did ownership of the land. The Duvall family owned it now, but that had not stopped the witches from meeting there for the Sabbats, which are the holy days of the witch's calendar, to put it simply. They wouldn't use the term holy, but I would as it helps give a real grasp on what they mean in witchcraft.

The lesser Sabbats coincide with the cycles of the earth revolving around the sun, two at the solstices and two at the equinoxes. The greater Sabbats, often called Esbats and which are sometimes celebrated more than the others for being the high energy times, are the midpoints between the others. In a few weeks, they would be celebrating a greater Sabbat, Samhain, which not only coincides with Halloween, but has influenced it in terms of decorations and costumes. And never mind how it's spelled. It's pronounced *sah-win* after its Celtic/Gaelic origin.

Richards had formally warned them not to perform any rituals or conduct meetings on Coven Ridge by way of letters from his lawyer, but he had never actually tried to stop them or have them thrown off, when they were out there. It was more a legal positioning thing to show he wasn't accepting of their trespassing, should any of them get hurt.

"Or perhaps he's afraid of the curse," Francine said with a mischievous grin.

Things were good for the witches in Willow Creek until about 1903. Sometime that year, as they were marveling at the first motor cars running down their back roads, the attitude of the town elders changed. Maybe it was that no one wanted such a silly and superstitious religion to be prominent in their area during the industrial revolution; it was never made clear.

Thus, the harassment started. There were no prosecutions or things of that nature. No one wanted to draw publicity to the witches. It was more subtle. Denying them credit at the general store where other families were allowed to run tabs in tough times. More strict application of zoning and other administrative laws. Outright shunning in public places. They were made to feel unwelcome in their own hometown. Eventually, most of them left. Only the one family still remained and that was comprised simply of Melissa, her grandmother, Francine, and two aunts with their families.

Melissa's mother had been killed a year earlier in a freak car accident that literally decapitated her. How odd it was that three woman had died of decapitation here, counting the recent murder and the woman killed in that industrial accident I told you about at the beginning.

That was when Francine decided to chill my spine to subzero. She paused in her packaging and looked me in the eye and said, "Stranger still, when you consider that both of those women were grandnieces of mine, Melissa's cousins."

"What?" I breathed before my throat tightened up. All three of them related? That was just too weird! Three women from the same family all killed by decapitation over the last few years. Had two of the deaths not been accidents, my imagination might have raced. It still wanted to, but I kept it in check. Maybe if I hadn't, things might have come out differently. But at the time, it seemed like Fate was being just crazy for them. So, I didn't say anything and made my mind calm down.

"Very odd," Francine remarked.

"Really odd," I emphasized. "I don't think I've ever heard of any more crazy coincidences."

"Yes," she said. "I don't know that I have either."

I totally missed then the glance she gave Melissa. I recall it clearly now as I write this, unless I'm imagining it. But I don't think I am. I just missed it then. I rolled my mind around the curiosity of the similar deaths and tucked it back, the investigative historian in me coming back to the point.

"Tell me about this curse," I said. "Melissa

mentioned it the other day and I've heard some talk about it. What was it the Duvall family allegedly did to yours?"

"They started the harassment," Francine told me. "At least, that's the lore passed down through our family. Some felt it was because they wanted to take Coven Ridge for their estate. Others felt it was because we somehow interfered with their businesses. They started to become even more successful at about the same time. These are the rumors that go around, though. The truth is our magic and spells are limited to the use of the energies in plants and minerals and what little we're allowed to use of the world's own energy. We're Green Witches. We wouldn't know how to bind souls to this plane, even if we wanted. Even if it was possible."

"You don't think it is?"

"I don't think it is," she told me. "Unless there's some powers that I've never heard about. I know the Lord and the Lady could bind you somewhere, if you deserved it. I don't see where a person could do that. The power doesn't exist."

"So it's all Hollywood, B-movie or pulp fiction stuff."

"Yes," she said. "It's ridiculous to think we could have or would have done such a thing. It's possible that someone's reincarnation may be blocked somehow, but it's laughable to think we would have caused it. It would be interrupting the cycle that is at the heart of our beliefs."

"I'd love to learn more about it," I eagerly told her.

"Come with me today, then," Melissa said. "I need to head up into the mountains for some leaves and flowers for an order. We'll have all day to talk."

"That sounds like a good idea," Francine added. "Especially since that little Scion of yours almost gave out on the slopes last time. That is, if you wouldn't mind driving, India."

"I don't mind," I told her. At least, I figured my Civic could do the job, plus all my gear was already in it and I didn't fancy getting stuck somewhere in a dead Scion. Mine hadn't shown any sign of laboring in the hills, but it was getting old. "I came to spend the day with you all, if you didn't mind."

Melissa made a dismissive sound and waved her hand to drive away my last comment. "Hardly," she said. "I was hoping you would."

"Cool," I answered with a smile.

"Come on up," Melissa told me. "We'll get some lunch ready to take with us."

She was on her feet and moving, so I didn't have much choice but to follow, had I actually objected. Arthur did, but hid his displeasure at being evicted from my lap in a tail-flicking close inspection of the straw for the boxes.

The upstairs was where Francine lived. It had a pair of small bedrooms, a living room, kitchen, and bath, all the room she really needed for the simple life. It was cozy and invitingly decorated. My own place was small enough to be called cozy, but not nearly so well-decorated. I hadn't made my place me so much as Francine had made her place her. I resolved to fix that when I got back.

Melissa had earlier started getting a picnic lunch together in anticipation of my joining her. It didn't take long to finish gathering the cheese and jams, bread, and some fruit. Francine Brindley was a vegetarian, but from the looks of the variety Melissa packed, she still ate quite well. Although Melissa confided that she wished her grandmother would occasionally allow her some meat while there. Melissa was not a complete vegetarian.

Our first stop was Coven Ridge, a bare knob of rocky earth overlooking a wide bend in the Marais des Cygnes River. It was, at most, a quarter of an acre of clear land with a thin stand of trees at the rim of the hundred foot sheer drop to the river at the rocky point. Cannons and muskets here would definitely have controlled river traffic. The only even ground between it and the road was the little track we'd driven in on and a slim grassy swath leading down through the woods to the Duvall home. They'd once used it for processions to this point, but now had to make them more symbolic than real. It was easy to see how the Union was able to hold it easily.

As we drove on, Melissa finished Francine's story of the harassment by simply mentioning how it lost its political and social appeal as the people of the area grew more worldly. Nowadays, folks just seemed to think of them as simple and perhaps misguided. Most in the area were Catholics or Baptists and preferred just to let them be. It wasn't hard, when so few of them were left in the area. The tale of the curse became just that, an old tale, and their lives were as normal as they wished them to be. There was nothing more to tell of it.

Richards had never tried bringing a trespassing action against them for using Coven Ridge; probably out of fear of a lawsuit for religious persecution. He had also rejected the idea of leasing the field to them because he didn't want to appear to be supporting them. He'd rather they just found somewhere else was their consensus. All in all, it was just a casual peace; an attitude of live and let live as it should be.

"Green witchcraft is folk magic and herb craft," Melissa told me, switching the train of conversation as neatly as I changed lanes to avoid a squirrel on the road. "It's nothing at all like you find in movies and books. It's very much in the vein of shamanic traditions and healing; all natural remedies determined from ages of use. Our focus is on nurturing and improving life, never harming anyone. We believe that sending a harming spell will ultimately result in worse coming back at us, but I think I told you that the other day."

"You did," I replied. "I read something about a three-fold return on the internet later."

Melissa smiled and nodded, a laugh held just behind her teeth. "Yes. It's been referred to that by so-called religious scholars who need to put labels on everything. Once for the witch you sent it against, twice for the Lord, and thrice for the Lady. They will punish you for having tried to harm another."

"So you never would," I repeated the end of that

thought from our earlier conversation. "Which makes the story of binding the souls to the basement ridiculous."

"Entirely ridiculous," Melissa said. "The green witch is close to the growing things of the earth. She honors the natural forces of the world. There is energy in everything; the plants, the rocks, the insects, the birds, the water, and the wind. She tries to work in synergy with these natural energies around her. By opening herself up to the world and becoming part of the flow, she tries to make the energies flow the way she intends through spell work."

"And those intents are always positive for everyone?" I asked just to hear her confirm it.

"Yes," she obliged. "Green witches are healers and naturalists. We live and work with the earth to nurture and maintain it and all the people on it. Witchcraft and all pagan faiths are much older and more extensive religions than most people realize."

"If this is a stupid question, forgive me," I started and she held up a hand to stop me. She knew what was on my mind.

"No," she answered the question I had meant to ask. "Everything you've heard or read about Black Magic has been dreamt up in Hollywood. If it ever existed, it is a lost art and we can be grateful for that."

"How can we be sure it's lost?" I asked. "We can't know everything that everyone is thinking, and it's something that people would be hiding. They'd be doing it in secret to benefit themselves with no one else becoming the wiser."

Melissa frowned at me over that question, then winked with a sudden grin. "I asked my mother that once, and my grandmother since. They both told me we'd know. We'd sense it somehow when things were not working within the natural order."

"So what about the basement then?" I asked. "What about the stories of the anger it makes people feel? I have to tell you I felt that way the minute I walked in and had no reason for it."

"There is something to it," Melissa answered as she directed me to turn from the main road and onto a dirt track. That and her answer made me frown. I was okay with driving the hills, but it was a Civic, not an SUV. The tire ruts weren't terribly gouged into the land, but they were lumpy and rocky. The rocking and bouncing it gave my suspension was making me worry.

"Are the Duvall men bound to the cellar?" I asked.

"I don't know about that," she replied. "But there is something wrong about that building. We've always known it and avoid it like the plague."

"Maybe there is some sort of black magic at work there," I concluded. "You said you'd sense it, as well as something else, there."

"Pull into that space," she instructed, pointing to a grassy spot beside the tree lined road. If you could call it a road. There was orange hunter's tape tied to the tree beside her that I thought she'd pull off, but she left it. Later, I would remember to ask her why and she would tell me that the hunter it belonged to used all of the deer for food or leather, and with fewer wolves left, had become the predator that helped keep the herd in balance with the forest. He was the custodian of this area. At the moment, our conversation stayed on the old mayor's mansion.

"That's an interesting question," she said. "I must ask my grandmother later. All I can tell you is there is something dark in that building. I cannot tell you how it came to be. There's no reason to assume it was created by a human."

"That's a good point," I had to admit. But remember, ghosts and witchcraft and all those metaphysical things were just intellectual concepts to me. This was all simply curious conjecture and fodder for my eventual novel. The reality of it was as likely to be it was an old, imposing structure that had left me ill at ease that first morning. The rest was likely power of suggestion after Sam told me the stories.

Hauntings? Please, I still wasn't convinced.

Nevertheless, Melissa was and she had a way of making you believe with her. Either that or I was simply not questioning my new friend. Besides, I did believe in herbal teas and natural remedies. After all, aspirin came from a flower in the Swiss Alps. It hadn't taken a modern lab with gas chromatographs and micron-telescopes and what not to create it. It had just taken a scientific approach to an herbal remedy. The types of remedies they applied as green witches were entirely in line with how modern scientists first discovered medicines. So who was to say they weren't using some that science hadn't yet tried? I could see where green witchcraft could be effective without believing it was magic. But the rest of it? Forget it. I wasn't buying it. I also wasn't saying anything against it to Melissa.

A few yards past the line of trees where we parked, the hill sloped steeply upwards and became rocky. Melissa began collecting herbs and hunting mushrooms as I started snapping pictures. There were a few places we came across that afternoon that were breathtaking. It was easy to understand feeling you were only a small part of it all when you were surrounded by such impressively rugged mountains. These were the ones in which Jesse James had once roamed. No wonder it had been so hard to catch him, I thought, intending to use it as background to the Duvall book.

At one point, as I snapped photos of Melissa in her winsome dress, looking perfectly elfin in the forest, I noticed how she was thanking the oak and the poplar trees for giving her their leaves and branches. She had been talking to the woods and the rocks and the earth all through the late morning, saying appreciative and even flattering or encouraging things.

"Do you always thank the trees and other plants?" I asked, presuming the answer would be yes.

She nodded. "We own nothing," she told me. "Whatever we have to use is given to us by the earth and we must never stop being grateful."

She was also scattering dried compost at the base of every tree she took a clipping from. Over lunch, she explained that to me.

"It is all a balancing. The world is not something you control, but enter into an agreement with. That is a basic tenet of green witchcraft, and a good lesson for life."

"That life is something you enter into an agreement with, rather than control?" I wasn't quite with her on that. I was directing where I was going.

"Yes. I take actions to move it in the direction I want, but I am not and never will be entirely in control of it. Life has its own ideas and plans for you."

Does it ever, I thought, musing over my current situation, one rejection letter too many away from losing everything I'd been working twelve years to build. So, yeah, I had to accept that she was correct. I was making the right moves, but control was not really mine.

In retrospect, I know it was the dawning realization I was not in control that was driving my angst at the time. It's what was up with me and was driving me to be pensive and moody. No one likes being forced to confront the fear they've been subconsciously ignoring for years.

For the moment, though, sitting on the blanket covered boulder with my beautiful new friend and having a lunch of fruits and cheeses and icy herbal tea, I was still only willing to accept there were twists and kinks to work out as I came to them, but the plan and direction were still my own.

"When we're alone, you can call me Guennean," she suddenly told me.

"Guennean?" I asked. "Is that your middle name or a nickname?"

"It is my craft name," she told me. "When you become a witch, that is, once your training is to the point you can practice solo and enter into the craft, you take a name to use in bonding and circles. I chose Guennean, the white spirit."

"It's beautiful," I told her. "Just like you."

And the smile on her face made my day, because I had obviously just made hers.

"So what are you gathering the oak and poplar leaves for?" I asked. "Can I know or does telling ruin the spell?"

She laughed brightly and told me it wouldn't. "They are for a person interviewing for a new and much desired job in Kansas City. Oak and poplar are among the plants that are good for success."

"What about the mushrooms?"

"For tonight's salad," she answered and I almost fell off the boulder for the laughing fit that gave me. Do I even need to mention what a great day that first Sunday together had become?

We drove to another area and wandered about as much as we had in the first. I was quickly filling my camera with photos and videos to capture the beauty and peace of the forest in the first of its fall colors. Melissa, or Guennean, began humming and then eventually singing in Celtic or some other old language. Her voice was pleasant and steady as she sang the lilting, warbling tune in words I didn't recognize.

"What language was that?" I asked. "Celtic?"

She shrugged. "I've never heard it before either. It was a tune the trees wanted to hear and I pulled it from their memories. I do it all the time."

Which sounded perfectly normal coming from Guennean even as it gave me the first real pangs of worry that she wasn't quite right. Being hippyish and in tune with nature was one thing, but plucking memories of songs in dead languages from trees was a little farther down that road than I was comfortable with. Maybe those mushrooms weren't quite the button or morel kind either.

There was Fate again, that frustrating side of her that always brought something up to make me worry when things were going so well. I didn't want my new, dear friend to turn out to be a nutter. But songs from tree memories? Okay then. Someone's feet needed pulling back down to the ground. I didn't say anything then. There would be a better time, when she wasn't so lost in her current moment.

The waxing moon would be rising before we headed back that evening. We had to stop one last time for her to pick some ash leaves from a stand of beautiful trees. That was the last of what she needed to gather that day, she told me and we drove in a peaceful silence back to the shop, other than her directions. I was hopelessly lost until the shop came into view in the deep twilight.

"Don't run away," Melissa told me, when we stepped from the evening's chill into the warm, gently lit store. There wasn't much need for light as there were rarely any customers in the store at night, particularly a Sunday. The tourists that came by during the day were all gone to dinner or sitting around their campfires once dusk fell. I hadn't intended to leave right away, so her request was easy to accept.

Melissa went to work on something downstairs while I sat with Francine and my new, purring paramour, Arthur, in her kitchen, cluttered neatly with utensils and drying herbs and bulbs. She served me a steaming cup of strong tea against the night chill. The October nights no longer held the warmth from the day. I was wishing I'd had enough foresight to bring a sweater.

"Did you enjoy the day?" she asked me.

"Yes," I told her. "Very peaceful and informative."

"A good walk in the woods is always cleansing for the soul," she told me. "If you let it, nature will remind you that you belong to her and not the other way around."

"I got that," I told her. "Melissa said she was singing songs from the trees' memories."

"She has that gift," Francine said to me and I didn't know whether to worry about her too or be less concerned about Melissa. Francine was a woman you could trust and believe. But still. She smiled at the look on my face. "You find it hard to believe because of your practical upbringing. Or rather, your scientifically practical upbringing."

"It does seem weird," I admitted. "Trees having memories."

"The world is a living place," she replied. "You've probably heard the term Gaia. It's been in the popular media for years now."

"The world as a living organism."

Francine nodded. "It is," she told me. "Gaia is a goddess, the Earth's grandmother. The term has been used to describe how the whole planet is a complex organic system, and there are energies and things science has yet to understand or even discover. The memories of trees are not like those of you and me, but more like ancient energies or rhythms that still pulse through the earth. Melissa has the ability to feel them and translate them into what we can understand and experience. Does that make sense?"

It did. Thank God, it made perfect sense. My friend was not insane. I had been using too narrow a frame of reference. In the back of my mind, I felt there was something wrong with that kind of thinking. Yet, it worked for what I wanted to believe and that was good enough. To this day, I haven't been able to put my finger on what seemed wrong about her explanation. I think it was just the scientific part of me not wanting to accept what had not been proven.

Does that make sense? If not, screw it. I accepted Francine's reasoning and was good with it.

As we spoke, Francine had been laying out the vegetarian dinner she had prepared for us all. I got up and helped her, because it felt less like I was imposing, but also because it seemed natural. Melissa came back up a few minutes later with a white cotton pouch, neatly hand sewn shut around some aromatic herbs.

"This is for you," she told me, handing me the packet.

"What is it?" I asked, holding it up to my nose to sniff. "Is that the ash leaves?"

"Yes," she told me. "It's a dream pillow for you. Ash collected under the waxing moon is for prophetic and insightful dreams."

I was struck dumb and paralyzed. I just sat there, staring motionlessly at her. I hadn't mentioned a word of my angst or inner turmoil to her and she was giving me something to help me have prophetic and insightful dreams. I couldn't respond beyond blinking at her.

"When we first met and I listened to what you were telling me," Melissa said, "and the more we talked today, I got the sense you are really searching for your path. I was hoping this might help when you dream at night. Those reveries often show you the way."

I was floored.

Until that moment, stories about the gifted had only been stories, like clinical reports on some person's condition. But with Guennean looking me in the eyes, smiling, and holding the hand that wasn't shaking around the sachet, I understood. It wasn't mind reading. She had looked into my heart.

She brushed back the tear that had formed at the corner of one of my eyes and a laugh escaped from me. It was a chuckle at myself for being embarrassed. A moment later, we were eating and talking about other things Wiccan and Willow Creek. They knew a lot about what had gone on the region over the last couple of centuries. Remembering and passing on the lore was part of the craft.

Melissa walked with me to my car after dinner and a course of sweet, dessert brandy Francine distilled in the cellar. The dream pillow was tucked safely in my purse. Obviously, I had been touched deeply by the gift and felt as close to Melissa as I had ever felt to anyone before. I set my purse on the hood of my car so it wouldn't get in the way of the huge hug I gave her. She returned it and the kiss on the cheek I gave her, before we released each other.

"Thanks," I told her. "The dream pillow means a lot

to me."

She smiled back and said, "I know I said it before, but I'll say it again. Enjoy the gift of life, India, the one you've been given, not the one you keep fighting to make. Whatever you are due to have in life, you will have. Why make it a struggle and miss out on things along the way?"

"We have to work to make things come about," I replied. "Plans don't accomplish themselves."

"By all means plan," she said. "Don't think of it as a defeat, though, if something doesn't go right."

"That's sound advice," I agreed. "I hadn't thought I was doing that, though."

She nodded. "I sense you feel beaten back when something doesn't work out."

I smirked. She was right. Hadn't I just been complaining about that earlier? Okay. Yes. It was time for a change of outlook. No more treating life as a struggle with Fate. From now on, we were going to work together. Or at least I was going to go with her flow a little less reluctantly from now on.

"Lunch tomorrow?"

"Yes. I'll call you with where to meet me," she said, which would become a routine. She'd give me directions to follow and we'd go to different places; sometimes the same place, but she'd send me on different paths. So silly. Such fun. She put a twist I looked forward to into every day.

When I got back to my room that night, I put the dream pillow under the fluffy one from the Wells the minute I walked in. When I laid down later on the cool, clean sheets after a quick soak to scrub the day away, I felt entirely relaxed and found myself wistfully ruing that Melissa wasn't a man. I gave myself a chuckle over that. If only I could get her personality into a body like Richards'. Wow. That would do me forever. Fat chance of that, though, right?

Smiling, I drifted quickly into sleep. I may not have dreamt that night or the pillow might have needed time to work. I didn't wake up with any revelations the next day.

Just the feeling that I was ready for another week of work.

The next week would be much the same as the first, except with the silly lunchtime adventures Melissa gave me. When I wasn't interviewing someone somewhere or working with Alice Duvall in their great home library, I was digging through the church and genealogy records in the mansion, or local newspaper archives in libraries and storefront offices. Lunch was a diversion with Melissa. Dinners were belt stretching affairs with my clients. Thank God the town was built into the hills and my runs, which I got in every morning, even in the rain, were made more challenging, i.e. calorie burning for that terrain.

Thursday's lunch, though, started as a bit of a surprise and a shock. Melissa's instructions had been, "Once you come around the sharp bend around the blue boulder, there will be a creek about thirty feet under the shortest bridge you'll ever cross. Driving at 30, count to seven after you cross it and then turn left onto the dirt road between the stands of lilac trees."

The trees were easy to spot; a little beat up from the recent rains, but still dripping with blossoms. I ran all the windows down as I drove between them, filling the car and my head with an intense perfume. Thirty yards down that closely hemmed lane, the sagging trees and tall grasses gave way to a riotous clearing.

Twenty feet in front of me, Melissa's Scion was parked in a garage so ramshackle it was better called a shed. Gaps in the walls and the roof let dappled sunlight in over her car. I parked behind it at the edge of a yard on my left that was a tangled mat of dandelions, thistle and heavy grass that hadn't been mowed in a month.

Beyond that yard stood a tiny house and a huge garden, stretching back toward the road and lost from sight in its own overgrowth. It might once have been magnificent, a show piece garden for the arbors and the ivy-encased gazebo at the far end. Now, it was its own master, deciding what grew where and how tall. Several healthy looking cats prowled the grounds.

The house was what gave me the shock. My apartment back in St. Louis might have been larger than this grayed, wooden structure. The worst of it was that the old mansion may have been in better shape than what I knew had to be Melissa's home.

She emerged from the garden with a basket of herbs and flowers on each arm and a dusty straw hat with a huge brim sitting askew on her head. In a flowing summer dress and sandals, she was once again the perfect hippie. All she lacked was the peace sign pendant hanging from her neck, I thought, and then saw that she was wearing a pendant on a leather cord. It was a Celtic knot. She was a modern hippie after all.

Arms full, she couldn't hug me. So I gripped her shoulders and we kissed one cheek and then the other, before heading for the house.

"Here, take this," she said and held out a basket. I took it, seeing that it contained leaves of various kinds, including what appeared to be lettuce and some small onions. She stooped to snatch up a few, brighter colored dandelion leaves as we walked. I figured this was going to be the salad portion of our lunch.

The steps were cement and not attached to the house. A half-inch gap opened between their edge and the frame of the house. Grass grew up around either side, standing taller than them and poking through that gap. Melissa happily led the way in, thinking nothing of what to me would be a structural flaw.

We entered into the back corner of a kitchen straight from the 1950s. Small, outdated appliances that I wouldn't have thought could still be working stood in front of me. Her stove was an apartment-sized one, about half the width of your normal range. Beside it was a small wood stove, which I imagined was more for heat than cooking. We set the baskets on the old wooden table and she gave me the tour.

There were only three rooms and a small bath with a cast iron tub from the 1930s. There was the kitchen, her little bedroom, and a large living room that was half the structure. It all sat on a platform, raised a couple of feet from the ground. There was no basement or foundation. What it did have was an impressive fireplace of natural stone in one of the long walls of the living room. From the hearth to the bottom of the mantel had to be a good four feet and the base went almost three feet back.

"You can have indoor bonfires in that," I remarked.

"That's how I heat it in the winter," she told me. "You'll see when you come to visit, right?"

It was a question and an invitation. I smiled and told her, "Of course."

Her grin was heartwarming. "It's not much, but I don't need any more. I spend a lot of time at the Herborium as well," she told me as we returned to the kitchen where lilac flowers and other herbs hung drying along the walls. A rust colored tabby cat had followed us in and was getting a drink from the trickle of water in the sink.

"Hello, Aubrey," Melissa greeted and scratched his head, but made no move to take him from the sink. "Grandmother is still quite hale for her age, but she doesn't move as quickly as she used to. We have to keep the business looking nice, so I tend to this place, when I'm not busy at hers."

"Did you live here with your Mother?" I wondered.

She nodded. "Slept on a sofa sleeper for most of my life," she said with a smile. "As well as imposed on Grandma."

"I doubt she considered it imposing."

Melissa smiled as she washed the leaves and bulbs she'd just harvested, then seemed a little melancholy. "Well, it was for the two months I stayed there after Mom died. It was hard to be here alone."

"I guess it would be." I had siblings. Melissa had been an only child.

"But I couldn't *not* come back," she told me. "This is my heart as much as any other part of me. My parents bought it as an abandoned house from the bank, intending to renovate and expand it. We got as far as clearing the grounds, starting the garden, and putting in the lilacs. Then, my father lost his job at the tannery because of health issues. Probably some chemical exposure although we're not really sure. He got disability payments from them and social security, but it wasn't what he'd been getting before, and he passed away a few years later."

"I'm sorry," I said. "How old were you?"

"Twelve."

"I was fifteen when Dad passed."

"So you have some idea then," she noted and we said no more about it. Nothing more needed to be said. Right then, nothing more needed to pass between us on it.

"Well, time undid most of my father's improvements, as you can probably tell. Mom and I kept the garden up, but that was about it. With her gone, it's too much for me, when I'm spending so much time helping Grandma. Though, I still get a lot of good things out of it," she motioned at the salad she was making, "but for the most part, I call it my rodent garden, because mice and other forest critters seem to get more from it than I do. But that's all right, the cats balance it out."

"Are they feral?" I asked.

"For the most part," she told me. "But they aren't wild." In emphasis, she nuzzled Aubrey, who had jumped from the sink to the counter beside it. He purred and seemed to smile.

"How many do you have?"

"Six or seven," she answered. "I wouldn't call them mine. They just stay here with me. There's chicken salad in the fridge for us."

I went and got the ceramic bowl that was probably as old as our ages combined. There was no lack of chill in the glass. The old fridge was working fine. At the table, I felt the floor board deflect under my weight with a creak.

"Going to have to shore up and replace that spot in

the spring," she commented.

I had noticed different colored boards sticking out from under the area rugs. Apparently, they had been spot repairing the place as necessary. Winters had to be a constant battle between the roaring fireplace and drafts through the floors and windows.

"Eventually, though, it's going to have to come down," Melissa said wistfully. "I can't afford to keep it up. I can't even insure it. We stretch our money, but there's only so much Grandma and I can do to keep two places up, and we have to keep the Herborium up. It's how we get our money in the first place. If it wasn't for the lilacs and some other perennials, we wouldn't need it. But we use the oils for the candles and soap. We figure I'll just move in at the Herborium permanently, once this house is unlivable."

"What about a loan to fix it up?" I asked. "Surely the land would be enough for capital."

"Maybe once my car is paid off," she said. "There's only so much money to pay loans back with."

"Good point," I said as she began slicing homemade bread for sandwiches. "Still, it's your parents' place. I'd hate to see it just fall to the ground."

"Yes," she said. "But no things last forever and we'd still have the garden, even if I couldn't live here. That was the most important thing to my mother."

"And to your father?"

She cocked her head to one side and smirked. "I guess for him the big thing would have been knowing that I was okay, wherever. I don't think it needed to be this particular house."

"Same here, I guess," I replied as I thought about it. Dad hadn't been overly sentimental; not even about pictures. So long as I was healthy and happy, it wouldn't have mattered to him if I was in Sitka or Katmandu.

We took our lunch out into the center of the haphazard, but beautiful garden, where she had cleaned off an old bench for us to sit and eat, while the cats prowled and the birds and the butterflies fluttered about us. Somewhere during our conversation, I found myself talking about doing the fall garden clean-up with her. It didn't feel so much like I was promising to help as it did that I was stating simple facts of a normal activity. I was going to help. Why wouldn't I have? As much as I love my work, I regretted having to get back to it that afternoon.

Memories would return that Thursday night. Recollections of a day I aged several years.

It happened in the spring, when the trees were in full bloom and the world was coming back to life after a harsh winter. The windows were open in our classrooms to let in some fresh air. Birds were cheerily twittering and fluttering in the shrubs below them. I was in front of the class, preparing to recite Robert Frost, when I came to a crashing halt.

There was no reason for it. I had recited before and had no problem with it. I'd been feeling fine all day and lunch had been good. There was no physical reason for me to have shut down as I did. Yet, I felt everything stop working, my mind, my mouth, even my body went slack. I simply and completely stopped functioning.

"Miss Hills," Mr. Duggan prompted. He wasn't the most understanding of teachers, but he was patient. He didn't get bent out of shape when I didn't respond. "Miss Hills, we're all waiting."

I just stood motionless, eyes staring past the page in my hand and toward the floor, while seeing nothing. His words were barely registering. The same with the singing birds and the fresh scent of spring. A breeze moved the paper in my hand, but I hardly noticed it.

He prompted me again. Then, he scolded me gently for wasting precious class time. Finally, he mildly threatened me by asking if I wanted to see the principal. Other students, those that knew me, asked if I was okay. They insisted to Mr. Duggan that something was wrong.

After several moments, Mr. Duggan called in the hall monitor to escort me to the principal's office. That student knew me and took me to the nurse instead.

"What's wrong?" the nurse asked me.

"Nothing," I said. "I don't know. I just..." I couldn't put it into words.

"Did something happen to you earlier?" she asked.

I shook my head. "I don't know. I just feel weird."

She did the usual checks such as taking vital signs and asking what I'd eaten and wrote it all down, finally declaring, "There's nothing wrong with you. Why are you acting like this?"

"I don't know," I said. "I'm not acting like anything."

So she called the principal to report the incident and her jaw dropped and her eyes widened. I started crying and couldn't stop. I would still be there, sitting hunched over in the hard, wooden chair and quietly sobbing, when my older brother came to get me.

It had been sudden; an aneurism no one knew he'd had. No one could have seen it coming. My father was just gone in mid-sentence at work. Many years later, I would learn of the therapy his supervisor had needed from the trauma of seeing him die.

I was lost for the next several days. I must have eaten and slept and bathed, but I don't recall any of that. I had been on auto-pilot, I guess. There had only been the haze of shock at knowing my father was dead; that he was just gone. I think I cried for three days straight, having started there at school.

It's hard to describe the sense of being lost and alone that comes from losing a parent. It's one of those things you have to experience for yourself. I don't wish it one anyone. I certainly hope it comes when a person is not so unsure of themselves and the world as is a fifteen year old, mostly introverted girl.

My coping was to become more withdrawn, retreating from most of my classmates. For the rest of my years in high school, I hung with a few core friends and never dated. I read a lot, which was probably where I got a sense of how things should be written. I came out of my shell in college with a new set of friends and already writing freelance to finance my living expenses.

When I think back on it, I don't believe I've ever really gotten over that day. I probably never will. Mentioning it to Melissa had caused it all to come back.

I called her from my room, wondering if she hadn't also been flooded with memories and finding that she had.

"I miss my dad, too," I said, tears trying to cloud my vision. You never really get over it.

"I know I shouldn't still grieve," she told me with her own sniffle of soft crying. "It's been fifteen years. I know he's been reincarnated to a healthy body and that his spirit is enjoying a new, good life. But it's still just so hard."

"I know, Mel. I've been tearing up tonight, too," I replied. "Fifteen years? My dad died fifteen years ago, too, in the Spring."

"Mine passed in the Fall," she answered. "How odd is that? They passed within months of each other."

"Maybe they came back together too," I thought aloud, "and they're best buds somewhere, chugging cold Cokes after playing baseball all afternoon."

I heard her laugh at that. "Dad loved his baseball, all right. Did yours?"

"He was into all sports," I said.

"What was he like?"

"He was funny, but stern," I answered. "Both my parents were realists. I mean, Dad felt that life was to be enjoyed, but not until after you got your work done. What about yours?

"He believed in setting aside time for both work and play," she answered. "Which is probably why our house never got fully repaired."

"But you got to enjoy it," I replied. "Where I'm usually working six days a week, morning until night."

"Funny how we become our parents," she said and I chuckled in agreement. Then the melancholy came back into her voice. "I still remember how I felt that day."

"Like nothing was right in the world anymore," I said, recalling the loss of all hope and joy in those first few hours.

"I couldn't grasp it at first," she told me. "I think it took hours for it to finally register."

"It was too much of a shock."

"Yes. I didn't even talk for a couple of days."

"I wasn't making much sense."

"I remember feeling like nothing would ever be right again," she said.

"It never has" I said.

"No," she agreed. "And no understands that hasn't been through it."

"No. They don't."

"And you've not found anyone like him or you'd be married," she remarked, which threw me for a loop.

Although, I answered in agreement, "No," my mind was left reeling by the sudden realization that no one I had ever dated had been anything like my dad. None had been anything like the man I had thought was the best in the world. Why was that? Why had I not dated the kind of man I respected? I didn't get it.

"Same here," she said. "Well, I should probably let you get to sleep. I just needed to talk a little. Thanks, Indy."

"You're welcome, Guennean," I replied. "And, thank you back."

There was a little laugh in her voice when she said good night.

Why had I made such disastrous choices? I wondered after ending the call. I couldn't fathom it. I made sure to put the dream pillow in place. Perhaps the emotions would bring about those prophetic dreams, I reasoned. If they did, I couldn't say. I didn't recall anything of my dreams that night.

Overall, though, it was a good second week. I made no secret of my fast friendship with Melissa and despite what people had said to me, no one made anything of it.

Richards seemed to be accepting a business-only relationship with me and Alice Duvall, surprisingly, turned out to be a rather humorous and clever woman to work with.

Per my plan, I popped back to St. Louis on Sunday to do laundry and to check on my place. Yeah, I was trying to be a little less anxious in my outlook. But I wasn't trusting enough not to check on my apartment every couple of weeks. I had wanted Melissa to join me, but she had already been committed to something in preparation for Samhain, or *sah-win*, in a few weeks. It was nice to sleep in my own bed and be surrounded by my own things even if only for one day.

When I left early Monday before the sun was up, I was ready for week three. I was looking forward to it and to really making progress. The outline and family member profiles were thoroughly done, and the timeline of their significant events had been laid out. It was time to go deep and get intimate with their story. I couldn't have known it was about to become a case of wishing I'd been more careful of what I'd asked for.

Chapter 5
The Encounter

When I say the first two weeks were good weeks, I mean in general. I got a lot of work done and was enjoying my stay in Willow Creek. Then again, not every single second was perfect. I was seeing shadows within the shadows at the mansion and couldn't shake the creepy feeling that the ghosts of the Duvall men were lurking just beyond the edge of the lights as I was shutting them off behind me. That uneasiness stayed with me the entire time, dampening my enthusiasm.

The rain came back that third Monday. The picnic lunch Melissa had planned ended up being on a blanket laid out on the Herborium porch, where the spray occasionally found us and chilled my cheek where it touched me. I had brought my sweaters with me from home this time so I was prepared for autumn temps.

The rain also put me a little behind schedule for the evening as I had to drive a lot more cautiously on the steep, windy roads. St. Louis has some topography, but nothing like Willow Creek in the middle of the Ozark foothills. It was already full on dark, when Sam bade me good night and headed home from the mansion. I continued my work, fleshing out the outlines into first drafts. The Mayor had gotten Sam to set me up with a large table in the records room, where I could leave whatever I was currently working with spread out. I even had some tiny speakers plugged into my laptop for a little music, another bit of what made the setup so sweet.

Then, thunder cracked loud enough to make me

jump and shake the building. The lights went out and I was lit up only by the glow from my laptop as it switched to battery power. Through the closed windows, I heard car alarms going off from the shock wave of the thunder. First, I questioned why anyone needed a car alarm in a sleepy little town. Next, I wondered if the old building had actually been damaged by the shaking. Sam's assessment of its condition, and the spongy floors I'd discovered in wandering around in it the last couple of weeks, had me doubting its structural integrity.

I couldn't see any lights from outside through the frosted windows, but I also didn't see any glow on them that a street lamp should have made. I opened one of the windows to look, got a face full of spray and snapped it back shut. I wiped my face with my hands as I went back to the table and the small grayish circle of light from the computer. The window hadn't been open long, but I hadn't seen any illumination from the street or other houses. It was a complete blackout.

Still, I thought, it was probably smart to check the circuit breakers, or, more likely for a building of this age, the fuses. I had no idea where they were, but it seemed logical to me that they would be at the back of the basement, where the electric service came in. I had noticed the conduit running along the ceiling of the stone corridor away from the store room. It seemed reasonable to assume the breakers or fuses would be at the other end of those runs.

Using the flashlight app on my phone, I went to the exit door and hesitated as a moment of fear hit me. My overactive mind's eye envisioned the entire clan of deceased Duvall men standing in the hallway, waiting for me to leave the blessed area and step into the darkness that they controlled. I chastised myself for being an idiot and opened the door. The light switch was just to the left of it. I figured why not give it try. Couldn't hurt. So, I reached for it.

Someone grabbed my arm with a grip so hard and

icy it burned.

I stopped breathing. I stopped thinking.

Then, I saw a man standing there in a high necked collar and old style fedora, snarling at me from beneath the handlebar mustache. In the pale light of my phone, he seemed to have a glow of his own. His right hand was clamped in an iron grip around my arm. He pulled and I started to fall.

Terror turned my body to fire and I screamed to prove it. There were more of them behind him, grim men in suits of long outdated fashion; their burial clothes. They meant to put me into mine. Two more reached out at me with gray, hard hands.

With another primal scream, I wrenched my body sideways, yanking my right arm free and swinging the door shut with the other. I felt it knock their hands back as the tears of pure fear fell from my eyes. I heard them claw at it, but sensed them quickly recede. They could not enter that room.

Relief filled me with exhaustion as the adrenaline subsided as quickly as it had come. I fell against one of the walls and slid down to sit on the floor as I cried, and then sobbed at both the terror and the sense of being safe. My right arm stung as though burned and I cradled it with my left as I sat there unable to leave and powerless to call for help. I had dropped my cell phone and knocked it into the hallway.

So on top of being terrified, I felt like an idiot. How incredibly B-movie horror flick was that? I'd dropped my damn phone and punted it into the hallway in the middle of the pack of ghosts that wanted to kill me. Just saying that sounded utterly ridiculous. What no longer sounded stupid, though, was the idea of ghosts. No more just believing in them as a curiosity for fiction writing. They were real. Melissa had been right. I should have accepted her protection. At that moment, I only wanted to call her and get her help.

I didn't know what she could have done. They all

avoided the building. From what I had gathered, she was not able to come in fighting like some Van Helsing character and wipe them out. I was stuck until morning and I knew it. It just would have helped to have been able to talk to her.

I ended up sleeping right there where I sat as the room grew danker and damper without the air conditioning. I dared not open a window to let the rain in with the old, delicate records around me. I never even moved. The laptop battery drained as I slept what little I could.

In the morning, I was stiff, and sore, and cold, and embarrassed. In the early sunlight, the attack seemed less real, less plausible. It almost seemed as though I might have simply passed out from fatigue and dreamt it. I packed up my gear and retrieved my phone, which thankfully had survived being dropped to the floor and bashed by the metal door. That gorilla glass stuff really worked. The device was out of power, but it came on when I plugged it into the car charger and drove back to the Willow's Wells.

In my room, as I pulled off the sweat dampened clothes from the day before, the possibility of having imagined everything continued to play in my head. I had been drowsy. Had I dreamt it? But the phone had been in the hallway, which would not have been the case, had I imagined it. Maybe the old wiring had been damaged by the thunder or the lightening and I'd actually gotten an electric shock off of the switch. That was entirely reasonable. I hadn't tried the switch, given the sun was up and I had been assuming the power was out.

Yes. That was probably it. I'd gotten an electric shock from the button and my crazy, over-active imagination had conjured up visions of dead Duvall men trying to do me in. Lord, I needed to be setting aside time to write that book while I was on this project, I thought.

Only, electric shocks didn't leave hand prints on

your forearm. Red, burn-like imprints in the shape of a man's hand encircled my still tingling right arm.

I almost fainted.

When my mind cleared, I found I was sitting in the armchair at the small writing desk. I picked up the phone and called Melissa, but got the message that the call could not be connected the three times I tried. The storm, I figured. Either lines were down or towers were out. I would have to drive out to her place or the shop.

But not right away. The dizziness was still with me and I felt like someone who had just slept on the floor of a creepy old basement. Which, of course, I had. I was nervous, perhaps as much as anxious. I was no longer terrified, though. Sensibility and perspective had returned to my thinking. Coffee, food, a bath. Rejuvenation. Those were necessary things, as well. I slipped on my sweats and went down for that big mug of coffee Mrs. Wells had already gotten into the habit of making me. My special morning beauty must have been exemplary that morning, I thought.

What pushed my already boggled brain further into a spin was finding Melissa coming up the steps to me as I was headed down for the coffee. Never mind the soup bowl sized mug. Mrs. Wells sent us up with a full carafe and a plate of heavy biscuits and gravy.

"I felt something was wrong," Melissa told me as we settled into chairs, me with my feet tucked in front of me on the love seat and her in the plush armchair. Everything in the room was soft and comfy, meant to be welcoming. I loved that room and was content to stay there.

I showed her the marks on my arm and recounted what had happened and how I had felt. "I thought ghosts couldn't really hurt you," I commented. "I thought they couldn't really influence this side."

"Then how do they slam doors and knock books from shelves?" Melissa responded. I had to admit that was a good point. I'd just never thought it through that deeply. I mean, why should I have when I hadn't believed in them until then?

"All those things you have heard are fables and wishful thinking," she told me. "They are the imaginations of film and TV writers looking to entertain and create what suits their scripts. A ghost can hurt you, India." She raised my injured arm as an example. "A ghost can kill you."

"I believe you now."

"Here. Wear this." She took a necklace of black and murky white stones bound in a leather cord from her bag. "This is what I wanted to give you in the beginning. I've kept it with me for this moment."

"What is it?" I asked as I donned it.

"Black tourmaline and selenite. The tourmaline will protect you from spirits and the selenite is for cleansing. You should come by the shop to get some salve for those wounds."

"They're just bruises," I replied. "Whoever he was, he had a strong grip."

"They are wounds, India," Melissa corrected me. "My grandmother will have a poultice ready for you once I get back and tell her what happened. We were afraid of something like this."

"That they'd attack me?" I asked and in the back of my mind found it curious that the thought of Francine Brindley knowing was not embarrassing to me.

"That the status quo would change because you were here."

"What do you mean? Like I'm some sort of catalyst?"

"Yes. Exactly that. You didn't mean to, but you have stirred the pot," Melissa told me. "You and that professor with all of his equipment, intruding into their space."

"We're making them mad."

"They were already angry. You're just providing a convenient target."

"This is my bullet proof vest," I said, holding up the crystal necklace.

Melissa smiled and said, "Something like that. I'll let

you rest and get some food in you. Come out to the shop. We'll be waiting."

I resisted the impulse to say, 'Yes dear.' Instead I smiled back and promised I would.

At the door to my room, she hugged me warmly and kissed my cheek. "Be careful," she whispered. "You're dear to me, you know."

I clutched her a little tighter, but didn't find the right words to tell her she was just as valued to me. She was. But the words didn't come to me and mimicking hers felt wrong. I simply told her I'd see her later and she headed out.

Alone in my room, I devoured the biscuits and guzzled the coffee, then fell asleep in a hot, sudsy tub with the crystal necklace clipped around my forehead like a pendant. I wasn't letting go of that sucker. No way, no how, not after that night. I had been converted to believing.

It was an abbreviated day. Alice Duvall and I had covered all of the family members and I'd collected most everything I needed from her by way of scanning into my laptop or borrowing a few pics and clippings. Most of that week was to be filling in from other papers and interviews with local historians. Francine Brindley and Marianne Wells had actually been two good sources of anecdotal history and lore. The first chapter of the book was about Willow Creek as much as the Duvalls to set the scene for the history to follow. Alice Duvall had been surprised and pleased at the first draft. It wasn't what she had been expecting at all.

It wasn't yet dark when I returned to the Willows Wells. I'd avoided the mansion most of the day, but had to stop in to get the few notes I needed for my interviews. I'd parked in my usual spot under the street lamp, switched off the engine, and then stared at the old house for a long time. Before, I had viewed it in a romantic light through the eyes of a writer looking for the words to describe its faded beauty. Now, I saw it as a façade; the beautiful, made-up face of the hag within.

It terrified me.

The unwelcome feeling came over me and grew stronger as I approached from the walk. By the time I mounted the first step, the sense of malice toward me was quite palpable. This time, however, I knew it wasn't my imagination. Sam was sweeping the storm debris from the porch. He'd said, "Hello," but it seemed to me that he was less than cheerful, as though he was sensing it, too.

I didn't take long getting what I needed and heading out. As I drove away, my arm throbbing, I began to think of other arrangements, like a work table in my room or the library at Richards' home, which they'd both offered several times. The problem was I liked being alone and away from everyone while I worked. The records room had been the perfect choice. I didn't know about that any more. But then, with the pendant from Melissa and maybe some other precautions I might be safe enough. I didn't know. It was a confusing day.

I let work fill my mind and push the experience back, clear it from my psyche to give me a cleaner perspective. One of my planned interviews that day was forty miles away, so Melissa and I had already figured on dinner over lunch. In a way, that was helpful. I needed some alone time to let my mind come to grips with how wrong I had been; how the world had gotten bigger in ways I couldn't have—and in some ways still couldn't—see. Part of me was lost that day, and I buried it in my work.

Still, it was a relief to see her at my door shortly after getting back to my room, even if she was frowning and pensive with me for not having gone out to the shop as I'd promised. Not enough time with all the driving, I told her, but there would have been had I not just wanted time away from everything else. I'd parked overlooking one of the lakes and just breathing the rain- scrubbed, fall-scented air for an hour. I had felt cleansed afterward.

"Well, I brought the poultice for your wounds," she

told me. "We'll do the first treatment before we head out."

"I'm sure it'll go away," I said. "It's just a bruise."

"That's your logical mind trying to reason it away," she told me. "You really didn't believe until this happened, did you? Maybe you did in your head, but not in your soul, not until they made their presence known."

"No, I didn't," I admitted. "It was like a scientific concept, a theory. The proof wasn't what I was expecting."

She smiled and told me to roll up my sleeve. The bruises were tender to the touch and I had to gently slide the arm of my shirt up rather than pull it as I had started to. I had not looked at the marks during the day, part of ignoring them, I guess. Instead of being red and well-defined, they had turned purple and grown wider with sickly greenish spots, the way bad bruises always change. They looked ugly.

Francine's poultice was white and a little grainy, smelling of familiar herbs that I couldn't place. Melissa told me a few of the things that were in it, but I didn't retain it. All I recall is that it was cool and soothing to the point of almost making me woozy for the relief. She wrapped gauze around my arm and salve to protect the sleeve she slid back down.

"How about sloppy barbeque tonight?" she changed the subject in a blink. "I want you to experience the best place this side of Kansas City, which we need to go to, as well."

"Sounds good to me," I said with a grin. It never ceases to amaze me how many absolutely fabulous little eateries there are scattered around small town areas, where one wouldn't have expected there to be a lot of business. But they're out there, all over the place. I've been querying publishers every year with the idea of a state-by-state backwoods eating adventures, but so far no luck. One day, hopefully.

Where Melissa took me was no exception to the rule. It looked like a collection of shacks dragged over from other places and cobbled together. Which was close to the truth as I found out. As it had grown, they'd inexpensively added on. We ate mounds of sloppy, pulled pork, baked beans, and coleslaw and drank sweet tea for what seemed like hours as we talked more about the realities of the spirit world.

There are real, unseen, and little understood energies out there that can, and do, interact with our physical world and our emotions. They can get into your head as well as your body. Knowing it and staying strong are the best protections. I was going to feel a bit better about going back into the mansion now. I knew how to guard myself mentally and had my protective crystals.

The rain was threatening as Melissa pulled up to the Willows Wells to drop me off. Night had fallen hours earlier and the deeply clouded sky was dark as pitch where the cloud lightening wasn't showing off ominous black billows. Thunder rolled heavily in the distance, like over-laden freight trains on uneven tracks. Another massive storm was brewing.

"I'd better get home before it lets loose," Melissa said and I gave her a quick hug from the passenger seat before making to leave. She caught my arm and held up a hand. Then, she invoked the Lord and the Lady and the good spirits of the land as she said a prayer of protection over me. She concluded it with light kisses on my forehead, cheeks, and lips, which last bit startled me. It didn't seem like that should have been part of the ritual, but my knowledge of witchcraft had been so bare.

"Blessed be, India," she told me. "Sleep well."

I guessed maybe it was some parting ritual or something. I didn't know. It had been a confusing day and I'd been forced to take in so much that I hadn't wanted to believe before. I just went with it for the moment.

"Blessed be, Melissa," I replied. "If it's okay for me to say that."

She smiled and laughed. "Of course it is. We're not a secret society, after all."

I laughed at my foolishness before saying good night

again and hurrying onto the porch under the growl of thunder and gray light from the clouds. When I waved from the open door, Melissa drove off with a wave.

It was warm inside the lobby and smelling of wood smoke. The Wells' had lit a small fire against the growing chill, but it was all but out now. Only a few red and orange embers glowed from the hearth where Willis stirred them up with the poker. He looked up from the perfectly Victorian setting of hearth and wing back chairs and smiled awkwardly. I was sure he meant it to be friendly, but his rough face and matter-of-fact demeanor worked against that.

"Good evening, Miss Hills," he said to me, sitting back with the book he'd been reading closed in his lap. "I've been waiting to chat with you."

"Hello, Professor," I replied. Why in the hell for, I wondered and felt instantly on my guard. It didn't help that the rain was beginning to fall and the rest of the building felt quiet.

"It has been more than two weeks now," he said. "I was wondering if you'd had anything odd happen in the old mansion, yes?"

"No," I lied as I sat in the armchair across from him, then thought better of it. Nothing at all happening might make him wonder if I was lying. "I mean, it's creepy there at night and I sort feel like someone is watching me when I leave, but that's to be expected in a creepy place like that, right?"

"Yes. The imagination does get carried away," he agreed. "But perhaps not. In my researches, many people have told me of having the sensation that there is someone else in the room, but you can't see them."

"So we can all sense ghosts?"

"To some extent, yes," he told me. "Or, at least, our bodies are able to detect the energy fields that are in some locations, just as static will make your hair stand up. The body does react to such things. What those energies are, is a different question, of course."

"I see."

"What about sounds or things moving?" he asked. "Even smells. Have you noticed anything in the mansion?"

I shook my head. "It's an old place. I don't really pay any attention to the creaking it makes. The thunder last night made it rattle like a kid's toy."

"Yes. That is a valid point," he said. "Buildings make noises of their own. It is not strictly paranormal. It can be so hard to differentiate the two."

"How do you do that?" I asked.

He shrugged. "Sometimes we don't. What about voices? Have you heard any voices? Seen any shadows moving?"

"Shadow figures," I clarified. Melissa had just been telling me that many spirits are fleetingly visible as black shadows darting by. "No. I didn't see any of those." Which was the truth. "I mean, it does seem like there are shadows in the shadows, but after staring at a computer screen for hours, who can say if it isn't my eyes playing tricks on me."

He nodded. "That happens to researchers all of the time; their eyes play tricks on them after being in the dark for so long. So nothing unusual has happened to you?"

"No," I lied again. He just gave me a bad vibe and I didn't trust him. "It's been the same the whole time. Sorry if that wastes your waiting for me."

"Oh no, quite the contrary," he replied. "It was important to know one way or the other. Two weeks with nothing occurring is very telling. Very telling."

"Oh, right," I understood. "It helps on the disproving side of things."

"Exactly," he said. "May I ask what you have heard from the Wiccans? What lore they may have told you."

"About the mansion? The same as we talked about before, that it was supposedly the Duvall men in some sort of Purgatory," I answered. "They've heard the stories, too, and said they don't have the magic to do it even if they wanted to. I'm sure you've heard all that, as well."

"Yes, yes," he said smiling. "Green witches could not do that. I am familiar with their ways."

"Part of your studies?"

"Not formally, just those things you learn along the way in working in a field," he said. "So Miss Ferrier and the others have not related any personal stories of encounters at the mansion?"

"No. They avoid it."

"Why is that?"

"They feel a negative energy coming from it."

"I see," he said, mulling it over. "Very interesting. I had not heard that. Perhaps it would be worth talking with them after all."

"You haven't?" I was surprised he left that source untouched.

He shook his head. "Not very scientific, their ways. Until you said that, I had thought the place was just a building to them, nothing special. I see that I have been somewhat misled or misinformed."

"They have a great deal of knowledge, Professor. I should think you'd want to consult them."

"Knowledge in what, my dear?" he asked. "Herbal remedies? Spell craft? Local history? Other than history, which is anecdotal to me, none of that really helps in my work. But the ability to sense low level energies, now, that could be useful. I thank you for mentioning it to me."

That kind of pissed me off because he bugged me and I wasn't pleased at accidentally helping him, especially since he didn't seem to view the witches as regular, intelligent people. I didn't reply with any courtesy.

"Well, it's been a long day for me, Professor."

"Yes, of course," he replied with his attempted polite smile and he rose from the armchair to extend his hand. I shook it and, of course, using my right arm made the bruises flare up sharply. I hoped I'd concealed the grimace, although he seemed to be studying me. I think he knew I was lying. "You will let me know if you do encounter anything?" he requested.

"Of course I will."

My suspicion of him began to clarify in my mind then. I got a grip on what was bugging me about him. If the ghosts were so strong and active that I felt them and had even been attacked, then how was he coming up empty in his research? Melissa had mentioned that intelligent spirits can hide and attack at will. Were they ignoring him? Had they been silent for the month he'd been working there? Seemed like it. Maybe they didn't like him either.

And then, it hit me as he walked out into the rain. When he reviewed last night's audio recordings, he was going to hear me screaming. He was going to know I'd been there all night. His recorders were battery powered. The blackout would not have affected them. However, it was too late to fess up, even if I had wanted to. He was off the porch and already swallowed up by the downpour as though dissolved.

I hurried up to my room. Melissa probably wasn't back to her home yet, so it was too early to call her. Moreover, my arm was stinging now from his firm handshake. I needed to apply some more ointment first. That would give her time to get home.

I took off my sweater and blouse rather than try rolling the sleeve up again. That had hurt. I unwound the gauze from the ugly-looking bruises. They were no better. The green spots had gotten greener and even a little black where the fingertips had dug in. Melissa had warned me it would get worse before it got better. I wondered if she had meant this much nastier.

She had given me the wooden spatula she had used to apply the ointment. I wasn't to touch the salve with my other hand, just use the utensil. Being left handed, it wasn't so hard. But it did give me that same light headed rush as before, as though something in it was mildly psychotropic and very fast acting. Putting the gauze back on was a bit of a challenge.

I wobbled a little as I stood from the desk, where I'd

applied it, and had a panic begin deep inside me. Not that I would fall over, rather from a sudden strong urge that I was being watched. It was the same sensation I had been getting in the basement, only enhanced by my dizziness.

Then, the weirdness started. I had to blink to be sure I was seeing what I thought I was seeing. The wall to the hallway quivered. I shook my head, but that didn't help. It trembled again, then seemed to ripple as if from something pushing it from the outside. The shivering went through the floor and ceiling before fading out.

I had backed up against one of the bedposts in the center of the room as I watched the undulations in the wood and sheet rock flow past me. The sense of malevolence and of a presence heightened in my spinning mind.

They were in the hallway outside my room, I knew it. They had left the mansion. They were no longer bound to the cellar as I earlier sensed.

They were here to finish the job they'd started last night.

My phone was on the desk. Beyond it, my eyes fell to the window and the blackness of night pushing on it. It rippled and settled to reveal a face at my second floor window. The gray face of an angry, scowling man. The face of the man that had grabbed me last night.

I stood there propped up by the bedpost as the dizziness plagued me and nausea made me gag. I was terrified, but I wasn't cowering. I had my pendant from Melissa around my neck and, it came to me, they couldn't enter my room. Either those crystals were incredibly powerful or something else was holding them back. I looked around at the floors and walls and ceiling. Under the bed, in the very center of the room, was a symbol drawn in charcoal. A sachet of something sat in the center of it.

Melissa.

While I had used the bath room and cleaned up before we'd gone out, she had quickly drawn this symbol and probably said a protective prayer over my room. I left it undisturbed and went to the desk for my phone. Her number rang without answer. The damned storms again. It should have gone to voice mail, not just rung twenty times each time I tried.

The face was gone from the window, but I dropped the curtains over it anyway. I wouldn't be leaving it open a crack tonight. As I stepped back from it, I heard the man's voice from outside it.

"You're mine, Hills," it whispered maliciously. "I won't let you destroy us forever."

"What?" I asked involuntarily. Destroy them? How? It didn't make any sense. Yet, there was no answer, only the pattering of the rain against the glass. The walls and floor seemed as solid as ever. The only sound was the shushing of rain falling on the roof above my head.

They had gone.

With a sigh, I changed into my sleep shorts and sleeveless T and crawled into bed. I was exhausted, spent mentally and physically, and Marianne Wells had put the most comfortable mattress ever made into this room. I remembered to slip the dream pillow under the fluffy down one before I was out for the night. If I did dream, it was pleasant. Because the sun was up when I opened my eyes again, and I felt refreshed.

Then I sensed the stiffness in my arm and, when I unwrapped the gauze, I gasped and half panicked. Instead of ugly, hand shaped bruises, my arm was encircled in black, near leathery-looking burn marks. Melissa had certainly been right. This was definitely worse.

Her number still rang endlessly.

Chapter 6
Richards and the Witches

I rushed through my morning routine, lotioning my arm liberally with the dizzying ointment and wrapping it securely. I told Mrs. Wells I'd overslept and had an early appointment. Then, I shot out for the Herborium, only to find the country road completely blocked by a number of downed trees. The trooper on the scene told me a tornado had ripped through there last night and torn out all of the phone and power lines.

He was also able to tell me that no one had been hurt. He couldn't put me in touch with them, but he did know for a fact that all of the Wiccans were safe and none of their homes had been damaged. Other troopers had already checked on them.

Thank you, Lord and Lady, I thought with a deep, internal sigh. Frustration filled me, but also relief so strong that it drained me. The shock of seeing the downed trees and flashing patrol car lights had flooded me with adrenalin from fears of the worst; of Melissa and Francine crushed under tree boles thanks to my active imagination. I was feeling the effect of its passing.

I turned around and headed for the Richards' estate. I needed some better answers from him. I needed to hear what he'd kept from me.

His Lexus was at the end of his driveway, about to turn out to head to his office, when I caught him. It felt surreal stopping him under the overcast, where stone columns held a gate that was rarely closed and stately trees, now showing their fall colors, dripped cool rain onto the cold ground. It was more like something out of an old English whodunit than rural Missouri.

"Can we talk about something?" I asked from my open window.

"Of course," he replied from his, totally perplexed by the look on my face and tone of my voice, but perfectly willing to appease me. "Have Agnes let you into my office. I'll join you there as soon as I get turned around and park."

"Thanks," I rushed up the winding drive, which I had all but memorized in the last couple of weeks, and skidded to a stop at the door.

Agnes was waiting for me. Richards had called from his car. Trailed by Ben and Jerry, she saw me into the warm, overly-furnished room with the juxtaposed styles and promised to return with coffee as quickly as she could make it. I stood alone in the office with the dogs peering curiously up at me for a moment as my resolve started to wane. The wax Chinese officer stared angrily at me like he'd lop my head off for saying the wrong thing.

Was it really such a good idea to confront Richards about it? What was I supposed to expect him to do about his dead ancestors? If it was them. But that face in the window, the man I'd seen in the hallway. I'd seen him in the photographs. I thought of going to the library to find it, but Richards came in at that moment, looking insanely right in his pinstriped suit and dark tie. He ran an import business. What could he know about ghosts?

"What is it? What's the matter?" he asked. "You look like something's happened."

I wasn't sure where to start. I'd thought about outright confronting him with the injury to my arm, but I had my doubts about sharing that with anyone else yet. Finally, I said, "Tell me about the haunting in the mansion."

"You've heard the stories."

"Tell me the true ones," I told him and he blinked and stared at me from behind his desk chair for a moment. I was standing in front of him with my arms folded and it got through to him that I wasn't joking.

"Something has happened. Hasn't it?"

"The haunting is real," I said. "I know that for a fact now. Tell me the truth so I know where I stand."

"Have you seen them?" he asked, seemingly afraid of the answer.

"Yes," I admitted. "The same man the last two nights. I'm sure I saw him in the photographs of your relatives."

He turned his head aside. That was the answer he'd been afraid of.

"Are the Duvall men condemned to that cellar?"

He looked back at me and said, "I'm not sure. I'm still not sure if I believe it."

"There's more to that," I said. "What have you experienced?"

"Nothing," he said. "It was my former fiancée."

I hadn't known there was one. They hadn't mentioned her. I sat down in one of the stiff chairs to listen. The dogs crowded on either side of me as though protectively flanking me, or keeping me in place.

"Her name was Phyllis," he told me, settling into his chair. "She was from a family like ours, but out of Little Rock. We met in college, so we'd known each other for years and dated for most of it. There was never any doubt that we'd get married."

"When was this?"

"Five, six years ago," he replied.

"What happened?"

"We were at a function at the old mansion. It was in better shape back then and we still used it for fund raising and other events. That particular day was another couple's engagement party. At one point, Phyllis and the other bridesmaids-to-be came in to use the restrooms."

He paused, so I prompted, "And?"

"They ran into a man in the kitchen," he told me. "They all saw him. He was dressed in an old, brown suit with a high collared shirt and had a big mustache. They said his eyes stared right through them." A chill ran through me at the description of the man I'd seen. "They all say he looked right at Phyllis, even leaned toward her, and growled at her, 'You don't want to be a part of us.' Then he disappeared into thin air and they came screaming out of the mansion. That was one of the last times we ever used it, and the last day I ever saw her. She broke it off that night and went back to Little Rock, married someone else a couple of years ago."

"But you haven't?" I noted.

"No," he said. "To tell you the truth, I was a little bit relieved. I know it sounds bad, but we were at odds over where to live. I wanted to stay here to be close to the business. She had wanted us to buy a place in Little Rock or Kansas City so we could spend much of our time in a real metropolis, rather than Hicksville Willow Creek. She never actually called it that, but it was the sense I got from her. We'd been looking at homes in the Kansas City suburbs. I would have commuted to the office, which I abhorred the thought of."

"Are you saying you weren't upset?"

"Of course, I was," he replied. "We had the worst fight of our lives that night and haven't spoken since. Some mutual friends have told me what she's been up to, but I'm over it. In the end, it probably wouldn't have worked out."

"Who did you blame?" I asked straight out, knowing it was a rough question. My anger and fear had been fading, but I still wasn't feeling magnanimous.

He observed me for a long second, seeming to ponder what answer I was looking for. Finally he said, "Who was there to blame? How do you blame a ghost?"

"What about the witches?" I asked. "Did you blame them because of the curse?"

"Of course not," he lied, averting his eyes. "That would have been stupid."

"But you did," I said knowingly. "A least a little."

"Well, okay, I felt anger toward them because of the old stories," he admitted. "But it's not like I was out to get them."

"You know the idea of them placing a curse is laughable," I pointed out, adding, "if you really understand them."

He nodded. "Yeah, I know. I don't believe in that crap. I'll be big and admit I felt some resentment toward them for a little while. Looking back on it, I know it wasn't anyone's fault really. It's just the way it was."

"Back to the point, though, you knew all of this and didn't tell me?"

"Well, you're not in any danger."

"How do you know?" Still, I didn't show him my injuries.

"It's just one ghost that shows up every now and then," he replied. "He can't hurt you."

"How do you know?" I asked again.

"Because nothing has ever happened," he said. "If it's someone that died back at the turn of the last century or so, and no one has ever been harmed in all this time, then he can't hurt anyone."

I was about to show him my arm, when Alice Duvall walked in. The door had been open. She'd caught the last of the discussion.

"What in the world are you two going on about? Why the conversation about this?"

"She's seen him, Nana," Richards told her. "Twice. The same one I described, right?"

"Yes," I said and nodded. Mrs. Duvall's arrival had put me off showing my arm. I didn't know how she'd react.

All she said was, "Oh."

She came in and took the second armchair at the desk. Her hand unconsciously settled on Ben's proffered head.

"He is a Duvall," I told her. "I know him from one of the pictures."

"Are you sure you weren't dreaming?" she asked.

"I was wide awake both times."

"I've told her about Phyllis," Richards added.

"What did he mean, 'You don't want to be a part of us?'" I asked. "This curse on the Duvall men?"

"Curse?" Alice Duvall appeared offended. "There's no curse."

"Then what did he mean?" I asked again. "What is he doing there?"

"That we can't tell you," she replied. "But you can't jump to the conclusion that all of the Duvall men are condemned to the cellar because one has been seen. We don't even know which one he is."

"I can find him in the pictures," I told her. "I'd really like to know why you didn't warn me."

"Honestly, dear, I didn't think you'd ever see him," she told me. "That incident with Phyllis was the first sighting in ages. I didn't think researching our family's past would stir him up."

"It has," I pointed out needlessly.

"I'm sorry, if he's frightened you, dear," Alice Duvall said. "But Robert is correct, he can't hurt you."

I was about to show them both my arm, when Agnes walked in with coffee and muffins. The sight of them reminded me that I'd skipped breakfast to go out to Melissa's right away.

"Anyway, you can come use the library here to continue working," Alice told me. "Just tell me you don't intend to add this to the book."

I didn't have an answer other than I hadn't even thought of the book. I was at that moment only concerned about my own skin, particularly the bit turning black thanks to this *harmless* relative of theirs.

Richards managed to surprise me then. "Hey, let's put it in," he said like he was having a brilliant idea. "People love paranormal stuff and it will add some color to the book. Maybe the man was some black sheep or something and this is his punishment. I think it would be cool."

"Robert, we don't want people thinking we're crazy."

"We're not, Nana. We have documented sightings by different people. I think it will be a fun part to read."

Agnes handed me a cup of steaming coffee fixed exactly the way I liked it. She'd figured that out during the dinners I'd taken here. I found myself sitting back to watch the emerging debate.

"Your ideas of fun have often perplexed me," she said. "You put that part in and you have to tell the whole story about the witches and the ridiculous curse story."

"What family can boast that kind of history?" he asked. "No one will be able to accuse us of being boring. Besides, it will make for a more accurate account, won't it, India? Otherwise, we're white washing things and sweeping it under the carpet."

"So long as it is an accurate account," Mrs. Duvall replied. "I trust you won't start editorializing, India?"

"Of course not," I almost spluttered over the coffee. Had she forgotten everything I'd told her about how we'd end up writing it together?

"You'll just show how we got caught up in some old feud?"

"What was the feud about?" I asked.

Alice Duvall shook her head. "I really don't know. It's been over a hundred years. Maybe you'll find something in the old newspapers, but as far as I can tell you, no one remembers."

"I can check," I told her. "I still want to know how you can be sure I'm not in danger."

"Danger?" Alice Duvall seemed surprised at the idea. "From a ghost? What can they do?"

"Knock books from shelves on my head maybe," I replied. "This man is not just a mist that people see. He's real. He can do things."

"Then don't work there," Mrs. Duvall said. "We'll bring everything to our library here."

"Well, the records room appears to be safe," I replied. "The church blessed the space, so that seems to keep them out. It's everywhere else that concerns me."

"What do you mean? Isn't it just the cellar?"

I hesitated a second, then told them. "The second time I saw him was outside my B & B last night." I left out that he was floating outside my window.

"What?" Richards sat up straighter, then leaned on his desk. "That's impossible."

"How is that impossible?"

He appeared confused for a second, then held out his palms as if to say it was obvious. "The story is that they're tied to the mansion."

"You told me the stories were wrong. That there was no curse or anything."

He looked like he was trying to figure something out. "He's never been seen anywhere other than the mansion."

"He has now," I pointed out.

Richards glanced over at his grandmother, who seemed equally lost. What they had known to be a fact all along, no longer was. They had no answer.

"Well then, how were you safe inside the B & B?" he wondered.

I pulled my necklace out from under my blouse. Richards figured it out instantly and pointed at it.

"You got that from the Wiccans. Melissa Ferrier, I'll bet."

"Yes. She made it for me."

Alice Duvall was stunned. "You don't seriously believe in that, do you?"

"He couldn't enter my room last night," I told them. "Something kept him out." I held up the necklace and kept mum on the symbol under the bed. They were silent, staring at the crystals as if wondering how much they could believe. I'd just changed their world. "Anyway, it couldn't hurt, right?"

"Dear, you need to put your faith in God," Alice Duvall told me. "Marianne Wells had the local monsignor perform a blessing when they opened the house. That's what kept you safe."

For a split second, I wondered if maybe she was right, that possibly Melissa's symbol had only seemed effective because of the greater power protecting the building. Then, I remembered sensing them—the ghosts—in the hallway and seeing the walls ripple. I also realized we were talking only about the one spirit. There were many. There were a lot of them.

"What other ghosts have been seen at the mansion?" I asked.

They thought and shook their heads.

"I've never heard of any others being seen," Richards said. I had the distinct impression he was lying. He knew more than he wanted to tell me. Was he really afraid that I'd be frightened off and not finish the book or something? Why else would he want to downplay the whole thing? Or was I being too critical of him still?

I was always looking for the man that was coming to take it all away, when things were going too well for me. Of course, I'd never expected that man to be a long dead relative of my employer. The deal truly had turned out to be too good to be true. But it was salvageable. The practical part of me was reasserting itself and reminding me I needed the income from this project to get through the winter. The records room was safe. My room was safe. I had the necklace and the protection of the witches. This wasn't a lost cause.

"I'm sure we can figure something out," I said. "Now that we've got a better idea of what's going on."

"There's some empty office space downtown, too," Richards suggested. "We could have the monsignor or Pastor Cogdon bless some rooms for you to work in, if you want to do that."

"That might be an idea," I conceded, although it seemed that the fewer spaces I worried about, the fewer times I'd be exposed as I went between them. I didn't know. I wanted to consult with Melissa and Francine first. They would know more about what danger there was to worry about.

I still had my doubts about Richards. I wasn't blind. I knew he'd had those kinds of thoughts about me. I'd admit that I'd had a few about him over the last couple of weeks, as well. So far I'd managed to keep it professional, but I knew he wouldn't hesitate to change that. As illogical as it sounded, at that moment, I felt if I opened up about the injury it would be too intimate a thing to do with him there. I wasn't experiencing that level of trust that morning.

It was a screwed up way of thinking and I guess I was kind of screwed up at that moment. By keeping my injuries to myself, though, I probably missed my first and best opportunity to alter the course of what would happen and keep some people alive.

However, Fate does as she pleases. She probably would have found another way anyway. I was making what seemed to be the right moves.

Obviously, though, I wasn't in control.

The trees had been cut up and pushed off the road and the power company crews were reconnecting the lines as I headed over to the Herborium. I was much better fueled on Agnes' coffee and banana muffins. That woman needed to be married and taking care of a family that appreciated her. Richards kept her on because she was eager to please and he probably liked surrounding himself with such people. Or was I being too harsh again? My thoughts were all over the board. I couldn't think one thing without the other and then admonishing myself for it.

The tornado may have missed the shop, but the hanging and potted plants had taken a beating from the slashing rain and wind. They were ragged and spent. This late in the year, they were finished growing and weren't going to recover. They would be done entirely within a couple of weeks after this pounding. But Francine was on the porch inspecting them when I arrived. I imagined she had something in mind to resuscitate them or combine them into something more vibrant until the snows starting falling.

Arthur came scampering over to greet me vocally as I stepped out of my car and scooped him up. Francine came down to hug me as I came toward the steps. With her arms still around me, she said, "I'm glad you're safe. Come inside and let me have a look at that burn."

Her arm around my shoulders as she led me in was warm and comforting. Arthur purring against my chest was relaxing. The aromas in the shop were just as soothing. Seeing Melissa at the counter completed the picture. When I set Arthur down and gave her a hug, I started crying from the ups and downs and twists of the last twelve hours since she'd dropped me off.

Over hot cinnamon-scented tea at the work table, while Arthur tail-flickingly looked on, Francine tended to my arm with considerable concern as I told them everything that had happened from the surprise visit by Willis to the conversation with Richards and Alice Duvall, and searching through the photos after.

The man I'd seen was apparently Samuel Duvall, who had been mayor at the time the so-called feud had begun. Even that bit of knowledge hadn't jogged Richards' or Alice's memories. The reasons for the feud, if it was such, were lost in time to them.

But not to the witches. I didn't miss the look between Francine and Melissa this time. It was one of resignation and wanting forgiveness. Francine sat down and took my right hand between hers.

"We owe you an apology, India," she told me. "We have kept this within our circle since it happened. You're a part of the circle now or you wouldn't have been attacked."

"What are you talking about?" I wanted to know. I didn't care that they'd kept it from me.

"It happened over a hundred years ago," she answered. "And it wasn't a simple family feud. It's a dark spot on our family's history as much as on the Duvall's."

She continued after drawing a breath. "There was a

male witch from Romania. Popular media likes to call male witches warlocks, but that's just a term they use. It's meaningless to us. A witch is a witch, regardless of sex," she explained. "His name was Baltus Sammic. He married into our family. He was strong in the craft, very strong. What we didn't know was that he had fled Romania because he had been caught learning the black arts."

"So there is black witchcraft?"

"You might call it that," she told me. "We prefer to call it black arts or spell work. I'm sorry we lied to you about that, but you weren't part of the circle."

"I understand," I said and that was the honest truth. Arthur slipped from the table and curled up in my lap as though to make it better.

"Sammic became stronger and more inured of the black arts," she carried on with the tale. "Our ancestors tried at length to dissuade him from those ways, but he couldn't be turned back. He liked the power he was gaining.

"And so the coven was forced to take drastic measures. His wife and her mother drew up a scheme to drug him, chain him, and force him to go through the cleansing rituals to rid him of those desires. Only, he was stronger and more alert than they had figured. He overpowered and killed them both by beheading. Holding their dying heads up in front of him, he swore to destroy our entire clan. He had become a raving lunatic."

"Beheading?" I was stunned and revolted at the same time. It was such a horrible way to die, and the fact that it had happened again to three more of them made my skin crawl.

"Yes," Francine understood my thoughts. "So who's really cursed? The Duvall's or our line? It's an uncanny coincidence."

"What if it isn't a coincidence?" I wondered aloud.

"You mean, what if it's really Sammic, still alive and strong after more than a century?"

Francine shook her head. "No one's magic is strong

enough to avoid death or come back. And where is he hiding? The sheriff has been scouring the area after Brianna's murder."

"Plus, my mother died down south a year ago," Melissa added.

"And Dianna was killed in an accident," Francine concluded.

"Looks like you gave this some thought," I said.

Francine nodded. "It's weird," she admitted. "But, Sammic's return just isn't possible. We lied to you about the existence of the black arts, but believe me, life extension or reanimation is not among them. He's dead."

"What about this Professor Willis?" I asked. "He gives me the willies."

Francine smiled and let out a small laugh, giving my hand a squeeze. "My dear, you do have an active imagination. I met him. He's weird, but he is not Sammic. He doesn't even look like him."

"You have a picture?"

"In the attic," she said. "I'll show it to you later." I would later add it to my collection of photos at the mansion. He was scary looking. But she was right, Willis was a completely different sort of disturbing. He wasn't Sammic. I'd been watching too many movies.

"So what happened after he murdered his wife and mother-in-law?"

"Our ancestors turned to the local authorities. Samuel Duvall was mayor at the time. Richards is a direct descendant of his. The sheriff was also a Duvall; his brother Adam. They betrayed us. They harbored Sammic and allowed him to escape. We can only surmise he reciprocated with a spell that started the Duvall fortune. They have been wealthy and powerful ever since.

"The coven made Sammic's crimes known to other witches, should they come across him. There was no coven in North America he could have innocently joined. No word came back to us, though. He disappeared completely. We imagined he went back to Europe or may even had gone to South America, but we had not been certain of where he went or what end he came to, until almost forty years later.

"We finally heard from a coven out in Montana. He had taken on the name of Harzchcuk, remarried, and had another family before dying about thirty-five years after he fled from here. Someone took a picture of him in his coffin and someone else recognized him from the photo we'd circulated all those years ago. They were good enough to tell us so we could close the chapter on him. His meeting with the Lord and the Lady could not have been good."

She would show me that photograph also. Sammic was dead and had been buried for sixty-five years.

"How do you know he swore to destroy the coven?" I asked. "Was someone else there?"

"Yes," Francine told me, "Sammic's daughter, Melissa's great-great-great grandmother, my great grandmother, who was five at the time. Sammic had not been aware of her presence. She had seen it all and told the rest of the clan. Perhaps it was her youth that made the Duvalls doubt. That doesn't account for hiding him and allowing him to escape, though, nor their sudden financial successes."

"What did your ancestors do to the Duvalls?"

"Nothing," she told me. "They reported the incident to state authorities, but they didn't care about witches. The harassment began and most of the clan was driven off, just as I told you before."

"Then it was to cover up what they did, not because they didn't want the old religion around."

"Yes," Francine answered. "Although the religious reasons would have played a part in it, too."

"What about the ghosts in the mansion then?" I wondered. "Who are they?"

"That's a curious question," she answered. "We know they are at least the Duvall first born males since the event. Perhaps it is their punishment, their Christian Purgatory for what they did to our ancestors. But we are telling you the truth that it wasn't us. We wouldn't even have known how to bind them and interrupt their reincarnation. We just avoid the mansion and try not to get close to them."

"Then how did they get there?"

"We don't know and never have," Francine told me. "It's just as much a mystery to us as anyone else. People condemned us for being in league with the devil, when nothing could be further from the truth. Witchcraft is a religion bound to the earth itself. We have many deities, rather than being monotheistic. In particular, we do not believe in the devil or Satan as some religions would like you to believe.

"Besides, and I've made this argument to scholars and others over the years, if the Christian God exists and is more powerful than we are, then He would be able to do whatever He wanted and our spells would be harmless. He wouldn't need public opinion behind Him before He condemned the past leaders of our town for what they did. He would have done it on His divine knowledge. So, if He had not undone any spells or curses to bind them to the mansion, then it was because He had already decided it was a just punishment. There was no point in blaming us witches, regardless that we couldn't have been responsible in the first place. Any condemning was being done or condoned by their own God."

"That's a really good point," I commented.

"It's possible, maybe even probable," Melissa said, "that you were attacked because they're afraid you'll do something to tip the balance, maybe uncover the proof of what happened. Any Purgatory is better than being condemned to Hell, which they would believe in, even though we, as witches, don't believe in it."

"They're not bound to the cellar like everyone thought," I added. "Now, we know they can leave it, if they have reason."

"Which is you at the moment," Melissa pointed out unnecessarily. I gave a frowning smirk in equally pointless acknowledgement.

"How long will it take you to finish your book?" Francine asked.

"I had figured four to six weeks overall, maybe eight for the initial research and some first drafts, which have to be done here," I answered. "I don't know what having angry ghosts after me does to that, though. I was hoping you could tell me what I need to do to stay safe."

"Are you sure you want to complete the project?"

I nodded. "I have to. One, I promised and don't want to break it. Never mind it would look bad for me for getting other jobs. But also, I really need the money."

Francine nodded. Whether she thought my reasoning sound or not, she never told me. She was a woman that let you be who you were.

"I'll make up a stronger poultice and have Melissa bring it around this evening," she said. "She'll probably need to redraw the protective circle. Mrs. Wells is likely to have scrubbed it off. She's a good woman and will do what she believes to be helpful."

"None of what I'm researching would prove the guilt of the Duvall ancestors," I said. "At least, I wouldn't expect it to. I'm not digging for any unofficial sources. I shouldn't see any accounts that contradict the official story, which says nothing about the incident with Sammic."

"They were unreasonable in life, don't expect them to be any less in death," Francine told me. "Melissa will bring you some more protective items for your room at the B & B. You will be safe at the mansion, so long as you wear your necklace. Whenever possible, leave before dark."

"That won't be a problem, trust me," I told her.

After lunch, a prayer for my safety, and a long and tight hug from Melissa, I went back to work in the mansion. I could feel them there, hiding in the shadows. But I was no longer afraid of them.

I knew what to do now.

Pastor Cogdon came calling at the mansion that

afternoon. He poked his head non-intrusively around the shelves that blocked my work area from the door and put on a pleasant smile.

"I hope you'll forgive the intrusion," he said.

"No intrusion at all, Pastor," I returned politely.

Still smiling, he came forward to seat himself across the table from me. "I was hoping we could talk about something," he began.

"The witches?" I asked. It struck me then that he was late in coming to address me about them. I'd been there two and a half weeks and my friendship with them was no secret.

"Mostly the curse tales," he said. "I spoke with Alice Duvall this morning and am concerned with how you will represent the haunting stories and the role of the witches here."

"It's not a story, Pastor," I told him. "I've seen Samuel Duvall twice in the last three days. I wouldn't be surprised if he makes it three in a row later tonight."

"My dear, I'm sure you've seen something, but surely it's not Samuel Duvall. He passed on a century ago."

"Physically anyway," I amended. "The rest of him is still here."

"There are no such things as ghosts," he told me.

Maybe I should have shown him my arm, but I doubted he'd have believed me. "I'm afraid I can't agree with you anymore, Pastor. I stopped thinking that two nights ago when I opened the door over there and he was standing in the hallway in front of me."

"A trick of the light or merely tired eyes," he said.

"A full-bodied apparition, clear as a bell," I corrected. "I was wide awake and he was really there."

"And last night, too?"

"He was outside my B & B," I told him.

"And you expect him to come to you again tonight?" He didn't believe me anymore than he did in little green men on the moon.

"I think he's just as concerned as you are about what I might write," I answered.

"Surely you don't intend to write anything about it." He sounded aghast at the idea.

"Richards has given me the green light on it," I told him. "He thinks it will make interesting reading."

"The devil he does," Pastor Cogdon was getting bent out of shape and I couldn't hold back a small laugh.

"Don't worry, Pastor," I told him. "I'm writing a family history, not an exposé. I'm not looking for bad guys and good guys."

"That isn't my point," he replied. "The point, or a major part of it, is that souls move on. Samuel Duvall cannot possibly still be here."

"What about Purgatory?"

"It is not a place on this Earth," he told me with an amused look in his eyes. I think he actually controlled himself from making a waving off motion. "That's a foolish notion to think a soul might serve Purgatory somewhere amongst us. That's simply not possible."

"Then what's he doing here?"

"He's not here." Pastor Cogdon insisted, the humor he saw in my position being replaced by the start of frustration.

"I saw him."

"I will agree that you saw something, but it cannot have been Samuel Duvall because Samuel Duvall passed on to where we all go one day."

I resisted making a joke about hoping I didn't pass on to this mansion's cellar. He wouldn't have appreciated it. Instead, I said, "I'm sorry, Pastor. I can't agree with you on that. I know what I saw."

And I knew who had tried to kill me.

"And you intend to write about it?"

"No. Of course not," I said, which I think really surprised him. "This is the Duvall family's history, not mine. I'm not in it."

He raised a curious brow at me. "What do you

intend to write then?"

"That some people have seen the apparition of Samuel Duvall in the mansion," I told him. "I'll mention the tales of curses, but that no one, not even the witches accept them as even possible, much less believable. It's merely to add something fun to the story."

"Fun from your perspective," he said. "Although, we don't want people thinking the people of Willow Creek are superstitious idiots from the nineteenth century."

I had to push back from the table and distance myself from the distractions of the computer and photos scattered about so I could put myself into a small space of my own to deal with that comment.

"Seriously?" I asked. "You really think people are going to think that?" I was as close to flabbergasted as you could get without babbling in incomprehension.

He simply nodded and looked at me as though I were the fool.

"Pastor," I said, "No one thinks that way anymore. Everyone looks at how people used to think that way as a quaint relic of our past."

"With all due respect, Miss Hills, your perspective is based on living in a big city where no one thinks that way out of fear of being ridiculed. People here tend to hold onto simpler ideas."

"Again, I disagree with you," I said. "I find it funny that I'm defending the intelligence of your flock to you. You've got college-educated people running your stores and working in Richards' offices."

"Are you a Republican or a Democrat?" he asked, surprising me.

"What difference does that make?"

"None," he answered. "It doesn't matter how educated you are, when you come to some subjects, like politics or religion or perceptions of groups of people. You believe what you believe and no amount of logic from the other side will dislodge your opinions."

"You mean, as in thinking all small town folk are

hicks from the sticks," I understood.

"Something like that," he replied. "It concerns me that you may, however unintentionally, cause people to view us in an incorrect light simply by mentioning that we ever believed in such things as curses and are a haven for witchcraft. We don't believe in witchcraft. Those women are misguided, even if they mean well, for which I'm sure God will be merciful to them."

"So you'd rather I didn't mention it at all." I don't think he heard the touch of disdain in my voice.

"I would be most grateful, if you left it out." To him, the best way to prevent people getting the wrong impression was not to explain it clearly, but to whitewash it, to cover it up.

His response raised my hackles. The only people whose gratitude mattered were the Duvalls. His gratitude had no place in this business. I counted to five internally to settle myself down, which only gave him the opportunity to continue. "What does it really add to their history to paint the town in a bad light by mentioning the witches and curses and hauntings? That's not the sort of publicity Willow Creek needs."

"First off," I began, controlling my voice as tightly as my temper. "The Duvall family and your local library are the only people who are ever likely to even see the book. So its becoming wide knowledge is extremely and ridiculously remote. Additionally, anything I write is already known and written down in other places."

I had never had to repeat myself about the scope of my work so much in all of my career as I had then. These people seemed to think the entire world was waiting to read the Duvall family history, when in reality there were only three people that would ever read the book from cover to cover, me, Richards, and Alice Duvall. Where did they get these ideas?

"Secondly," I continued, my temper easing off as I ticked off the points. "I'm not saying anything about the present day witches. It's not their story either. We're talking about an entry in a chapter of old family history. I won't be making anything big of it, just saying how it gave birth to the quaint, but disbelieved legend of the mansion being haunted."

It was basically going to be a lie, the way it would be written into the book, given what I'd learned from Francine and Richards himself that morning. It was a family history, after all, not a ghost story and after a hundred years, what did it matter? Everyone responsible was dead and gone, or serving their time for it in the old mayor's mansion. Someday, when I wrote my real novel, I figured I would incorporate parts of it. For now, it didn't need to be in the Duvall history. There really was nothing to be gained by doing so.

"Well, that's good," Pastor Joe said. "Because, otherwise, you're stirring up muddy waters that are best left still."

I could have made an argument that a tale of a haunting based on past wrong-doings was a quaint thing that would be good for tourism; give people something memorable to talk about when they got home. But, I left well enough alone. Stop negotiating once you have agreement, I'd been told on first starting out. Put pen to paper and get signatures on it. There wasn't anything to be written down here, not even a handshake on it.

"I'm relieved," he said. "You know, once you add a dose of reality to legend or rumor, it goes from being just a story to a reflection on those involved. Or in this case, their ancestors. It becomes news, rather than a tale, and taints them. Do you know what I mean?"

He was still negotiating. I grant that he had a point. People could be quick to assume. It only took a small, even misinterpreted fact to cause bad assumptions to be made and stick with people.

"Third," I told him. "Alice Duvall will have final say over how we write it in."

Pastor Cogdon gave a start in surprise. "Oh, really? I wouldn't have thought."

"It's her story," I reminded him. "I'm simply helping out with the research and the writing."

"Well, when you put it in that light," he said, the somberness leaving his mood and reddening a little in his cheeks. "I feel a little foolish for having been concerned."

I wanted to, but didn't tell him that he should be. He was rising to leave. I stayed in my seat and edged a little closer back to my work.

"I guess I'll be on my way then," he said needlessly. "Sorry to have disturbed you, but thank you for your reassurances."

"You're welcome," I said and he nodded with a smile before bundling off. That was the only way to put it. He was a larger man and when he exited, he pulled his sport coat around him as though wrapping himself like a package.

He left me with two thoughts, one not so flattering of him and the other curious. The first was that there I was with the ghosts trying to take my soul, the witches attempting to protect it, and the Pastor only worried that it had pure intentions from his perspective. The other was one that hadn't occurred to me before. What if he was right and Purgatory was on some other plane? What if it couldn't have been here on Earth; couldn't be in that basement? If that were true, then the ghosts were not there to be in Purgatory. It wasn't God doing the punishing. And, it wasn't the witches. So, what were they doing there?

Was it their choice? Was there really a curse and releasing them from it would mean their condemnation to Hell for their sins? Naturally, they would prefer endless exile on Earth to eternity in Hell. I had to wonder then... who placed the curse? The witches did not and never had the ability, even if they had been so vindictive. No one else would have had a reason.

The only one in this mix that could have had the power would have been Sammic himself, but that made absolutely zero sense, given he had rewarded them with the prosperity spell. They had sided with him and he had done completely the opposite of cursing them.

There was no logic to thinking there was a curse. Nonetheless, if neither man nor God were binding these ghosts to the earth, then it had to be by their own choosing. They must have chosen this exile.

Could spirits purposely remain, rather than go to Heaven or Hell? Why would they do that and choose a dank cellar to inhabit? What was there about this building? Its meaning and prestige from the bygone era? Their favorite place in life and so the same in death?

My overly-active imagination thought up the possibility that there were documents somewhere in this records room that would prove their guilt, ruin the family reputation, and get them condemned openly by the current leaders, perhaps drive them to the Hell that they had earned for themselves. They were there to protect the family's reputation and to safeguard the secrets. That was why they had attacked me. That was why they wanted me dead insomuch that they'd left the mansion to try to get me.

I calmed myself down for the idiot my imagination could make me. The records room had come long after they had passed and chosen to remain in the mansion. Some seventy or eighty years after Samuel Duvall had died in his forties, young like all of his male siblings and heirs. I was being ridiculous.

Then, why had Samuel Duvall said he wouldn't let me ruin them for all time?

The feeling that they wanted me dead remained. There was no shaking it. I didn't think it mattered whether there was proof in those old records or not. They didn't want anyone else knowing or delving into their past. Knowledge was power. They didn't want anyone holding sway over them even in death. Of course, with my arm still black and aching when I overused it, my thinking might have had just a touch of melodrama thrown in.

By this time I had long missed my last chance to

run and avoid the coming storm. There had been no stopping it, of course, never had been. It would only have played out differently and not done what it was about to do to me.

Chapter 7
Melissa

Dusk was forming as I got back to my room at the Willow's Wells. Marianne had indeed washed away the symbol on the floor and the sachet was gone. For a brief moment, I felt a wave of panic that she had also tossed out the dream pillow. However, it was where I had left it, safe in the drawer of the nightstand. I'd not had any prophetic dreams in the week and a half since Melissa had given it to me, but thought that perhaps I hadn't needed to with everything going so well, up until this week.

Or maybe I wasn't remembering them when I woke up and was merely having my moods pushed by them. I'd been feeling stronger and more at ease. Conceivably it was the effect of dreams that didn't linger in my memory as much as it might have been because there had been no problems before. Who knew? My imagination was capable of coming up with just about any reasoning possible. I was glad I'd never started believing in conspiracy theories. Someone would have needed to lock me up in a padded room.

There was a knock on my door and Marianne asked if I was there. A look of concern was on her face, as I let her in. She was holding the sachet from under the bed, trying hard not to twist her hands around each other in anxious thought and maul it. I wondered if anyone had talked to her, as well, but suspected it was her own discovery of the item that had her upset.

"That bothers you?" I asked about as needlessly as any question ever.

"Well," she began, trying to keep her words polite

and calm. "I know you and the Ferrier girl are friends now, and I guess that's all right, but..." Her words tailed off and she raised the sachet slightly. "It bothers me when I find things in my Christian home."

"It's for protection," I told her, "from the male Duvall ghosts in the mansion."

The look on her face said she didn't know what to make of my words. There was both surprise and satisfaction at my acknowledging she was right about the ghosts in the mansion, and yet, I could see it was perplexing to her to think of the witches as helping me. She let me take the sachet from her without resisting.

"You believe me now?" she asked. "You see that I wasn't being foolish?"

"I saw one of them, Mrs. Wells," I told her. "Twice. Melissa gave me this necklace and drew that protective image in the middle of the floor to keep me safe from them."

"If she wants to keep you safe, then why not get rid of them?" she asked. "They put them there. They control them."

Her brow furrowed as I shook my head before she even finished talking. "They didn't put them there and they have no control over them. No one does. Apparently, they aren't bound to just the mansion either. The second time I saw Samuel Duvall was here, right outside this window."

I walked over to the desk to set the sachet on it. Marianne followed me a few steps, but then stopped at my words and looked even more worried.

"They came here?" she sounded terrified.

"They couldn't get in," I said, and then clarified, "Or at least, couldn't get in by me. They were in the hall the other night, but the amulet or whatever we should call it kept them out."

"What? How do you know this?"

"They tried to get in through the walls," I told her.

"Are you sure?" she asked. "How can you be sure?"

"I just am," I said.

"Well, I'm sorry, but you'll have to keep Ferrier and the others away from here then," she said. "I can't have this happening here."

"It's not Melissa," I insisted. "It's me. They're after *me*."

"Are you serious? Are you sure?"

I thought about showing her the marks on my arms, but since I had been keeping it a secret from everyone else in the town, I had second thoughts. Even though I respected her I knew she would tell people and it would eventually get back to Richards and everyone else I kept it hidden from.

"As sure as I can be," I told her as I continued to mull it over.

"Well, I still think you should think twice about letting the witches in here," she said. "I already said you never know what a witch wants. You can't be too careful around a witch. You don't know what they'll do."

I asked, "If the witches were so powerful and could do whatever they wanted, then why haven't they? Why haven't witches taken over?" I paused for her to think for a moment, and then continued, "It's because they can't really do whatever they want. They're bound to what they know, what energies are really available to tap. The rest is just imaginative minds entertaining or after something. What would they be after anyway?"

"Control. Your obedience. Who knows?" Marianne rejected my answers. "Witches aren't normal people. They don't want the same things as the rest of us. There's no way you can tell what they want or what they will do to you, if you cross them."

"Don't worry," I told her. "We're friends. If anything, they'll protect me, not hurt me. And, that includes your home, as well. As long as I'm here, they'll protect it."

"The Lord will protect it," she replied. "I had the place blessed the day I opened it."

"That didn't keep them out of the hallway," I pointed

out.

Marianne Wells made a face of dismissal and shook her head. "You must have been mistaken about that. I will let you do as you think best, but I'm not comfortable with them around and I'd appreciate it if you didn't let them mark up my place with heathen symbols."

"That was just temporary," Melissa said, startling us both, from the doorway I'd left open. "Until we could put better protection around her personally. I'm sorry, if it upset you, Mrs. Wells. I was only concerned about India."

"This house is under God's protection, Miss Ferrier," Marianne said. "I'd appreciate it if you refrained from practicing paganism here."

"If that's what you want," Melissa replied, "I won't redraw the circle. I will, however, put this lotion on India's burns."

"Burns?" Marianne's anger deflated in an instant and she turned to me. "My God, dear! How did you get burned?"

"You didn't tell her?" Melissa sounded surprised. "India, they followed you here. She has the right to know."

"You mean the ghosts?" Mrs. Wells asked. "She did tell me. What do you mean burned? Did they burn you? How could that be?"

I showed her my arm and told her what happened. She wanted to call a doctor to look at my arm.

"It's okay," I tried to calm her down. "It's doing much better and this lotion is helping. Besides, it's not a burn, it's a bruise from Duvall grabbing me." I gave Melissa a look hoping she'd get what I was thinking. Bruises were easier to let be and heal than burns. If Melissa insisted it was a burn, Mrs. Wells was going to insist on a doctor. I don't think she did get it actually, but thankfully she chose not to argue about it. She set about getting ready to apply the lotion with the small, wooden spatula.

I had a sudden thought and asked without rethinking, "Can you keep this a secret, Mrs. Wells?"

"What? That you were attacked by the ghost?"

"Yes," I told her, "only until we figure out why they would want to attack me." I didn't have any logic for giving that reason. It simply sounded good.

"I guess," she said reluctantly. "If you think it would help."

"The fewer that know the better," Melissa chimed in. "We don't want rumors starting and people talking. But you deserved to know."

Maybe she had picked up on my thoughts. It sounded like a good reason to me. Apparently, it satisfied Mrs. Wells. She understood gossip.

"I got it," she said. "It would muddy up the waters. Get people thinking and talking about all manner of stupid things."

"Yes," I said, because you shut up, when you had agreement.

"All right then," Mrs. Wells agreed. "It'll be our secret. I have your word, Miss Ferrier, that there'll be no more spells or hexes or anything done here?"

"Yes, ma'am," Melissa replied. "With the exception of a protective prayer for India. At least let me do that much."

"Prayer?"

"Just asking the Lord and the Lady to look over her."

"No more drawings and things?"

"No, ma'am."

"Well, I guess a simple prayer would be okay," she said. "It's not a ritual or anything like that?"

"No, ma'am. Just a prayer asking for protection."

"I guess that will be okay," Mrs. Wells relented in the face of Melissa's gentle respect. "I'll leave you two alone then. I've got to get David's supper out of the oven before he dies of hunger."

"Thank you, Mrs. Wells," I said and she shut the door as she left. As her footsteps receded toward the stairs at the back, I turned to Melissa with a smile and asked, "You're going to do a spell for protection anyway, aren't you?"

"Of course," she said. "As if I wouldn't do whatever was needed for you."

Her sentiment warmed my heart and I was about to say something along the lines of doing the same for her, when she began lathing on the poultice. That instant warmth was as surprising then as the first time had been. The lightheadedness followed a second later, but passed as she wrapped the gauze around my arm.

"How about just the diner in town tonight?" she asked, completely and casually changing the subject.

"Sounds good to me," I replied. I wasn't all that hungry.

Dinner was simple. We talked about a number of things, how life came to you in snippets like this when you were on the road but weren't working. Our conversation ran all the way back to our childhoods as we told the other more about ourselves that night, staying away from anything paranormal. Although it came to us briefly as Professor Willis had been dining there, as well.

"Good evening," he said, pausing at our table as he was leaving. "Those are interesting necklaces you both are wearing." I had the impression he clearly understood their purpose. "I'm close to wrapping things up. Still nothing to report?"

"Nothing," I answered, though I had the feeling he knew I was lying. I figured he'd probably listened to the recorders from the other night and had heard me scream and slam the door shut. He couldn't have known why I'd screamed and shut the door, of course. However, I would have expected him to ask. That he didn't seemed odd. Then again, he was an odd man. Or perhaps he simply hadn't listened to the recordings yet.

I commented on how strange he was to Melissa after he had said good night and left.

"Some people and things just have to be let be what they are," she said.

I simply nodded and shrugged my agreement. She

was right about that.

We linked arms for the stroll back to the Willow's Wells. It was dark and we'd had a touch too much wine with dinner. We felt safe under the street lights. The male Duvalls were there. We both felt them lurking just out of the reach of the lights, surrounding us and chaffing at being held back by the necklaces we wore. Their voices, whispers of threats, and venom came to me like distant sounds on the wind. I could almost make them out, but I let them pass by and over me, refusing to let them get to me emotionally.

In my room, we had the last two glasses of wine in the bottle I'd opened the other night, as Melissa applied the poultice again. The warmth shot through me and the dizziness was amplified by the wine. Melissa caught me as I swayed. Then, the walls rippled again.

I gasped. "Did you see that?" Was I imagining it? Had I conjured it the night before, too? Was it whatever was in the poultice? Something psychotropic?

"They're trying to get in," Melissa said. Okay, she had seen it. I was not hallucinating. "Sit down."

I was a bit heavy dropping onto the sofa. The wine or the medicine or both had me woozy. Melissa stepped away toward the rippling wall and drew a shape in the air as she declared the room protected. The walls fell still. The hall beyond seemed vacant. The air outside the building felt empty of them. I sensed it more than knew it, that they had given up and gone away.

"Stay with me tonight?" I asked anyway. The temporary loss of balance was fading as quickly as it had come. Whatever was in the medicine didn't last long either.

"Yes," she said, coming back to me. She frowned as she looked at me. "You're a mess, India. You're tense as hell."

"Wouldn't you be?"

"Of course," she said, making me smile. "I brought some relaxation oils. I figured you'd need them."

"Do I use them in the bath?" I wondered, thinking of commercials I'd seen.

"No, silly," she told me. "I give you a massage with them. Take off your blouse and I'll start on your shoulders."

I complied as she brought out a dish to warm the oils by a small, lavender scented candle. A glass of wine was all that was needed, I felt, and we had just about finished ours. So, I opened my last bottle and poured us some more on impulse more than directed thought. I was going into autopilot and putting myself literally in Melissa's strong hands that rubbed the scented oil along my shoulders and upper back.

I slipped my arms from the bra straps to get them out of the way and sipped the wine while she worked warmth and freedom into my shoulders and back. After a few minutes, she pulled at the latches and asked it was okay to undo them. It was and it wasn't. I was so enjoying the massage, but her undressing me seemed awkward. My head was nodding, while my brain was doubting, and she released them. My eyes saw my bra on the table a second later as though my mind had detached and was merely observing now.

Melissa appeared to sense that because she starting saying things like, "Yes. That's what you need to do, India. Let your mind take a break. Let your instincts lead you."

I began to feel much warmer for the heated oils and her massaging hands and for the food and the wine in me. I was feeling safe from the ghosts while Melissa was with me. I was guarded from whatever was outside of that room. She was working on my neck, loosening the knotted muscles. I saw massage from an oriental standpoint, that you were releasing the blockages in your energy when you worked out the knots. It certainly seemed that way as the liveliness entering my head was making me dizzy again while it relieved my back.

Melissa was chanting, sotto voce, a rhythmic spell; hypnotic in quality. I knew it was one for relaxation and I completely gave into it, and yet I was energized as Melissa's hands moved over my back and shoulders. She seemed to be drawing the fatigue from my body. I was warm and almost meditative, like my body was asleep where I sat, while my mind drifted.

Through the trance, I was aware that Melissa was sitting beside me and whispering the spell into my ear. One hand of hers was caressing the fronts of my shoulders as the other arm was around my back. I realized that she was also topless and was pausing in her whispers to kiss my cheek. She must have felt the tension coming back into my shoulders as she began whispering for me to let my instincts guide me again.

"No," I said. "I'm not." Yet no more words came out. She continued to hold me and gently caress me. My mind wanted to know what she was doing, how she got that idea. My voice and my body wouldn't cooperate.

"It's okay to feel weird," she told me and whispered more soothing words in a language I didn't recognize, like when she had sung the songs of the trees. "Let your mind go. Let the energies flow that you've been stopping with your worries. Allow yourself to feel the world without thinking."

I still wanted to protest, but my head sagged back as she kissed my shoulders and the front of my neck. Her calming voice kept coming through to push back any conscious thought I had.

"Forget I'm another woman," she whispered. "Lose yourself in the sensations of your body. You carry too many worries. Let them go."

I already was. That was what was freaking me out internally. Physically, I was relaxed and open.

"Doesn't it feel nice just to have gentle hands on your shoulders and arms?" she asked soothingly.

It did. She was moving. My eyes were closed. I felt her slowly standing.

"Don't my lips on your neck feel good?"

They did. God, they felt good. Soft, giving more

pleasure than they seemed to want to take. She was in front of me, leaning forward to cup my face in her hands. Her lips touched mine.

"Isn't it good to be kissed?"

"Yes." I found my voice coming to me as an echo, something coming back to me after it had already been spoken.

"Isn't it good to kiss?"

"Yes." I heard myself again. My arms were around her as she sat in my lap straddling my hips, arms around my shoulders. I didn't need any more words. I was entranced and my body obeyed Melissa, kissing warm, soft lips, even as my mind disconnected, as though simply observing myself.

I won't tell the details of what happened that night, because to me our love making was and will stay private. I'll leave it to your active imaginations. When she left me at daybreak, she kissed my cheek tenderly. It was more loving and sincere than any such kiss from a man that had ever left me before dawn.

I continued to feel that way in my dreams and slow waking state. But that was it.

On waking fully, I sat up sharply in bed and began shaking in a wild riot of emotions over what I'd done.

It was hard to describe my spinning feelings and thoughts: embarrassed, disgusted, horrified. It was a big jumble in those first few minutes. A bad case of the shakes overwhelmed me. I skipped going down for coffee and climbed straight into the tub where I scrubbed and cried away the shame and horror of what had occurred. I couldn't believe it. What the hell was wrong with me?

And somewhere in the back of mind, I couldn't help but laugh at myself. I couldn't help but lament how I'd originally regretted that Melissa was not a man. Just what the hell was happening to me? What was wrong with me? When all the other emotions had calmed down, I was left with fear. I was afraid of what was going on with me.

Was this how a nervous breakdown started?

Chapter 8
Reactions

Thunderheads mirrored my insides that morning, dark and in turmoil. My day began with a meeting with Alice Duvall to review the drafts so far, to be sure the style was still acceptable, as well as to look at the additions I'd made to the outline.

The wind rocked my little Honda and splattered rain against it like pebbles. A few times, I lost my vision for its intensity. A couple of other times, though, the water welled up in my eyes rather than across my windshield. Flashes of lightening and roll after roll of thunder came down through the hills, as though falling from the mountains above as a landslide.

The people in the town would fear flooding. I was already flooded. *Why* had she done that? *How* could she have done that? I was heartsick at the thought of it.

By now, I was parking out back, where an old oak tree provided some protection from the rain and wind. But not perfect protection. Agnes, the darling that she always was, had been watching and dashed out with the canopy-sized umbrella to usher me in. Still, our lower legs got soaked from the few seconds of upward spray from the heavy drops bursting on the pavement.

Inside, I paused to wipe my legs with a kitchen towel before taking a hot mug of perfect coffee from Agnes. I caught her noticing how I was dressed and I will admit I'm not entirely proud of having done so. I wore a shorter skirt, not a mini, but above the knees and my blouse was white, thin, and cut to show what figure I did still have. I'd left it one button fewer done up than I might normally have. The sweater to keep my back warm was light and unbuttoned. Mostly though, it was that I had gone braless.

It was stupid, but I intended to get a rise out of Richards. I wanted to see a man desiring me. I needed mentally to deal with repelling such attention so I could forget or push away thoughts of the night before. Dumb, I know, and I wasn't really thinking that at the time. I was looking for affirmation from a man that everything was normal. That morning I had gone from having something up with me to being on the edge of manic.

Richards was there, of course, just as I had expected. Storms like this often kept him at home, working from his overbearing office. The sight of him made it worse. Whatever the back of my mind had been thinking, it hadn't thought it through. I don't know if that charcoal gray suit was Armani or some other designer, but he looked so damned good in it that my pulse quickened and I was sure my expression betrayed my thoughts. I saw him react to it. Either that or to my own state of expressive dress. He followed me into the library, where Alice Duvall was waiting.

He sat in one of the arm chairs, hooked an ankle over the other knee and draped an arm along the back of the chair as he asked what was in store for the day. If Johnny Depp had been sitting there in that suit, my attraction would have been no more intense. Desire was stirring and was going to need satisfying, smart choice of partner or not. It frightened me to be losing control completely like that.

I had to get my mind off of him, off of trying to forget the night before. I had been drunk and overcome with relief and grateful to Melissa. Her healing spell had been hypnotic. If it had been only a healing spell. That was ridiculously melodramatic, wasn't it? Wasn't it childish to believe such things? Then again, weren't the burns on my arm proof that such things were real? If ghosts were real and could hurt you, then why couldn't a witch cast a spell of seduction? Which thought sounded really over-the-top melodramatic? I recalled Marianne Wells' repeated warning, 'Who knows what a witch wants?' and I thought, maybe she wants your body.

How could she have done that, when we were friends?

"India? Are you okay, dear?" Alice Duvall asked. She had been saying something, but I hadn't even heard her.

"I'm sorry," I replied. "I guess I'm a bit tired today and that storm is really distracting."

"It is blowing and booming, isn't it?" Richards commented and suddenly the most horrific crash came from outside and we all jumped out of our chairs. Ben and Jerry dashed out the room barking. That had been no thunder clap. It had clearly been the sound of wood breaking against metal and shattering glass. "The solarium!"

It was attached to the dining room, right behind the library. Ben and Jerry had run to the source of the disturbance and were barking loudly. We ran in to find a jumble of branches and sopping red and yellow leaves flapping madly in the tangle of limbs from the huge, old pecan tree that had stood beside the house. Through the spray of the pounding rain, the tree itself was visible, lying flattened along the ground; it's broken roots a jagged mess of shattered wood and mud at the far end of it.

The wicker furniture nearest it had been smashed while the rest of it and the non-weather proof photos and paintings were getting drenched. Agnes came running in as we pulled the rest of the furniture back and got the decorations out of harm's way. It was frantic, crazy work with no one giving directions, just everyone grabbing stuff and moving in the straightest line to safety, dodging the less than helpful but erstwhile dogs. I hadn't even notice that Richards had gone for a tarp until he returned with it and a short ladder. Together, we tied it off on the still solid parts of the metal frame, top and bottom with it stretched over the limbs. Spray and full drops continued to find their way around the edges and into the room while a lake-sized puddle was forming on the floor. We were able to keep the worst of it out.

The four of us were drenched to the skin. Richards had shed his suit coat, but only onto a chair that had soaked up almost as much spray. His red tie hung limp and dripping like a rag. Ben and Jerry shook clouds of water from their coats. Alice Duvall was panting and trembling from the shock and effort. She didn't look physically drained, but she accepted Agnes' arm around her in support.

"Nana," Richards scolded. "We had it under control."

"Like hell," she replied, surprising me a little with her curtness. "It's still getting in. Call the board up service. I'm going to go change and get some hot tea." She made a sound of being relieved and exhausted and waved her hand at the offensive limb. "I'd never wanted that damned tree anyway."

Agnes led her out as the first shivers ran up my spine. In the heat of battle, so to speak, I hadn't noticed that the rain was freezing cold. Now, I stood there sopping like a mop with my hair flattened to my scalp and everything plastered to my cold skin.

Richards had some muscle, I noticed through his white shirt, now gray for being plastered to him, too. He looked at me and tried not to freeze or gulp. I didn't need to look to see what had his attention. My white blouse had become transparent and skin tight and he didn't need any imagination. I knew the cold rain and the excitement of the moment, as well as the sexual tension building inside of me, was making my nipples hard and showing through the thin fabric of my blouse, maybe even straining at it. I knew he couldn't keep from looking and I wasn't trying to stop him.

In the back of my mind, it was dawning on me that I'd dressed to get a reaction from a man, from him, after the night with Melissa, to try to put things back where they belonged. Maybe it was still the need to reassert my real sexuality that had my heart pounding. Nonetheless, I wanted to make love with him. It was not so much him as it was the need for a man at that moment, the pure sexual need.

Of course, I wasn't thinking so clearly then. It was more like a voice in my head that I could barely hear trying to tell me what was going on. I was still a complete jumble inside, not acting like myself. Basically, I was losing control, like when you're so angry and know you should stop yelling, but you can't help yourself.

He was trying to pull himself together, to be the gentleman. Already breathing hard and pumped full of adrenalin, my excitement was shifting from the moment past to the one coming and I made the move.

It was wrong, but there it is.

It was me. I was the aggressor this time.

I kept my arms at my sides and let him see as I stepped forward without rushing. I was close enough to feel the heat coming from his body, and knew that was fuel to his fire. Part of my mind was telling me to stop. Yet, a greater part was feeling affirmed; I wasn't gay.

He was about to give in.

"Miss Hills," Agnes called from the other side of the downed limbs. Richards stepped back and I hurriedly crossed my arms over my breasts to hide them as she came around the still dripping leaves. She was drenched, but dressed properly underneath. "Mrs. Duvall said I should show you to the guest room, so you can get warm and cleaned up."

"Thank you," I said, though I was already very warm. "I appreciate it."

"I'd better call the board up service," Richards said and I could hear the struggle for control in his voice. I'd gotten to him completely and I cannot explain how good that made me feel or the surge it sent through me. Maybe it was wrong to feel that. I did, though, and there wasn't much right happening that morning.

I followed Agnes upstairs to a room at the front,

which turned out to be large enough for a small sitting area at the window and had a decent sized private bath. There was a long built-in wardrobe along the wall that abutted the hallway. The four post bed looked thick and warmly blanketed with a quilt work comforter. Oriental throw rugs covered the hardwood floors everywhere you needed to walk.

"There are some clothes in the closet," Agnes told me. "They should fit you well enough."

"Thanks," I said again, even though that part of my mind in the back of my head that was trying to remain clear noted that it seemed a little odd there was a closet full of clothes that would fit me. I was thinking more of the warm shower. Moreover, the idea of finding which room was Richards' filled my head. God, I was just gone at that moment. It was as though whatever had been in that poultice had taken away my reason for good.

As Agnes retreated toward the stairs, I was in the open door and watching when Richards came up, shirt still plastered to his lean frame and dripping coat and tie over his arm. "You should go clean up, too," he said to Agnes. "Don't worry about us."

"I need to get some tea on for Mrs. Duvall," she said. "And the boys are a mess."

By *boys* she had meant the dogs. "You can get cleaned up first," Richards replied. "Nana will likely fall asleep for a bit anyway."

"I can at least start warming the kettle," Agnes said as she descended the stairs.

I wondered for a second if those two had slept together. There was definitely the opportunity. There would certainly have been times of need, like I was feeling. Need and proximity. Why shouldn't there have been?

He saw me standing sopping and barefoot in the doorway and stopped to stare. My hands were working without me needing to direct them. I had already peeled off and dropped the dripping sweater to the floor of the suite's bathroom. I undid the few buttons of my blouse and began to open it. I teased him by turning first, and then lowered it just enough to show off my back as I went into the room. I didn't close the door.

He did, though, a few seconds later. I stood halfway between him and the bed, my bare back to him, my blouse on the floor. I glanced at him over my shoulder and the tension in him was enough to convince me to go on. In that moment, I was in control of what was happening, if not myself. I turned my face away and slowly unzipped my skirt, letting it fall as I made my way to the bed.

How he completely undressed in the three steps it took him to get to my side was something I would never figure out. But there he was, cold and wet and burning up against me. I had given in to Melissa. I abandoned it with Robert, and it wasn't long before we were both sweat drenched and spent with the scattered bed linens hanging from the bed. I lie atop him, still kissing him and nipping at his neck and shoulders. Once I'd caught my breath, I could have gone on and on.

Then, all of a sudden, my mind switched itself back on and I heard myself asking, "What are we doing?"

"Taking a break?" he asked playfully, but I felt him react to my stiffening up.

"No. We can't be doing this," I told him and extracted myself from his arms and the bed. My clothes were still sopping wet. It was pointless picking them up to dress.

"Don't start going on about employer and employee," he said, propping himself up in the bed as I dashed for the bathroom. "You know it's not like that anymore, not after these weeks of getting to know each other."

Good words, I thought. It must have been what he'd been thinking over during the weeks as we had gotten to know each other; that it would be okay to take it to another level, to take the next step. Admittedly, so had I in the back of my mind. Well, maybe not so much in the back of mind given I'd been actively trying to control my usual urges and attractions.

"There are people here," I said as softly as I could from the bathroom and still be audible. "It's still the morning!"

"What does that have to do with anything?" he asked. "You don't think anyone in this house is going to be upset, do you?"

"We have to get back to work," I told him and although I couldn't see him, I was sure he was rolling his eyes and sighing at what had to seem silly to him. I wrapped myself in a thick, soft, warm bath towel and ventured as far as the bathroom door.

"No, seriously," I said to him. "Not that it was wrong. This just wasn't the time for it."

"I don't follow you, but," he started to say, then a huge frown came over his face and he pointed. "What the hell did you do to your arm?"

I had completely forgotten about the burns. The edges were faded now, making them appear more like bruises, so I lied. "I must have done it in pushing the tree out."

"They look old though," he noted.

"No," I continued lying. "I bruise easily. I'm sure it just happened. I'm going to get a shower." I backed into the bathroom and closed the door.

I heard him say, "Good idea. I will, too." Anything more he might have said was lost to turning on the hot water.

Never before; that was how many times I had wanted a tryst to end so quickly. Like any girl, I enjoy lingering and cuddling, keeping the man close. But there was nothing normal about that morning. I was in his house during the day with people around and hadn't wanted this to happen, much less to become known. I didn't want to be gone long from people's sight. It was enough that I had dispelled the night before.

It didn't need to get any more complicated. Our absence could be explained by each having gone to clean up after getting soaked by the rain.

Dispelled? What an odd choice of words that was, I thought as I stepped into the flow of water hot enough to billow steam. Agnes had unwrapped a rose-scented bar of soap for me and I applied it liberally. It was as though the hot water and rose-smelling soap were washing the lunacy from me as I felt my mind clearing from the last twelve hours. I felt logic and control returning and saw I had now made two big mistakes.

As to Melissa, I told myself again that I was mesmerized. I was tired. I was relieved. I was drunk. I didn't what I was or what the hell happened. I wasn't myself last night. However, making love with Richards was my emotions really getting out of control and I desperately needed to pull it together. How could anyone, as smart as I normally was, lose it so completely in such a short span of time? What the hell was this place doing to me?

Of course I wasn't gay!

I hadn't needed sex with Richards to prove that! I had been drunk and thankful and Melissa had known how to use her voice and hands to mesmerize me into that state. Why had she done that? Why had she presumed I was like that? That I would have wanted that? I had liked Melissa as a close friend, the beginnings of sisterly feelings had been there.

Now, I wasn't sure. There was undeniable anger at being misused and having made love with her was distressing, but there was more. There was disappointment. There was regret. I hadn't wanted to lose the new friend I'd made. I had intended to keep in touch with Melissa once I finished the book and left Willow Creek, to stay friends and visit her little farmhouse in the winter.

That wasn't possible anymore. You couldn't be friends with someone who wanted to be more. Especially a woman! It saddened me. I had lost what should have been a great friendship.

Why had Melissa done that? Why had she ruined such a perfect friendship?

All that talk about letting life be what it would be and stopping stressing over someone coming to take it all away, when it started going good; and then it was Melissa herself who had come along and taken it all away. A string of invectives went through my mind. I went from angry to regretful to livid.

Because on top of that, I had gone and made love with my employer out of pure idiocy! Not just any kind of love, but mad, passionate love like he had been the man I had been waiting for. What was he going to think and expect now? How was I going to maintain control of this altered relationship?

What an idiot!

Let myself get a little nuts over something. Then break something else, trying to fix the first thing. What a mess. All wasn't lost, though. I knew I could fix it. I wasn't sure how, but I knew I could, as long as I calmed everything else down. In retrospect, I knew I had been half-thinking about the second part of my fee and how badly I really needed it. I let the prospect of being set for the winter get to my thinking and became a little foolish. I convinced myself that it would work out.

The pain in my arm brought me out of my heavy thoughts. I had gotten too aggressive with the soap from the intensity of my thinking and aggravated the burns. Yes, I was admitting they were burns and not bruises. I thought to myself there was my excuse for everything that had happened in the last twelve hours. It hadn't really been just the last twelve hours, of course, when I thought about it. It had been everything since Monday night, when my entire life's paradigm had been upended and plowed under.

What should I have been expecting from myself after having been attacked by something I hadn't even believed in? The only certainty in my mind was I was caught up in it now and completely on the witches' side. No way would I have run out on them, even with Melissa's betrayal of sorts, and, in retrospect, the horror to come would have been more awful if I had.

A knock at the bathroom door preceded Anges' muffled voice, "Miss Hills, did you have any dirty clothes in there? I'm going to wash everything."

I was done showering and switched off the water. With a thick, wonderful towel wrapped around me, I went dripping to the door and opened it a crack. Thank God I'd kicked Richards out. Of course, Agnes was there to collect the laundry. That was her job.

My breath caught and sickness rose in my stomach at the sight of the rumpled bed behind her. I almost couldn't talk. She followed my eyes and read my expression.

"I won't say anything," she told me. "I was kind of wondering if it was going to happen."

That had surprised me. "What?"

Agnes smiled in a conspiratorial way between women. "Forgive me for being too familiar, but I saw it between you. I'm not sure that Mrs. Duvall did, but I did."

That didn't make me feel any better. I didn't have a reply.

"Are these all of your clothes?" she asked me, the bundle of damp material in her arms.

"You don't need to wash them," I told her and I think I was a little harsh. Surrender to Melissa. Give in to Richards. And be obvious about it all. I was about to hit the roof. I liked Agnes and immediately felt bad at snapping even the slightest at her. "I mean, I've already got a pile back at the Willows Wells. I'll just throw those in with the rest."

"It's no bother, Miss Hills," she said, silent apology accepted. "I brought up your purse for you, by the way."

"Call me India, please," I told her.

"Well, maybe when no one else is around," she agreed.

"I wanted to ask you about those clothes you said were in the closet," I said, ducking behind the door to drop the towel and pull on the heavy, terry robe hanging on it. I padded barefoot into the bedroom as Agnes went over to open the doors to show me. "Why do you have a closet full of clothes that will fit me?"

Agnes almost giggled at the thought I saw a conspiracy or something in having gotten clothes for me. "No. They were for Phyllis. You're about the same size," she explained.

"She left a closet full of clothes?" I wondered, half embarrassed at myself for thinking they could have been meant for me, half not understanding why Phyllis had abandoned her wardrobe.

"Actually, I think she never saw them," Agnes answered. "They were gifts that Mrs. Duvall had gotten her as an engagement present. That was the day she saw the ghost at the old mansion and bolted."

They were high quality clothes. The materials felt good and I didn't recognize a couple of the labels. They may have been from small boutiques. I browsed through them, my eyes falling on a white dress with blue bands around the shoulder and joining into a stripe down each side. I rather liked it.

"Why didn't Mrs. Duvall donate them or give them to you?" I asked.

"I think she hoped Phyllis would think twice and come back," Agnes told me. "She did offer them to me about six months later, but I didn't want them. I'm a denim and cotton girl. I couldn't wear these. You'll look fabulous, but I can't see myself in them."

"I could," I told her, then gave her a sideways look of assessment. Something I'd been wondering about was at the forefront of my mind at that moment. "Sure it doesn't have anything to do with who they were meant for?"

"What do you mean?"

I knew she caught my drift and was being coy, so I asked straight out just to be sure. "There wasn't anything with you and Richards?"

Her eyes got round and she fell a step backward. "No! Of course not!" She almost sounded offended. "There was never anything."

"I was just wondering," I replied. "I mean, knowing him."

She smiled and recovered her composure. "I suppose he wouldn't have minded," she said. "But he's not cowboy enough for me."

"Oh?"

"I've learned about fine things working here," she told me. "But I'm all country at heart. Dress me in blue jeans or a nice cotton dress, but don't be looking for me in silk or chiffon, because those don't go well in the saddle." She winked and made me laugh.

"I'm going to borrow this one for today," I said, choosing the white and blue number. It was so simple of line and design that it was really elegant. It was one of the designers I didn't recognize. Agnes just shrugged at it when I asked. She didn't know the places Alice Duvall had shopped at and had never been interested obviously. "Is there a sweater of something for my shoulders?"

Despite the hot shower, I was still feeling the chill that was in the autumn air that day. There was no sweater unfortunately. The chill was still a hint of the coming season and the rain was already blowing over. The sun would be out and it was probably going to be warm enough. I asked her to wait while I put the dress on so she could zip me up and that was when I unthinkingly showed her the marks on my arms. I told her I caught it in a file cabinet at the mansion; just a clumsy moment. I wanted to tell her the truth, but was afraid she would have said something to Richards.

After she left, I went to my purse for my comb and brush. There was a hair dryer, but I wasn't using a brush left behind by Phyllis. Clothes she had never worn or seen, okay, but not a hair brush, thank you. My necklace from Melissa was at the top, where I had set it on arriving there that morning. I had been thinking that I hadn't wanted Mrs. Duvall or Richards to see it again as they really weren't okay with my friendship with the witches, but maybe, as I let myself think critically, I had really just been removing anything that would have interfered with Richards' view of my cleavage.

Yes, I admitted to myself. I had purposely dressed to provoke. And yes, I had been attracted to Richards, still was. So maybe, subconsciously, I had used the night before as an excuse to be with him. Maybe I'd even let the night before happen to give myself an excuse.

Or maybe I was letting my wild imagination run rampant again. I was going to work myself into a serious state of anxiety, if I didn't contain it.

I put the necklace on under the higher collar of the dress and went downstairs; the grandson's new lover in the dress of a previous. Yeah, the melodrama was still running freely in my mind. I was permanently afflicted with it.

Chapter 9
Twists

I heard noise coming from the Solarium and headed there. The board-up crew had arrived and were building a wooden frame to clamp to the metal beams, while others were firing up chain saws to cut up the limbs for removal. They'd nail the plywood sheets to the makeshift frame to keep out the elements, while replacement glass panes were brought in. The dogs barked their disapproval from Richards' office, where they'd been confined.

Richards was overseeing the work, although there wasn't much for him to do but watch. A shock went through me on seeing Sheriff Levinson beside him. Why in the world did he call the Sheriff because a tree fell through the window? He and Richards were wearing heavily serious expressions.

"Miss Hills," Levinson called on seeing me. "I was wondering if I could talk to you about last night."

"Last night?" A lump formed in my throat and my stomach sank through the floor. My only thought was that Mrs. Wells had told the entire world of my sick, kinky tryst with Melissa and the prudish small town was about to brand me the devil and send me packing. I was the proverbial one more thing away from screaming and needing Valium and Prozac both.

"Let's go somewhere we can hear ourselves think," he suggested, pointing away from the sudden roar of a chainsaw.

We went across to the music room on the other side of the house, the room I in which I had first met my employers. My mind and pulse rate had calmed in the minute it took to walk there. The surge of panic had passed. I wasn't wondering how many people knew, convincing myself it didn't matter. Why should it have? One part of my hyperactive mind even considered it a good thing, because it would probably turn Richards right back off and solve that problem. Although, getting kicked out of town without finishing the job or getting paid, paying back the partially-spent first payment... well, that was still going to be a problem come the winter.

Chill, I told myself. I knew I wasn't in any kind of trouble, but my crazy thoughts wouldn't stop. Could it turn out to be the person to take it all away was going to be a man after all, namely the Sheriff? Maybe I'd gone from anxious to panicky.

"Has something happened?" I asked, trying to play it cool.

"Yes, there was a fire."

"A fire?" How in the world could I be blamed for a fire? Then, a horrible thought hit me and I couldn't help the gasp that escaped. "Not the records room?"

"No," he replied and I couldn't help the sigh that came from me. However, his next words stopped my heart and my lungs. "Melissa Ferrier's place burned to the ground overnight. Nothing but ashes and twisted bits and bobs of metal left."

"What?"

"Fortunately, she spent the night at her grandmother's place," he added.

I felt an absolute wave of relief. Melissa had lied about where she had been. She was still protecting me, even if out of a different affection than I had first thought. Melissa would have had no second thoughts about our friendship or relationship. There was no lack of love on her part.

So, the guilt at thinking less of Melissa began. My already racing mile-a-minute mind went into warp drive with a bazillion new questions. What if Melissa had just misunderstood? What had I done to tell her I was like that? Or to tell her that I *hadn't* been like that? It could have been my fault. Maybe what I had considered normal affection had led her on. I didn't know. Just knowing she'd covered up for me just to be on the safe side threw me back into the jumble I'd awakened to.

"So, what did y'all do last night?" he asked.

"We went to dinner and then back to my room because she gave me some lotion for this rash on my arm." I pointed out the muted marks. It could have passed for a mild rash that was clearing up. I told him Melissa had brought it over and wanted to apply it with an incantation. I shrugged as I said that, as if to say, 'So what? It couldn't hurt.'

In the back of my mind, I wondered if the Sheriff and Richards would compare notes, because I had now impulsively given three different explanations of the marks on my arm to three different people.

Yeah, sure, I'm in control here, I thought sarcastically.

Control had become like a super ball, and when I'd lost my grip on it, it had careened off wildly out of the room and down the road, and was probably still bouncing crazily and half way to China already.

"Did you talk to anyone or see anyone?"

"The only person we talked to was Willis, that paranormal researcher," I told him. What an odd fish he was, I thought again.

"What did you talk about?"

"It was just, 'hello, anything to report,' and then he was off," I answered.

"Did he seem like he was on good or bad terms with Miss Ferrier?"

"No, he didn't seem to get along with Melissa, but given they are on opposite sides of the spectrum," I replied. "He's a pure scientist with all his electronic gear and she's an old world herbalist with wooden boxes and handmade tools of her craft. It's not surprising they didn't associate." I had started to say "see eye-to-eye," but that would have made it seem like there was friction. There hadn't been. There was non-interaction. There was nothing. Melissa just let him be. Like I should have been doing with regards to Melissa myself. "You don't think that's enough to burn her house down, do you?"

I'd been suspicious of him myself earlier. I had needed Francine's reassuring to keep from seeing him as a suspect behind Brianna's murder. What was I doing trying to suggest the opposite to the sheriff?

Fool, let him investigate the man and be sure of it, I chastised myself.

"I'll certainly try to find out," Sheriff Levinson said officiously. "You never know, when it comes to rivalries and all."

"That's a good point," I said by way of erasing my earlier words.

"Did you talk to anyone else?"

"No. That was it. We weren't out very long."

"Did you notice anyone else around or anything that seemed out of the ordinary?"

I shook my head. "This wasn't an ordinary fire, was it?"

He shook his head. "It was definitely arson. Someone was clearly upset with her."

"Arson?"

"Yes," he explained. "It wasn't merely the house. They burned the garden and her lilac trees, too."

"No," I said, horrified and saddened to real grief. I had loved that garden. It had been Melissa's last link to who her parents had been and the life they had wanted to give her. She had to be devastated, and that hurt me to think about. I did still love her as a friend.

"Luckily, she wasn't home," he said.

"Yes. This is awful." My heart dropped.

"Thanks for your time, Miss Hills," he said, standing. "If you recall anything else, please call me right away."

"Of course," I promised and shook his hand before he left.

Then, I fell back into the armchair, the same one I'd sat in that first day, and felt sick to my stomach. My head ached and I had a growing need to cry. Even as a friend, I was being horrible to Melissa. She had only been herself and I had been upset with her for it. Now, the home she loved had been taken from her. Who was the one really at fault here? Who was the one being bad?

"Hey, you okay?" Richards asked as he came into the room.

"Yeah," I told him, realizing I'd been sitting with my head in one hand. "This morning is turning into one of those days."

He smiled understandingly and sat on the sofa near enough to me to reach over and put a hand on my knee. What would he have thought if I had told him that Melissa and I had made love? Would he still have been wearing such an understanding and caring smile?

"Well, you know I don't care about your friendship with her," he said. "But, we do need to be careful what we say around Nana. I'm sorry, but she doesn't entirely approve, regardless of what she says."

"We?" I asked. "What's with the *we* already?"

He looked startled and unsure, yet he didn't move his hand. I didn't make him either. "Okay, you," he corrected. "Just trying to say I'm with you on it."

"The feud is still going on, isn't it?" I snapped at him. I was angry. It was mainly with myself for the messes I had made and the fool I had become, but I was aiming it at him.

"Well, sort of," he admitted. "It's not like it's anything open or serious, but yes. My grandmother does carry some of the old grudge against them."

"I had a feeling you hadn't been entirely straight forward the other morning when we talked about Phyllis," I said. Intimacy made it easier to talk about this, or rather to argue about it. Some part of my imagination saw where a progression had been going on all along. My current mood helped, as well.

"I'll admit that in older, less enlightened times my ancestors, including my grandfather, more than half believed in the curse," he said. "Nana still hasn't completely shaken the prejudice of them that she grew up with. It's nothing to be proud of. But there it is. I don't think she wants to feel that way; however, she can't help herself."

"What about you?" I asked. "Why do you have something against them?"

"I don't," he replied. "I have no reason to associate with them, either."

I sensed he was lying, but it wouldn't do any good to press him on it then. He must have seen the doubt on my face.

"No, seriously," he said, "I really don't have anything against them."

"Is that why you let them use Coven Ridge?"

"No. I'm just not really bothered by them," he said. "Besides, if I ever tried bringing a trespassing action against them, I figure I'd lose on religious grounds, that I was infringing or denying them the right to practice their religion, or some other such legal language."

"You've never tried to stop them?"

He shook his head. "The city tried to by declaring that section of the road a no parking area. That law was struck down for the very reason I just stated."

"I know a little about property laws," I said. "Enough to realize they may have some ownership claim from all the years of use. They've been using it for centuries."

"Ownership rights were not at issue and so weren't decided in that case," he said. "I also rejected the idea of leasing the field to them for fear of seeming to support them. Really, I'd rather they just found somewhere else, but haven't really wanted to force them to do so. It seemed more trouble than it was worth."

"What about Phyllis?" I asked and his brow

furrowed. "The other day you told me you didn't, but do you blame the witches vicariously for the curse that scared her off?"

He smiled a little sheepishly. "I admit I was mad at anyone and everyone I could think of for a few days. But no, I don't blame them. Like I said, it was probably for the better, so maybe I should be grateful to them instead."

That had a wrong ring to it. "I should get back to my room and do some writing," I told him, standing quickly and heading for the library to get my stuff.

"Dinner is at seven," he said, following me.

"Don't start assuming things," I told him sharply and was proud of myself for it. I'd never been a bitch before, but saw now where the line was between that and standing up for yourself. Being angry at the world helped. I was still full of rage for everything that had happened since dinner the night before and being short with him was easy right then. It felt good because I knew myself. With men like this, I gave and they took. This time, I wasn't giving. Or at least I wasn't going to let him start dictating already.

Already? What was I thinking? This wasn't a relationship. I had over-reacted. Made a mistake. I was going to fix it. Not repeat it. Who was in charge of me after all? It was me, not the small town prince.

"Why are you so mad?" he asked.

"I'm not mad," I answered, although no one was about to believe me.

"Yes, you are," he replied. "Is it because you weren't expecting this?"

"Stop it, Robert," I told him. I could have gone on about there not being a *this*. All I wanted to do then was be by myself and settle my mind down.

He sighed, clearly frustrated. To him the morning had been a breakthrough; how the big city girl had finally dropped her attitude toward the country boy or some such. He'd come to want something and saw it as having started. The only way to save myself from another disaster was to become the bitch I hated being, which he didn't deserve. Because I was the one that had been an idiot and gotten him thinking that. What a damned mess I was making of things.

The storm was still grumbling high up in the clouds as I walked to my car under the dripping oak tree. Red and golden leaves liberally speckled my car and the ground around it. I didn't bother cleaning them off. I used the wiper to clear the windshield and drove away.

I was thinking how the research was all but done and would be finished in two or three weeks. It would be mostly the writing after that. And really, there was no reason I couldn't finish it from my apartment in St. Louis. I didn't need to be here with either of them, Robert or Melissa. Well before Thanksgiving I would be back in my cozy apartment and focusing on the writing. A couple of more months and maybe a handful of trips for interviews, and I would have this project wrapped up and the balance of the fee in my bank account and would be able to forget this little town even existed.

Of course, it wasn't that simple. This wasn't just a hypothetical little town with boring, stereotypical, small town people. It was a real place with souls that had touched mine. I had become involved. By the time I got back to my room, my mood and thoughts had completely done another one-eighty.

I wanted to call Melissa and see how she was feeling after losing her home. I also wanted to avoid Melissa. That made me feel guilty. I still liked her as a person and as a friend. Needing to tell her I only wanted to be friends was actually disturbing to me. It was crazy, but I was really stressing over it as much as I would at having to tell a man the same thing. You would think it would have been easier. It wasn't. I still didn't want to hurt the other person's feelings. In fact, I dreaded it even more because I did still want to be friends with her. I just didn't know how to do that.

I sat at my computer, trying to work, yet finding I

was too distracted to get much done.

My cell rang after a while and I saw it was Richards. He asked if I wanted to come to dinner and told me it was okay if I didn't. He didn't give any explanation for his change of attitude. Maybe he was still as confused, only he was trying to be understanding. I told him I was on a roll and wanted to keep working.

After dark, I had settled down enough to have gotten some work done. It was a peaceful night weather wise and I kept the windows open a crack, but with protective crystal chains from Melissa hanging from each latch. A gentle breeze seeped in and filled the room with a heady fall scent. Somewhere out there, the Duvall males still lurked in the darkness. The necklace and pendants kept them at bay. Samuel Duvall could no longer get close enough to menace me from the windows.

I was eating some olives and cheese and sipping some Pinot Noir, when my cell rang again. This time it was Francine Brindley.

For a second, I was reluctant to answer. Francine equaled Melissa. It meant facing the things I'd worked all day to forget.

"How is your arm?" she asked, when I did answer. "Are you using the lotion?"

I had completely forgotten about it. I was truthful and told her I hadn't. "It's gotten a lot better, though," I told her.

"Are you one of those people who doesn't take all of their antibiotics because they feel better?" she asked me. "You have to use the lotion until the burns are gone."

I felt sheepish. "Okay. I'll put some on in a minute."

"Promise me?"

"Yes. I promise," I told her and meant it, although I could see her sitting there with a look on uncertainty on her face. I hesitated another second, and then finally asked, "How's Melissa?" I really did want to know.

"She's fine," Francine told me. "Sleeping right now. It was a long day for her."

"I guess she'll be staying with you for the time being then."

"Yes. She's moved in. There was no insurance, as you know, so there's nothing for her to buy a new place with," she told me and a heartsick guilt wracked me that I had not been there for her. She had literally lost everything and I'd avoided her. "She could have done with seeing you today, but I'm sure you were busy."

It hit me then that Francine, of course, knew where Melissa had really been the night before, because obviously she wasn't at either her own place or at Francine's overnight. As much as I knew I was being a bitch to Richards, I felt even worse over ignoring Melissa, especially when she needed her friends, the people she loved, and those she expected she could count on.

"I'm sorry," I said and the tears started. I tried to say something to explain, but the words wouldn't form.

Francine seemed to understand though, "Even as intuitive as she is, Melissa gets a little impulsive and misses things the rest of us would pick up on. That is nothing to worry about. You should come by in the morning so I can have another look at your arm."

"I will," I promised. Those few words from Francine had filled me with relief as much as remorse. Obviously, this was not the first time Melissa had done something like this. Francine was the kind of woman that always seemed to know what to do. My own grandmother had died young, before my parents even. Right then, I liked to think she would have been exactly like Francine Brindley.

I slept peacefully that night, after crying softly for some time, the dream pillow under my head, hoping for something to come to me by the morning.

Chapter 10
Turns

I decided to settle in for a few days of writing, if only to avoid stirring up anything more. In letting things settle down over the next few days, though, I may have missed my second and last opportunity to affect what might have happened and keep some people alive. But I'll let such thoughts go now. We were probably well past when anyone could have done anything more.

I headed out to the Herborium as promised first thing that Friday morning after breakfast. I had applied the lotion with the wooden spatula the night before and again after bathing that morning. I didn't know if the dream pillow had done its job or not. There were no prophetic thoughts in my head that morning. It may have been working only I'd been expecting too radical of a sign to notice. I didn't know.

"These are healing nicely," Francine said of the wounds on my arm as she inspected them. "They should be gone within a week. Just keep using the lotion twice a day. Promise?"

"I promise," I told her. She seemed to have caught on that I couldn't break a promise to her.

"Good," she said. "I've got some orders to get ready for FedEx, so I'll leave you two to your tea."

We were in her kitchen above the shop. Melissa was sitting quietly on a stool across the table from me. Her hair was loosely brushed to look a little wild this morning, and she was all but hidden within the huge sweater shirt she was wearing. It could have almost qualified for a baggy dress. The look on her face was uncertain. I imagine so was the one on mine. We remained silent for a few seconds as Francine descended to the shop, Arthur following in her wake as though even he knew to leave us alone for the moment.

After a few more seconds of abortive eye contact, she spoke first. Her voice was soft and contrite and sad.

"I'm sorry," she told me.

I wanted to say the same words, but couldn't find a tone of voice that wouldn't have come off as accusatory or final.

"I had a feeling it was too early in our relationship for that," she told me and I flinched internally at the word relationship. "I thought you really felt the same, only you needed a little push to get past the stigmatism of being with another woman."

My throat was too tight for words, which I didn't have anyway. I just shook my head.

"I also had a nagging feeling not to go home," she added. "As it turned out, I was right. I guess I still could have come here. Thing of it was, I wanted to be with you."

I couldn't frame the right response. I pursed my lips and frowned, trying to come up with the words to describe what I felt without hurting her.

Me, a writer, verbose in any other situation, was at a loss for words.

"You have nothing to say?" she asked.

I finally found my voice. "I don't know what to say."

"You don't hate me, do you?"

"No," I answered quickly. I didn't. My feelings hadn't changed at all, other than not knowing how to handle the altered friendship and the knowledge that she wanted more. "I don't hate you."

She gave a relieved smile. "I don't blame you for being mad," she said. "I guess I should have talked with you more about it. I misunderstood what you meant when you asked me to stay with you that night, especially when you'd let me kiss you the night before."

I remembered the light peck that had confused me. I

had mistaken it for a parting ritual, when it had been her tentative first move. I had asked her to stay, as well, after seeing the walls ripple and from not wanting to be alone out of fear. Had I said it in a way she misunderstood? I was a little drunk and out of it. Maybe it wasn't fair to blame her entirely.

"Yeah, I didn't mean that," I told her. "I'm sorry if I gave you the wrong impression."

She gave a small smile, a glimmer of the beginning of being her usual happy self again. "Just so long as you don't hate me. Can we still be friends?"

I felt a wave of relief at the question I had been afraid to ask. The wall that I had put up came down with a sigh and a smile. "Yes. Of course, we can still be friends. I really do like you, Melissa, but not that way. I don't go both ways. Men do it for me. It's not a best of both worlds thing for me."

"Well, it's whatever you feel it is," she said, echoing the types of words she used in seducing me. "These are not things you apply logic to. I can respect your feelings, though."

"Thanks," I said, although I wasn't sure if I hadn't just been scolded somewhat. "I guess I shouldn't have..." The words escaped me.

"Responded?" she suggested.

"Yes," I answered. "I shouldn't have responded like I did, but I was drunk and scared and that lotion makes me high or something."

"Are you suggesting we pretend it never happened?" Melissa asked and I could see that the idea bothered her. Like Robert the morning before, she had felt it was a moment of connecting.

"No, it happened," I answered and was then lost again. If I said anything about it being a bad experience, it would crush her. If I said anything about it being a good experience, she would wonder why I didn't want to repeat it. I'd talked myself into a Catch-22. I tried for something middle of the road. "I'm not ashamed so much as I'm shocked at myself. I'm not like that. I really do prefer men."

"Fair enough," Melissa replied, though I could see she was lying and still hurt. Obviously, she wanted to be forgiven and remain friends. She really liked me, and so I felt bad anyway. It looked good on the surface, but we were both still hurt and reeling a bit.

"Well, if it helps any, I've also been with men," she told me and I wasn't too sure how to take that. "It's not a gender thing, but a personal thing for me."

"Oh," was all I managed to utter. I hadn't expected this.

"I have to be in the right mood for a man, you know," she told me, "to want something more physically intense than emotionally connecting."

"You can connect with men," I replied and then almost instantly wondered about that because I hadn't had any luck so far either.

"I hope so," she said. "I'll need to marry soon and have a daughter, but I don't know where to find someone. I certainly haven't here."

"Kansas City isn't that far," I said. "You can still visit me in St. Louis."

"That would be nice," she said. "I like Kansas City, but haven't been to St. Louis yet, believe it or not."

"It's such a short drive away."

"I know. Silly, right?"

Over which we shared a tension-freeing giggle. My shoulders and brows relaxed. My stomach began to settle down. I had feared facing a screaming, rejected woman. What I'd found was someone that cared enough to do what it took to keep me in her life. That sounded melodramatic, but that what she was doing.

Then, she asked the question that almost made me fall out of my chair. "So tell me about Richards. How was it with him?"

I was sure I was mimicking the movie The Mask, where his jaw dropped right through the table to the floor.

Melissa giggled in delight at my reaction.

"Okay," she said with a grin, "I have a confession to make. My first encounter with another woman was my senior year in high school. It was nothing more than a short kissing and heavy petting session, but I went home feeling mortified later. The next day, I made out with one of the guys from the wrestling team. I didn't even like him, but he was cute and fit and all that."

"So why?" I asked, knowing the answer.

"Because I had to show myself that I was normal and got off from men," she said. "I'm expecting you had to do the same thing, and Richards was the closest and probably next man you came into contact with." She smiled and nodded from how deeply I blushed. My face felt red hot and there was no denying it. "I don't blame you. He is dishy for what we have to choose from around here, although I never wanted him seriously."

"Might have ended the feud," slipped out of my mouth.

Melissa laughed instead of taking affront, and then I chuckled just out of relief that the angry encounter was not going to happen. Francine would later tell me that she heard us down in the shop and smiled from ear to ear knowing the two girls she cared about the most were going to be okay, no matter what relationship they sorted out. Do I have to even mention again that I'd already adopted her as my pseudo-grandmother?

"Are you going to dish or not?" she asked me of Richards. "I know it had to be tawdry."

"I don't want to talk about it," I said and totally admitted it by saying that.

"Oh, come on. Don't leave me hanging," she said. "How did it start? Who went after who?"

"Melissa!"

"Were you inside? Were you outside?"

"Both, sort of."

"What?"

"That old pecan tree toppled in the storm and

smashed through the solarium. We all got soaked throwing a tarp over it and moving the furniture out of the way. So we were inside, but exposed to the outside."

"Sopping wet and panting," she said imaginatively. "Then what?"

"Melissa!"

"What? Tell me. Don't leave it to my imagination!"

"Well, I had on a thin shirt and I wasn't wearing a bra," I told her and couldn't believe I had. Then, I thought, Why am I reluctant to tell her? I would have told any other close female friend. Was I afraid of getting her desires stirred up? On the other hand, how could we go on as friends if I couldn't talk about anything at all to her?

When she said, "Ooooh!" to my last comment, I dished and when I'd finished, she sat back and fanned herself with her hand. "You will get us a double date in St. Louis, won't you?" she asked.

"Melissa!"

"Well, I want to have fun, too."

I rolled my eyes and made a sound of frustration at that. "It wasn't about fun. If anything, it was a mistake and I wish I hadn't done it. I enjoyed it at the time, I'll admit, but I'm not going there again. I was a fool."

"Yes, but a normal fool," she said. "Just like the rest of us."

"Yes. We're all fools at times, aren't we?" I replied wistfully and then saw the truth in it. Weren't we ever?

The odd thing of it was I felt more embarrassed at having been with Richards than Melissa, because at least I liked Melissa as a person. Richards was good looking, yet I still didn't like him all that much. More perplexing to me at the moment was how I was accepting the night with Melissa as something I didn't need to be embarrassed about. Maybe talking with her and sorting it out took away the fear factor that it was a pivotal event in our friendship, that I had let it be completely destroyed. I know, melodramatic again, but my mind was still going a mile-a-minute.

What I'm getting at is the differences I was seeing. Melissa loved me; I could clearly see and appreciate it. Yet, she had no jealousy of Richards and no expectations that she and I would ever be together again. Whereas Richards, on the other hand, had already spoken rather ill of Melissa and was expecting me to fall in line as his woman. With Richards, it had been pure sex, pure need. With Melissa, it had been about connecting. When I thought back on it, on her calming voice telling me to forget she was another woman and free myself to the sensations, I realized it had actually been nice. It had even felt safe.

Not that it was going to happen again. This was just how I was feeling and what I was thinking then. Or more accurately, what was utterly confusing me then.

"What now with your house gone?" I asked to change the subject. We had agreement, of sorts. It was time to stop discussing it. "Moving in here sooner than expected?"

"That's the only plan there ever was," she told me. "Good thing I had some clothes here. There was nothing left over there."

"Lucky thing you weren't there," I remarked, hoping I hadn't just reopened our prior conversation.

"We aren't so sure," she replied. "Grandmother thinks whoever did it would have seen I wasn't home. I mean, you've seen it, it's not big enough for anyone to have thought I was somewhere far enough inside that you wouldn't have seen me."

"They knew you weren't home?"

"That's what she figures," Melissa replied. "Whoever it was wanted to keep me from going back there."

"Why would they do that?" I asked. "Did you have something really special there?"

She shook her head. "Nothing really, just my personal altar and you know it wasn't anything out of the ordinary. I can replace all of it this afternoon if I had somewhere to put it."

"It doesn't make sense, then, unless they were

mistaken and thought you were home," I said.

"You're thinking this has to do with Brianna's murder, aren't you?"

"Aren't you?"

She nodded. "Seems awfully coincidental otherwise."

"Have you talked to the sheriff about that?"

"He agreed there could be a connection, but wondered if it wasn't something in the family."

"As opposed to a hate crime?" I asked. You could see it as attacks on two cousins or on two witches. Levinson seemed to prefer the family angle from what Melissa had just said. I supposed it was more plausible. I mean, the witches may not have been highly respected or taken seriously, but no one I'd talked to had given me any reason to think they were hated. They kept to themselves and did no harm as was their creed. What reason could anyone have had for hating them?

"Of course, it makes just as little sense to think it's a pissed off relative," Melissa noted. "I mean, we know better than to do harm to another practitioner. You'd have to be really mad or just plain nuts to do this, if you're one of us. There's no one in the family that's either."

"Yeah, but how do you know that?" I asked. "Obviously, if it's happening, then someone is."

"Which is the point we can't get around," she told me. "We know it has to be somebody, but there's nobody we can figure it would be."

"Are we sure it's not the ghosts?" I asked, feeling really stupid just thinking it. "You said they could kill."

"We wondered about that, too," she said. "But, my place was torched with gasoline or something similar and Brianna was decapitated. You can't do that without using physical things; weapons and gas cans. You have to bring those things with you. It's hard to see ghosts doing that. They could manipulate something that was already around, but to bring something to the scene? We don't think so."

"That really means a hate crime," I concluded.

"Somebody has it out for you."

She smirked and nodded to one side. "The sheriff figures it could have been someone trying to muddy the investigation of Brianna's killing by making it look that way. He figures it may have been someone she rebuffed. That's why the guy, whoever he is, burned my place when I wasn't there. He didn't want to hurt me physically, but made it look personal by destroying everything."

Which seemed to me to be making it too complicated. Something else was going on.

"I'm sorry about the garden and the lilacs," I told her. "They were all so beautiful."

She smiled wryly. "I'll be able to replace it all. The lilacs may come back. They're very hardy."

"I hope so," I said. She seemed calm about it. Her father had planted them for her, after all. I would have been distraught over losing them. Or was it just me being overly dramatic about it? That seemed par for the course for me.

"Did you make plans for dinner?" she asked, taking me out of that line of thought. Evidently, they were okay with the sheriff's theory and weren't concerned. I wasn't so sure, but wasn't going to argue the point with my little knowledge of the people and the area. Maybe it was someone they'd both said no to. Or, the sheriff could be on the right track. I was uneasy letting it go, but I did because they weren't concerned. It still bothers me that I did.

"Dinner with the clients," I told her. "We lost yesterday thanks to the tree incident."

"Among other things," she teased with a wink that lightened my mood.

"So, we'll be recapping the week tonight," I finished, trying to squash the grin that was forming on my face.

"How's it coming?"

"Almost done here, really," I told her. "The research is almost finished and the outline is written. It's mostly down to the hardcore writing after that. I'll be doing that back in St. Louis, once the research is done."

"How much longer will you be?" She clearly was not pleased with the prospect of my leaving soon.

"A couple of weeks, maybe three," I told her. "We're going to St. Louis next weekend, though."

She brightened up. "Oh yes?"

"I've been going back every other weekend," I told her. "Come with me next time."

"That's right before Samhain," she realized. "We'll be preparing. The rest of the clan is coming here this year."

"No. It's the weekend before that one," I corrected. "You couldn't get away for just one night?"

"And a double date?" she added playfully.

I failed at suppressing another grin. "Maybe," I said.

"I'm sure I could," she said with a smile of her own. "This will be fun."

"Yes. It will," I said.

"I'm actually partial to soft spoken, deep thinkers," she offered.

"I'll see what I can do," I told her, relieved at her resilience in adjusting to staying friends. We'd always be friends. The rest of it was for our male counterparts, when we found them.

Did I know any soft spoken, deep thinkers? He was going to need a wingman, too.

"How about dinner tomorrow night?" I asked her.

"Join us here," she told me.

"Sure," that sounded great actually. "I'm going to knock off around four. Okay if I clean up and come right over?"

"Of course," she told me.

"Cool," I replied. "I really need to get to work now, though."

"Okay. I'll see you tomorrow night. Have a productive day."

I laughed and promised I would, then awkwardly started, stopped, and then finished stepping into a hug with her. It was me that was the problem. Melissa was fine and better at adjusting with her outlook of letting life be what it will be. I was still wrestling with life not wanting to obey me. I managed to relax into the embrace and hesitantly, placed the same kiss on her cheek that would normally have done.

She giggled. "The first time you did that made me feel awkward," she confessed. "I didn't know if it was just friendly or otherwise. I promise I've got it straight now. We're straight."

"Yes, we are," I said, letting the sudden tension her confession had given me go. The double meaning of the word straight made me relax again. I didn't need to be jumpy. I needed to be more like her. "See you tomorrow."

"I'll be here," she quipped.

I positively bounded down the steps in my relief and joy from not losing our friendship. I made Arthur grumble for the vigorous, two handed face rub I gave him. I gave Francine a huge hug and kiss on the cheek as I went out.

The sun was trying to peek out through a thin cloud covering and lend a little warmth to the day. The weekend was supposed to be decent, perhaps the last really nice one of the year. If my mood was any indication of that, it was going to be a gorgeous weekend.

I did have a productive day, cranking away in the old mansion's basement and not even bothering with lunch.

It was a little after six, with dusk dominating the eastern part of the sky, when I let myself into the kitchen at the Duvall's. I still felt a little odd doing so, but they had insisted and with my present mood, I was less bothered by it than normal. Or maybe it was the aromas I walked in to.

Agnes was pulling out the stops it appeared. She had pasta going with homemade sauce and huge meatballs sizzling in the skillet. She was mixing the dressing for a massive salad of just about everything she could think of. Above it all was the mouth-watering scent of roasted garlic. She had made her famous garlic bread.

At least it should have been famous. When she opened a restaurant, I was going to fight everyone for first in line.

"What army are you cooking for?" I asked looking at the sheer volume of food she was preparing.

"We have guests tonight," she told me. "Didn't anyone mention it?"

"Guests?" I was standing there in a blouse, blue jeans, and tennis shoes with the blue and white designer dress hung over my arm. I had changed out of it immediately on returning to my room the other day.

"The Mayor, Sheriff Levinson, and Pastor Cogdon and their wives," she informed me. The heavenly triumvirate of Willow Creek. No one had said a word. Afraid I would have been scared off? I glanced at the dress over my arm and she said, "Yeah, India, I'd put that back on if I were you. You looked good in it."

"Thanks," I said as my imagination wondered if they'd said nothing so I'd be forced into wearing the former fiancée's fine clothing, some sort of showing off that I was becoming part of the family, part of the town's elite. I was permanently afflicted with melodrama. It was like a syndrome. Chronic MD Psychosis.

No one saw me slip up to what was sort of my room after the morning before, although I could hear them talking and having cocktails in the boarded up solarium, probably telling the tale in several different ways. I changed back into the dress and checked myself in the mirror. It did look good on me, especially with a bra holding things where they were supposed to be. There were some heels in the closet, too. I wasn't all that used to heels considering my line of work, and Phyllis had about a half size smaller feet. However, they worked better than tennis shoes with the dress.

I wobbled my way back down the steps and took shorter strides through the dining room and into the solarium where the assembled party were onto their second pre-dinner cocktail. I would have to promise to catch up.

"There she is now," Alice Duvall announced on catching sight of me. "We've been discussing what to do with all the pecans that fell off the tree. We have way too many for pies and pralines. You look quite lovely in that dress."

"Thank you," I replied almost as an aside. My practical mind was more interested in the question posed. "Don't pecans keep?"

"Not ten bushels worth," she said. "I guess the squirrels must have been getting them every year. This time, they literally fell into our lap."

"Feed them to the squirrels then," I said. "They're probably relying on them being there like always."

"Exactly what I was saying," chimed in the highly-permed, blonde wife of the Mayor. "We need to be conscious of what we do to the environment, including the animals."

"They'll find something else," Sheriff Levinson said. "That's what wild animals do."

"That wasn't the only pecan tree around," Robert said. "And not to be heartless or anything, maybe the animals should be relying on the forest, not anything men are growing. That would be more sustainable, wouldn't it, Meredith?"

"For fewer of them," replied the Mayor's wife.

"Introductions, Robert," Alice Duvall scolded mildly and Richards stopped to introduce me to the wives. As he did, Alice poured me a glass of the champagne they'd been drinking.

"What are we celebrating?" I asked and had an odd feeling it had to do with me, the house, and the dress I was wearing.

"Friday," Mrs. Duvall told me lightly and they all twittered at the joke.

I grinned and felt stupid for my active imagination. They didn't need an excuse to drink champagne. This was their normal lifestyle.

"Hurry up," she told me. "You're already two glasses

behind."

"Just give me a chance to get warmed up," I quipped. Where it came from, I haven't a clue, but it got a laugh and that was good enough. The last thing I was about to do was try to catch up on being tipsy.

The conversation then turned to other local happenings without resolution to the pecan question. True, it was a very minor subject. When you're given a question, you tend to want a final answer. Or was I being too nitpicky? I hated when stuff was left hanging.

Dinner was fantastic. I was serious. I'd fight anyone for first in line if Agnes ever opened a restaurant. However, that was the end of the lightness for me. I always had my guard up, expecting something to go wrong, when things were too good. Maybe they'd figured me out and this evening had been structured to put me off my guard. Because the after-dinner conversation was not more of the same as before.

"So, India, how much longer do you expect this project will take?" asked Mayor Baker to start it off.

"Two or three more weeks here," I answered and my spidey senses, as you might call them, began to tingle. "Then just the writing."

"Then your interviews with folks are done then?" Sheriff Levinson asked.

"For the most part," I said. "Why?"

"Not to beat around the bush," Mayor Baker answered, "but we're a little concerned that maybe the interviews and the research haven't gotten a few people upset, maybe more."

"Have people complained?" I was just shy of being astounded. The only people I'd interviewed had been local historians, other family members, and some folks that might have remembered things from the past. They'd all been happy to help and excited at getting to have a voice in the history of their town. Why would they turn around and complain?

"Not as such," he told me. "Not outright complaints.

A few folks on the council have been wondering if having you researching the Duvall history hasn't caused some of the old hatreds to flare up."

"Seriously?" escaped my mouth before I could be more tactful. Thank you champagne, wine, and intoxicating food. "I mean, that was over a hundred years ago. Why would anyone make a big deal of it now?"

"I might have asked the same question," Sheriff Levinson replied, "if it weren't for Brianna Tate's murder a couple weeks ago and now Melissa Ferrier's place being torched."

Which point made me stop to think. Something was amiss in the logic there, but it wasn't obvious.

"It's apparent someone has something against the Wiccans," he added. "There wasn't anything happening until you started work on the book."

"You can't be blaming her," Robert immediately chimed in in my defense. "She didn't cause it."

"That's our concern," Levinson returned. "It started the night she got here."

That was the flaw in the logic. "Exactly," I said and surprised them as for a moment they would have thought I was agreeing with them. Then, I explained, "Brianna Tate was murdered the night I arrived. That was days before I started interviewing anyone. So, it couldn't have been any interview that set someone off."

"That's a good point," the Sheriff conceded and leaned back in his seat with a thoughtful expression. "It does mean that it was already starting."

"Maybe India's talking with people made them stop," Robert offered. "Until the other night, when whoever it is burned Ferrier's house down. She wasn't even there, so he burned down an empty house."

"He might not have known that," Levinson noted. "Now, more of the Coven is starting to gather at Brindley's place."

"That's for Samhain," I told them. "They had already planned on being here before anything happened."

"Are you sure about that?" Levinson asked.

"They told me so weeks ago," I answered. "They were all planning on celebrating here."

"Out on Union Bluff again, I imagine," the Mayor said.

I thought about saying something about it being Coven Ridge to them, but decided not to be argumentative. Instead I asked, "Are you worried about them doing something?"

"Wouldn't you be?" Baker asked. "Tate's murderer hasn't been found. No offense, Gus, but we haven't a clue as to who did it or why other than maybe the old hatreds."

"You mean the curse?" I asked.

"No, of course not," Baker replied. "Besides, the only person that fairy tale might affect would be Robert here as the existing Duvall male."

"We know he's not off chopping people's heads off," Levinson said, "Even though he's got that Chinese sword back there in his office."

Which was all my wild imagination needed to have that thought planted in it. The creative neurons fired like mad and came up with him intending to wipe out the witches in hopes it ended the curse. I had slept with the madman hell bent on slaughtering my dearest friends. I pushed those certifiable thoughts to the back of my mind.

"Not with what it cost me to buy it and get it here," Robert said as they laughed about it.

"Then, what do you mean?" I asked. "Was there other trouble from the shunning and driving them out?" Even as I asked it, I wondered why I hadn't thought of that before.

Mayor Baker held out his hands, palms up. "Old hatreds," he said. "I won't say that's what's behind Tate's murder and all, but something is. And with Ferrier's house getting burned, it's got some of the Council not wanting to deal with anything that touches on the subject."

"Meaning my research for the book."

"Or just writing it... period," Mayor Baker said.

"Mind you, it's not any of us in this room that thinks that way. We're still all for the idea."

"Still?" I asked. It implied a potential changing of their minds.

"Entirely," he corrected, but the admission had been made. They wanted it wrapped up. "I've got to deal with the Council and the City Attorney."

"What is he saying?" Robert asked. I got the sense that there was some bad blood between them.

"He's afraid we may be creating a risk our insurance won't cover," Mayor Baker told him. "He says our insurance coverage of the old mansion did not include long-term invitees, a legal term for someone taking more than a few days to look into something. He's urging us to cut off your access, India. We're not, but other Council members are in agreement with him."

"So, I need to hurry it up before I get kicked out," I summed it up.

"They're planning on bringing it to a vote at the next meeting," he replied and both Alice Duvall and Robert were aghast.

"What? This is our book. They've got no right to interfere," were the words that came out of them.

"I'm just telling you what's happening," Mayor Baker replied. "I'm voting in your favor, if it comes to it. I can't make any guarantees, though."

"When is the meeting?" I asked.

"A couple of days," he told me.

That wasn't enough time to wrap it up. I said, "I need three more weeks to finish here. There's a chance I'll need to conduct some follow up interviews later, but probably not many and I'll only need to be able to double check something at the mansion. Once the research is done, it's all writing." I was getting tired repeating myself.

"Are you saying you won't need to be at the mansion much anymore?" he sounded hopeful.

"I will do the writing back at my place in St. Louis," I answered. "I'll need to have access just in case. I'll be able to give you advance notice of that."

"I think that would do it," he said. "They're mostly afraid of what might happen to you on the property."

"I can understand that," I replied and felt the burns on my arm tingle. They didn't really; it was all in my head. The worst that could have happened to me there had already occurred. Their worries were foolish compared to reality.

"Might I ask what you intend to say about the Wiccans?" Mayor Baker asked.

"Sorry?" My social filter was not working well that night. I let my instant irritation show. Politely worded or not, one doesn't ask to have input on how or what a writer included in a work that had nothing to do with them.

"We know you're friends with them," he said. "Which is no big deal with us."

"But these Nervous Nelly Council members..." I said, leaving it open.

"I agree with you," Robert said. "We're not the ones to be mad at, though. We just have to deal with them."

If he hadn't been right, I would have been furious with him for butting in. I still wanted to smack him for it. A part of me saw where he was trying to keep an argument from starting, and probably ending badly. Another part of me was getting even angrier for feeling intimate enough with him that I would even consider smacking him. My insides were roiling like lava rising to the quiet volcano's surface.

"You can tell the Nervous Nellies not to worry," he continued. "Nana and I have seen the outlines and the drafts. Hell, Nana is editing the drafts. It's going to be an interesting part of our history, not a condemnation on anyone."

"No one is saying it would be," the Mayor started.

Alice chimed in this time. "Oh, you know perfectly well they are. They're all afraid of how it might reflect on the town and their family's reputations, once it gets written down."

"Actually, so was I," Pastor Cogdon finally spoke up. "But Miss Hills put my mind at ease about it, when she pointed out that Alice is editing the book."

"That's right," she added. "I've seen what India intends to write and it's rather clever. It's like we're almost poking fun at our ancestors for being silly. You can tell Martins and the others not to be such wimps."

"Martins?" I wondered.

"The worst of the worriers," she told me and left it at that. I assumed she meant a Council member. "Now, that's enough of this at dinner."

And that ended that. In Alice Duvall's house, you listened to what she said. At least, they did that night. I doubted it was always like that. The evening ended on a brighter note, although my mood had been altered enough. I barely touched the after-dinner brandy and stayed to the side while we were entertained by music from the pastor's wife on the piano. She was a classically-trained musician as well as the choir director and had a rather pleasant voice.

Me? The only way I'd make money singing was from people paying me to stop. However, a similar lack of talent didn't stop the others from joining in for an hour of rather amusing sing-along. They were bad and they knew it and they cracked themselves up over it, especially when Ben and Jerry joined them in particularly off key tunes. I wasn't quite comfortable enough to make a fool of myself with them, and they were polite enough not to insist, when I declined, although they did get me to take a few dance steps with the Mayor and with Robert.

It was almost ten and threatening rain again when the party broke up. That struck me as an early hour, but I wasn't about to complain. My feet were killing me in those heels and I was tired from the emotions of the last few days. That ultra-comfy bed back at the Willow's Wells was calling my name. I headed up to my pseudo room to change as the others filed out. Robert followed me up a moment later and rapped at the door frame.

"Can I come in?"

I was sitting on the bed rubbing my bare feet. "Yes," I told him and he entered quietly, almost like a predator. He had that look in his eyes.

"Want help with that?" he asked, glancing at my feet.

"Phyllis had smaller feet," I told him. He started to come over, but I waved him to the plush chair by the window. "I'm fine."

He leaned against a post of the foot board. "I'm sorry about the conversation. I didn't know they meant to talk about it at dinner."

"You knew they were concerned though?"

"They told me earlier, but I assumed I'd talked them into leaving it for tomorrow," he said. "I thought they'd agreed to an informal meeting in my office here."

"I guess their agenda didn't allow for that," I sniped.

He grinned at it. "Even small towns have their politics."

"What is it with you and the illustrious city attorney?" I asked.

He smiled again and sat on the edge of the bed beside the post, a couple of feet away from me. "You caught that, did you?" I nodded. "He's the one that drove Phyllis home that night."

"And you've never forgiven him."

"He was always an ass," Robert said. "We were always rivals for some reason; all the way back to high school. It's not like his family doesn't have money either. It was just that for some reason we always competed."

"Alpha males," I said.

He gave me a sideways glance. I'd hit a sore spot there, or a chink in the armor. "Are you always so hard to keep things from?"

"That's why I'm good at what I do," I replied. The alcohol was still running through my head and half-controlling my words.

"You are that," he said.

"Did he sleep with her that night?"

"I don't know about that," he said, "but I'm fairly certain he did at some point."

"Politics *and* drama," I commented.

"Do you not like us?" he asked. "Me?"

"Oh, I like you all fine," I half lied. "It's been a bit of rough week on me."

"Because of yesterday morning?"

"And other things."

"Do you want to tell me about it?"

"No. It's okay," I answered. "I think the champagne and brandy are talking more than I am right now." Fortunately they weren't telling him about Melissa. He probably wouldn't have been ready to hear that.

"We did go at them a bit, didn't we?" he said with a small laugh. I simply smiled. He turned and looked at me with a hopeful expression. "Stay with me tonight?"

I half considered it. That less than confident look on his face, I had to say, I rather liked it. It made him appear less like the ass I had been pegging him for all along. I wasn't saying he'd stopped being what he was. At the moment, though, he seemed like any normal man with normal doubts. I smiled, but shook my head. I had already gotten myself into enough trouble going there. Some distance was necessary.

"I need time," I told him so as not to hurt him.

"We've only got three weeks," he quipped and winked, taking it well and making me smile. He stood and turned to me with complete ease in his posture. "Well, you know you can stay in this room rather than head to town with the champagne and brandy co-driving."

That made me smile a little more. "I'll be fine, Robert."

How many people said that as their final words? Or before something bad happened to them? How could I have known they were about to become fateful?

"Okay," he said and leaned forward to kiss me, softly and lovingly. It was the kiss you'd want from a man that was into you. "Be careful."

"Night, Robert."

"Good night, Miss Enigma," he surprisingly said. "You're the most baffling woman I've ever met. And, I mean that in a good way."

He left me smiling at his words, and wondering if he meant it. I'd rather thought he really had, which left me feeling good. I wasn't sure if it was Marilyn Monroe who said it or not, but a woman does like a man who makes her feel different. Although, I'd say it was more that a woman appreciated a man that liked the difference he saw in her.

I changed into my jeans, blouse, and very comfortable sneakers, leaving the blue striped dress laid across the bed. Agnes had told me to do so, so she could send it to the dry cleaners for me. No point my paying for it, she had said, when they had so many other outfits to be dry cleaned every week. I slipped out the back quietly and headed back for town.

Chapter 11
Taking Shelter

Despite the fine mist, I had driven with the window open. It was dark and most of the town was quiet; just a few lights on here and there in the homes and the sounds of television programs drifting through the open windows of some. That was the scene as I slipped gently into the parking spot that had become mine by the Willow's Wells. Through its window, I saw the kitchen lowly lit and flickering with the light from their television. I heard the familiar voice of Jimmy Fallon and his audience laughing.

I took a moment to relax in the peaceful evening and drink in the scent of mist-dampened leaves. It wasn't perfectly silent, but the sounds were muted and respectful of others, rather than the harsh blare of the city I was accustomed to. It was peaceful and I breathed in deeply to savor it, and to relish the calm I felt returning to me.

I wasn't sure what alerted me, some sound or odd scent on the breeze. But I turned my head toward the front, toward the walk I would have been out on, had I not taken that moment. There were two of them and they were huge, like Great Danes with the stoutness of Mastiffs. They had come around the corner and stood now on the walk, staring at me with red eyes. When an animal's eyes catch and reflect the light, they glow greenish or white. They don't glow red. Nor were these two in any light to be reflecting.

I went cold and my throat dried up.

At the first low growl, I fired up my old Civic and spewed gravel up against the house as I floored it back out. They were at my door as I shifted and floored it again, tires screeching as I peeled away.

These weren't dogs. I didn't know what they were, but they weren't anyone's dogs. Hot breath and burning saliva hit my arm and neck as one almost got its head in through the open window. The other rocked my car as it bit at the spinning tires. A living dog would have been killed doing that. These two gave chase.

They were on my tail for the first couple of blocks, keeping pace with my old car. I'd bought it thinking of saving on gas mileage. Never in my dreams had I expected to be running for my life from hellhounds. That was what they had to be. I simply knew that. The ghosts hadn't been able to harm me once I'd started carrying the amulets, but these beasts were a different matter.

I was repeating, "Oh my God! Oh my God!" relentlessly without even realizing it at first. I was asking myself over and over why I hadn't anticipated this. Why had I not expected some sort of escalation? I kept the accelerator down even when the engine shuddered up a hill. My muttering fell to simple gasping as the hounds fell behind me.

However, they didn't break off. They fell farther and farther behind, yet they didn't give up. Like lions wearing out their prey, they knew it was only a matter of time before I had to quit running. I could feel the front tire rocking the entire car. It had bitten a hole in the rubber. The tire was or had already gone flat. There was only so far I could go on it. I was going to make it as far as I could on it, though.

I thought only of getting to Melissa and Francine. Only the beasts had forced me to start out in the wrong direction. I was headed back toward Richards.

The tire got me a few miles down that road until I lost it with a huge bang and a violent lurch rocked me toward a spin. I saw the rubber go flying away from the rim, as I lost control and slid off to the left and into the scree of a rock fall, crashing up onto a boulder and wedging it under the engine, which instantly quit on me. The smell of hot oil poured heavily through the vents as the sound of hissing came from below the engine. I knew enough about cars to know I'd shattered the oil pan. My Civic was as dead as I was going to be if I couldn't get away from those hounds.

I hit the ground running, knowing I had miles to cover. The sedative effects of the champagne and brandy were long gone by this point and I was running all out on adrenaline. There was nothing peaceful about the misty silence now. There was only an anxious hush and the sound of my hot breath and sneakers smacking the pavement.

About a mile on, I thought I heard a howl, but it may have been the blood in my ears. More likely, it had been the engine of the pickup truck that suddenly came up from behind me. He had to have come off of one of the side roads.

He pulled up alongside me and said, "Hey there, girl! What's got you running like that out here in the dark?"

I didn't ask permission. I yanked open the passenger door and jumped in.

"Drive!" I yelled. "They're right behind me!"

He accelerated rather slowly, crept along the road and kept checking his rearview mirror for anyone coming up on us. "What are you talking about? Who's after you?"

"Not who," I said and ran the passenger window up. "It's dogs. Wild dogs."

"Wild dogs, you say," he replied nonchalantly and checked his side view mirror. "Well, dogs is nothing for this truck. We're safe in here." He stopped to take a better look at me, and I knew what was coming. I was barely better off. "You're that writer girl from St. Louis, aren't you?"

"Listen to me," I tried to be calm. "These aren't ordinary dogs. You need to start driving."

The idiot put the truck in park. "That a fact? You city girls know things, don't you? Show me some of them and I'll drive you all the way to the White House, if you want."

"Seriously," I continued trying to reason with him. "We're in danger. We can talk gratitude later, but if you don't start driving, we're both going to be killed."

Just saying the word made my heart drop. For a second, I felt nauseous.

"Well, I don't see any danger," he said. "There ain't nothing around us and there ain't nothing getting into this truck. So let's you and me work out some arrangements first. Show me a little something." He pointed at my breasts.

"Dude, would you please just drive me to the Richards' estate!"

"Come on, girl. A man deserves something for his time," he told me.

And then he got it.

The passenger window was closed. But his wasn't. While one hound scratched and scored the window by my face, the other got its teeth into his shoulder. With a scream of pure horror and pain, he tried to wrestle it off. When it released his shoulder, it got the side of his face. Tears of fear and agony melded with his ear-shattering cries as the truck rocked with their wrestling.

I put the vehicle in gear and floored it from the wrong side, steering as best I could with a panicked man wrestling the hellhound slamming into me. It fell off, losing its grip on him as he continued to yell and cry and moan. I drove flat out, not sure I could keep it on the road, while he thrashed and screamed in shock. His shrieks dropped off the further we got, until it fell to nothing but labored, pain laden panting once the shock wore off.

"Who are you? What were those things?" he yelled, blood running from his jagged wounds.

"I tried to tell you!" I screamed back, doing my best to ignore those horrifying gashes in his face. "We're almost there. We'll call for an ambulance."

"Fuck you!" he yelled and shoved me into the

passenger door, wrenching my shoulder, then slamming me forward into the dashboard as he stomped on the brakes and screeched to a stop. "You did this to me, you bitch. Get out! Get out of my truck."

Bleeding all over me, he leaned across, jerked open the door and pushed me out onto the pavement. It skinned my palms as I broke my fall and grunted in pain. Tires spun and stones flew as he gunned it. I rolled aside and away from the rear tires as he nearly ran over me in getting away. Over the roar of the engine, I heard them.

It wasn't my imagination this time. They were howling as they bounded up the road below from where I lie on the cold, wet pavement. The chill in my body was more than the ground could give me.

Richards' driveway was on my right. I had gotten as far as the entrance to their estate. It was a half mile of winding pavement with trees tight on each side and no lights to show it. Fortunately, I'd learned its curves over the last several weeks. I'd jokingly thought to myself that I was getting to where I could have driven it blind folded. I was about to find out.

I leapt to my feet and ran like no one had ever seen me run before.

I had the mansion lights to guide me every few seconds through the trees, the brush already thinning as Fall progressed. Behind me, the howls grew louder and then ceased. They were saving their breath for the final chase. If they hadn't already seen me, I was sure they had gotten my scent.

As I broke from the last of the trees with a hundred yards to go, I thought I heard their claws scratching on the pavement as they dug in. I drowned that out with the sound of my own yelling. I screamed out all of their names and "Help" and "Open up" with every spare breath I could take. It seemed pointless to shout at the dark house. No one was awake. They were lost in alcoholic slumber. No one was going to hear me or unlock that door for me. But I yelled just the same in pure desperation and fear.

As I hit the steps, my legs wobbling at the end of their strength, the light came on and the door opened to Agnes, my best friend in the entire world at that moment. I literally went flying into the lobby where she caught me going limp and fading.

"Indy?" she started, before the growls and footfalls of the dogs caught her attention. With a shriek, she kicked the door shut, leaving them skidding to a stop on the red brick stoop. The door shuddered as they growled and clawed at it.

Alarmed, Ben and Jerry alternated between howling in fear and barking in anger, and racing from room to room. More lights came on in the house and Robert came running down the stairs in his robe, hushing the dogs to stop the growls, grumbles, and bouncing nervously around him. The hounds were no longer outside the door, but we couldn't be certain they had gone.

"You're covered in blood!" Robert exclaimed, but sounded far away.

I think I fainted in relief.

The next thing I knew, I was on a blanket on the sofa feeling weak for fainting, as well as completely spent from the run. Robert was on the phone and Alice Duvall was sitting at my hip on the sofa, patting and rubbing my hands to wake me. Agnes came racing back in with both the brandy and a bottle of Perrier. She had told them what she had seen.

"Huge ones," Robert was telling someone. There was blood on him from carrying me in. "Rabid maybe. Agnes only got a glimpse of them before she had to shut the door. Indy's got blood all over her, but it's not hers. She isn't hurt."

"Drink this, dear," Alice said as she poured me some brandy.

"No, the water," I rasped. I was shaky and bone dry. Agnes fumbled the cap off. She was shaken, too. "You better get something for yourself," I told her.

Then, she surprised all of us by taking the brandy

from Alice's hands and slamming it down. "Whoa," she said gratefully and held out the glass for another. Mrs. Duvall obliged as Agnes settled cross-legged on the floor.

Robert came over, cell phone to his ear, as I sat up unsteadily. "I'm on with Gus. He's getting every deputy out to hunt for those things. What the hell happened? Whose blood is on you?"

"They were waiting for me back at the Willow's Wells," I said and wished I'd phrased it differently.

"Waiting for you? What do you mean waiting for you?"

"They were outside of it when I pulled up," I said. "They came right at me."

"That doesn't mean they were waiting for you."

"No. You're right. I guess I'm a little shaken."

"No wonder," he remarked. "Where's your car?"

"A few miles out of town. They bit through one of the tires and it came apart before I could get very far."

"So you ran all the way here?"

"No. There was some guy in a pick-up. Jesus, Robert, they bit the guy up really badly. It's his blood on me."

"What? What did he look like?" Robert wasn't sure what to do, but he meant to think of something.

I sighed and leaned on my knees, rubbing my head at the sudden pain of fading adrenalin. "I don't know who he was. I just knew the things were chasing me, so I got in his truck. Only..."

"What?"

"He wanted to discuss payment for the ride first," I told him. "The hounds caught up to us. I drove the truck from the wrong side until he came to and pushed me out. Then, I ran the rest of the way."

"Jesus," Robert whispered and related what I'd said to the Sheriff.

"This is absolutely crazy," Alice Duvall said. "I've never heard of such a thing. Whatever is happening around here?"

Agnes offered her the empty glass. Alice gave it a half seconds thought, then took and poured herself some of the brandy.

Robert gave the Sheriff an accurate account of what I'd told him, then added a name of who the injured man might have been, saying it sounded like him, before they ended the call and he turned to me.

"Needless to say, you'll be staying here tonight," Alice told me. "We can't risk you going anywhere with those things out there."

"I appreciate that," I said. She was right. I wasn't going anywhere before the sun came up.

Alice chimed in. "You know where the guest room is. Agnes, would you mind helping India get settled in?"

"Not at all," Agnes answered. "I think a hot bath is a good idea."

It was. All the more because that run had taken everything out of me. A soaking was going to be good for my muscles and my nerves, as well as to clean the blood from me. I followed Agnes up the flight of steps that felt a lot taller all of a sudden. I sat on the toilet seat and took off my shoes as she began drawing the bath.

"You're all in, Indy," she noticed. "Frazzled."

"I was never so scared," I told her.

"You're safe now," she assured me.

I nodded my agreement as I started on the buttons of my blouse, my eyes on the warm water filling the room with lavender scent from the oil beads she'd tossed in. She was watching me and given how Melissa had interpreted my undressing in front of her, I paused. She may have liked cowboys, but I wasn't sure that she didn't also like brunette, lady writers.

"They chased you all the way up from town," she said. "That's strange. They didn't look like normal dogs or wolves either."

I was reluctant to level with her. I didn't want to get her involved. As long as she didn't know the truth, she was safe, I felt. Silly, but that was what I thought at the moment.

"Mrs. Duvall also mentioned that you saw the ghost of Samuel Duvall," she went on. "It's like they don't want you to finish this book."

"Somebody doesn't seem to like me," I admitted.

"Well, I do," she said and for an instant I started to panic. What was with the women around here? "You can imagine there aren't many women that come here who I'm comfortable talking to. I'm usually stuck with just having my day off for that, when I can hang out with my sisters."

"I'll bet your sisters are a blast," I said. A cadre of down home, country girls; they had to be a hoot.

Agnes smiled. "Boy, if that isn't the understatement of the year," she remarked. "I'm just saying be careful. I don't get what's going on, but it feels like it's getting out of hand."

It did at that, I silently agreed. I promised to be careful and Agnes left me after setting out soap and a wash cloth to wipe away the blood and letting me know where her room was if I needed anything during the night. Not that I hadn't already learned where most everything was in the kitchen. There were PJs in the dresser, she told me as she headed out. Mrs. Duvall had completely prepared to have a grand-daughter-in-law-to-be in the house, in a proper manner that was, not shacked up with her grandson. I was beginning to feel like a surrogate.

Despite the hour, I pulled out my cell and called Francine and Melissa to tell them about the hounds. Thankfully, the clearer skies let the call go through.

"Clearly something more supernatural than ghosts is at work," Francine said, sending chills through me. "Plus, if they're after you, it's clearly not someone Melissa and Brianna said no to, like Levinson thinks. This goes way deeper and is focused on us. I'm sorry that pulls you in, dear." I was going to tell her not to be sorry, but her next words made me go silent. "I'm going to alert the other covens. Here's Melissa."

That she felt it necessary to alert the others filled me

with dread. I heard Agnes' words again, saying how it was getting out of control. *What* was getting out of control? What had I gotten involved in?

"I'm worried about you," Melissa told me. "You're not safe there without proper protections."

"The hounds weren't able to get into the mansion," I reminded her. "They couldn't get through the door and ran off when more people showed up. And you can bet Ben and Jerry will sound an alarm if they do come back. I'll be safe."

"You'd better be or I'll kill you myself," she remarked and made me chuckle.

"I'll haunt you, if you do," I threatened.

"Promises, promises," she returned. "Just be safe. Please?"

"I'm not setting foot outside until the sun is well above the horizon," I said.

"Good. I'll see you tomorrow."

"Night," I said and hung up.

I sponged off and then soaked for maybe thirty minutes before I had to give up fighting to keep awake. I wasn't going to win and didn't want to wake up in a cold tub looking like a giant prune at three a.m. I shook myself alert and dried off with a warm, thirsty towel, then padded barefoot in the thick robe to the dresser. I would have preferred flannels, but my PJ choices were red, green, or black silk. I chose the green, found some stretchy slippers and went down to the library with the heavy robe around me to find out if we'd heard from Levinson, provided anyone else was still awake.

Mrs. Duvall was pacing the library. A few inches more were gone from the decanter of brandy. I could smell it on the air.

"Robert's gone out," she told me matter-of-factly. "He's with Levinson, looking for whatever attacked you. The paw prints outside are the biggest I've ever seen."

"I'd never seen hounds so huge in my life either," I told her.

"Levinson brought your purse over for you," she said and pointed to it on the table with the photos and family records. "They had your car towed to the shop for repairs, too."

"That was nice of him."

"Well, you didn't expect him to leave it blocking the road, did you?"

"I mean, instead of impounding it."

"Why on earth would he do that?" she asked me. "It's not like you had much choice. Is that how they do it in St. Louis? Impound your car after you've run for your life?"

"Well, I guess if they knew the circumstances."

"That's one nice thing about a small town," she said. "We have the time to take to see what's going on."

"Any word about who that was in the pickup?" I asked. Idiot that he was, I was still concerned. They had bitten him up badly.

Alice Duvall waved a condescending hand. "Don't worry yourself over that Jeremy Schmidt," she told me. "He's as dense as a rock and just as tough. Stereotypical farm stock. The EMTs found him half passed out in his bathroom, trying to use Band-Aids to cover the wounds."

"Band-Aids?"

"I'm surprised he wasn't trying duct tape," she quipped. "He's of that mentality."

"He's going to be okay though?"

She nodded. "Nobody said he wouldn't. I imagine they're stitching him up as we speak. He'll be hitting on the nurses by morning."

"I take it he's known for that."

"That's how we knew who it was," she told me. "Funny. We've all said it would get him killed some day. Here it was how we knew to save his stupid ass."

Drink was making her curt. I didn't say anything more about it.

She meandered over to the table and sifted through the photographs absently. "So many memories, so much history. So many families that don't chronicle it, but let it pass into memory, where it probably belongs." She looked up at me with a half rueful expression.

"Did Robert tell you I had always been reluctant to have our story written?" she asked. She seemed for the moment to have forgotten that she had told me so herself at our first meeting. She continued, "Not all memories are good. Not all of a family's past is spotless."

She was drunk. Her melancholy was deep and almost addictive.

"I can leave the part with the witches out then," I offered, as much as it would have ruined that chapter.

"It's not the being written down part, but simply the being dug up and trotted around part," she told me. "I'd always been reluctant for fear of reopening old wounds. Maybe Baker and Levinson are right. Whatever, I let Robert talk me into it after all these years. I must be getting soft."

I took a deep breath and said, "I'd understand if you wanted to stop the project."

Alice Duvall smiled and answered with a chuckle. "No. We may as well finish it and have something to show for the pot we've stirred."

"Yes," I agreed. "It would a shame to stop now."

"Thank you for being understanding," Alice Duvall said to me. "You'll have to excuse me. I'm tired and need my bed."

She left me alone in the library with a drink I'd helped myself to as little as I needed it. As she went, she turned and commented, "How nicely those clothes suited you at dinner. How I wish their originally intended owner had been so level headed as you. Good night, my dear."

"Good night, Mrs. Duvall," I said and surreptitiously followed to watch that she tottered safely up the steps. With this big house and everything in it, you would have been justified in not feeling sorry for her in her self-pity. And then again, you wouldn't have. Not all memories are good. Not all of a family's past is spotless. They'd let a murderer escape and were still paying the price for it.

I wasn't quite sure of how to take her last comment about Phyllis. Was Alice Duvall suggesting I get together with her grandson, to step in where the other woman bailed in superstition? Or was her comment exactly what it seemed; the wistful, passing thought of a lonely and inebriated widow?

Back at the table, I saw the photo she had paused on, Samuel Duvall in his finest, and phantom pains went through my arm from where he had grabbed me at the start of this insane week. They couldn't get me themselves. So they'd set these hounds after me.

Melissa was half in a panic over me being in danger and Robert was out hunting whatever had attacked me. As for my earlier point about any control I had over the situation having bounced half way to China, well... at this point, I was thinking it had made it there. I didn't know what to expect next.

Fatigue was heavy on me by then. I tottered myself to bed, hanging the robe on a post. For a moment, I stared at the turned down covers and contemplated sleeping naked rather than in silk as the surrogate granddaughter. I also debated whether or not to lock the door against Richards, but eventually decided to leave it unlocked to see what he did. I was certain he wouldn't force himself on me. He could be a cad, but not a rapist.

I did go to bed naked, as though that was leaving my options open. Honestly, I really didn't know if I would have told him no or not. I didn't know what was wrong with me. I just knew that my instincts or impulses were beginning to rule my actions. I couldn't say why, but it was as though I really had no control over myself anymore, and I wondered again if I wasn't on the verge of a breakdown. Too many years of stress. Too many years of fighting with life to make it into something it didn't want to be. Melissa was right. I was wading neck deep against a flow that had been getting deeper as my savings ran dry.

It was time I changed, let things be what they were

going to be and work with my Karma. I could have been lying dead and torn to pieces in a ditch that night, rather than snuggled into a warm bed. What saved me was Fate putting me in the position of pseudo granddaughter and welcomed here. That made my earlier negative thoughts about it somewhat hypocritical.

I missed Melissa. Because Melissa really cared about me. How could you not want that? Or not want anyone that just wanted you for you? I wasn't sure why Robert wanted me, if it was simply the conquest notion or if Miss Enigma had really gotten to him. I did know that I didn't reciprocate. Yet, the hypocrite in me had left the bedroom door open an inch as an invitation, not to draw a cross breeze from the open window as I'd been thinking then.

Hell, never mind all that. I had just been scared out of several years of my life. It was a night I hadn't wanted to be alone, like the first one that put me in Melissa's arms and led to his. I needed to leave Willow Creek and never come back. But, I couldn't yet. Financially, I couldn't walk away from this job.

Fate had set me up to be here. Whatever I'd gotten into wasn't over yet. All my remarks about missing my chances to run or change how things might have come out were more wishful or magical thinking than anything. Because I wasn't merely the observer and recorder this time. I was part of the cast.

I lay there for a long time, listening to the soothing rustle of the wind in the trees, but not sleeping as these thoughts kept cycling through my head. I couldn't conclude how I felt about anything, only that I'd stepped into a real mess.

Morning came cool and windy and I regretted leaving the window open. I whipped on the robe and rushed to close it. Heading for the bathroom, I noticed the door to the hallway was shut. Probably blown shut, although I imagined Robert had returned and taken the invitation, only to find me snoring and unattractive, or had stood at the bed and watched me sleep for few moments before deciding not to bother me. Either way,

I didn't feel all that rested. Too few hours after too much stress.

I cleaned up, dressed, and stumbled down for coffee. I found a fresh pot brewing and a stomach growl-inducing aroma of cinnamon rolls. To Agnes, these were comfort foods. She had figured I'd need some as much, if not more, than she after the night before. The sight of those hounds was going to be with her for a long time, as well, she'd told me.

An exhausted looking Robert and Sheriff Levinson shuffled in a few minutes later. Robert was still in the same clothes as the night before and obviously had been out with the Sheriff all night. That answered the question about my bedroom door. The wind had shut it. Robert had not returned and hadn't checked in on me. For some reason, that bugged me. Where was the romance in that?

The thoughts that had kept me awake started over again.

"No sign of them," the Sheriff reported. "The tracks are still out front, but they've gone deep into the woods. It's going to take hounds and a small army to flush them out."

"What about the guy in the pickup?"

"In the hospital," Levinson said, thanking Agnes for the cup of black coffee she poured him. "Said it was wolves that attacked you. Too big for coyotes."

It hadn't been wolves. How did I tell them that without seeming like a nut case?

"We'll have to hunt them down before someone else gets hurt," the Sheriff said.

How could I tell them that anyone hunting the beasts would probably get hurt, perhaps killed? I knew they wouldn't believe me if I told the truth. They'd probably want to lock me up for observation in the local loony bin. I could only hope the hounds would ignore them because I was their only target. They had been sent to kill me. There was someone that wanted me dead or out of the way in this mix. Why, I didn't know. Francine and I had come to that conclusion last night.

My mind went to Willis again because of the odd fish that he was. Even though we had already established that he was just a Professor and had been back up in Ames, when Brianna had been murdered. He was simply the obvious and convenient choice, and peculiar enough to elicit an instinctive suspicion of him.

So who was it then? Who was there that could free the souls of the Duvall men from the mansion and conjure up hellhounds to come after me? My mind reeled at the craziness of that thought, but the facts were there. This wasn't about the ghosts at the mansion. There was a person behind this.

One of the other witches?

"I'll run you back to the Willow's Wells," Robert told me. "We had your car moved to the better repair shop. You'll be taken good care of."

"Better repair shop?"

"The guys initially towed you to Altman's, the big, local shop," he told me. "I had them move it at no cost to Wilson's, the smaller shop we use."

By *we*, I sensed he meant the wealthy people. "I don't follow."

"The other shop does so-so work," he told me, "but he charges the insurance companies less and pays the adjusters kickbacks. Unless you have enough money to be above Altman's socially, your car ends up there. I'm sure that offends you, but there it is." He was too tired to put it tactfully.

I wasn't offended, nor even very surprised. Why shouldn't there have been car insurance and repair scammers in the boonies?

"You need some sleep, Robert," I said. "Someone else can run me back to the B & B."

"No. I'm good."

"The lady's right," Levinson said. "I've got to run back to town anyway. I'll take her."

Riding with the Sheriff didn't sound like that much better of an idea. I wanted to get some more sleep and away from anyone that might have stuck more insomnia-inducing thoughts in my head. I had actually hoped to impose on Agnes or call Melissa to come get me.

"Thanks, Sheriff," I said anyway.

"Hell, you should be calling me Gus by now," he told me. "Despite what we talked about last night, you're part of Willow Creek now."

"Thanks," I said. I managed to sound sincere, then thought that would be hokey and suspicious, so I added, "I think."

The men smiled and Gus said he was ready whenever I was, which was the minute I'd finished my coffee before they'd arrived. I headed out for my first ever ride in a Sheriff's cruiser, riding shotgun. Literally, it was in a rack at my left, where an officer could have grabbed it easily. I was too tired to resist, so I asked, "Have you ever accidentally blown a hole in the roof?"

He bust out in a good natured laugh and I felt a surge in my liking for the man. Tired, Gus Levinson let his lawman's guard down and let me see the country boy behind it. His narrow focus remained, I was sure. Yet, the harshness was gone.

"Safety's on and there's no round chambered," he told me, which was so obvious that I felt stupid for asking and laughed at myself.

He had me run through the events of the last few days on the drive back. They hadn't made any progress on the arson of Melissa's house either. It was as though whoever it was could vanish or erase all traces. It was just weird how they couldn't find a thing, he remarked. Not if there was something supernatural at play, I thought, but kept that crazy sounding thought to myself.

Being the proper gentleman that he was, he walked me up to my room to make sure it was safe. What we found was that it was empty of all of my electronics. Computer, scanner, printer, even my hand written notes; they were all gone. I dropped my purse and barely held back the tears.

Levinson had a Deputy come over and we wrote up the report and they interviewed everyone in the building. Marianne Wells was all but in a state after the screeching of my tires the night before as I peeled away. She had jumped to the window in time to see the dogs chasing me down the street and had phoned the Sheriff's office. I hadn't known it, but help had already been on the way. What little aid they might have been against the hounds. That could have been a horrific disaster in the making.

"What now?" he asked as they wrapped up. "Can you start all over?"

"Don't have to," I told him. "I'm anal about backing up." I pulled a thumb drive from my purse. "Even if I've only changed one word, I back it up and I carry this with me everywhere. It's got my life on it."

"So you haven't lost anything but equipment?"

"A few of my written notes," I said, "But nothing I can't remember."

"Thank God for that," he said and I saw he meant it. Of course, it could have been because it still meant I'd be done and gone in a few weeks. "Well, get some rest, India. We'll call you if anything comes up."

"Thanks, Sher- I mean Gus. You should get some rest, too."

"I will when I can," he told me. "Goes with the job, you know."

He went out, closing my door gently. I heard him going heavily down the steps and out the front door. The grumble of his overworked cruiser sounded and faded as he drove away. There was a bit of sunshine trying to peak through the clouds, but it wasn't much for my mood. Instead of sleep, I called Melissa to tell her what had happened.

Chapter 12
Taking Sides

Twenty minutes later, she was hugging me in my room and the world started feeling better. I felt like crying, but also too tired to cry. When you're worn down to where nothing more can affect you... I had gotten there. Only the tight embrace of my friend kept me from breaking down.

"What now?" she asked, slowly releasing me. "You said you have a complete backup?"

"Yes. All I really need is more equipment." "Can you afford it?"

"I have my credit card," I told her. "Everything was insured. Hopefully, I'll get that check in time to pay off the card."

"That's a relief," she said. "There's no store in town, though."

"I'll get my car back tomorrow, I guess," I said. "I'll run back to St. Louis and get what I need."

"I have a better idea," she said. "I'm stuck eating vegetarian at my grandmother's. There's a great fish and chips place in Kansas City."

"Road trip?" I attempted some humor.

"Brush your teeth, comb your hair, and let's go," she said cheerfully and I felt a smile breaking across my face.

Snap out of it, Indy, I said to myself. *Start moving.* "And a change of clothes," I said. "I'm wearing a dress today."

Damn it! I was going to be happy and just deal with it.

Her little Scion rattled and puttered us up to Kansas

City, where I used my phone apps to locate the closest store. On the way, she had told me the garden had not been completely destroyed. Two lilacs still showed green and seemed to be bouncing back. That had relieved her sorrow. She had already resigned herself to knowing the house would eventually go; therefore, she wasn't so upset at losing it, so long as she hadn't lost the lilacs and the rodent garden.

She had also seen the cats prowling the edge of the forest and what was left of the garden. She had tried to bring Aubrey over to the Herborium, but he had jumped back out of her car before she had started it up. She figured to put up some sort of structure for them by winter. The cats would be okay.

I didn't buy the super systems, but I needed relatively high end. I think Melissa actually gulped at the total. I was back in business, though. It was a matter of re-downloading the software I used and loading up from the thumb drive. Actually, having all new equipment was exciting.

Francine called as we shopped. She had gotten in contact with a Witchcraft Scholar outside of KC and the woman had agreed to talk with us about the hellhounds. GPS got us there easily enough, if perhaps not by the most direct route.

The house was like any other on the rural block. We were well south of town and it was past the time we had expected to be diving into a plate of battered, fried cod and greasy chips with malt vinegar. Much longer and my stomach's growling would be imitating the hounds. We went up the walk and were met by an older woman in a faded floral house dress and gray sweater before we could knock.

"You must be Francine's granddaughter, Melissa," she said with a smile. "I finally get to meet you. Come in, come in. You must be India Hills."

"Yes, ma'am."

She waved a hand at me. "Name's Delia. I've got

some tea on. Come on into the kitchen."

The house was something of a library and museum to Wicca and other pagan religions. Before I had met these women, I might have said Occult, which carries a negative connotation. That would have been an entirely wrong description of them.

"Tell me about these hounds," she prompted as she poured tea. "Tell me the entire story, what you saw, felt, smelled, heard, and thought. Everything."

So, I did, which was the first time Melissa had heard it firsthand. I could tell it chilled her. Delia furrowed her brow a bit.

"Doesn't entirely match the legends of hellhounds," she said. "In lore, they are generally shaggy with black fur and glowing eyes. You say yours were more like Great Danes or Mastiffs, only shorter haired?"

"Yes."

"Curious," she noted. "The tale matches relatively well to that of the Gwyllgi, a Welsh legend. The Gwyllgi is said to resemble a Mastiff with red eyes and horrible breath."

"I remember the breath," I said, recalling it hitting my face and shoulder as I had barely managed to turn before it got its head into my car.

"It's called the Black Hound of Destiny and prowls rural roads at night to terrify travelers."

"Destiny?" That sounded ominous. "What does that mean?"

"They're also called the Dogs of Darkness," she replied in an academic voice. "They can be dangerous, but not omens. Most hellhounds of legend are guardians of the gateways to the dead. These are not part of those."

"What are they doing in Willow Creek?" Melissa asked.

"Good question," Delia replied, which did nothing for the chill in my spine. "The better question is how did they get there?"

"You mean from Wales?"

"For you to be seeing them so far from their natural habitat, if that is what they were, it means someone or something brought them there."

"That's what we've been trying to figure out," I told her. "There's a person behind all this. We just can't figure out whom."

"Well, hopefully knowing what they are will help narrow that down," Delia said. "It worries me some that they attacked. The legends speak mostly to them wanting to frighten people, but not really hurt anyone."

"These two wanted to kill me," I told her. "I'm sure of it."

She pursed her lips and frowned. All she could say was, "Be careful, dear. Don't go out alone at night. Not in such a rural place."

"Trust me *I* won't," I told her and that was a fact.

There were no specific protections against the hounds, she told us. General protections, much like Melissa was already providing, and common sense precautions were the best we were going to do. Mostly, we simply needed to try to avoid them and hope for the best.

We left for the restaurant and didn't talk about it. We each had to take it in. A Welsh legend; it was mind warping. Three weeks ago, ghosts and evil witches had been fun things to talk about on Halloween. Suddenly, they had become real and burned my arm, and now I was prey for the Black Hounds of Destiny. Could it have gotten any crazier? I thought, and felt that it probably would.

Over our late lunch, Melissa suggested I move in by them. "We can protect you better that way," she said.

It made sense, although I had more room to work at the B & B. "Besides," I told her. "I'm not sure how well that would go down with some parts of the Town Council."

"Town Council?"

I told her about the prior night's dinner conversation while her face screwed up in bewilderment.

"Seriously? They're worried about some feud restarting? What century are they living in?"

"Their own, I guess," I replied. "It'll be alright. You've protected me so far. I'm sure we can continue on the way we have."

"I suppose," I could see she wasn't too certain. "I can bring some more appropriate protections over."

"I'm not worried about the Gwyllgi," I told her. "I'm more worried about what the next surprise will be." If we defeat the hellhounds, what comes next?

"I hadn't even thought of that," she admitted. "I guess we'll have to put our heads together on that. Some of the women from the other covens are going to arrive today. You're about to have a platoon of witches protecting you."

Three weeks ago, that would have made me smile in utter amusement. Now, it filled me with gratitude and relief.

Back at the Willow's Wells, Melissa helped me bring up the new gear and get it hooked up after drawing a different protective circle on the floor. She knew her way around computers well enough. As she had said, they were twenty-first century witches. Once it was up and the first of the software was downloading, I felt relaxation beginning to soften the muscles of my body and I sighed.

"Not so tensed up now?" she asked.

"It was obvious?"

"Very," she answered. "I would suggest a hot bath. I brought you a sachet of rejuvenating herbs and some natural soap."

I made a sound of delight. "Sounds perfect."

"I figured you'd need it," she said and headed into the bathroom with a pouch she pulled from her bag. I heard the splash of water start as I followed her in. She set them on the edge of the sink while the water warmed up. "Just toss it in, when you start filling the tub. What time should I come get you for dinner?"

I answered by taking her face between my hands and kissing her. I hadn't planned it. I hadn't even thought of it until I found myself doing it. It just came out of me and when she gave me a confused look, I kissed her again, longer and sensed her responding. Her arms were around my waist; mine were around her shoulders, our foreheads together. I could feel the heat of her breath getting deeper and the growing urgency in her body.

"I don't get it," she said.

"Neither do I," I told her. In the back of my mind, I was wondering what I was doing, what was coming over me. I didn't feel in control. Hell, face it. I *wasn't* in control of myself anymore. I didn't know what was happening with me.

"Are you sure?" she asked. "Because if you're not…"

"I won't hurt you," I cut her off, instinctively knowing what she was going to say. It would have been too much for her, if I wasn't serious about this.

I was. I couldn't have told you why then. It was still coming to me. The long and the short of it was Melissa had gotten under my skin. It wasn't a case, as some may think, of my relationships with men always failing because I was really meant to be with another woman. That wasn't it at all.

I was falling for her heart.

"You were right," I told her. "I did need a nudge." It had been the stigmatism of being with another woman that had bothered me. I couldn't say it wasn't still a source of angst. I was still feeling unbalanced. But I was also feeling things I had never expected to feel.

"Okay, now I'm scared," she told me.

"Me too," I admitted. "My entire world has been rocked and shaken since I got here. I almost feel like I don't know who I am anymore."

"Will you still love me when you figure that out?" she asked.

"I think loving you is part of who I am," I told her, finally seeing it for myself. "I think I'm just finding out who I am."

"Indy," she whispered, but words escaped the feeling

she wanted to express.

"Mel, you know what we're doing?" I asked, with a hint of playfulness. "We're wasting hot water." She smiled and chuckled at that. "Put the plug and the sachet in for us."

She nodded and did so after another kiss. When she turned back, I wasn't there. Although, my dress was on the floor. Later, she would tell me how her mind was being blown by my sudden aggressiveness. She hadn't seen it coming. Truthfully, neither had I. When I returned, it was with wine and glasses. I set them on the sink and proceeded to unbutton her.

Our love making was a private thing. Suffice it to say there was nothing kinky in it. It was more loving and simply sensual than anything else. When I undressed her completely, I caressed her slowly for her as much as for myself, as much for her to savor the touch of my hands on her body as for me the feel of her skin.

It wasn't the largest of tubs, but neither of us were the largest of people. The hot, aromatic water. The silky feeling soap. The strong Merlot. The abandonment for hours, there and the bed, after to feelings that seemed to come from nowhere. It was a catharsis from my controlled life.

I felt carried along. Swept up is a real event that happens to you. My involvement with Melissa was specific to her, not to women in general. I still had no feelings toward other women, even the most attractive. In fact, I oddly still felt repulsed by the idea. Men still made my pulse quicken and warmed my blood. It was just that I was getting into Melissa for some reason I couldn't then fathom. Melissa was different. I couldn't really explain it. Like Melissa said, it's not a thing of logic. Nor was it so much a physical thing as it was a person to person thing.

I didn't like Richards that much personally, but I was turned on physically by him. I didn't feel any compelling physical attraction to Melissa, but liked her beyond explanation. It was weird, really. Once more, I found myself wishing if only Richards had possessed a heart and soul like Melissa's.

It was late afternoon, when the ring for Francine sounded on Melissa's cell, waking us from napping in each other's arms.

"Hey there, Granny Franny," she answered, something I hadn't heard her say before. She must have been in as good a mood as I was.

I could hear Francine asking what in the world had happened that was so good. She obviously understood the expression well.

"The world just feels right today," she said.

"Are you talking about you and India?" I heard her ask.

"Things are good," Melissa cautiously answered.

"Well, that's good to hear," Francine replied and I took the phone from Melissa's hand as I rolled on top of her.

"Hey, Francine," I said. I think there was still some sleep in my voice. "What's for dinner tonight?"

"You're heavy," Melissa complained loudly enough for her grandmother to hear.

I heard Francine laugh. "Dinner will be a surprise," she told me. "Just like this phone call. Two hours give you enough time?"

Melissa gave me a look as if to ask if that was enough time.

"We just need to finish waking up," I answered and Melissa pouted. I whispered to her, "You have to bring me back later," and she smiled.

"Okay," Francine said laughing. "I'll see you when you get here. Bye."

"Bye," I said and hit the end button as Melissa shouted her goodbye.

"That was my Granny Franny," she jokingly complained. "You didn't let me say goodbye."

I dropped the phone on the bed and kissed her in

reply.

As we dressed a while later, I noticed I had a voicemail on my phone. I hadn't noticed it ring, so it had probably been while we were in the bath. It was from Richards, having heard from the Sheriff about my equipment being stolen. I called him back as Melissa dressed quietly.

"It was insured for theft," I told him. "I'll file a claim on Monday."

"We've got some equipment at the warehouse you can probably use in the meantime," he offered. "Thank God you had it all backed up."

"Yeah, nothing lost," I replied. "I've already replaced everything."

"You have?" he was surprised. It hadn't dawned on him that I could have done it so quickly. "How did you manage that?"

"Don't be upset," I told him. "Melissa drove me up to Kansas City this morning after I got back here."

"Why would that upset me?" he wondered.

"Because last night, it sounded like people were afraid I was taking their side in the feud, including you," I answered. Looking at Melissa buttoning up her dress, there was no doubt in my soul that I had chosen her side. "Like there is a feud at all."

"Forget what the fogeys on the Council think," he told me. "They can make a lot of noise, but they wouldn't dare defy Nana. If there's any feud, it's there."

"A little power struggle going on?" I asked and knew I should have kept my mouth shut. I could see him cringing on the other end of the line.

"Nothing you need to worry about," he replied a bit stiffly.

Melissa was distracting me by dangling one of my sun dresses, suggesting I wear it to dinner. I nodded and waved at her to be still. She went about selecting the rest of my ensemble. That was a twist I hadn't anticipated; a woman could pick an outfit for me when every man I'd ever dated had been clueless. It threw me a little.

"I probably should have told everyone last night that the witches really look on the whole haunting and curse thing as a joke. They aren't a party to it and actually believe everyone else is misguided for believing in it."

"You told me the other day and I told them for you," he said. "The mayor thought it was funny, but figured the city attorney wouldn't be amused. He'd probably agree, but he hates being told what to believe just on general principle."

Melissa started untying the sash to my robe and mouthed the word, "Hungry." We'd rather worked off our sloppy, calorie and grease laden lunch. I slapped softly at her hands and damn it if Richards hadn't heard it.

"What was that?"

"I dropped a notepad," I lied and shooed her away. She was grinning like an imp. I didn't know what was coming next, but was sure something was. I tried to hurry up the call. "I'm getting everything set up and downloading the software I lost."

"I'll let you go then," he said. I had completely forgotten about the software once we'd started the bath. All I'd managed to download was one item, not even install it, when I probably would have been done otherwise. I gave Melissa a sideways grin that made her hold up her palms and wonder why. Richards was still talking, "You know, I'd feel a lot more comfortable if you would stay at the house. You and your equipment will be a lot safer here."

That was a point I couldn't deny. "I work best if left alone," I told him. "This B & B is the perfect place."

"So, work there, but spend the nights under our roof," he suggested.

"That's an option," I had to agree. "Let me think about it."

"I can do that," he agreed. "Should I come get you for dinner?"

"No thanks. I need to rest."

"You mean you're dining with Melissa," he wasn't

fooled. "No biggie. Tell her and Francine hello for me."

"What?"

"Seriously," he replied. "I have no animosity against them. But you're right. I'm kind of stuck with our small town politics."

Attitudes was more like it. I let him slide with calling it politics. I pushed End and looked over at Melissa holding up the dress for me by way of telling me to hurry up.

"He says 'hello.'"

"Let me guess, the option was to stay at his place instead of here."

"Jealous?" I asked, knowing full well she wasn't. I was still feeling playful.

"Pffft!" she replied. "I still say you'd be safer staying with us. You'll have the protection of the entire coven."

"Where would we be alone?" I teased.

"No fair," she complained with a smile. "Seriously, though. I'll give up our privacy for you to be safe."

Our eyes were locked for long seconds. The sincerity of her words and look wrenched at me. I began to see what was happening then. Melissa made me feel the way I'd always wanted a mate to make me feel. Treasured. My eyes may have watered a bit.

"There's always St. Louis," she reminded me. "No rural roads for any Gwyllgi there."

I smiled. "As soon as I'm sure I won't need to double check anything in the library or the records room," I promised her. How I would regret that later is something that may always haunt me.

In the moment though, my roller coaster ride continued as I felt my emotions flip-flopping again. The thought of taking Melissa to live with me in St. Louis as my lover made me feel the conflict again between who I had thought I was, a normal, heterosexual woman, and who I seemed to be becoming. There was both excitement and trepidation at the thought of Melissa coming to live with me. If Richards had come to me the night before, instead of spending it chasing the Gwyllgi, I would have taken him into my bed. There had been a need and I would have given in to it.

The point was that with Robert, it would be an affair. Melissa was becoming a relationship. It may seem that such was normal for this day and age when we're mostly accepting and open. But when it was changing your own paradigm about yourself, it was unnerving.

Chapter 13
The Storm Brews

A knock at the door broke our trance and we both gave a start. The Sheriff announced himself. Melissa hopped off of the bed and scampered barefoot into the bathroom, forgetting her purse. I tossed it in to her as I pulled my robe tighter and padded barefoot to the door.

"Hi," I said, opening it for him to enter.

"Did I disturb you?" he asked solicitously, noticing the bed and my unbrushed hair.

"No. I was already up," I told him. "Just deciding what to wear." I motioned at the dress Melissa had picked out and noticing a couple of embarrassing things she had laid out beside it. As much as I wanted to kill her for it, it also excited me and left me wondering just how crazy of a relationship this was going to be.

Levinson was tactful enough to ignore them. "We tracked the wolves into the woods," he told me. "But we lost them there."

That was a relief. No one needed to confront those things.

He kept talking. "If they're still out there, though, people are alert to them and watching. They'll be spotted eventually."

I really hoped not. At least not by anyone who didn't know what they were dealing with.

"I won't go jogging outside of town anymore," I told him.

"I'd suggest you suspend your runs until we find them," he advised. "They were in town last night when you came across them after all. Can you remember anything more of it?"

I went through it again, telling the exact same story as the night before and the morning, when he had driven me here. There was nothing new to come to mind. I remembered every detail and still do. There was no forgetting that night.

"How's the driver of the truck?" I asked.

Levinson smirked. "He'll live. I don't know that he learned anything, but he'll live."

"I hate to stereotype anyone," I started. I wanted to say something along the lines of he had it coming, as well as he'd had gotten more than he'd deserved.

Levinson chuckled and surprised me again, "He's my cousin, India, and there never was a bigger stereotype. He's home now; wouldn't stay in the hospital. You can bet he's sitting on his porch drinking beer with his antibiotics and pain killers."

"Well, still more than he deserved," I commented.

"Maybe. Nothing will ever be enough for him to learn his lesson, though. That's just Jeremy," Levinson assured me. "You have nothing to worry about. His blood tests came back negative for anything you might have had to worry about catching from it. No HIV, Hepatitis or anything like that."

I hadn't even thought of that. I still said, "That's a relief."

"I see you're all set up again." He motioned toward the new equipment.

"Almost," I told him. "I'm getting the software situated now." Very slowly at that, I thought.

"So, you'll be back at writing the Duvall's story again tonight, it looks like," he remarked, then caught me off guard with the next question. "That the only book you're writing about Willow Creek?"

I gaped for a second and that gave me up.

"Yes?" he asked.

"I'm keeping a diary," I confessed.

"For a book one day?"

I could only smile. There was no hick in this small town Sheriff. "One day. But no names or real places."

"On your honor?" he asked.

"Well, maybe a disarming and sharp country Sheriff named Guy," I replied and made him smile.

"Nobody calls their kid Guy what lives around here," he told me. "Well, I'll let you get on with your evening. I just wanted to come by and check on you."

"Thank you, Sheriff," I said and got a mildly reproachful look. "I mean Gus. Thanks."

"Night, India," he said and then looked past me to call to the bathroom, "Night, Miss Ferrier." I think I might have jumped at the certainty in his voice. He grinned again as he glanced at me. "Everyone knows her little, white Scion. And I know you couldn't have walked to St. Louis or wherever for this equipment."

"I think I have a main character," I told him.

He grinned again and actually tipped his hat to me as he put it back on. I shut the door behind him and turned to see Melissa standing in the bathroom doorway. She had a wry grin on her face, amused at ourselves as well as curious.

"Gus?"

I simply smiled back and went to dress. A plot was forming in my mind for a story about a clever country Sheriff trying to solve a crime of supernatural origin. It was half written already. Like any good story, it was writing itself and the ending was yet to be determined.

Melissa came and sat on the bed with an almost wicked grin. "Okay, so he likes you, too. Who doesn't?"

"Melissa!"

"Never mind that. Tell me about this diary."

I was trapped now. I had written about her. How I had found someone I felt connected to, a friend for life. How I had been grateful for her concern and protection. I had noted how I wished she had been a man. How I had become conflicted and worried about losing her friendship after that first night. All my ramblings as I had tried to sort it out in my mind were in that diary.

I would have told it all to her anyway. So it was no secret what I had felt or thought.

"When we go to St. Louis," I told her. "For now, let's go eat."

She helped me finish dressing and before we went out we kissed one more time and held each other for several moments. The following weekend, when I would bring her to my home, felt too far away.

It was dark when we pulled up at the Herborium. The lights shining from within and the lanterns hanging on the porch illuminated the grounds for a dozen yards all around. We stepped from the car into light that was at odds with the heavy autumn chill. It seemed like it should have been warm and smelling of fresh grass and flowers, not cool and damp with the air laden with sodden leaves and trees.

She hooked her arm through mine and I hugged hers to me as we went up the steps and into the warm, glowing shop. Over the usual scents of herbs and candles came the smell of Francine's cooking. Vegetarian or not, her casseroles were to die for. It helped, of course, that she was a big fan of cheese.

I heard another woman's voice as they talked upstairs. It sounded calm and sturdy, like Francine's.

"That's my great aunt, Carla," Melissa told me with a big grin. "She's my grandmother's sister. Two of them are still with us."

I smiled in anticipation of meeting her. I had no doubt she'd be as pleasant and welcoming as her sister. You could hear it in the lightness of her voice.

Of course, when it came to their family, I was already very biased.

"There they are," Francine announced on seeing us ascending the steps. "We can call off the search party."

"We aren't that late, are we?" I asked.

"Of course, we're not," Melissa said. "Family is never late."

"They are when someone is waiting for her hug," returned a plumpish woman with a gray mop cut. Carla Foster held her arms out for Melissa to run into a bear hug.

"Missed you, Aunt Carla. You don't come around often enough."

"Ain't so easy on these old hips anymore, darling." Deep, dark eyes, much like Melissa's were turned on me. "You must be India. I've been waiting to meet you."

"Sorry we kept you waiting," I said with a grin and stepped up to shake hands, but received a bear hug instead. Which, I guess, I should have expected. I was part of the circle, at least, if not family by now.

"I've heard so much about you from Francine," she told me and surprised me by pushing up the sleeve of my sweater to inspect the fading burns. Her smile disappeared for a second as she gave them a serious eye, then it returned with a nod. "Gone by the end of next week."

"I hardly notice them anymore," I told her. "The poultice is working. What's in it, by the way? It makes me dizzy, when I first put it on."

"It's more than what the ingredients are," Carla told me. "It's the spells said over it and the love put into it."

"I'm beginning to understand," I told her. I mean, it was easy to say I got it. How they were combining medicine with the metaphysical, pulling in energies from the planet that science has ignored. When you start to live its effects and have your world rocked as mine had been, you begin to *feel* the truth of it. That was what I meant by understanding.

"Let's eat while it's hot," Francine said and we gathered around the table, laden with food and the workings for magicks and charms she was getting ready. I grabbed a quick hug from her before taking a seat next to Melissa. We sat close together, like a new couple would. It was not lost on either of our elders, but they left it to glances and smiles between themselves; the matrons happy for their young ones.

I recognized most of the vegetables, but a few were unfamiliar. Francine told me what they were and how she'd prepared them. I wasn't converting to a vegetarian, but I could see making it a bigger part of my diet. Melissa was a committed carnivore. I half expected resistance from her on it. Although, I could see making the yellow beet and quinoa salad a staple.

"What about these hounds?" Francine asked. "What did you find out from Delia?"

"She said it resembled a Welsh legend, the Gwyllgi," Melissa reported and gave an accurate account of what it was.

The older sisters frowned and exchanged thoughtful looks.

"Doesn't quite match up," Carla noted.

"Why are they suddenly here?" Francine added.

"Me and the book?" I asked, knowing it was the truth. What else was there?

"Something to do with your research," Francine concurred. "Something about the Duvall history that we don't know about."

"Or are overlooking," said Carla. "The fact that these hounds don't match any known legend and were never here before is enough to tell us that someone brought them here, either by spell work or opening a portal. Or both."

"But who?" I asked. "Who would want to keep me from writing a family history that next to no one will actually ever read?"

"It's probably more fear of what you'd uncover." Carla said.

"That was a hundred years ago," I replied. "The one that grabbed me was Samuel Duvall, Mayor back when Sammic killed your ancestors. What is he trying to keep secret? That Sammic cast a prosperity spell on the family? I think we all know that. Even if I did find proof who would care nowadays?"

"Samuel Duvall probably doesn't see it that way," Carla told me. "He and the other male Duvalls trapped here still think the way they did back then. Proof of their deal with the Devil would be condemning to them."

"True," I agreed. "That would explain why he said he wouldn't let me ruin them for all time."

"He told you that?"

"Yes. He said I was his and he wouldn't let me ruin them."

"Definitely sounds like he hasn't changed since then," Carla noted with a hint of amusement. "Physical death is a change of planes, not of heart."

"That still doesn't explain who bound them to the cellar, or at least to Willow Creek," I pointed out. "Nor does it provide any clue as to who could have brought those hounds here and sent them after me."

"Yes," Carla said. "It doesn't."

"Could the Duvall men have developed the ability in their current state?" I asked.

The women looked at each other over this new thought and nodded.

"Perhaps," Francine said. "We don't know what it's like on that plane, so we can't know that they couldn't have."

"They may have let loose the hounds on me once they knew they couldn't get to me themselves."

"Plausible," said Carla.

"Except that still doesn't explain why their ghosts remain here in the first place," Melissa reminded us. "There's a big piece missing."

"I know," I said. "And the only person in this whole mix that had the power to do either is Sammic himself, and we know he's dead. I mean, if I were writing the story, his returning for revenge would have been the perfect plot."

"We have proof of his death," Francine reminded me.

"No one can come back or prolong their life for a

hundred years," Carla noted. "At least, not without others like us being able to sense it in him."

"And you've met Willis," I pointed out. We'd already ruled him out.

"Willis?" Carla asked.

"A paranormal researcher out of Ames," Francine answered. "He's been here for a few months, collecting data on the mansion to prove the haunting."

"Old and scary looking," I added. "He would have made the perfect Sammic, still alive after a hundred years."

Francine shook her head and said. "I talked with him a few times. He's odd, but there's no aura and he looks nothing like Sammic."

"Sammic is dead," Carla said. "Uncle Jacob dug up his corpse and confirmed it."

"I didn't know that," Francine remarked.

"Well, it was never talked about," Carla said. "I only found out a few years ago. Uncle Jacob didn't have permission."

"Sounds like him."

"The only one we know could do it, couldn't have done it." I said.

"Besides," Melissa pointed out, "what would he have wanted revenge for? He's the one that got away with murder and went and lived a full life somewhere else."

"Yeah, that is another hole in the theory," I agreed. "So, who else would have had the motive?"

"Well, let's focus on the current people," Carla suggested. "Figure out who could bring about those hounds, and hopefully that leads to who bound the male Duvalls to the cellar."

"Shit!" I blurted as a thought came to me. "Someone that lost out because of the Duvall prosperity puts the curse on them in revenge."

"If you had the power to place such a curse," Carla shot my idea down, "then why not cast your own counter prosperity spell?"

"Right," was my deflated response.

"Maybe it was their Christian god," Melissa chimed in. "Perhaps He is punishing them."

"Possibly."

"And it could be they have learned how to conjure hounds," she added.

"That fits the facts," I agreed. "If they were only in Purgatory here, though, they had no reason to want to kill me. They'd know they only need to serve their time before going to Heaven."

"True," Francine replied. "Which is conceptually hard for me actually, because we don't believe in a Purgatory or a Hell. That, and the fact that they aren't just waiting out their time, suggest it's something more."

"Well, let's go down the list of the people involved," Carla said. "We can probably rule out the Duvalls themselves. Why bring you here just to stir everything up?"

"Unless they hoped stirring things up would help break the curse by bringing it into the open or something," I offered. Marianne Wells had suggested that my first day in Willow Creek, I recalled. "The book was a way of feigning disinterest and disbelief in the ghosts and the curse, while they worked to break it or carry out their family's revenge." It sounded foolish even as I said it.

"Revenge for what?" Melissa asked. "They were the ones who betrayed us."

"Just break the curse then," I replied. "Maybe Richards was hoping something would come of it."

"Possible, but contradictory," Carla told me. "If they were able enough in the arts to call up hellhounds, then they would not have been naively hoping things would be fixed by your stirring things up. They would have fixed it themselves. Have you seen any signs that they are secret practitioners?"

"No," I answered, somewhat deflated at my idea being killed so easily. "I've been all through the house and read everything they have about themselves. They've never dabbled, not even to try removing the curse themselves. Now that I think about, why would they be trying to scare me off, if they wanted me to stir things up and find the solution for them? It can't be them."

"No, it's another practitioner," Carla said, "and a powerful one at that, deep into the dark arts as Sammic once was."

"But who and why?" Francine posed. "The only living person with anything to gain was Richards, as he's destined for the curse."

"Even if he did believe in it," Melissa reminded us. "He's never asked for it to be lifted and has never bothered us."

"He said he doesn't believe in a curse, even though Samuel Duvall has been seen in the old mansion," I told them. "He says he has no animosity toward you. He was angry at everyone when Samuel Duvall chased off his fiancée, but claims he got over it."

"Do you believe him?" Melissa asked.

I didn't have to think about it. "Yes. I do."

"I was suspicious of him too," Carla admitted. "I thought perhaps he had killed Brianna and was intent on wiping the coven out, hoping the curse would be lifted when we were all dead. Like you said, though, why have you here, if that was his plan?"

"Who else is there?" I wondered aloud.

"What about their housekeeper?" Carla asked and I almost laughed.

"Agnes? No way," I told them. "She's a total sweetheart. Not a malicious bone in her body."

"Is she sweet on Richards?" Carla asked and I couldn't keep the grin off of my face.

"Not cowboy enough for her, she told me," I replied. "College degrees and silk ties count as marks against you according to her."

"There was never any Cinderella fantasy going on there?" Francine asked for confirmation.

I shook my head and gave a little sigh. "I think

they're all hoping the future Mrs. Richards is me."

"Excuse me?" Carla asked and Francine actually let out a small, highly amused laugh.

"I'm not surprised," she said. "Knowing him. Always bringing the world to Willow Creek. Of course, he'd be looking for someone from somewhere else. But you're...," she indicated Melissa and left the question open.

"Yes," I said and I swear Melissa began to glow. I was sure my sudden change of heart was still leaving her with doubts. However, hearing me admit it to her family dispelled most, if not all of them. To myself, as well.

"How have they gotten that idea then?" Carla wondered.

"I kind of complicated things," I admitted, staring down at the table.

Melissa laid her hand over mine. "I kind of put you in that position."

I turned my hand over to interlace our fingers. "I'm over that."

She squeezed my hand and said nothing more about it. But her great aunt was left with a confused look on her face. Francine waved a hand at her sister to tell her to forget about it; she'd explain later.

"Who's next to gain anything?" Francine posed.

We looked from one to the other blankly. Who else in Willow Creek had the skills and the motive?

Mayor Baker? Would he benefit somehow by having the mansion cleaned of the spirits? Was that holding up some renovations or removal of the records? Some other planned uses? The appearance of Samuel Duvall had been at a function. Maybe fear of a repeat was keeping them from fixing the mansion up for use in other money making ventures, such as a haunted house.

Pastor Cogdon? His visit with me that day had revealed his unreasonable concern over how people would view his flock if it became known that they believed in ghosts and witchcraft. It all had negative connotations to him. He'd want the last of the witches gone and my work stopped.

Sheriff Levinson? He might have wanted me to stop stirring the pot, if he felt I was. He had no reason, though, for wanting any harm to come to the witches, much less to murder Brianna. He was the least likely of them all to be behind it, which, in perfect crime fiction genre, would have made him the most likely.

Who else was there? The City Attorney? The Council? We knew they had concerns. Might they also have doubts, even objections to my writing the Duvall history? Only what motive could they have had to kill Brianna and burn Melissa's house down? That was so nineteenth century that it made no sense.

As far as we knew, none of them were practitioners. They had no skills and little motive, if any.

"We'll need to try to find out discreetly if any of Willow Creek's finer citizens are practicing in private," Carla concluded.

"How do you keep something like becoming strong enough to call the hounds quiet for so long?" I asked. "Surely, you would have seen some signs."

"You would hope," Francine said.

"It gives us something to work with," Carla said. "We'll start later tonight and try to divine who it might be."

"There wouldn't be anything like a rival Coven, would there?" I wondered aloud, my active imagination at its artistic best.

That almost made them laugh. "You don't really think that, knowing what you know about the Green ways?" Melissa asked.

"I know," I replied. "You don't compete."

"Exactly," she said. "The very nature of a Green Witch is compassion and cooperation."

"I know. I'm talking about some other kind of witch. Obviously, he or she would have to be, if they released the ghost and the hounds."

"They wouldn't be a rival Coven, though," Melissa corrected me. "Even if there was another coven that wanted to bring harm to us, it would be something much more than a rivalry to cause them to break the rule of three."

"We've actually already asked around," Francine told us. "Once the Duvall men started haunting our woods and the hounds chased you, we knew something more was going on than ever before. We started investigating. So far nothing. No one's heard anything."

"Why would some other witches want to harm you anyway?" I asked. "What have you got that anyone could want? The land or the shop?"

"No one's ever asked to buy them."

"Maybe they never wanted to buy you out."

Francine gave a shrug to say it was possible. "There's nothing special about this land and there's only an acre. Our family has owned it since the first of us settled here. No one else has ever wanted it."

"You've made it into something more," I pointed out. "It's a haven."

"Any good witch can do that," Francine replied. "As possibilities go, it doesn't make sense."

"Are there minerals under the land?" I asked.

"Maybe. Who knows?" she answered. "But there's no mining going on anywhere nearby and mining companies generally aren't into witchcraft."

"Good point," I told her.

"Nor would they be after you," Melissa pointed out. "No. This is something to do with our history here with the Duvalls. There's something out there that's still volatile enough to make them want to keep it quiet."

"They're afraid I'll find it in the old records."

"Seems that way."

"Maybe I should start looking and see if I can't nip this in the bud, then," I said.

"That might be a good idea actually," Francine said. "It's as likely to get you kicked out for snooping. But if we could figure out what this is all about, it would make things safer for all of us, especially you."

"I'll start peeking through the old records on Monday," I said. "I don't know what more I can find, though. I already got all of the newspaper reports on the Sammic events and anything else minor and of significance for the Duvalls. I've basically already dug up everything there is to dig up about them."

"Evidently not," Melissa replied. "Or they wouldn't be trying to stop you."

"I'll see what I can find," I said.

"We'll make sure you're protected," Francine promised.

I was grateful for that sentiment. How they were going to protect me from those hounds short of a shotgun with silver deer slugs or something was beyond me at the moment. My only hope to be safe from them was simply not to be out anywhere after dark or get too far from my car, once I had it back.

They had promised Monday afternoon, Tuesday at the latest. For the moment, I was dependent on Melissa. Which changed nothing at all, given we would have spent the weekend together anyway. She drove me back to the Willow's Wells after dinner. It was getting late and very chilly with another round of storms threatening.

We waited for several minutes in her car, listening and watching the dark surroundings for signs of the hounds. When we didn't see anything, we opened the doors and stood in them hanging open for almost a minute. When nothing continued to happen, we silently closed the doors and then dashed up the steps and inside. There was no guarantee we would be safe in there, but it just felt that way.

The front hall was silent and dimly lit. The Wells were in their quarters in the back, probably already asleep. I hadn't seen any lights from the outside and the usual, muted sounds of their television drifting down the hall were absent. The fireplace was cold and empty tonight as I was the only guest at the moment and I'd told them I'd be out all evening. The parlor and hall were blanketed with a hush that evening.

We slipped silently up the heavily padded, carpeted stairs on tip toes anyway and opened the door to my room quietly. It was warm and still the mess we'd left it in. Clothes from the day on the floor or over the backs of chairs. Bed unmade and thoroughly rumpled, which gave me a rush remembering why. Computer still running as I had left it extracting and installing software, when we left. There were still a couple of applications to finish up before I was completely back in business.

"Go ahead and finish that up," Melissa told me. "I've got my reading to do."

She produced a large tome on oriental religions from her shoulder bag.

"Converting to Buddhism?" I asked.

"Studying," she told me. "I'm doing on-line classes remember."

She had told me the other day about her academic goals. She'd been taking various classes on-line as well as a few at the University of Missouri. Her goal was one day to write a compendium of all religions with grids that showed the common themes of celebrations at common times. The world's religions, it turns out, have a number of common threads.

"Halloween came from Celtic traditions and the Day of the Dead actually came from ancient Aztec rituals that survived and were merged into Catholicism," she told me as the rain began falling again in a constant shushing and occasional rap at the windows. "It's really quite fascinating.

"Samhain is a Sabbat representing death with the promise of rebirth. It marks the end of the harvest season. It also coincides with the Christian holy day of All Saints Day, the Mexican tradition of Day of the Dead, other veneration of the dead celebrations in Asian and African cultures. There are many curious similarities between our supposedly different religions. Makes you wonder if there was once a common religion or if we are all just subconsciously tuning into the natural rhythm of our planet."

"It does," I agreed. "When did religions begin?"

"Some say when primitive man had gotten intelligent enough to become aware of his own mortality and start to wonder if there wasn't more than this," she told me. "But the big criticism of that is that it's too complex. That the first religious thoughts would have been simpler."

"What do you think?"

"That the naysayers are right," she told me. "I think primitive peoples had an experience such as yours. They came face to face with one of their dead ancestors and had actual proof there was more than this world, rather than clinical surmise out of fear of their own mortality. That's why they started burying utensils and all with the dead; so they'd have what they needed, as far as primitive man was concerned, so that they wouldn't be coming back."

"A practical approach to a frightening problem."

"Simple and clean," she told me. "No overthinking by scholars or primitive peoples required."

"Can the scholars handle a theory without overthinking?" I asked.

"I've been told to continue my studies," she replied.

Her phone rang as we chuckled over that.

"Hey Granny Franny, we're here safe and sound," she answered and the smile dropped from her face a second later. "The Duvall spirits are patrolling the woods around her place," she told me. "Right. Okay. I will. Goodnight."

Melissa set the book aside and hopped off the bed to begin digging in her bag.

"She said for us to make sure our protections were in place," Melissa related. "Apparently, the ones at the shop are keeping them at the edges of our property, away from the house, and out of the gardens. I'll draw us a circle for tonight. I'll clean it off before Mrs. Wells finds it."

"What do I do?"

"Come stand in this circle with me so I can draw the protections around us."

I immediately got up and stood where she directed. Francine had mentioned it at dinner, but it hadn't sunk in then. The spirits had progressed from being released into the town to being able to roam freely everywhere. The same questions began whirling through my mind again.

Why were they coming out now? Why were they becoming aggressive and dangerous all of a sudden? Was it really something about them that I might find out? Would it be enough to damn them forever over waiting out their purgatory in the old mansion? Who released them and brought on the hounds?

Most importantly... *what* had I stirred up?

Chapter 14
Quiet

The next day it got weird, because things stopped happening.

Just like switching off a light bulb, the witches no longer noticed the Duvall males anywhere and all traces of the hounds simply disappeared. The week passed as quietly as had the others before I was attacked and the hounds had shown up. I got my car back in perfect condition. The insurance claim on my stolen equipment was filed and unlikely to raise any red flags, my agent said.

We had gone to Melissa's burned down home that Sunday. It was just like one of those old movies where the heroes find something in the old ashes of a burned out homestead, where all that was left was the chimney. That was what Melissa's place looked like. Her 1950s appliances and even the heavy bathtub were just twisted and blackened tangles of scrap metal in one corner of a low pile of black coals and ash, faintly smelling of smoke. The massive hearth and chimney, however, still stood tall and strong, as though waiting for the house to be rebuilt back around it.

If there had been insurance, I was sure we would have been planning that.

The lilacs were mostly charred stumps. Except for two of them. Those still showed some sign of green on unburned branches. If they survived the coming winter they might come back in the spring. The rodent garden was a mess, but not a total loss. Patches of it had been spared by the rain or the wind or just the vagaries of the way things burn.

We poked around finding those spots and clearing the debris from around them to give them a better chance of making it. After several hours or dirty, sweaty labor, we had the garden as restored as we were going to get it and a pile of burnt and nasty brush in what had been the back yard.

Aubrey sneezed disgruntledly at the debris, but we were satisfied with an afternoon well spent and further delighted that Melissa had counted all of the cats. They were sheltering in the intact, if you could call it that, garage, where Melissa had rigged a heavy tarp as a small tent. Come winter, though, there were going to need a place that provided some heat. The Herborium was the only option, of course, unless Carla and the others could take some. Aubrey trotted away again as we got set to leave.

We shrugged and headed out. Once it started to get really cold, we figured, the cats would change their minds about coming with us.

I kept on working away that week, although I avoided the mansion at night. For all that mattered anyway. The Duvall men could go anywhere they wanted to now. The weirder part was their absence. I didn't sense them anywhere. Nor did any of the witches. By Friday, we would begin wondering if they hadn't been released from the curse somehow. It seemed like they were gone.

That didn't fit with anything that had happened before. It was more likely, to my active mind, that they were lying low; staying out of sight while something bigger built up, as though they were waiting on something or someone. What that was remained a mystery. Nothing Francine or her sister tried allowed them to determine who, if anyone at all, was the other practitioner. Whoever it was, was smart enough to know we would have started searching.

I found nothing in the old records other than some

of the original photographs and notes used in the newspaper articles of the time. They were wrapped in an oil cloth and placed at the bottom of a crate. If there had been anything incriminating in them at the time, it was lost to me now. I already knew everything that was in the notes and had seen the photographs. It was curious they had kept it. Perhaps Samuel Duvall had done so as a reminder of his crimes, or more likely, as some sort of safety valve. If anyone had ever tried to delve into it, he had the *proof* in these papers and photos, which left out anything negative. Maybe the incriminating thing was in how clean they were. It was impossible to say.

The relationship with Melissa was much as any new relationship would be. We went to lunch during the week and saw each other at night, when I wasn't working. A part of my mind was still coming to grips with it while another part was wholly stunned and surprised at how normal it felt, how comfortable I was with it. It was as though some part of me had awakened.

Overall, though, it was an unbelievably, uncannily, and unnervingly normal week. The peace was putting us on edge, waiting for whatever storm was going to follow that calm. None of us could have known it was going to be one of the worst we had ever endured.

Melissa and I left out late on Friday afternoon to get a fair distance from Willow Creek by nightfall as well as to have as much time as possible together in St. Louis; our first weekend at what we were both beginning to think would become her new home away from Willow Creek. The Herborium and Francine were still going to need the majority of her time, of course. Francine needed her and I wanted her to be there for Francine, my pseudo grandmother. St. Louis to Willow Creek was not too long of a distance.

The first thing she said on walking in the door and taking a first look around was, "You're missing a cat."

Every witch needed a familiar after all. Hers were still running wild, although at least Aubrey had turned up at the Herborium during the week.

The weekend was glorious and special. I'll leave it at that. Friday dinner was a greasy pizza, a bucket of lite beers, and a long talk about life and fate, specifically how part of me was still struggling with the idea of a love affair with another woman. With her forcing me to think about it, the little pieces had been coming together.

"Before he got sick, Dad would bring home a pizza every Friday night," she told me. "They'd let me drink enough Coke that I started feeling sick." The smile spreading across her face brought out an equal one on mine. "The earliest I remember was when I was eight. I ended up feeling so sick, but Lordy, it was so good! Afterwards, we'd catch fireflies in the summer or play board games in the winter. I was the Clue champion. What about you? Did you have a game night or anything like it?"

Warm memories came back to me. "It was Sunday for us," I recounted. "Mom would get up early and put a roast or a big chicken in the oven to slow cook, while she was at church. Dad did yard work or fixed whatever had broken that week. He'd bought a hobby more than a house, he used to say. I would sit in the sunniest spot and read. I loved to read and they let me have all Sunday morning to myself to do so."

"Sounds heavenly," she remarked.

"It was," I replied. I was never happier than those Sunday mornings, lost in the latest story I was reading, smelling the building aroma of slow roasting dinner. "After that early dinner, it was movie time, usually something rented, but occasionally we'd go to the theater."

"We never had a TV," she told me. "We did go to the movies once a month. Even after Dad got sick, we'd still manage the odd trip to the theater. I still go once or twice a year."

"I haven't been to a movie in a couple of years, come to think of it."

"Let's go tomorrow then!"

"Okay. I don't even know what's playing."

"Me either," she said. "I guess we'll find out."

"I guess," I said and the memories turned bittersweet. "Eventually, it became me cooking for Mom on Sundays."

"After your Dad died?"

I nodded. "My brother started hanging out with his friends on Sundays. His way of coping was to start doing something new."

"I think a lot of people do that," Melissa said. "We started going to Grandma's on Fridays, after Dad died. Once I got older, I realized it was because Fridays without my dad were very hard on my mother."

"So was Sunday cooking for my Mom," I said. "That's why I took it over. It became our time."

"Yes," Melissa nodded. "That's when I really started getting to know my grandmother and learn about the Herborium. I mean, I knew it was there and all. I was a preteen. All I really grasped before then was that she ran something like a flower and gift shop."

"But then you started to become a part of it," I saw.

She nodded. "I've come to love it as much as she does. We can replant my garden and hopefully those lilacs did survive. It will all be for the Herborium."

"I spent a lot more time reading afterward. Probably where I learned to write," I told her. "I even shrank my circle of friends. I didn't need to. I could probably have been just as active. I just lost interest in doing a lot of extra things."

"Stayed with what was important to you," she understood.

"Yes. I simplified my life to enjoy it more."

"That was smart."

"When my brother went off to college, it was just my Mom and me," I went on. "I stayed at home while I went to a community college. I already knew I wanted to write. What I needed were classes on genealogy and how to conduct historical research. I didn't need an expensive college for that. You, on the other hand, are going to need a major school for your religion degree."

"I am taking classes," she reminded me.

"One or two here and there is not going to get you where you want to go," I pointed out. "I get that you don't need to be obsessive with your goals, but you need to have some kind of plan."

I could see by her expression that she knew that, but had been comfortable with her slow pace. By conventional standards, Melissa was drifting through life with some vague goals, but no real drive. True, she was stress-free, happy and healthy; living at her own pace, or rather at the pace life wanted her to go. I could see how that was a better way to live to some extent. It was getting her nowhere, however, with respect to the things she wanted to accomplish, in particular her compendium of religions. She needed to start a proper course of studies and get a degree in World Religions, starting with the upcoming winter semester.

Through a frown and a smirk she said, "Grandma has been telling me the same thing. She told me to get a road map together."

"Well then, I guess that's what I'm here for," I replied, thinking of how people come into your life for a reason. For Mel, I was there to give her the structure she needed, if she was ever to accomplish the things she wanted to do.

"What about me, then?" she asked. "Why do you think I'm in your life?"

I didn't have to think long. She'd touched on it the day we'd met. I was chuckling and smirking as I answered, "Probably for the opposite reason."

"Yes. You are way too hard on yourself," she said again. "You need to stop worrying that someone is going to come and take it all away. Why do you think that way?"

It came to me at that point in time. Maybe I had known it in the back of my mind, yet I had never given it conscious thought, much less voiced it.

"I guess because when Mom died, I did have it all

taken away." She stopped eating and took my hand. "I guess I've just been expecting that to keep happening to me."

"That's not your lot in life, Indy, darling," she told me. "You will be okay."

"I hope you're right," I replied, squeezing her hand. "It's just that I've worked so hard to get here and I'm still only a single lost job from losing it all."

"You're going to be all right."

"This job for the Duvalls could do that," I told her. "This one could finally get me to where the down times aren't always lean times. If I can just get a normal number of assignments over the winter, I think I'll be there. I've worked too hard to fail now."

"You're not going to fail, Indy," she told me. "It's like you're punishing yourself for things that *could* happen, but probably won't."

"What if they do?" I replied, my stomach turning into a brick at the thought. "I've never worked another job, Mel. I have no work history to find any kind of job."

"Indy, you made it this far. You'll be okay."

"Back in the beginning, after Mom passed," I related, "I kept food on my table while I got my freelance career started, only because of my share of our parents' estate. That cushion is gone. I used it to get here. I'm still not making it on my royalties. Honestly, when you look at it, I am already failing. I haven't wanted to face it, but I am and it makes me physically ill."

"Indy, you're acting defeated," she told me. "Stop it."

She was right. I feared defeat so much, I was preparing myself to face it, like I was being sucked into it. My negativity had gotten that bad, she made me see. I was spiraling toward depression the way I was going. My willingness to be honest with her was causing me to be honest with myself. I had been gradually failing. I would utterly if I lost this job.

"I hope I'm making the right moves," I said with a sigh. "Honestly, I don't know that I ever have."

Her words right then will always be with me. "Just because your life would be different, if you could go back and change a mistake, doesn't necessarily mean that it would be better."

That was so simple as to be profound.

For a moment, I had nothing to say, lost in the numbing reality that even my smartest moves were often no match for Fate. It was foolish of me to fight it so much. And really, things had always worked out somehow. I would continue to find ways to solve any problems that came along. There was no point in worrying myself to an early grave over it.

Finally, I smiled and squeezed her hand. "I'm glad you're in my life, Mel."

"Same here, Indy," she replied. "I guess we've come into each other's lives to give the other balance."

I nodded. "We're definitely good for each other."

"I think we're going to make a great team."

I smiled and gave her hand another squeeze before releasing it.

"You know," I admitted. "I still don't understand why I was ever attracted to the Robert Richards' of the world. They're completely the opposite of my Dad and anyone that was important to me."

"So you said before," she noted. "Were you afraid of settling down? You know, picking guys it could never work with so you could really focus on your career and all."

That felt like a revelation. It was as logical as anything else I'd ever thought of. Then she surprised me again.

"He is good looking, though," she reminded me. "You are still physically attracted. Don't lie to me."

She was smiling, knowing it for a fact.

I had to confess that my attraction to Richards had not dissipated. Although I no longer felt any need to fulfill it. Even if I had, it would only have been physical.

"I understand now what you meant about being in the right mood for a man," I told her and received an impish grin in response.

"Perhaps we should take him together one night," she joked. "Maybe he'd get over his attitude toward us witches."

To which I almost choked on the beer I was trying to swallow.

Then, our conversation lightened up as to what kind of movie to see and what else to do over the weekend. I had cathartically voiced what frightened me and it was okay. It was all going to be fine.

While we were enjoying that moment, we would later learn by phone from Francine that signs of the hellhounds prowling the woods around the Herborium were being seen again, and the Duvall men were again roaming the entire town and surrounding area. The Sheriff had had no more luck in tracking the hounds than had the witches in learning who the unknown practitioner was.

Both were like shadows.

We headed back a little late Monday morning after dawdling over breakfast at a small place I liked to frequent, when I could afford it. It was still before noon when I dropped her at the Herborium, leaving me enough hours to get something accomplished on the book. It was going to be a working dinner with Alice Duvall that night, so lunch the next day would be my next time together with Melissa. I kissed her in a way to let her know how badly I was going to miss her.

She gave me that smile and fanned herself, telling me to hold that thought and then headed into the shop. I grinned all the way back to my room at the Willow's Wells, where I knuckled down to work.

Chapter 15
The Curtain Falls Away

The rains fell again that day, stripping the trees of their final fall glory. The area was beautiful that time of year; breathtaking when it wasn't raining. I didn't take any foliage pictures that day, but I was keeping a photo album along with my diary of this trip. It had actually been rather exhilarating to be taking pictures while out in the lesser storms. Until the Duvall men and the hounds had been set loose. My photography had been ended by that.

The one pic I snapped that day was of a man I hadn't seen before who seemed to be watching me. I took the photo the third time I spotted him walking along the street outside the Willow's Wells during a break in the rain. I emailed it to Richards to forward to Levinson. I had no reason to think there was anything wrong other than the fact odd sort of things had been popping up at me regularly. That and a healthy paranoia over what might be coming next.

I watched from the desk in my room when a Deputy came along and picked him up. The man went quietly enough. I almost got the impression he had been confused, even dazed, when talking to the Deputy. He was a good hundred yards away at the time. His face wasn't all that clear under the once again thickening overcast and the Deputy was quick about taking him off to the station.

The rain forced me to dash to my car between outbursts when I headed out to dinner with my clients. Even without the threat of flooding, this weather wore on a person. It was oppressive, even more so as the edge had returned to my nerves on returning to Willow Creek. I could have done most of the work at home and just scheduled two or three research days in Willow Creek. However, that would have meant being away from Melissa, and she was busy with Francine with preparations for Samhain in a week and a half. She had to be there.

Agnes stuffed me silly once again on pot roast and root vegetable casserole filled with the sweet of carrots against the tang of parsnips. I should have asked her for that recipe, but I didn't trust my culinary skills to match hers.

"He was a drifter," Robert told me of the man that had been watching me. "He said he thought he recognized you from somewhere and was trying to place you before talking to you."

"Really?" I wasn't buying it. The ghosts couldn't get me for the amulets. The hounds had missed me and I knew how to avoid them. The next logical step was a live person; someone I wouldn't have looked at twice. Except I had gotten into and not left my room before I'd spotted him. It was pure luck that this third try had missed.

Or was it just my active imagination at work again? I mean, I was talking about a possession of some sort, wasn't I? How else did you get an otherwise typical person to blindly stalk someone? Wasn't it more logical and more sane to think that he was a simple drifter who was a little or a lot off kilter and he'd gotten fixated on me for some reason? Wasn't the latter the least crazy possibility?

I tried calling Francine and Melissa from the library when I had a moment to myself. I couldn't get a connection with storm raging outside. The phone service was horrible here during these storms. The land lines seemed to be down more than connected and cell service had little line of sight for the towers to work amongst the rocky hills. The storms only made it worse.

The rain was absolutely pounding down when we wrapped up for the night. Alice Duvall and I had spent a very productive four hours going over the drafts to lay out edits and flesh out some of the thin spots. I was pleased with how few follow-up interviews it seemed I would need to conduct. I could see the light at the end of the tunnel for the project. The part about the witches was drafted as was Alice's own generation. We were working on her son's era now. Robert himself was next. Two more weeks was looking like a good estimate.

"Sometimes it seems like there was more to our history than I realized," Alice commented during the evening.

"It's a lot to try to remember," I told her.

"Yes. I guess this book was a better idea than I thought, even if it's just for us!" she added with a grin and a chuckle. "You think you remember it all, but you can't."

"Some of it you may not have known," I pointed out.

"Like Cousin Al publishing that book of poetry in the nineties," she replied and then shook her head. "I still don't know why he never mentioned it. You'd think one would brag about something like that."

I'd learned of it during my interviews from a different cousin. He'd not told much of his family because he hadn't felt very connected to them and felt no reason to brag about it to them. I left that out of the book, of course.

Robert came in toward the end of our evening after watching Monday Night Football. He made a comment about a real defensive struggle, but I confess that football does not capture my interest, so it didn't click much. What registered was the decanter and glasses he carried in. Nightcaps were a very regular thing in the Duvall household.

Tonight was that fiery brandy I'd had previously. With the wind howling and the rain splattering loudly against the windows - that and the small fire he'd lit - were perfect for the evening. Thunder shook the house and startled Mrs. Duvall. Ben lifted his head from where the boys lay by the hearth and growled at the storm, but then he grunted, yawned, and put his head back down.

"That wind is horrendous tonight," Mrs. Duvall

commented, clearly ill at ease over it. "I suppose we'll lose some more trees."

"Just when we got the solarium fixed," Robert quipped. He'd had a few drinks during the game, it seemed.

"Is it supposed to go on all night?" I asked. I hadn't been watching the weather reports.

"Could," Robert said. "It's another massive storm. Thankfully, it's too cool for tornadoes because this one could have generated a few."

"You'd better figure on staying the night here, dear," Alice Duvall told me. "It's not a safe night to be driving anywhere."

"No argument from me," I replied. Thunder up in the mountains punctuated my words. I tried to look out the window to see how badly the trees were swaying in the gusts, but couldn't see that far through the rain. Visibility would have been measured in feet trying to drive in this.

"I'll have Agnes make sure the guest room is ready," she said and started to turn.

"I'm sure it is," I replied and caught a sideways glance. I only saw it in her reflection in the window we were trying to look out through. For a second, I thought she was going to offer the information, but I had to ask after all. "Why have you kept that room ready? Did you expect Phyllis to return?"

"At first, yes," she told me after a slight pause. "I'd hoped she come to her senses and not call it off."

"But she did call it off."

"Yes."

"You sound hurt by that," I observed. It wasn't so much the brandy talking as how comfortable we had become speaking about family things and herself. "You loved her, too."

"Yes. I did," she admitted. "She fit in with us so well. I never imagined her leaving us."

"You took it personally," I noted lowly, so only she could hear.

"Yes," she admitted as quietly.

"That's why you didn't throw the clothes out or give them away."

"I couldn't," she said and I waited for her to explain.

Robert chimed in from his seat near the fire. "What are you two whispering about?"

We ignored him. Mrs. Duvall sighed. "I couldn't bear thinking she'd not wanted to come back."

"You mean that she didn't love you as much as you did back?" I asked, even more gently. She knew I meant nothing mean in the question.

She thought for a second and then nodded. The sadness had come back near the surface.

"Did you just close the room off until you felt you could deal with it?"

"Something like that," she said. "Mostly, after a while, I didn't want to be bothered with it."

In other words, she hadn't gotten over it. "Why did you open the room to me?" I asked.

"I didn't," she told me. "Agnes did. When you got drenched, her first thoughts were that someone could finally use that room and those clothes."

"That must have made you mad."

"Oddly, no," she answered. "Agnes had asked a few times what we were going to do with the stuff. She didn't want it, but she hated seeing it go to waste."

"So you were okay with it?"

She gave a lopsided grin and nodded. "Yes. I guess I was waiting for something to happen to make me deal with it."

"Or for someone to come along that might step in, where Phyllis chickened out?" I asked and she gave me a long look, trying to figure out where I stood, before answering.

"Have you?" she asked. "Are you trying to tell me something?"

"No," I told her. "I'm not stepping up. Robert's okay, but that's as far as it goes."

"I know there's more between you," she told me. "I'm not stupid. I know something's happened. It's in the way he treats you now." Our eyes were locked in the reflections on the window. "Decide for yourself, dear. But know that you'll always be welcome here, regardless of your choice."

"Thank you, Mrs. Duvall," I said. What else did you say to something like that?

"I'm all in," she said, turning from the window and patting my arm. It was a gesture she had begun in the second week of working together. Until this night, I had not realized the significance of it. She had not given my arm the slight rub she did tonight. I hadn't realized before I had been accepted as more than the family chronicler.

"Goodnight, conspiratorial Nana," Robert jokingly said.

"Sounds like I need to check the level of the bourbon," she said in return.

He looked over at her with a clear-eyed smile and winked. "I won a thousand on the game from Henry."

She made a sound of dismissal and waved it off. "He'll never pay up."

"No. He never does," Robert agreed. "It's still fun besting him."

"Goodnight, Robert," she said and walked out shaking her head.

Robert turned his gaze back to the fire. His shoeless feet were extended lazily toward it as he was settled comfortably, almost slouching along his spine in the plush armchair. Like the house, the furniture wasn't extravagant in design or style, but just a little larger than normal.

"You going to tell me what you two were whispering about?" he asked.

"No," I told him from the window. I wasn't trying to watch the storm anymore. There wasn't much to see beyond sheets of rain in the few outside lights they kept on. I was observing him from behind, trying to assess whether he was the man I had taken him for on first sight or if there was something more to him. Not that my feelings for Melissa had waivered. It was more of a clinical question from my overly-curious mind, which I'd never really been able to control, than an issue I needed resolved.

He grunted. "Figured as much."

I walked over by him with a smile on my face and set my empty glass on the tray by the decanter.

"I'm off to bed," I told him.

"Care for company?" he queried. "Comfort from the storm?"

I smirked at him. "I'm a big girl. Storms don't scare me."

"What if I need comfort from it?" he asked playfully.

I rewarded him with a slight grin, but said, "You're a big boy. You can handle it."

He smiled back; the one that always slayed me in the past. Now it was simply pleasing. My next words were there without me thinking them.

"Besides," I told him. "I know which room is yours, if I change my mind."

Then, trailing an impish expression, I left him sitting startled and uncertain in his overstuffed chair by the warming fire. I went up to what was basically my room now feeling good. It was satisfying to be the one in control for a change.

I tried calling both Melissa and Francine before and after I changed for bed. The silk pajamas didn't seem like overkill that night. There was still no phone service. It was definitely out until after the storm.

Dawn crept uncertainly out from under the cloud cover on that Tuesday. The rain had stopped, but the sky hung low and menacing. The wind kicked up now and again and had gotten much cooler. Fall was rumbling in that week. It didn't seem all that happy to have been awoken from its yearly slumber.

I picked out a basic yellow blouse and blue skirt that morning from Phyllis's would-be wardrobe. Nothing fancy or pretentious. With my tennis shoes from the day before, I looked a lot like a Bobbysoxer from the fifties. It was a cute style and I was rather pleased with it, while at the same time feeling disturbed over it. It hit me I was becoming a little too comfortable with the idea of wearing those clothes. I thought of changing back into my jeans from yesterday. Yet, at the same time, I didn't need to be uptight about it. Everyone knew it meant nothing and the clothes were otherwise going to waste.

After a breakfast of strong coffee, cinnamon rolls, basted eggs, and thick, crispy bacon, I felt fortified for the day and needing a run to clear the cholesterol from my arteries. I wasn't about to go running in this weather, but I got a good ten minutes of mild exercise clearing the leaves that the storm had plastered to my car. The pavement was covered with them as it seemed the trees had been all but denuded in the night. I drove away carefully so as not to skid on them.

I tried calling Melissa and Francine both from the car, my fourth attempt that morning. Nothing. The lines were still out. This was definitely the catch that came with such a beautiful place to live. I wasn't sure I could do it much longer even though they were paying me.

Sam was out front of the mansion raking the colorful display of sodden leaves from the lawn. I suggested he wait for them to dry out some, so they'd be lighter. At his age, they should have given him a riding mower or vacuum to handle them.

"It'll be worse tomorrow, if I leave them," he told me. "More storms coming."

Which struck me as apropos. My mood at being back, plus out of touch with Melissa even for the one night, was turning ominous. I couldn't lie. I was still rattled by the attack from Sam Duvall and the hounds, and perhaps the missed one from the drifter.

This wasn't over.

I was still watching from the corner of my eye and trying to peek around corners and doorways before going around or through them. I needed Melissa's calming influence to keep my imagination and fears at bay.

I patted Sam's shoulder as I passed. "Don't work too hard and I mean that seriously."

"I'm pacing myself," he assured me. "Watch the porch. It's slippery today."

I could almost see the shine to it, like the drenching rain had acted like a wax. A couple of shingles sat to one side of the steps. I glanced up but was too close to see the roof. Yes. The place wasn't going to last much longer. In fact, I began to doubt it would make it through the winter. I made a mental note to mention it to Robert later. The records were going to have to be moved before it snowed.

It was a typical morning, once I got inside, checking on some questions that had come up in last night's session and continuing the writing. When noon came and I still had not heard from Melissa, I went to our backup plan. The cell service had been so iffy from the start that we'd always figured on the diner we'd first met at, if we couldn't connect on where to meet. The idea was to take the same booth, if it was available.

When thirty minutes had gone by without her showing, the worry began in earnest. Up to then, I'd been keeping it under control, blaming everything on the storm. With the tempest blown over, I was worried. Storm or no storm, she should have gotten word to me somehow or showed up at the diner. I'd left her safe at the shop and she wasn't going to leave until this morning to meet me for lunch. Of course, nothing could have happened to her. Yet, that didn't start my out of control imagination from knocking my calm aside.

As I raced to my car and sped out to the shop, I was seeing images of it burning to the ground or trees falling on it and trapping them both. By the time I hit the country roads, I was envisioning the hounds or the Duvall men breaking through their barriers and rushing the house. I was seeing it burnt, smashed, and destroyed. I wouldn't let my mind picture what might have happened to them.

The thoughts forming were bad enough.

The storm-ravaged forest didn't help. Leaves and branches were everywhere alongside and on the road, as though the storm itself had been the beast sent after us this time. A rock scree had fallen at one point and rain water still poured down the limestone hillside like a small waterfall of blood from the land. The hills appeared weak from having been battered and wounded.

Yes. My mind was racing.

I came around the last turn and down the slope to their valley and there stood the beautiful white house, its yard and plantings the worse for wear, but standing calm and peaceful with curling wisps of smoke trailing from the chimney. Had it been a snowstorm, it would have been a Currier and Ives moment. I relaxed and breathed a sigh of relief until I realized there was no white Scion next to the green Cavalier.

I went in at a half run and rushed to the back of the house to find it empty. I heard footsteps on the stairs and ran toward them. Francine descended with her usual smile that melted on seeing my face.

"What?" she started, but didn't want to face what came to mind.

"Where's Melissa?" I asked and realized I was starting to sound frantic.

Her answer was the words I hadn't wanted to hear. "I thought she was with you."

"No. I haven't seen her since yesterday." I was now sounding frantic. "She was supposed to meet me for lunch today."

"I haven't seen her," Francine told me. "She wasn't here when I got up. She didn't leave a note, so I assumed she had gone to meet you. She would have told me where she was going otherwise."

"Oh God," slipped out and I felt myself starting to shake. "What if she had an accident in the storm? Or worse?"

"Don't get yourself in a state," Francine told me,

while her own fear was evident. "Maybe you just missed each other in town. She's probably at your room, waiting for you."

"No. She would have called or met me at the diner," I told her. "Something's wrong. Something's happened."

"All right, I'll call the Sheriff," she said. "Take a seat. I'll make you some soothing tea."

"I don't want tea," I snapped as my reason began to leave me. "I want to find her."

"Okay," she said calmly. "You drive the route she would have taken and see if you can find her. I'll still call the Sheriff."

"Okay," I said. "Okay." But I hesitated a second out of fear of what I might find, before hurrying back to my car.

I drove slowly, watching for signs of skidding or a crash into the trees or undergrowth along the road. If she had gone off the edge of one of the steep, rocky slopes, what that would have done to her little car, to her? I forced my imagination not to conjure any images. I stopped a couple of times to look down some of those slopes. But there was nothing. I found myself back at the Willow's Wells without having found anything. Marianne Wells was dusting the parlor when I walked in.

"There you are, dear," she said with relief. "We missed you at breakfast and I got a little worried when I found your room unused. I guess you rode out the storm up at the Duvall place."

"Yes," I answered almost absently. "Have you seen Melissa? Was she here earlier?"

"No. I could have missed her, but I haven't seen her or heard anyone in the house. Has something happened to her?" She was genuinely worried and that was all I needed to be pushed over the edge. Fear gave way to panic and I needed to get to my room so I could get myself under control.

Sheriff Levinson would be looking for her by now. He and his deputies would have responded to Francine's call and would be fanning out to find her. I should have felt comforted by that thought. It was just that I was terrified of what they might find.

I ran up the stairs to my room and shut the door behind me, leaning on it to try to settle my mind and heart down. All the fear I had felt when Samuel Duvall had grabbed my arm was swiftly coming back. I was beginning to lose it, I knew. That terror I'd been bottling up was near to bursting free. I had to relax. I needed to calm myself down.

I needed to stop crying. I hadn't even noticed it start. With a couple of sharp breaths, I half brought it under control and headed for the bathroom to wash my face.

And there.... I found Melissa's head staring vacantly at me from the bathroom sink.

Marianne Wells was the first one to me, so they tell me. I was gone, completely and utterly hysterical and out of control. She found me in the hallway outside my room, collapsed onto my knees and wailing out my grief. I was screaming out my rage and despair with the world.

At some point, I became aware that I was in a clinic or something and being given a sedative. From there, it was a dreamlike drifting to the Duvall mansion. The deep bed was turned down for me in my cozy room, but I preferred the oversized, over stuffed armchair near the window where I fell into a drug-induced doze, watching the drizzle outside while I stayed warm under a blanket Agnes had tucked around me.

I came out of it as dusk pooled between the trees. The rain had fallen off to a steady mist, making it hard to distinguish that from the evening's gloom. Still in the yellow blouse and blue skirt, wrinkled for wear, I padded in stocking feet toward the voices I heard in the hall.

Richards and Sheriff Levinson had been quietly talking, but turned and sighed on seeing me. Whatever they'd been discussing, it needed my input to finish.

Richards came over and put a hand on my arm.

"India, you shouldn't be up."

"I'm okay," I said drowsily.

"The doctor said to make sure you rested and stayed off your feet the rest of the day," he told me.

"What did they give me?"

"I don't know," he answered, "just that it was strong because you were hysterical. He was afraid you'd hurt yourself or have a stroke."

"I'm sorry," I said, although I had no idea why I should have been.

"Come on," Robert said, directing me back into the room. "We can talk with you sitting. I don't want you falling over."

I let him help me back to the chair and pulled the blanket around my legs and lap. I shivered over being chilled, probably a result of the drug. Robert sat on the ottoman at my feet protectively, while Levinson stood a respectful few paces away.

"I'm sorry, India," he said sincerely. "I knew the two of you had become close."

I nodded weakly. The after-effect of the drug was fatigue.

"Are you up to talking about it?" he asked.

I gave him a weak smile. I didn't know what I had said or what other people had discerned, but Gus Levinson knew for certain that we had been more than close. He'd basically caught us, even though Mel had been in the bathroom, that first day, and kept it to himself. It wasn't meant to be a secret, but I did wonder how many other confidences the man had learned and dependably kept.

"I last saw her yesterday when I dropped her at the Herborium," I told him. "We were supposed to have lunch today."

"Where were you before you dropped her off?"

"St. Louis," I told him. "She had stayed the weekend with me at my place."

"So, the last time you were in town was Friday?"

"Yes," I told him. "We headed out right before dark. We were afraid of running into those hounds."

"When was the last time you talked to her?"

"When I dropped her off," I said. "I tried to call, but couldn't get through. I thought it was because of the storm."

"It probably was," he replied.

"Do you have any idea when she was killed?"

"No," he told me. "She was killed somewhere else. We're trying to locate where that was."

"You don't have her body?" It was important to me that she was found, so she could properly be laid to rest.

"Not yet, I'm afraid. There's a lot of ground to cover."

"The storm would have washed away any traces."

He frowned. "Very probably did," he admitted. "It's not going to be easy, I don't think."

"He didn't hide Brianna's body," I noted.

"No, but there's a lot of places we need to look," he said. "Assuming it was the same person."

"It *had* to be," I said. It *had* to be whoever had released the Duvall men and sent the hounds after me. I didn't know how to explain that to them. He didn't argue the point, though. He was thinking the same thing.

"Do you also see that this was a warning to you?" Gus asked.

"Gus," Robert said in a tone admonishing the directness.

"You know it is," Levinson said to him. "You agreed with me five minutes ago."

"I know, but we don't have to be so harsh."

"It's okay, Robert," I told him and put a hand on his arm. "I'm all right."

"You might want to consider going away for a bit," Levinson advised. "Maybe finish the book from St. Louis."

"What?" Robert asked.

"I'm not saying you're the cause of this trouble, India," Levinson said. "However, it did start up when you got here. You're the catalyst."

The drugs spoke for me as I shook my head and waved the thought away. I unwisely replied, "The trouble has been coming to you for a long time."

"I'm sorry?" he replied.

How to explain that comment without getting into the curse, and the haunting, and the first attack on me, and ending up looking like a loony? I should have kept my mouth shut. I did rally with a reasonable response. "Whoever killed Brianna down by the river was here before I ever arrived and started working."

"True," Levinson agreed. "What I'm saying is that you and the other women of the Coven might be safer if you weren't here. I don't know how or why, but somehow your presence has gotten someone stirred up."

"I don't believe that for a second," Robert chimed in. "It's just coincidence. Look, she can stay with us. She'll be safe here. There's always someone here."

Which was fine with me. For all my earlier misgivings at getting comfortable in that room and with another woman's clothes, I *never* wanted to go back to the Willow's Wells again. I *never* wanted to see that room again.

"I know it's probably coincidence," Levinson said. "I'm just trying to think of ways to keep everyone safe; India and the Coven."

"I appreciate that, Gus," I told him. "Francine's sister is with her. She's not alone either. Mel must have gone out for something. I just can't figure why."

"Francine said she left early in the morning," Levinson said. "We're trying to find someone who saw her so we can try to recreate her moves."

"I tried driving her route to the Willow's Wells," I told them. "I was watching for signs of an accident or something. I didn't see anything."

"We figured that," Levinson said. "Then, you spoke to Mrs. Wells before going up to your room. Was there anything out of the ordinary in it?"

I didn't want to think about it, but I had to. I tried to recall how the room looked as I had leaned against the door and tried to control my breathing. Nothing came to me. It had seemed the way it had always been.

"I don't think so," I told him. "I can't recall anything different about it."

"Well, right now is probably the wrong time to ask," he noted. "Maybe later, when you've rested and the sedative wears off."

"Maybe," I agreed, but doubted it. I hadn't been in the room in three days and Marianne Wells had cleaned it thoroughly over the weekend. It had just been your ordinary, neat and clean room. The killer had slipped in, left his warning, and slipped away as though he was the mist falling outside. It was unnatural, which was the most logical solution. How to tell him that?

"All right," Levinson said. "I'm going to get back to the search. Just rest up, India. Let me know, if anything pops into your memory later."

"I will," I promised.

"Take care," he said and went out, leaving me alone with Robert.

I leaned back in the chair with my arms loosely folded over my lap. He reached over to touch my leg under the blankets.

"We'll keep you safe," he promised. "Don't worry. I'll take care of getting your things moved here. You do like Gus said and just rest. I'll have Agnes bring you something to eat later."

"I'm not hungry."

"I wouldn't expect you to be," he told me with his warm grin. "You still need to eat something. I'll leave you alone. I'll be in my office, if you need me for anything. Okay?"

I nodded. "Thanks, Robert."

"Not a problem," he said and rose, leaning over to kiss me on the cheek. He wanted to say something more, but words failed him for once. He had enough sense not to be smarmy or trite. Or maybe he was afraid of how Miss Enigma might take it. He just smiled again and went out, gently shutting my door.

I pulled the blanket up over me and drew my legs in tighter. It was silent in the room. One thing about their house was the heaviness of the construction. You could sense its solidity in the way sounds didn't carry from room to room. The triple glazed windows shut out the sounds of the world, if there were any coming through the suppressing mist. The fading light seemed to be carrying sounds as well as colors away with it.

I thought about everything that had happened since I'd arrived at Willow Creek. I mulled through a mental list of all the people I'd met and everything I'd learned about the family and the town and those events a hundred years ago. I went over the predictable affair with Robert and the unexpected love for another woman. There had to be a clue somewhere in all of that to tell me who could be behind this. Unless I had been asking the wrong questions. Perhaps the answer lie somewhere other than the Duvall family past.

Or maybe I just wasn't up to figuring it out. I'd been so addled by Sam Duvall's attack from the other side that the only sane part of my mind was the bit way in the back that was still wondering how I could have gotten involved with another woman. I had just expected my internal questioning to fade with time. As I sat there, warm and comfortable in the growing gloom and heavy silence, and as the drowsiness stole back over me, I felt that old mode of thinking easing forward to reclaim control of me.

As always, something had come along when things were looking up to take it away from me. I felt as cursed as the Duvall men. This time, though, I also felt as though I could do something about it. Tomorrow, when the drugs wore off, I was going to start poking my nose into places it didn't belong, using the book research as an excuse.

I was going to find the bastard behind it all.

Despite the medications weakening my body, my

mind and heart were energized as grief fanned anger. I don't have words to describe the utter horror at finding Melissa's head. I had screamed at the top of my lungs as though I was the one being killed. Part of me did die. It took me three days and dozens of attempts to write this part of the story. The wound will never heal. In that moment, though, in the seeming peace of the quiet room, it fed my emerging rage.

I wanted vengeance.

Melissa had told me I fought with life too much, that I needed to work with what it brought me. I wasn't planning on fighting it, however. I was planning on owning it.

I woke up fairly early Wednesday. The drugs had put me out for the count sometime in the early evening. I was still in the chair. My suitcases stood at the foot of the bed. Some fruit and cookies and a bottle of water sat on a table near me. I hadn't heard anyone come in. I remembered how a friend once told me that she'd woken up from a day surgery just long enough for her husband to drive her home, then gone back out until the next day. They must have given me something that strong.

I changed the grubby, wrinkled blouse and skirt for some sweats out of my suitcase and went down to see if there was any coffee ready so early. All I wanted right then was to get cleaned up and presentable enough to go out to the Herborium and be with the family. My thoughts of owning Fate and my desire for revenge were still with me, but under the control of my returning reason.

I heard voices coming from the kitchen as I approached it. I recognized Gus Levinson, but not the other two. The aroma of coffee flooded the hallway and my pace may have quickened at it. The unfamiliar voices belonged to two men in basic, blue suits and looking a little weary. Gus and Robert were clearly exhausted. Appearing as though she'd just woken up, pulled on her uniform dress, and hurried to the kitchen, Agnes poured coffee for the men. She took one look at me and pointed at the counter.

Their kitchen had two of everything, including coffee pots that brewed into thermos pitchers. A latte cup sat ready next to the second pot, which I knew would be the strength I preferred.

"Right on cue," Gus remarked. He was more than exhausted. He hadn't slept at all and was getting punch drunk. "These are Special Agents Halloran and Minkoe from Kansas City."

"FBI?" I asked.

"Yes, ma'am," said the one named Halloran. "Sheriff Levinson notified us per protocol."

"For a serial killer," I realized.

"And a possible hate crime against the Wiccan women," the agent added.

"Right," I replied as I poured my coffee. They were finally willing to look at that, for what little good that theory would do them. What value were any conventional theories going to be?

"We were just debating if we should wake you up," Gus told me. "We need your input to continue."

"Have you found her yet?" I asked.

Gus shook his head. "Sorry, Miss Hills. Not yet."

I nodded and gave him a thankful smile. I was sure he'd been out looking personally, as well as his Deputies. I took a seat next to him, across from the FBI agents. Robert was the furthest away at the head of the table, as though mediating the lawmen's session. The stove timer dinged as I sat and Agnes pulled a pair of trays of perfect-looking biscuits from the oven.

Hunger swooned through me. I hadn't eaten since breakfast here the morning before. Was it the morning before? I had to stop and think. Yes. It had been here less than twenty-four hours ago, before the world had shifted on me once again. God love her, Agnes ignored the men to give me the first plate with honey and gravy and soft, sweet butter to choose from. A minute later, I realized they were watching and waiting for me to be ready to talk.

"Sorry," I said around half of the fourth biscuit to fall to my hunger.

"Did you eat at all yesterday?" Robert asked, concerned.

"Not since breakfast," I said.

"I'll get the sausages on and you just tell me when," Agnes said and went to work.

Halloran explained, "We're interested in knowing the whole situation, Miss Hills, not just yesterday. If you would, please, tell us everything you've seen or heard since you got here."

As I ate and drank strong coffee until I felt I might burst, I told them the story of Willow Creek as I had learned it from the incident with Baltus Sammic to the present time. I left out the part of Samuel Duvall attacking me and described the hounds as rabid wolves or something. I kept the story within the realm of the believable for them.

They took Sammic as a curious coincidence, but not as serious fodder for a copycat killer after a hundred years. Still, they promised to report it to their profiler. Stranger things had happened, they said and I thought how little they knew.

"You and Miss Ferrier became fast friends in a hurry," Halloran noted and the inflection in his voice was not lost on me.

Robert was about to object, when I decided to put it out there. I wasn't ashamed and the man on my immediate right already knew. I didn't want him to have to keep what didn't need to be a secret.

"We were more than just friends," I told them and the room got silent for a second other than the sizzle of more sausages and gurgle of yet another pot of coffee brewing.

"We were wondering," Halloran said.

"I wondered a little, too," I admitted. "It never happened before and probably won't again. It was her. She just got to me."

"You couldn't help yourself?"

"No," I admitted. It felt both weird and cathartic to say it out loud. "I couldn't. I fell in love with her."

In the corner of my eye, I could see Robert sitting back with the most beautifully baffled look on his face.

"That explains some of what they tell me you were screaming yesterday," Robert said.

"What was I screaming? I don't remember too much other than that I did."

"You were cursing out Fate for always taking away the best things you ever got," he told me.

"Yes," I said and the grief surged. I didn't say the words that came to me about how that had always been my lot in life. I felt Gus's strong hand squeezing my shoulder.

"That's okay, India," he told me. "If you're not up for this..."

I shook my head. "No. I'm okay. What about that Sandoval Willis? He's odd."

"We checked him out," Minkoe told me. He had the open file in front of him. He was the detailed one. "He is a tenured Professor of Parapsychology and Forensic Anthropology in Ames. He has witnesses that put him up there all weekend and through to last night."

"Forensic Anthropology?" Agnes asked.

"Figuring out the customs of ancient cultures through their artifacts and writings," I told her. "I've interviewed several for my past books. You're *absolutely* certain he was in Ames?"

"Yes, ma'am," Minkoe said. "He's odd, like you say, but he's not the killer."

"He finished up his investigations and left last week," Gus told me. "Plus, he was in Ames when Brianna was murdered. He's alibied out both times."

"What about that drifter?"

"He's sticking to his story that he thought he knew you from somewhere and wasn't sure how to approach you. He wasn't sure if it was good or bad between you," Levinson answered. "We also checked his hotel room and everything. There were no traces of blood or a murder weapon. We confirmed that he was two states away when Brianna was killed. It's looking like we'll have to release him this afternoon when we get to having held him for twenty-four hours. On top of that, he was in a cell by four yesterday. Francine Brindley says Melissa went to bed around eleven last night. So, it couldn't have been him. We'll just see that he moves on later today."

"Checking the timeline," Minkoe said, glancing over his notes. "You dropped Miss Ferrier off at the Herborium about eleven Monday morning, then spent the day working at your B & B, then out here until the next morning. Yesterday, you were at the old mayor's mansion until noon, and then went to the diner, where you expected to meet Miss Ferrier. When she didn't show, you became worried and went looking for her."

"Yes," I said. Although, actually, I had been worried all along. That had amped up to anxious, when she didn't show, and then to hysteria in the last moments.

"You didn't leave here at all that night?"

I was floored. "You suspect me?" I was so stunned for a second that they could have suspected I would kill Melissa that all thought left me.

"A crime of passion is what they're thinking," Gus broke the silence that had fallen. "That's why they wondered about your relationship with Miss Ferrier."

"Sheriff, if you're going to interfere with our investigation," Halloran began.

"Can it, son," he cut the agent off. "You saw the clear space out back. If she had moved her car, that is if she had gone anywhere that night, the whole back pavement would have been covered with leaves. She never left here."

"We've been using the alarm since those wolves showed up, too," Robert added. "You can't open a window enough to get through at night without tripping it. She never left. We already covered that. Why upset her with these questions? She's been through enough."

"Not to mention a lack of motive to kill Brianna," Levinson added for good measure. "Don't give me that bull about needing to ask all the questions when the answer is obvious."

"No, I'm okay," I said to diffuse the argument. I got the feeling they'd talked about it earlier, but not reached an agreement about going easy on me. "I was just startled, is all. Really, Agent Halloran. I loved Melissa and there was nothing wrong between us. I'm more insulted than anything that you even thought that."

"Well, I do have to ask all the questions, difference of opinions aside," Halloran said.

Levinson gave him a disapproving look. His character in the book I was planning was getting some new facets. He wasn't going to be anything that you expected at first.

"I was here, sound asleep, thanks to a long day, a good dinner, and late night brandy," I told him in a half frustrated tone. But not with them. The guilt was beginning to settle in. Guilt at having been warm and happy and safe, as my love was being brutally murdered.

"Have you remembered anything odd about your room at the Willow's Wells?" Halloran asked. "Now that you've had time to sleep."

I shook my head, even as I tried to recall it. I had noticed nothing, having been too caught up in my own anxiety. They could have painted the room purple and I probably would not have noticed in the state I'd been in.

"Nothing. I really didn't notice the room at all," I told them. "I was in a panic at that point."

"Mrs. Wells used that same word," Halloran told me. "She described your reaction as pure horror and despair."

"It was," I told them. "That's the only part of it I can recall clearly."

They stopped asking questions as a tear formed in the corner of my eye. I might not have answered any more anyway. My heart was growing heavy again as I thought about it more and just wanted to leave and be with Francine and the family. They had become my family.

"Well, if anything comes to mind, please tell us," Halloran told me.

"We don't have anything, do we?" I asked, looking at Gus.

He almost seemed embarrassed, but did appear sorry as he shook his head. "We have no good suspects. Everyone we can think of, and the only other stranger in town, have verified alibis. It looks like we're going to be relying on combing the area and hoping to come across someone that saw something. Miss Ferrier's car is still missing, as well."

"Thank you," I told them. "I'll be at the Herborium, if you need me." Then it dawned on me that I had not driven there. "Oh," I said, turning to Robert. "My car?"

"Agnes brought it over after packing your things," he told me. "It's out back in a temporary shelter. We should have put it up earlier for you."

"Temporary shelter?" What had he bought?

"One of those pop up tents for cars," he told me. "It's been sitting in the garage for years. I'd forgotten all about it until we were thinking of what to do for your car with you staying here."

"Thanks," I said.

"I put your keys beside your purse," Agnes told me. "Did you get enough to eat?"

"More than enough, thanks."

"Coffee for your bath?" she asked, holding up the pot. I'd only spent a couple of nights there and already she knew me. I didn't really need it and the bath was going to be quick. Still, I handed her my cup and received a perfectly prepared cup of coffee in return. She really knew her business and I was very glad she had been the one to pack my personal things rather than Robert.

Chapter 16
The Gathering

Dressed in jeans and a gray sweater for the turning weather, I drove out to the Herborium a short while later. The men had already gone, but Agnes saw me out and offered what help she could give me. She'd suspected something of the truth about me and Melissa when I hadn't continued anything with Richards. She'd known there had to be a reason. I gave her a hug before leaving. The first sympathetic one I'd received from anyone.

Tears ran softly as I drove. My vision blurred here and there. Fortunately, I was familiar enough with the way now.

"Franny," Carla called to her sister from the work table as I walked toward them.

Francine appeared to my left from behind the candle and wreath display she had been setting up. She came straight to me with no words, just open arms and love in her eyes. I fell into her embrace and let the tears come freely. I was no longer hysterical or drugged up. I was just me and I was with my family. I buried my face in her shoulder and we cried until there were no more tears left in either of us.

I found that I was in the center of a group hug with Carla and two other older women that I had not seen before. Sisters by blood or by faith, I figured, and accepted them as was the way of Green Witches. I didn't consider myself a witch or a Wiccan, but I felt connected here, to them, the shop, and the land it sat on. I couldn't say how, but it was as though Melissa had come home within me.

"We have some tea at the table," Francine said and walked me to the work table with her arm around my shoulder and mine around her waist. "Are you hungry?"

"No. Agnes fed me enough for a horse this morning."

"Good. Have a seat. You can help us, if you like."

The table was covered with dried leaves and herbs, willow branches, and thin, green florists wire. Several fall wreaths sat on it in different stages of build. This was their way of coping and grieving, I assumed; keeping busy.

"I think I'll be all thumbs," I told her. Truth is, I never was a very skilled person, when it came to crafts. I didn't want to mess them up, when she was obviously making them for sale. She smiled and went to work weaving in the leaves and dried flowers. Arthur jumped into my lap the moment I sat down.

"These are for Samhain," she told me. "We had planned on gathering in a week and celebrating on Coven Ridge this year. But we're gathering early now."

"Strength in numbers," I commented.

"Exactly," Francine replied. "By week's end, there will be dozens of witches in the area, support from other Covens in the Midwest. None of us will go anywhere in groups smaller than three."

"That's making the Sheriff nervous," I told them. "He's afraid you'll retaliate somehow."

"The FBI as much as warned us against doing anything this morning," Francine told me. "They were here for hours, combing the grounds and going through her room."

"They won't find anything," I opined. I had no reason to believe they wouldn't, but I was certain of it.

"I'm not placing my hopes in them," Carla added.

"He's still out there," I said.

She nodded grimly. "Yes. He is."

"But we have proof that he died."

"Definitive proof," she replied.

"Sammic is dead," I voiced the name. "There is no doubt of that. But the evil that was Sammic is back.

There's no doubt of that either."

"Yes," Francine replied. "It seems your intuitions were correct, India. You thought it. I didn't see how it was possible. I still don't know how it's possible."

"If his ghost came back, he might be possessing someone." I said. That sane part of my mind that was slowly reasserting itself did a double take at me for saying that. It was still coming to grips with everything, with unreality taking place.

"We've been wondering that, too," Carla replied. "The question we can't answer is why would he come back? Why sixty-five years after his death? Particularly when he got everything he wanted a hundred years ago. What grudge could he be holding? It should be us holding a grudge."

"Maybe he still wants your entire Coven dead," I said. "The sixty-five years part, I can't answer though. You'd think he would have come back right away, if he wasn't going to the meet the Lord and the Lady. Unless, I'm not understanding part of that."

"No. You've got it right," Carla said. "It's the same question we're asking. Why wait two more generations after dying; four or five after the one you tried to wipe out? We're coming up blank on that."

I pursed my lips and stared at the table as I thought. Because I felt a thought coming to me, forming out of the vagueness in my mind. Why so long? Why would he have needed so much time? To develop a plan? To wait for the right time? What made now the right time? Was there something he had needed first? And with that, the thought gelled.

"What if he hadn't been strong enough?" I asked.

"What do you mean?"

"Maybe it's like Sauron in the Lord of the Rings," I suggested, "if you'll forgive that reference. Maybe he needed time to build up his energy, or life force, to be able to return."

"He hasn't returned, though," Carla pointed out.

"It's still just his spirit we're talking about, possessing people."

"What if he's become more than just a spirit?" I said. "What if he really is out in those woods, not quite back, stalking us with the Duvall men?"

"Mel said you had quite the imagination," Francine replied. "I'm not even sure if such a thing is possible."

"He was practicing a different kind of magic," I reminded them. "There's the chance that something he did allowed his spirit to endure and slowly regain strength."

"Reincarnation is one thing," Carla said, disbelieving, "Reanimation is quite another."

"It's not even reanimation," Francine noted. "He's not reanimating his body. This is creating an entirely new one from nothing but the energy of the earth."

"Right," Carla saw the point and looked aside for a second as she considered it, then screwed her face and shook her head. "Not possible. Only the Lord and the Lady can breathe life into the world. None of us, no matter what we know, could take that power from them. When Sammic died, his spirit left his body and went to the Lord and the Lady."

"Should have," I corrected. "But we have the Duvall men outside to prove that ghosts exist, that not everyone goes straight to that meeting."

"Good point," Carla credited. "Yes, he may have been able to stay and postpone that meeting. But the fact remains that no one, once mortal, can usurp the power of creating life from the Lord and the Lady. He can't re-create himself. He can only take possession of someone."

"But who and where?" Francine posed.

"I know," I agreed it was frustrating. "The Professor and the drifter were eliminated as suspects, which leaves only local people."

"Drifter?" asked Carla and I told them about the man that had begun to stalk me.

"Oh, well, that brings up an entirely different possibility," Carla said and I saw a light come on in

Francine's eyes. The sisters were so thoroughly in sync as to catch the others thoughts.

"Sequential possessions," Francine said and Carla nodded.

"Wait. You mean maybe he's been possessing different people as the need arose?" I wondered. "I thought when you got possessed, that was it, just you. Are you saying ghosts can jump from person to person?"

"I've never heard of it before," Carla told me. "It would make sense as to why you couldn't pin a single suspect down. Like you said, he practiced a different kind of magic. Maybe this was a power he could have had."

"It could be another drifter or anyone at all," I noted.

"It would have been whoever was best suited at the moment," Carla said. "Honestly, though, that's probably a worse theory than your Sauron one. It requires an enormous amount of energy in Sammic's spirit to roam and possess so many people. If he had been that strong, then why did he wait sixty-five years? Why not have done our mothers in back right before or when we were being born? The stronger you make his ghost, the more you go back to it not making sense to wait so long."

"There has to be a reason," I said. "We're just not asking the right question."

"Which is probably the only thing we can be sure of," Carla quipped.

I had to agree with her. So much of what had happened to me and around me since I'd arrived at Willow Creek had been unexpected and unexplainable. I was getting to the point where there wasn't much I was sure of anymore. One of which was me. Either I hadn't ever really known myself or this had changed me. Well, of course, it had changed me. How could it not have? To have had an affair with another woman and be grieving the loss of that love with my new family of Green Witches, to find my greatest solace in a Coven I hadn't known a month ago? That was still a little overwhelming to put it mildly. No wonder my sanity was only hovering at the edges. It was afraid to get any closer.

I thought for a second, what might have happened had I not arrived? In retrospect, coming events would have been altered. But only in that different people would have died. Melissa would still have been among them. Our love would still have been lost.

Levinson had put it bluntly and correctly. *I* was the catalyst. Things had started happening the moment I arrived. But had they? Brianna had been killed my first night there. Only a handful of people knew I had been in town at that time.

Then, my jaw dropped.

There was our suspect pool: the few people who knew when I'd arrived. If you accepted that I was the catalyst, that is.

"What is it?" Francine asked. "You've thought of something."

I told them what Levinson had said and what had just hit me. My imagination was swirling. Who were the suspects? Who had known I was coming into town? The Mayor, the Pastor, the Sheriff. The Wells, Agnes, Sam the caretaker. Who else? The possibilities were growing and perplexing, and heart breaking when I considered Sam or Agnes.

Gut wrenching, when you considered Richards himself. Richards and that prized Chinese sword. How could I get it checked for blood? Dear God. Had I slept with the man that had murdered my lover?

"That is a curious twist," Francine noted, breaking my darkening thoughts.

"The question is why," Carla added. "Why would your arrival to write a book about the Duvalls trigger someone else in town to start targeting us?"

Which was a face full of cold water on that idea.

Still, it was worth pursuing, I thought. Nothing else that was happening followed a clear thread of logic. Why should we expect the killer's motive do so?

Robert's nasty-looking sword was the obvious

weapon. Could I anonymously mention it to the FBI for them to check out? It needed to be done. I wasn't being melodramatic. It wasn't having been in the killer's bed. It was about being under his roof.

I couldn't die mysteriously within the mansion. That was a risk he couldn't take, right? If anything, checking the sword would get my imagination back under control. As much as I ever could control it. Sometimes my creative streak was an awful bane.

To give myself and my mind something to do, I took the empty tea pot upstairs to brew another. I knew where everything was and felt comfortable being in the kitchen by myself. While the tea brewed, I sliced the bread that Francine or Carla had baked that morning for the day. It was still warm inside. I was no good with wreaths and what not, but I could handle myself in the kitchen.

I needed something to keep me occupied and to help make me feel better. There was the book, of course. However, this was a day for family, not work. Francine had told me what she had intended to make, so with Arthur supervising I set about preparing lunch for the four women downstairs and the others that were expected within the next couple of hours. When they arrived, all that would be needed was to pull trays from the fridge.

After a while, though, my active, wandering mind betrayed me. I found myself wondering what Melissa had gone out for. We knew it was dangerous to be alone. She had told me she was not going to the leave the Herborium until lunchtime. What had been so important that she had broken her promise?

Had she gone to check on her cats? Had she needed a flower or a leaf for a charm or a spell, and item that needed to be collected at sunrise or while covered in dew?

Dear God, what if it had been for me? What if she had gone out to find something for me? I felt my heart and stomach sinking. Or what if all those times I tried calling them suddenly showed up as missed calls? What if she had gone out to find me and see what was so urgent? I had to put the knife down. I couldn't see what I was slicing. I found the chair beside me, slumped into it, and cried into my palms.

There had been no other reason for her to have gone out. Whatever it was, it had been because of or for me. And, she was dead because of it. I had lost her because of her love for me.

Levinson was right. I was the catalyst.

It had started when I got there and Melissa's death was directly related to me. The evil and the hell that were coming to Willow Creek may not have come with me. It had probably been there all along. Yet, somehow I had awakened it, and it was killing people because of me.

The cruelty of Fate was harshly clear in that moment. So much bad had happened to me and around me for so long, I had often wondered if my lot in life was to be the female Job of whatever Bible would be written of our times.

Melissa had tried to stop me from feeling that way. I had wanted to try. But that morning, my soul felt as dark as it ever had. In that moment, my mind took it to an even deeper level. I began to feel as though all of the grief that seemed to follow me was not because Fate had chosen to torment me, but because she had chosen me for her agent. Everything that had and was happening around me was being done through me by Fate. I brought people's fate to them. I had become Fate.

A soft touch on my leg roused me from those dark thoughts. Aubrey leaned both front paws on my thigh and looked at me with worry on his beautiful face. A quick laugh escaped me at his seeming understanding.

"Don't worry, baby," I told him. "Momma's not cracking up."

He grrr'd at me as if to say, "We'll see," and then strolled into the room that had been Melissa's.

"At least, I sure hope she isn't," I added.

I dried my eyes, blew my nose, and was determined not to let my thoughts get to me. As I washed my face, I couldn't keep from wondering what her last thoughts had been.

Had they been about me? Had she been terrified? Had she rued her decision to go out? Regretted that she would never see me again? Or over losing our life together? Or had she been idly and happily thinking about whatever she'd been preparing for when it had all just ended?

I didn't know. I was a basket case by that point. I stood and cried again at the sink, until the sound of someone arriving down in the shop snapped me out of it.

I had gone upstairs for a reason, not to wallow in self-pity and whine. They were counting on me for lunch. I shook myself, washed my face again, and pulled it together and somehow finished prepping lunch without slicing my fingers off.

A few teardrops still found their way down my cheek. I was okay with it now, though. I had settled down. It was probably going to be happening over the next few days anyway; having good moments and bad moments.

Fatigue caught up with me after lunch. I didn't know if that was an after effect of the drugs or from my earlier big cry with Francine or in the kitchen or from letting myself fully relax, or probably all of that. I found I needed a nap later that afternoon, so I lay down in the bed that had been Melissa's and wrapped myself in the sheets smelling of her soap and the oils she used on her skin, and drifted slowly to sleep with watery eyes. Aubrey had already been there, probably loving the scents of her too, and he curled up against my back and purred us to sleep.

I dreamt of her. We were walking through the colorful hills that day when the sun had been shining and the days were still warm. We didn't talk about anything. We walked and shared smiles and giggles as we enjoyed the world around us and simply being together. I wanted to keep that feeling and those moments close to me. I wanted to keep that safe feeling of her being near me.

Francine looked in on me, waking me accidentally. The light was murky. Twilight was already falling. The glow from the kitchen was bright and warm and I heard the voices of still more women in the house. Their voices were low, but they seemed serious, as though they were preparing for something.

"Do you feel up for a ritual?" Francine asked me.

I couldn't vocalize how that lifted my spirits; to be asked to join all of them in their practice. They felt like family to me, so this made me feel that it was mutual. Groggy and blurry-eyed, I followed her into the kitchen and the welcoming smiles of Carla and eight other women, all middle-aged or older. They smiled and bade me hello.

"Come to the living room," Francine led me into the adjoining room. "We've prepared the altar here."

In witchcraft, I had learned, you didn't need consecrated grounds or special houses to hold your services. Witchcraft celebrated the earth, so anywhere would do.

The altar was just an oak table, covered with a white cloth, candles, a bowl, figurines, and flowers, both fresh and dried, particularly some of the lilacs from Melissa's garden. A short stool stood in front of it and Francine had me sit there. That was when I realized I wasn't observing or passively participating in the ritual. I was the focus of it. That startled me, but I trusted Francine.

"What are we doing?" I asked calmly.

"A spiritual healing ritual," she told me. "For Melissa to move on, India, you will have to release her spirit. That's not the same as forgetting her or getting over the pain. But you do need to let Melissa go at a spiritual level, to wish her peace in her rest, before she is returned to the world in a new life."

"You mean reincarnated?"

"Yes. Until you release her, a part of her may remain here with you," Francine told me.

"A part of her spirit?" I asked.

"You were joined in these few weeks," Carla explained. "Her memory and your love for her are good things to keep. We must let her go on, though."

"Of course," I said. I remembered stories about spirits attaching themselves to people and places. Why wouldn't it have been possible that Melissa, or some portion of her, was attached to me? Or, that I might have been holding it to me unknowingly. *Like my dream had meant*, I thought. Was that why it had felt so real?

There was no doubt I wanted Melissa to be able to move on, so I opened myself up to follow Francine's instructions to a T.

"You also need to let go of the burden," she told me, laying her hands on my shoulders from behind.

"Burden?"

"What bothers you other than missing her?" she asked.

"I don't understand. You mean that she was murdered?"

"No. I mean what else is hurting you?" she explained. "Are you blaming yourself?"

"No," I answered. "I mean, how could I blame myself for Sammic?"

"You know what I mean, India," Francine chided. "I want you to say it."

I didn't want to.

Instinctively, I knew where she was going. She was too smart not to have guessed what was troubling me. Holding it to myself and keeping it secret, helped me hold the guilt down by not facing it. Clearly, I was only fooling myself.

Still, I didn't want to voice it.

"Release it, dear," said Carla.

Anger flared through me. I didn't want to release it. I didn't need to be made to face anything. I was okay. It was just normal grief. It would pass in a few days. It wasn't my fault, she had gone out early and alone.

"We know that," Francine said and I realized I'd said that last bit aloud. "We just wonder if you really do."

Of course, I did, I thought angrily, but this time, I managed to keep from saying it. I felt Francine's steadying hands on my shoulders. I had made to leave without even thinking.

"Let her know," she told me.

"Her? Melissa's here?" I asked. "How can you tell?"

"She hasn't left you, India," Francine said. "She won't go until she knows you'll be okay."

"I will be okay," I told them. "She knows that."

"Does she? Have you told her?"

I hadn't even thought that I needed to. I mean, why should she have wondered otherwise? We were bonded. She knew what I thought, how I felt. Meaning, I realized, she would have fretted over my pain and angst and want me to release it. My eyes closed and my face dropped as I sighed.

"Why did you go out?" I asked, hearing the tears and tremor in my voice as though I was back to observing myself act with no control. "Why didn't you stay here where you'd be safe? What was it? Was it something for me? You said you'd stay here. You *promised* to stay here. What was more important than keeping safe?"

There was anger in the last part. Yes, I felt guilty, but I was also livid. I was so mad at her for not sticking to the plan. We'd had it figured out. We knew how to stay safe, to stay alive. She couldn't do it, though. Not even just for one morning.

Why didn't you do as you said you would? Why did you break your promise? Why did you get yourself killed? You threw away everything we were going to have and for what? What had been so God damned important?

Francine held me from behind. Some of it, at least, had come out aloud again. I leaned into her, letting the tears return and facing the pain I had wanted to bury until it had calloused over or been burned out in getting revenge.

"It wasn't my fault," I said. "Was it? Did this happen because of me?"

"Nothing has happened because of you," she assured me. "You are here because you were meant to be a part of this. Whatever is going on, you're not the catalyst. You're a part of it somehow."

"Everything works out the way it's supposed to." I said, seeing her point.

"With our help," she added. "Don't blame yourself that Melissa went out that morning."

"It wasn't my fault."

"It never was," she told me. "Can you accept that and not be angry at either of you?"

"I guess," I said. I certainly didn't feel as irate. I'd gotten it off my chest, so to say, and it was easier to deal with and put into perspective. We were never going to know what she'd been thinking, and stressing over it was only hurting me. That wasn't doing any of us any good.

"Good," Francine replied with a hug. "Now, come help us pray for her swift journey to the Lord and the Lady."

I got off the stool and joined them in a circle, holding hands, around the altar, which was a mini-shrine to Melissa with photos, her hair brush, the dried lilacs from her trees. I was struck by the similarity of theirs to Christian prayer circles, and by the words we spoke, together and individually, asking that she be received with love and open arms.

"Please accept my love into your arms," I requested, when my turn came. "Please keep her in joy and in peace, until it's time for her to return."

I did feel as though I was freeing Melissa, while still keeping the thought of her in my heart. It was hard to explain the sensation of releasing something I had been grasping with my soul physically, while retaining the memory of her in my heart still.

It was healing. It was relieving. It was as though I was opened up to the world as they knew it and I was able to feel a small part of it, become connected momentarily with the natural world on a new level. I felt larger inside. I could say without embarrassment that it was a moving and pivotal experience.

One that was suddenly broken by the howl of the hounds in the distance.

I opened my eyes as the room fell silent. Standing in a circle, we looked at each other with apprehension and a sense of battle rejoined.

"He's out there," I said with all certainty. No one refuted my conclusion.

"You'd better stay here tonight," Francine told me, glancing toward the front windows as though she might be able to see the beasts through the sheer drapes.

"I think we all better stay inside tonight," Carla added.

"I'll help with dinner," I offered. "I feel better. Thank you. All of you."

Francine hugged me to her hip. "So do we, Indy. Our sister can find her rest."

"Her meeting with the Lord and Lady will be glorious," I said.

"She will be welcomed with love and open arms, as you asked, Indy," Francine said. "There's no doubt about that."

We heard a car pulling up outside and trooped down to see who it was. A pair of deputies were waiting in the shop. They seemed taken aback by the number of women, eleven of us counting me.

"Hello, boys," said Francine in a familiar, welcoming way. They were younger than me, I thought. Boys was a good description coming from Francine.

"Miss Brindley," they greeted with a tip of their wide brimmed hats. "Sheriff Levinson said for us to come over and keep an eye on y'all. Someone's heard them wolves out in the woods again tonight and we knew you was gathering. Didn't realize you were all here already."

"We're not, Ricky," she replied, clearly knowing him. "Not yet anyway. You boys hungry? We were just going to start dinner."

"Thank you, but we'll just stay outside and keep watch." Ricky seemed a little unsettled that still more women were coming.

"We'll bring you something then," Francine told them. "Thank you for being here."

"No problem, Miss Brindley," said Ricky with a finger to the brim of his cap as they took a step back and turned to step out.

"Levinson is a better man than I first thought," I remarked.

"He's a natural protector," Francine replied. "It's his instinct. I told him he would make for a powerful witch, if he'd care to learn."

I smiled and then a dark thought hit me. "You don't suppose he's..." I didn't complete the thought.

We glanced at each other as the idea was silently considered. Who better? I could see the thought on all of their faces. It was strong in my own mind, too. As calm as the ritual had left me, the tension and the heaviness came back. Which was sickening because I had started to like Levinson. It was not easy to consider him a suspect. Until Francine's words, he had not been a serious possibility but if he really could have been that strong.

"Well, not so much strong as good," Francine corrected herself. "Spells work better for those that really care as well as believe."

"So, you meant he'd have been strong as a Green Witch?" I asked. We were just getting jumpy.

"Yes. That's what I meant," she replied. "If anything, it might make him harder to possess."

That was good to know. What faith I could give to law enforcement, I was putting with him. The majority of my trust was already given to these women around me.

"Well, I'm ready to start dinner," Francine announced. "Big rituals always leave me hungry."

It was getting late. Night was deep and you could sense the cold from the troopers' postures on the porch. Shotguns still kept at the ready, they were huddled into their jackets, probably wishing they'd dressed warmer. Levinson arrived then to give us an update, which was to say he had little more to tell us.

The FBI had even gone so far as to examine Richard's Chinese sword and found it hadn't been used. No blood was found on it, not even a trace, and it wasn't clean enough to have just been thoroughly scrubbed. There was still trace oil on it from when it had been packaged for shipping. I was a little startled that what I'd been thinking had actually been done. They weren't leaving any stones unturned.

It made me feel a little better. Although, when you already know the truth and it's nothing they can help you with, feeling better doesn't amount to much. I was considering telling Levinson to see what he would say, if he would change anything that he was doing. He was a matter of fact kind of guy. He didn't believe in things like ghosts and reincarnation and possession.

At least, such was what I was assuming. I'd never asked. Basically, I'd stereotyped him and he was certainly proving me wrong in that. I didn't want to ask him in front of the congregating Coven. That was, I didn't want to put him in a possibly awkward position in front of people he didn't know. I could do so back at Robert's. I started to ask, if he was headed by that way, when he beat me to it.

"If you wanted to head back to the Duvall's house, India, I'll escort you," he told me. "I'm bringing the sword back to him."

"Thank you, Sheriff. I was just going to ask."

"Whenever you're ready then."

"I'll just get my purse," I told him, but of course that was a twenty minute process of hugging good night and figuring when we'd see each other next. A memorial for Melissa was being planned, but was on hold until she was found. Witch funerals involved burial in a white-cotton wrap so that the body could return to the earth for re-creation. That wasn't possible without her body. No one actually said those words, but we all knew it. No body, no ceremony. It wasn't hard to figure out.

Aubrey jumped off the roof of my car, where he'd

been guarding it, and I followed Levinson back to the Duvall's. Knowing about my spot out back, he led me straight there and parked his big, heavy cruiser in such a way as to form a barrier between the dark woods and the rear door. When I stepped out of my car into the harsh spot lights illuminating for fifty yards or better, he was already out of his with a shotgun perched on his hip. The nippy wind kicked up leaves and put sound into the forest and a chill along my spine. It was like something out of a movie.

How was this really happening? I suddenly doubted my own sanity and my decision to say anything to Levinson. He waved me ahead of him and half backed to the door behind me, never looking away from the tree line. Tarantino was going to yell, "Cut," the minute I walked through the door and we were all going to go to our trailers for coffee and cocktails. What I'd been sure of half an hour ago seemed ridiculous in that moment.

The warmth of the familiar kitchen helped to soothe my mood. It was empty for the moment, but still held the aromas from dinner tonight and maybe all the nights since I'd arrived there. When I heard the solid click of the deadbolt on the heavy door, I felt secure again. I also felt hungry. I'd skipped dinner with Francine to return and the aromas were getting to me. Now, I was wishing I'd stayed there.

Levinson propped the shotgun by the door and headed for Robert's office with a gun case that presumably held the sword. I followed as the Sheriff gave one rap at the open door frame and walked in. Robert was at his desk, looking over some papers and silently nodded as Gus set the case on the desk in front of him.

"They said it was filthy," Gus told him and I knew he was kidding. "There was dust from the Fifteenth Century on the hilt still."

"Funny," Robert replied.

"Suit yourself," Gus said and turned toward the door. I was in it and didn't move.

"What did I miss?" I asked.

"Mr. Richards, here, seems to think I should have convinced the FBI that he couldn't possibly be a suspect and to leave his precious sword alone."

Robert was obviously hurt. "You didn't even say a thing."

"It was a reasonable thing to do," Levinson replied. "Anyone could have taken it."

"What anyone? Only we could get in here."

"And delivery people and the cable repair guy," Levinson replied. "Anyone could have gotten in here."

Robert screwed up his face in anger and disagreement, but wasn't going to say any more.

"He means you didn't defend him, Sheriff," I said. "Or his family."

"Like you need defending," Gus remarked.

"What the *hell* does that mean?" Robert demanded.

"Nothing," Gus said. "The hell with it. I've been up thirty-six hours. I'm getting some sleep." He went out angry and in a rush, and with him my chance to talk.

I stood leaning against the door frame with my arms folded and a frustrated smirk on my face. Just when I'd decided to try something, it got messed up by the two of them arguing like school children. That was always the way with my life. Melissa had counseled me to try to work with the way it flowed. It felt like it had just gushed away. How do you work with that?

"What are you upset about?" Robert suddenly asked over my expression, his tone insinuating that I had no reason to feel upset about anything.

I didn't react. Normally, I would have done and said something to make him feel better. Tonight, I thought about walking away and leaving him to his mood. I also considered telling him to get some sleep like Levinson. He didn't have a lock on sorrow. Did I need to point that out to him that I was the one that had just lost her lover? I could have been the one demanding attention for my grief, but I was focusing on the good she had done, as Francine and Carla had wanted me to do.

I didn't say anything.

I unfolded my arms and walked over to his desk. Without asking I reached out and unzipped the gun case, finding the sword wrapped in oiled cloth within. His eyes stayed on my hands. He didn't look up as I removed the shining blade and took hold of the hilt with both hands. There was some weight to it, but not so much that you couldn't have wielded it throughout a long battle. I wondered if it had ever tasted blood in the past, if it had ever taken another man's life. I suspected it had.

"I do like history and historical things," I told him needlessly, holding the gleaming blade in front of my face.

A smile slowly formed at the corners of his mouth as I inspected the sword. His mood was shifting again, lightening on its own without me making less of mine.

"Is that a hint for Christmas?" he asked quietly and finally lifted his head to meet my eyes. "I'm sorry, Indy."

"You're tired, too," I replied. "I know you were up with Gus last night."

"No. I mean I'm sorry about Melissa," he told me. "I didn't know you were…"

"In a relationship with her."

"Yes. After that morning, when the tree fell, I guess I didn't see it coming."

"Honestly, Robert," I confessed. "Neither did I."

"You said it had never happened before?"

"It hadn't," I answered, shaking my head and walking over to the figure to put the sword back. "Never even an inkling or feeling for another woman before."

"It was just her, like you said."

"It was her heart, Robert," I answered softly. My back was to him as I made sure the sword was correctly balanced in the display.

"I guess I can understand that," he replied and I turned to gaze at him.

"Do you?" I wondered and studied him. The look on his face was complex. He was fatigued and plagued by thoughts from all angles: the work papers on his desk, the FBI investigating him, my affair with Melissa. Somewhere in there, I thought I saw that he really did get it.

"There was a girl before Phyllis," he told me. "Marie DeSalle. We were in high school together and I was madly in love with her like only a fourteen year old boy can be. I didn't care that she was black or that she was smarter than me or that her dad was an activist from way back. Not that any of that is wrong or bad, but consider where we are and my family's heritage. It was a little scandalous still. Shouldn't have been, but it was."

"What happened?"

He frowned. "They moved to Japan. I never heard from her again. I suspect she's married with twenty children or a rocket scientist at JPL or something equally successful for what she wanted."

"Why didn't you try to find her?"

He shook his head. "I guess because I went to college, got involved with Phyllis for all those years, and then found myself in charge of the business. Life did what it does best, right? The point is that I do get what you're saying about Melissa. I mean it, when I say I'm sorry."

I felt a tear form at the corner of my eye. "Thanks, Robert."

"You're welcome, Indy," he said. "I suppose it's time I call it a night. I can't even see these papers any more my eyes are so blurry. We set the library up for your office."

"Thanks. I'll go have a look."

With a smile and a suppressed thought of kissing him for his understanding, I headed for the library.

The central table had been cleared of the scattered photos. They were neatly stacked in card boxes or piles at one end. My laptop, printer, and scanner were set up in the center of the table in the same manner I'd had them laid out at my room at the Willow's Wells. That thought made me think to ask how Marianne was holding up. I understood she had gone in to see what had shaken me up and been horrified, as well.

With my notes and everything where I liked them, I was as well set up here as I had been anywhere yet. It had Agnes written all over it. She was the only one who would have been worried about first noting how I had it set up and then duplicating that. I went up to my room and found that Agnes had not only finished moving me in, but washed my laundry, as well. Even the dream pillow was there on the nightstand. Plus, a note letting me know there was a plate in the fridge, if I was hungry.

I went down and found dinner, a thick pork chop, green beans, collards, and mashed potatoes. Down home comfort food. I certainly needed it. Quiet and security were what my soul needed that night. I loved Francine, but staying there amongst the ten of them would have been more than I was up for. I wouldn't have minded chatting with Agnes, though, I was thinking, when I heard her voice behind me.

"There you are. I thought I heard you," she said. "Do you want me to heat that up for you?"

I was already setting the plate in the microwave. "Nuking I can handle," I answered with a smile. "Everyone calling it an early night?"

"It felt like a long day," she told me. "Some coffee or tea?"

"Tea if it's herbal," I said. "I don't need any caffeine."

"How about chamomile?"

I smiled and nodded. A belly full of hot comfort food and soothing tea were going to be just what the doctor ordered.

"Your admission really rocked Robert," she told me as she went into the cabinets for the tea and kettle. "I heard him muttering this afternoon about not knowing who anyone was anymore."

"That's kind of odd," I noted. "Who else was he talking about?"

"The Sheriff for one, I guess," she answered. "Robert was livid when they took the sword to test it."

"I saw the aftermath when Gus brought it back."

The microwave beeped and I took it out to flip the food around for the second heating. "What about you? Did my confession bother you?"

"No," she told me. "I never got that vibe off of you, if you know what I mean. I never felt like you would come on to me. Am I making sense?"

I nodded. "Perfect sense. You don't feel threatened."

"Exactly," she replied, then winked with a smirk and added, "Besides, you're not cowboy enough for me either."

That gave me the first big smile since returning that night. It faded though a second later as I asked, "What about Mrs. Duvall? What did she say?" Her disapproval scared me. Not just over the job, either. I'd developed a lot of respect for her over the weeks. I feared disappointing her.

"No one has said anything to her, so far as I know," Agnes told me, which surprised me, and which was both relieving and disconcerting. It was disturbing in that her disapproval was still a looming prospect. "I'm not sure if she's guessed either."

"What do you think she'd say?"

Agnes pursed her lips and thought for a second. "Honestly. I think she'd be confused. I think the idea of the relationship would bother her, but she likes you. I don't think she'd know what to think."

"She's bound to find out."

"Well, it won't be from me, if she does," Agnes promised and turned to get the boiling kettle off the flame.

I was smiling as I took the hot plate from the microwave and sat at the table. She had heated enough water for two mugs and sat across from me with a cup of chamomile for herself, as well.

"How is Mrs. Brindley?" she asked.

I'd never heard her referred to with the honorific. It just showed you what a good heart Agnes had that she thought to ask about her.

"She's okay," I answered. "Her sister is there as well as a lot of other witches. She's got a lot of support."

"I'm kind of surprised you didn't stay there tonight."

"Too much support for me," I admitted.

"Oh! Did you want to be alone?" she suddenly realized.

"No. No," I assured her quickly. "Just not with ten other women around. This is more what I needed. More peaceful."

"Good," she told me. "You know I'm really sorry."

I smiled. There were tears that threatened to come. Agnes had become a sure friend. Her support lightened my heart. The ritual and prayers with Francine and the others had stabilized my emotions. I was able to simply and warmly say, "Thanks, Agnes," and keep it together.

It was helped greatly by the first bite of pork chop. "Oh, my God. What did you marinate this in?"

"Coarse salt and sparkling apple cider for a couple of days," she said simply.

"You should really open up a restaurant."

"I've been saving up for ten years," she told me. "A few more years and I should be ready. Kansas City, probably."

"I'll be first in line," I promised her. "Where did you learn to cook like this?"

"My mom got me started," she answered. "From there it was books, TV shows, and the internet. I love it, obviously. It's been my life pretty much and this has been a great place to hone my skills."

"Definitely," I said. "You don't seem to be lacking for anything. I didn't even know twenty-four inch butcher's knives existed." I pointed to the massive knife secured to the magnetic rail.

"That one is kind of like cooking with a sword," she joked.

"Robert and Mrs. Duvall are going to miss you."

"Oh, they want a piece of the action," she said with a wink.

"That sounds like a good idea," I had to say and Agnes grinned.

It was good talking fun things, future things. It helped me keep perspective, rather than succumb to feeling my life had been ruined. Yes, it wasn't going to be what it would have been with Melissa. There would be joy one day. It might be a while, but it would happen and more than likely in some unexpected way.

We talked about cooking and her expectations of running a restaurant. When I had finished eating and the long day was taking its toll, she shooed me out of the kitchen and up to my room. On the way, I snatched a healthy brandy to sip in the bath. It was a little odd to be helping myself without anyone else there. While at the same time I had the sense that it was more than just acceptable, but expected, even preferred that I act with such comfort and familiarity. I may have been just that tired, though, and my whacky thought patterns were at it again. It wasn't long before I caught myself nodding off in a still very warm tub. I put an early end to my soak and headed to the thick bed.

I tucked the dream pillow under the fluffy pillow and then slipped under the heavy comforter in my borrowed silk pajamas. The fatigue was making it feel surreal. In a way, it didn't really seem like my life rather that I had stepped into someone else's in this huge home with a housekeeper, designer clothes, and the softest PJs.

That also made the last two days a little easier to bear.

Chapter 17
The Breather

I found I was able to keep working with my usual focus. My grief had not lessened and tears came at odd times. I still wanted retribution against her killer. Yet there was a sense of peace at knowing that Melissa was now at rest until it was time for her soul to return. I know her meeting with the Lord and the Lady had been a blessed one.

People also left me alone mostly. Marianne Wells came to see me to see for herself that I was fine. It was just a short visit ending with a hug and a promise to stay in touch.

The FBI had gone back to their Kansas City offices after gathering some evidence and talking to the witnesses. There wasn't much for them to go on, though. Everyone, including the creepy Professor, had been accounted for. They couldn't find anyone with a motive to kill the witches, especially in a copycat style, *if* it was a copycat crime. Serial killers didn't think like the rest of us, but a hundred years was a long time to look back. It seemed hopeless without some sort of break.

Francine and I talked on the phone every night and we had a memorial for Melissa on Friday. Her body was still missing and it was doubtful it would ever be found. There were caves and slim ravines and the river to have dumped it into, if it hadn't been buried. The same was true for her Scion. Buried or in the river, her body would be going back to nature as was their custom. Having it to bury for ourselves would only have helped with our own closure. Melissa had already been returned.

I thought we at least we had part of her to bury, but we didn't. The coroner was holding onto her head because it was all they had for evidence. We didn't know how long they would keep her. So, we held the memorial for our own sake, en masse in Melissa's slightly recovered garden, with most of her cats also in attendance. Aubrey even rode with me back to the Herborium as though my company comforted him in his own grieving over Melissa's loss.

The danger was still lurking in the woods and alongside the roads. I still sensed the Duvall men prowling about the town and outside the Duvall estate. I wondered what it was that kept them out of it. Had the curse also included their not being able to return home? It seemed plausible. Why was there a curse in the first place? That we couldn't figure out.

So much still didn't make sense.

More disturbing, Levinson reported they'd been spotting the wolves' tracks every now and then. I didn't try explaining that they were hell hounds. I had changed my mind about seeing if he was open to supernatural possibilities. To him they were very large wolves. Missouri Animal Control had even brought in some hunters to try to track them down, but it had been difficult between the rain and the animals' pure caginess. I prayed they wouldn't come in contact with the hounds. My money was not on the hunters.

I don't know if it was that lack of safety or the fact that Melissa was gone for good had sunk in, but by the end of the week, that feeling of peace was wearing away. The sadness wasn't as raw as at first, but it was weighing on me again. My prose was not so poetic by Friday morning. The words were not flowing freely from my mind. I decided to go back to St. Louis for the weekend for some alone time.

"That's probably a good idea," Robert told me after breakfast on Saturday. I was getting an early start to beat a threatening storm as much as just to get away, and be alone as soon as possible. "Has to be hard for you to think with people constantly around."

Constantly watching me, I thought. We were in my room, where I was packing what I might want for the weekend. I wasn't packing everything. I had no intention of quitting. Robert was watching me from the oversized chair I had slept in that night.

"Yeah. I need some time alone."

He nodded then commented, "On the other hand, I wonder if you should be."

That made me pause and look at him across the bed where I had my bag open. "What do you mean?"

He held up a palm as if to ward off my response. "I'm not suggesting anything. I'm just thinking you've been keeping to yourself. Maybe someone to talk about things with would be a good idea, too."

"What things?"

"I want you to finish the book," he told me. "However, I'm concerned that continuing would be bad for you, given what's happened to you personally."

"I'm fine, Robert," I told him. "Writing is therapeutic for me, you know. Work helps."

"Good," he said. "I wanted you to know that I'm cool with it, if you needed to take a little break."

"Are you politely firing me?" I asked, mostly playfully, but a little worried.

He smiled that cute smile of his and gave a small laugh. "No. Of course not. I'm just trying to be understanding."

"Thanks, Robert," I replied. I kind of thought there was another issue here. "Are you still freaked out at my relationship with Melissa?"

"A little," he said. It was preying on him. "It wasn't what I expected."

"Me either," I admitted. "It just sort of happened."

"That's what you said the other day," he reminded me. "I confess it still sort of confuses me."

"Because of what happened here?" I pointed at the

bed.

"Because of the way you went at it," he told me. "That was the hottest and heaviest I've had for a while. I certainly wouldn't have suspected that you could..."

"Go the other way?" I asked.

"Yes," he said. "All that passion. For me. A guy."

"It was the situation," I told him. "I got carried away by it."

"Then I'm going to get some trees ready to crash down," he told me and I smiled for him, not telling him the entire truth of the situation I meant. I would never tell him how much of that passion was a result of disgust with myself from the night before.

"I'll be all right," I told him. "Don't mess with any of these beautiful trees. I'll decide if it's what I want without their help."

"Fair enough," he replied, although I could see he was just speaking words that sounded right. The mind was calculating. He was thinking about more than an affair with me.

"Was there something else?" I asked, expecting an evasion.

I got a surprise instead. He said, "I don't want you to be next."

Shock froze me for a second. All of the witches and I were taking precautions not to be alone or unprotected. We knew that any one of us was potentially the next victim. The one with the largest target on her, though, was me. Ghosts, hounds, the drifter; what was coming next?

"That's makes two of us," I quipped to soothe my own fears.

"No. Seriously," he said. "I'm worried how safe it is for you to continue."

"Robert," I said seriously. "No one is trying to keep me from writing your family history."

"No, but someone seems to have targeted the Wiccans and you're becoming part of them," he pointed out.

"You don't become a Wiccan overnight," I told him and resumed my packing, a little forcefully from anger at insinuating there would have been something wrong in that.

"I mean you're with them a lot," he tried to explain. "You're associated with them now. It doesn't matter whether you've decided to convert or not. You're perceived as being a part of them. That could make you a target. Do you see what I'm saying?"

I was getting a little hot with him. "Are you asking me to stay away from them?"

"Of course not," he replied. "I just want you to be aware that you're probably putting yourself in danger. Forewarned is forearmed, right?"

"You're suggesting I don't associate with them anymore?" I asked.

"For Christ's sake! No, I'm not!" he all but shouted. "I'm trying to ask you to be safe." He launched himself from the chair and strode for the door. "Jesus, India. Sometimes you make it hard just to be your friend."

He stopped short of the door where he sighed, but kept his back toward me.

"What have you got against me?" he asked, frustration clear in his voice. "I'm not a complete hick. I can see there's a chip on your shoulder. Is it my wealth? Where I live? What?"

My back was to him, as well. I wasn't sure I wanted to have this conversation. Because what *did* I have against him? All the guys like him that came before? How fair or smart was that? It wasn't, was it? This was turning out to be a journey of facing up to things. Melissa had wanted me to let things be what they were. That meant letting go of prejudices, didn't it?

I was still learning how hard that was to do.

"It's all the Roberts I knew before you," I told him.

"I'm not sure how to take that."

"As an apology," I told him. He was silent. But he didn't leave. "Something evil has been released, Robert, and it's growing worse."

He twisted to look at me and I turned toward him. "What do you mean?"

"I didn't just see Samuel Duvall at the mansion," I finally told him. "Those marks on my arm were from him grabbing me."

"What?" He slowly came over by the foot of the bed. "Are you saying he attacked you?"

I nodded. "Those are no wolves the Sheriff is chasing after. They were hounds of some kind. I saw them close enough to know."

"That's hard to believe," he said. "Are you sure this isn't just the scare making it seem larger?"

"It's real," I told him. "I know the dangers better than you do. The only things keeping me safe are what I've gotten from Francine and Melissa. You want me to stay away from the only people that understand and can protect me here."

"India," he said. "I really have a problem believing in these things."

"You didn't see them," I told him. "I didn't believe in them either when I first got here. I can't deny them now."

"I don't deny you believe it," he told me.

"But you don't believe me either."

"I'm trying to," he told me. "You know I care about you, so I'm trying to understand. It's hard."

"You saw the marks on my arm," I pointed out. "You saw what happened to my car. What more proof do you want? The ghosts attacking you?"

"I'm trying to fathom why one of my ancestors would have attacked you. That would help me to believe," he said. "Why would they do that?"

"To drive me away," I said. "Maybe there was something they didn't want me to know or they didn't want me stirring up the old pot. I don't know. But Samuel Duvall attacked me in the mansion and tried to do it again at the Willow's Wells. He told me he wasn't going to let me ruin them for all time."

"That doesn't make any sense."

"I'm a threat to them somehow, Robert," I told him. "They attacked me and they've been stalking me since. The only things keeping me safe are the protective spells and charms of the witches."

"I don't believe in any of that stuff," he told me.

"You don't have to," I replied. "I've seen proof of it. I've seen things that I never would have believed before. I'm still having trouble accepting."

"I guess you should take a few days to relax and think after all that's happened," he told me. "Let your mind clear some."

"You think I'm confused or losing my mind?" I asked.

"I think you need some time to think about things," he said, but the look on his face told me he had been wondering. He didn't understand my actions. That made my logic and ability to reason suspect. Maybe he wasn't entirely the stereotype I'd been pegging him for. He was still enough of it that he doubted the mental capacity of people that acted in odd ways to him. "Just promise you won't decide until we can talk about it some more next week," he requested.

"I'll come back," I said. I didn't tell him it was because I figured whoever it was would eventually come after my head for knowing about him. I wasn't sure how it would end now. All of my chances to run I've talked about before were long gone at that point.

"I'll let you get out of here, then," he said and took a step toward me, opening his arms with a questioning look. I accepted his embrace and a gentle kiss on my forehead. He had the sense not to try anything more. "Take all the time you need, but call me once a week at least. Okay?"

"I won't be gone that long," I said.

"Well, if you are," he said and let go of me. "I'll be here."

"Where else would you be?" I quipped.

"Wherever you ask," he answered and I didn't

respond. He was already walking toward the door. He left it open as he went out. I heard his footsteps go down the hall to the stairs and lost them as he descended the carpeted steps.

I finished packing and left with a brief hug goodbye with Agnes. Mrs. Duvall had already headed to their Country Club. She was part of the Halloween Party Committee and it would be next week.

The first five minutes at home were horrible. Being alone in my quiet apartment, after having shared it with Melissa caused the grief to surge. The pain of knowing I would never see her again came crashing home, undoing the healing ritual of the witches. We had made plans for the place for when she came to stay, which was to be with the start of the winter semester, when she started her classes for that religion degree. Without really saying it, we'd been planning for her to move in.

That had been taken away from me again by hateful Fate. My initial resolve to own my fate had also faded, crushed by the stinging reality I couldn't control everything that was thrown at me. No one can.

Worse, the part of me that had still been freaking out over a lesbian relationship was relieved the stressor was gone. I no longer needed to question myself and could go back to being who I thought I was. I cannot even begin to describe how horribly guilty I felt at thinking that. Especially on top of not having been there the night she was killed. Maybe she would not have been attacked had she not been alone.

I dropped all of my gear and clothes on the bed and sat on the end of it, my face in my hands. I fought back the tears. I hadn't come here to wallow in self- pity. I'd come here to get away from the people and the questions; to clear my mind and maybe view the problem from a different angle. I was hoping for a moment of clarity when it would suddenly make sense and I'd know who to blame. That wasn't going to happen if I succumbed to grief.

I set about my mundane routine of doing laundry, what little there was with Agnes having done it during the week after they moved me in. I realized as I shook out the clothes I'd brought for the weekend that I had one of the outfits that had been for Phyllis. Where was my mind? Why would I have presumed to think these clothes were mine? Agnes had mixed them together in doing the laundry, but I know I should have sifted them out. Maybe Robert had been right. Maybe my mind wasn't hitting on all cylinders. That was to be expected, though, wasn't it?

My normal routine also consisted of going to the local markets for fresh foods to make a home cooked meal, something I didn't get much of on the road. In this case, Agnes had been feeding me some of the best meals and Marianne Wells had seen to my breakfasts. The idea of eating out didn't appeal to me either though. Honestly, in those first few minutes, I didn't feel much like eating. I figured on just picking up some take out or something later.

My first order of business on returning most, of the time, would have been to go for a run in the park, because a lot of my runs on the road were hotel treadmills or abbreviated by not knowing the area. But after the hills of Willow Creek, the park seemed bland and pointless.

So I drove over to Babler State Park to hit some of those trails for the first time. It was a coolish day with sprinkles of sunshine and little wind. It was perfect for a long run and a lot of thinking. I set off with no particular route and tried to let my mind clear out. How, though, did you clear out a mind and heart full of grief, doubt, regret, and guilt? My simple job to save me financially had turned my life and my soul inside out, twisted and ruptured my heart, and had me questioning if I knew who I really was and how I was running my life.

Nothing was right anymore.

It hadn't been a person or an event coming along to take away what had been going good this time. It had been an entire town and it had taken my whole life as I knew it.

Maybe I didn't need to go back to being the susceptible girl I'd been. Although, I'd been content, even happy for the most part. I didn't feel capable of returning to that life anymore, and I didn't know what life to try to make.

I spent the entire afternoon running with little emotional relief until dusk loomed and, despite being a couple hundred miles away from the hounds, I hurried back to the lights of St. Louis. I wouldn't call it paranoia. I'd call it accepting that the unexpected was likely to happen.

I still didn't want to be in my rooms, so I headed out for that pick up dinner after a good hot shower, and ran into Shirley, a casual friend from the neighborhood and about my age.

"Hey you," I heard the familiar voice shout. "Where have you been?"

"I've been away on a job near Kansas City," I told her.

"This is my friend, Indy," she told the half dozen or so of her friends that were with her. "The writer."

I found myself shaking hands with a bunch of people whose names I was lost on in the first few seconds. That only added to my wonder about where my mind was since I was usually good with names. They all remarked on my name and Shirley repeated the age old joke, "I keep telling her that someone named Indy should be a writer for National G, exploring ancient ruins."

"This is Tim," Shirley introduced me to a quiet-seeming blond guy a few years older than us. I caught that he was the center of attention. "We're giving Tim a sendoff tonight."

"Oh? Where are you going?" I asked politely.

"Nowhere," Shirley said with a sly grin. "He's opening up a coffee shop on Halloween. We're never going to see him again for how busy he's going to be."

Which was apparently the joke for the night as they all laughed and Tim gave a wry grin of his own.

"Come on and join us," Shirley said.

"Thanks," I said. "I'm just going to get some Chinese and head back-"

"Sure you are," she said, cutting me off and hooking an arm around mine. "You're already a martini behind."

I let her drag me along with them because it was a perfect distraction and exactly what I needed; a chance to shut down and reboot. It was actually a perfectly normal night out, which made it seem all the more surreal.

Sunday seemed a little less odd. I sat sipping coffee and eating a croissant at my dining table as I perused the paper like normal. I thought of Tim's intended shop as I drank my strong coffee; Poet's Coffees and Teas, full of swap shelves of books, poetry slam Monday nights, kids' story reader Saturday mornings, treating book donations to a literacy group as coupons. That would have been the place for me that Sunday, my reading day.

I spent the day alone, letting everything that had happened go to the back of my mind to work itself free. I felt sure if I left the problem alone for a bit, then gave it a fresh look, I'd figure it all out. There was no doubt I was returning, regardless of any commitment to finish the book. Because, like a widow staying in her home, there was some comfort in the familiar places you'd shared. There was security in my pseudo-family at the Herborium. Even more than that, as Holmes would say, the game was afoot and I needed to see it through. I had regained my emotional strength.

When I headed out the next morning, though, it was all still a confusing mess to my mind. The critical clue had not magically appeared before me. A great detective, I was not.

Chapter 18
The Lowering Clouds

I was back early Monday in my room at the Duvall's home; nicely cleaned with fresh linens and a full closet awaiting me as though this were home and I'd spent a weekend away in St. Louis. There wasn't much to unpack, so I was in the library at my computer within minutes of arriving and put in a very solid day.

Robert came in later that afternoon, having left for work before I'd returned.

"I'm glad you're back," he told me. "I was wondering if you might not."

"I have a job here, remember," I replied.

"Yes," he said. "But, it's one you could probably finish elsewhere; somewhere safer. I'm still afraid some harm might come to you. I've been thinking you could work from home now that we're so far along."

I thought I caught the hint that he would come visit, but ignored it. My need for comforting after losing Melissa had been met by the healing ritual and, despite the bad moment when I had first gotten home, my strength had rebounded. I was comfortable being alone.

For once, I didn't think badly of him for thinking that way, if he actually had meant it that way. I wasn't sure. I may have just been expecting it from him. Who knew? Perhaps thinking of me as a lesbian had done something to his desire for me. I didn't know. I just wasn't feeling any interest at the moment.

"The records and all are still here in the mansion and the interviews aren't quite finished yet," I reminded him. "It will be easier to complete the research from here. Unless there was some reason you wanted me gone?" He was making me wonder.

"No! Don't be ridiculous," he returned. "I only want you to be safe."

He sounded sincere and I appreciated it. I told him so and wondered again if I hadn't misjudged him. It crossed my mind that my past relationships may have been disastrous for that very reason. Or was it more along the lines of what Melissa had been teaching me, that I fought to control life too much and with an alpha type male, that was a war waiting to happen. Possibly, maybe probably, she had been right in that I unconsciously picked the wrong sort of man to avoid anyone who reminded me of my father. Because then I could carry on with my life and not have to change it or my goals.

Whatever. The answer was not in Willow Creek.

I had about two weeks of work I needed to complete here left. Samhain was in a couple of days. I would celebrate it with the witches. By mid-November, before the cold weather set it, I would be back home, polishing the writing, and thinking about the next project. I was already drafting the query letter in my head for a book comparing the similarities of all religions. I'd even written the foreword and dedication to Melissa.

"This book was the idea of and is dedicated to Melissa Anne Ferrier, aka Guennean, a peaceful soul who taught me that love is not supposed to be encapsulated in stipulated roles."

When I said no more, but continued to work, Robert got up from the chair he'd plopped himself into and said, "Well, I'm glad you're back. I'll see you at dinner, I guess."

"I'll be here," I told him.

He nodded and went out. His anxiety was bothersome. I had my own bottled up. I didn't need him adding fuel to my fire and getting me tensed up again. Despite returning my attention to the computer, his visit had broken my concentration. I stood up and went over to the window to look out at the gray sky, turning slowly to gun-metal ugly as evening approached. Dark blemishes roiled with the low clouds, threatening to dump frigid rain. The evenings seemed to grow cooler quicker so late in the month. The fall colors had peaked and all but a few of the leaves had fallen, spotting the forest floor with reds and yellows amongst the fading greens. Brown and black were beginning to assert their year-end dominance.

It would have been idyllic for late afternoon runs, had the hounds not still been on the loose. I was going to be making use of that treadmill in the basement workout room starting tomorrow morning because I knew Agnes was preparing to stuff me to the gills again, and Alice Duvall would pour me at least two after-dinner brandies. I was going to need that treadmill.

Mayor Baker stopped by during the first of those brandies, taking one for himself as he nestled into an armchair in the library. Robert had another small fire going, crackling and snapping nicely. He was snug in the other armchair. I was between them in the desk chair they had brought in as part of my makeshift office. Alice Duvall was standing by the edge of the hearth, beside Robert.

"The council is giving me more grief about your use of the mansion, I'm afraid," the Mayor told me. "They insist on setting an ending date."

"We've talked about that," Robert said. "You can't put an ending date on something like this. Besides, it's our business anyway."

"They disagree," he told us. "Too much has been happening since you got here, Miss Hills. A man grievously injured by wild dogs that were chasing you, but haven't been seen since. Melissa Ferrier murdered in your room. We're not normally superstitious people, but they're saying they know when someone is bad luck."

"Are you serious?" Alice asked.

"I told them they sound like a bunch of superstitious old women," he said. "No offense, Mrs. Duvall. They won't listen. Fate just picks some people, they're saying."

That word again: fate. I had never felt in control of mine and now it seemed even more malevolent.

Robert spoke in my defense. "Most of the work will be right here in our library. She's almost done and won't need to be in town much anymore."

"Yes," I said. "There might still be a need to run over and check something, but for the most part, the work can be carried out here or by phone interviews."

"There's no point in getting all superstitious and worked up," Robert added.

"I'm not so sure it's superstition, actually," Baker replied. "I've heard the ghost of Samuel Duvall and a bunch of the others attacked you. I was there when Phyllis saw him, Robert, and I saw him, too. I know he's there. Between that and the Wiccans being murdered, the Town Council and a lot of the residents have become concerned that India's stirring things up somehow."

"That's ridiculous," Robert said.

Mayor Baker pressed on, "If the ghosts could attack Hills, they're thinking, then they could be killing the Wiccans."

"That's beyond absurd," Robert ridiculed with a frustrated wave of his hand. "The Council needs to grow up."

"Well, how else do you account for the murderer simply vanishing into thin air?" Baker asked. "That's their logic."

"*Their* logic?" Alice wondered. "I'm getting the impression you believe it, too."

"In any event," Baker stated, ignoring the rebuff. "It would be for the best if Ms. Hills finished up the book and went back to St. Louis where they could be sure she wasn't stirring things up. Or better yet, finished it back in St. Louis."

"I could probably start finishing it up from home, beginning next week," I said by way of compromise. "I want to be sure I have all of the research and longer interviews done."

"Okay. That should appease them," he said. "I'm sorry to have to be this way."

"It's no bother," I assured him. "No one should be uneasy about this."

"Thanks for being understanding, India," he said. "They've got me in a bad position. Thanks for the drink, Mrs. Duvall."

"Any time," she said although her voice clearly stated her exasperation with him.

The Mayor left after a few more pleasantries. I still had my key to the mansion.

"What superstitious fools," Alice Duvall was remarking on returning to the library after seeing him out. "I'm embarrassed for them, India."

"Great Uncle Samuel, or whatever he is, really did attack India, Nana," Robert told her softly.

Alice Duvall froze in her tracks and gaped at her grandson for several seconds, then said, "Robert Richards, have you taken complete leave of your senses?"

"It's true," I told her. "I was afraid to tell you both before because I wasn't sure how you'd react. Those marks on my arms were burns from where he grabbed me."

"What?"

"Francine's ointments and Melissa's talismans kept me safe."

"Seriously?"

As I nodded, Robert added, "Those weren't wild dogs that attacked ole Jeremy either."

"The devil you say."

"Not quite," he replied. "It seems something like him at least."

"Something's going on," I told her. "We just don't know what."

It had started right as I got there to write the book. That the two were related seemed inescapable, although I could scarcely figure out how. There was nothing in their past we hadn't already gone over. We all knew their ancestors let Sammic get away, presumably in return for a prosperity spell. We were leaving that out of the book. Was there still something more I had missed in my researches? I didn't think so. If there was, it had never been written down and no one living remembered it any more. So, again, it was a dead end, no matter the pun.

I had to wonder if Samuel Duvall and the others simply didn't want the book written. Finishing it would put an end to their haunting me. Yet, that didn't explain why they would have been murdering the witches. If it was them. We'd considered that before that it made some sense given how no living suspect could be found, but it had and still seemed too implausible. I was going to have to ask Francine about that again though, when I went back to my room after a while.

Alice lowered herself onto the edge of the chair the Mayor had vacated. Her expression was one of confusion, dismay, and a refusal to believe. She stared silently at the fire for several seconds, shaking her head as she tried to take in what we'd just told her.

"To answer your question, India, I don't know how to react," she finally said.

"I guess I'm still trying to cope with it, too," I told her. That and more.

"You're saying that Samuel attacked you? That he grabbed your arm?"

"Those were burn marks on my arms from his hands," I told her.

"And these hounds were somehow conjured to kill you?"

"Followed, probably, by that drifter," I replied. "I don't know how, but I'm sure something influenced him. I'm sure he would have attacked me."

"This is all very preposterous," she said, seemingly wanting to believe us, but having serious trouble.

"I know," I told her. "I'm going through it and it's still hard for me to take in. But, it is real. I seem to be some sort of focal point. I don't know why, but I am."

She turned a troubled expression to the logs and flames and thought for long moments. We all said nothing, leaving her to sort those thoughts out. Her eyes were on the crackling fire, but I don't think she was seeing it.

"I think I'm going to go do something I rarely do anymore," she told us finally.

"What's that, Nana?" Robert asked.

"Pray over it," she said and Robert gave a start. This had to be a monumental action on her part. "If you're saying all this is real, then there's only one place to turn. God."

Robert moved his mouth, but wasn't able to come up with any words. Alice Duvall excused herself and went out. Robert swallowed uneasily.

"Maybe we shouldn't have said anything," he said, worry creasing his forehead.

"Praying is a big thing for her?"

He nodded. "She only does it, when something has scared her terribly."

"Damn," I said. He was right. Maybe we shouldn't have said anything. She had a right to know, didn't she? I thought she did. It was her family, even if she couldn't do anything about them. It was confusing to my tired mind, dulled by wine at dinner and brandy after. A bad combination for someone that wasn't turning out to be much of a detective.

"Maybe we should do some sort of exorcism," occurred to me.

Robert shook his head. "We thought about that after Phyllis was run off. The psychic or whatever she was said exorcisms were for entities that did not want to leave, and so might not have worked on those that were trapped. For them, you had to find what released them."

"Which we still don't know."

"No. We don't," he said with a smirk. "I've tried to find out. Believe me, I've tried."

"I believe you," I replied. "As the Duvall male heir, you're next. That is, if the curse is true."

"I tried not to believe it," he told me. "That was hard to do after Phyllis' sighting. Even more so with what's happened to you."

"You were hoping my research would uncover the key you'd missed."

"I was running out of options," he admitted with a nod. "I hadn't counted on liking you."

"That's a complication how?"

He reached over and took my hand. "Because it puts you in harm's way," he said. "I hadn't known that would be the case when I commissioned you. But it's worked out that way. It's your safety versus the needle in a haystack. You've pretty much sifted the entire haystack already. So now we need to worry about your safety."

"Unless I was looking at the wrong things," I suggested. As touching as his concern was, finding an answer that put an end to it was the smart thing to do. "We can go through it all again to see what didn't seem important to the history."

A light came into his eyes, that proverbial glimmer of hope. "Yes. Maybe I should have said something sooner."

"I would have thought you were nuts," I told him.

"Okay," he said. "Only, either work here or the mansion, if you're not going to do it in St. Louis. Stay where we can be sure you're safe."

"Such as not going out to Coven Ridge to observe Samhain with the witches?"

He smirked at me. "Yes. I really wish you'd reconsider and come to the costume party at the club with us. It's not that we object to your friendship with them. We don't. It's just that we're concerned for your safety."

"I'll be perfectly fine, Robert," I assured him, while my active mind reminded me that was what the next victim in a slasher movie would say. "Where safer could I be than surrounded by a score of women that know how to protect me from what's out there?"

"I suppose," he wasn't convinced. "If you change

your mind, just say so. We can certainly put together a striking costume for you from all the parties before."

"Striking?" I asked and there was a good bit of a leer in the smile now. I gently took my hand back. "Time to call it a night, I'd say. A separate night."

He pouted playfully, but then smiled. His next question was a surprise. "May I come visit you, when you shift the work to St. Louis?"

What was a surprise was that he was asking. I would not have expected anything less aggressive than showing up unannounced with dinner reservations made for us. Maybe I had gotten him wrong. Or maybe something was different about him too.

"Of course you can," I told him without giving it much thought, although I was thinking I probably should have. I was picking up on him thinking about me first, rather than his own plans. "Are you falling in love with me, Robert?" Before Melissa had opened me up, I never would have been bold enough to ask that question.

"I don't know," he confessed. "You're different from other women."

"Are you just saying that?" Again my own directness surprised me.

"No," he said with a shake of his head, "In fact, you even seem to have changed from when you first arrived, or at least have turned out not to be what I had expected."

That much was true, I had to admit, as his words were echoing my own thoughts over the last several days. "So, what are you saying, then?"

"That I don't want the end of the book to be the end of knowing you," he said. "I don't really get what I'm feeling other than I don't want to say goodbye to you in a week's time or whenever it is when you've finished."

"You won't," I assured him. "I have to admit you're not turning out to be exactly what I expected either."

"So, are you saying yes to my visiting?"

"I'm not making any promises, Robert," I clarified. "I'm not telling you there's anything more than curiosity there."

"Curiosity," he said with a sideward glance and a nod of his head. "Yes, that's what it is. I've never known anyone that's made me so curious before."

"I suppose that's a good thing," I replied.

"It was meant to be," he told me. Smiling, he stood and stretched with a long, fatigued breath. "It's definitely been different since you arrived. I'm still trying to take in everything that's happened."

"That makes two of us."

He headed for the door. "Well, I'll leave you to finish up for the night. Sleep well, if you're not coming in to help me sleep well."

"Go to bed, Robert," I told him half-playful and the other half-admonishing.

Fatigue had robbed him of his usual swagger. Either that or there really were too many thoughts running around in his head. I hadn't expected him to be capable of such deep self-reflection. I was beginning to think I had been wrong about that. Or perhaps his world had been rocked as well and it was less reflection and more simply being lost.

I gave some thought to sneaking into his room later, but my senses were that it would be an unwise move right after that conversation, as though I would be telling him that there was actually more than curiosity there. Logic and caution were slowly returning to me, and somewhere in the back of my mind, that suspicious girl was warning me not to be taken in by the charm and the careful use of the right words. Wait it out to be sure he's for real before you end up merely rewarding his salesmanship. Be sure he wasn't like all the Roberts before him.

I went to my own room, to my own bed, in my own sleepwear.

That night, the dream pillow did its job.

I dreamt of being married to Richards and the mother of two perfect children, a handsome preteen boy and a pig-tailed girl in summer dresses. They played on a swing set out back of the estate as I picked fresh tomatoes and basil from the garden for Agnes' famous sauce. There was peace in the woods beyond the property line and calm across our grounds. Robert came home from work and the kids ran to him.

The dream morphed to the library, where he sat with feet extended to the fire and a well-tapped brandy bottle to his left. A storm raged outside like an angry lion wanting in, but being frustrated. I was safe and warm inside and feeling loved, until Robert spoke.

"I only needed to get married and have children to carry on the blood line," he told me. "You were there and willing."

I couldn't think of anything to say. The building seemed to shake and begin cracking apart as he spoke. The fire hissed and cackled like an old hag. Cold rain began soaking the area around me.

"Realizing how Melissa's death had ended their blood line had gotten me to thinking I needed to do something fast to preserve ours and your curious nature made you the choicest woman in Willow Creek," he concluded. "That's all there was to it."

And then, I was standing alone on Coven Ridge with the bloody Chinese sword in my hand and looking down at an angry river slamming through the rocks below. The storm was all around me, but still did not touch me. The wind battered its way through the trees and tried to push me over the precipice, but it hardly stirred my hair as it broke around my body. I had somehow separated and isolated myself from it all.

I felt nothing. Not love or anger, nor hope or despair. I became a hole in the world; a void without emotion or thought, seeing but not seen. What came to me, I dealt with dispassionately. I could no longer be affected. The world I had known no longer existed. I was Fate and I was cruel.

I awoke feeling horrified, not at Robert's duplicity,

but at the feeling of having had no compassion left in me. The storm had abated, but the wind and the rain were still busy in the pitch dark forest. It was still the middle of the night and there was nothing to see but deep black. Careful not to trip the alarm sensors I cracked opened the window a hair to get some fresh air and was weakened by waves of relief that came at smelling the clean rain and heady forest scents. It was as though I breathed in my lost love for the world with them.

After a few minutes, I had shaken the feeling the dream had left me with. I had gotten a little chilly from the cool air blowing in, but rather than closing the window, I pulled the heavy robe under my chin and tucked my feet under me in the big chair and continued to breathe the real world in. I fell asleep for while in that position, only to wake with cramps in my legs and neck a couple of hours later at five a.m.

I didn't feel like sleeping anymore, despite being tired still. I didn't fear another dream. There was just an aversion to getting back into bed. It was too dark and wet for a run outside even if it had been safe, and too early to hit the treadmill in the basement. The noise would have awoken everyone and the neighbors half a mile away. I opted for soaking in a hot tub, where sleep found me again for a while.

Agnes noticed at breakfast that I wasn't my usual chipper self, as much as I ever am in the morning. All I told her was I'd had a bad dream, but was okay. I headed off to the old mansion to work to be away from anything Richards. I'd regained my sense of compassion. However, the feeling of having been duped, even though it had just been a dream, remained.

The dream itself stayed with me during the day, nagging at me as though I should have been seeing something from it. Great detective that I wasn't, the hunch didn't finally gel until halfway through the afternoon. I'd kept thinking about how Robert needed to find a wife soon and about how Melissa had said she had needed to find a husband soon so as to have a daughter and carry on the line.

Bloodlines.

One now gone and another close to dying off. It all seemed to relate to bloodlines.

That was when my crazy connection-making mind came up with the thought that scared me and spurred me to switch over to my genealogy website accounts. There had been another involved in everything a hundred years ago.

I typed in the name Harzchuck and began tracing the second line of Baltus Sammic. He had indeed remarried and begun another family out west. The line had been thin, though, without many children and branches to it. It did lead me horrifyingly to the first grandson of Sammic's first grandson. That second grandson was a childless widower with the distinctive name of Sandoval Willis.

The paranormal investigator had alibied out for both murders. But what did that mean, when you were strong in the black arts? When perhaps you could influence the minds of others?

I heard yelling in the hallway, but it wasn't from anyone living. As goose bumps covered me and chills rattled my spine, I recognized Samuel Duvall's scream of rage from the hallway. I had learned what they had feared.

I collected my breath and forced myself to remain calm. I knew who and in general how, but this was going to take some proving, particularly to the FBI. So, I printed everything out in a nice, neat chart to bring to Richards and Levinson, while I called Francine to tell her.

"I'm such a fool," was her reaction. "Why didn't I think of this? Of course, he would have taught the black arts to his male heirs."

"Well, maybe not so much taught," I said as something from the chart caught my attention.

"What do you mean?"

"Sammic, as Harzchuck died on the thirteenth birthday of his first grandson," I noted from the chart. "That grandson later died on the thirteenth birthday of his first grandson, Sandoval Willis. What do make of that?"

"Sequential possessions," she said. "The theory we rejected as requiring too powerful of a spirit to take over several random people. Only it wasn't random and it was long term. I can see where that was possible. In fact, I don't see why it wouldn't be."

"He passed from one body to the next as the grandsons came of age."

"Yes. And now he's come back."

"To finish the job," I said. "He had no children. So his line has ended. He came back to make sure yours did too, which was why he went after Mel and her cousins, those of child bearing age."

"That leaves just Richards," she pointed out. "He may not believe you, but you need to warn him. Be careful, Willis had two reasons to want you dead. One, to keep you from finding this out; and two, which he still has, because you're of child bearing age and Richards likes you."

I hadn't thought of that, but one reason was enough, wasn't it? There was just one thing that still didn't fit.

"Why would Sammic have bound the male Duvalls to the cellar here?" I asked.

"I don't know," Francine replied. "That still doesn't make sense, given they sided with him and helped him escape. Something is still not quite right. You still need to warn Richards."

"On my way," I told her and hung up.

As I rose from the table, I heard the growls from the hallway and froze for a second. For that one long moment, my mind's eye saw the hounds standing just outside the door. But the growls, I was certain, had been those of men not beasts. I walked over to the door and listened at the jamb. There were no sounds beyond it.

Carefully, with my entire body behind it to force it shut if necessary, I gingerly cracked it open. No hounds. No sounds or even scents from the hall other than old dirt and ice cold stone. I opened it more and looked out and gave a start.

Samuel Duvall stood a foot from the door and sneered at me. Behind him were others I had seen in photographs. They stood as though intending to block my way. The thing was I had lost my fear of them with the necklace I wore. I only feared the hounds now and they were not present. Perhaps they couldn't materialize during the day or so close to the blessed room I was in. I didn't know and I wasn't going to wait around to see.

I shut the door and rushed back for my equipment. Samuel Duvall and the others would still be there when I opened it again, I knew. There was nothing they could do now. I released the door confidently on my way out. He was still there as expected.

"What did you do?" I asked impulsively, the idea simply coming to me as I asked. "What made Sammic curse you all?"

He didn't answer. He simply glowered. If he had been real, I probably would have shouldered past him. The memory of the burn from his touch and the nearly healed marks he'd left on my arm gave me pause. I knew the necklace would keep him from getting near to me. No one had ever said what would happen if I touched them.

"You can't stop me now, Samuel," I told him. "Tell me what you did and maybe I can fix it."

"You can't stop anything," was all he said and his tone made me half believe him.

"Get back, then," I told him and took the necklace from under my blouse. Keeping it around my neck, I held the stones out toward him and advanced. He stepped back and it took everything I had to keep my poker face and not sigh in relief. He kept begrudgingly retreating as I came out of the room and pulled the door shut behind me. I had room to get past them now. I let the necklace hang loosely and turned away from them, feeling my back itch in expectation of being grabbed again as I walked away. But, they couldn't touch me.

I walked up and out of the basement as calmly as I could manage and out onto the porch where I paused in the chilly sunlight to take several calming breaths and make sure the hounds were not waiting for me out there. When I was sure it was safe, I went down the steps and away from the old mansion for the last time, although I hadn't known it would be so at the time.

Despite how crazy it would sound to him, I went straight to the Sheriff's office. It was late in the day and with the long hours they'd been putting in, thanks to me in no small part, Levinson had left a little early. There was going to be an All Hallows Eve, or All Saints Day, service at the Baptist Church that night. He had gone to rest a bit before attending.

I had them try calling his cell, catching him out in the hills picking up his grandparents for the service. The connection barely held together as I tried to explain it to him.

"I know who the killer is," I told him and immediately thought how stupid and TV-like I sounded; the writer figuring out the whodunit for the cops. "I know it sounds crazy, but it's Sandoval Willis."

"We've already cleared him," Levinson sounded annoyed.

"Baltus Sammic was his grandfather's grandfather," I explained. "He's a blood relation."

"What? Are you sure?" He took me seriously now.

"I have the genealogical records to prove it. Willis has become his great-great grandfather and has come back to finish the job from a hundred years ago."

"That's just on the edge of plausibility," he admitted. "The only part that's confusing is that Willis packed up and left town the week before. Why leave before he finished the job?"

"Maybe he figures he has," I answered. "With

Melissa and her similar aged cousins dead, there are no more women of child bearing age in the family. He's ended the bloodline from Bernadette Sammic, too."

"I guess that could be a motive," Levinson replied. "We'll need to see what the FBI profiler thinks. Then, we'll have to figure out how he managed to be in two places at once. Remember, he was teaching class in Ames, when Melissa and Brianna were killed."

"I think I can explain that, too," I told him. "It's a bit much for the phone, though."

"Are you coming to services tonight?" he asked and I suddenly felt that it would have been bad form to not have been planning on going.

"I'll bring what I have to the church, then," I answered obliquely.

"We'll be able to talk in the back."

"Okay. See you there."

"Willis?" asked the Deputy that had overheard my half of the conversation.

"Yes," I said and handed him the genealogy chart with Willis' name circled. "He wants the FBI to see this."

"I'll fax it right over," he said and went to do so. I was sure Levinson was going to be angry over that. I hadn't actually asked the Deputy to do so, and I hadn't told him anything that wasn't true. I had given him the idea, and I was sure Levinson would. I would have to argue that time was of the essence, as lawyers said.

Chart back in hand, I headed for Richards. Dusk was falling as I rolled around to the back. It was quiet. I could still see through the tree line relatively well. That wasn't going to be the case, when I came back out. If the hounds had been there just then, I would have seen them clearly. In another twenty minutes or so, they were going to have the advantage. I parked as close to the kitchen door as I could, which was about five feet away.

Richards and Mrs. Duvall were already gone. There were involved in some charity event that preceded the services and so had gone over an hour ago. They had invited me, but I had been non-committal. It had seemed like the last step to being assimilated into them and I couldn't take it then. Now, I hurriedly changed into something suitable for services from the Phyllis collection and rushed to the back door.

I looked out the slim windows on either side of the door to be sure the coast was clear, then hopped out and into my car and was on my way. Still, I arrived a few minutes after services had started. The usher walked me forward along the outer aisle up to where Alice Duvall and Richards were sitting with Mayor Baker and his wife. It was little embarrassing, being inserted amongst them toward the top of the pecking order. However, I slipped in alongside Mrs. Duvall quietly and tried to follow along.

I wasn't much of a church person. In fact, I've never really been much of an organized religion person. Perhaps that was why I was more inclined to accept witchcraft. Because the order that it had was meant to be in line with the natural order of the world and of people. I could accept that.

The Willow Creek Baptist service, like so many I've experienced, was another of the self-re-affirming theologue kinds. They believed in the one true God and practiced the one true faith, so they were good people. Everyone else needed their pity and to get their acts together before it was too late. I was jaded on formal religions and had been for a long time.

I was wearing the necklace from Melissa, after all. It didn't catch on fire or scar my neck or anything in God's house. He must have been okay with it and the witches, so they had to be cool people, I mused. I'd admit it was snide. I've never understood how a religion can claim humility, while being self-righteous about it. That always seemed to be a contradiction to me.

As the service ended, I leaned toward Richards and told him I had something for him and the Sheriff. The look of happiness that I had joined them as one of the family bled from his face, replaced by one of confusion and worry. He slipped past Alice, who had been between us and followed me toward the back, where Levinson found us.

"What have you got?" he asked and I produced the family tree for Sammic/Harzchuck. Richards glanced over his shoulder and his eyes bugged out on landing on the circled name.

"You're sure about this?" Levinson asked.

I nodded. "I used a couple of sites. Both had the same records. We can get the birth and death certificates, if we need them."

"This is incredible," Gus said. "I feel a little embarrassed I didn't think of it."

"It came to me in a dream last night," I told him. Melissa's dream pillow had done nothing for me in all the weeks I'd had it, yet, in the end, it led me to her killer.

"Had to be some dream," Gus remarked.

"Yes, it was," I said.

"I would say not to tell the Wiccans until we run it past the FBI and get their opinion," he said. "I don't want to get them worked up over it, if the profiler said it wasn't plausible. But...you told them already, didn't you?"

"Yes."

"You told them before you called me, didn't you?"

"Yes."

"Is your Sheriff Guy going to have an exasperating pseudo helper?" he asked, making me grin a bit sheepishly. "What else does she do?"

I think I flushed. It was like being caught using crib notes by a favored professor instead of actually reading the assigned book. I answered with slightly averted eyes, "She kind of has a Deputy fax the chart to the FBI."

He pursed his lips and for a second I wasn't sure if he was going to be angry or laugh. "He tells her to leave law enforcement to him, I suppose."

"She's sorry for getting carried away."

"I see."

"What are you two talking about?" Richards asked.

"Nothing," Levinson told him. "This may give us motive. We still don't have opportunity. We have witnesses that place him back in Iowa."

"I know."

"On the phone you said you thought you had that figured out," Levinson reminded me. "Did you mean accomplices? People lying about him being at the university? Because he was teaching a class when Brianna was killed."

I was backed into a corner. I opened my mouth and now I had to go through with it. I know I had said I wanted to try running the paranormal reasons by him before, but I had wavered toward being cautious again.

"You're not suggesting he was in both places at once, are you?" Richards asked.

"Something like that," I told them.

"What?" Levinson asked, leaning in on my reluctance.

"Obviously, he was here," I said. "The people that said they saw him in Ames were made to think they'd seen him."

"You mean hypnotized?"

"Something like that."

"The FBI is going to want a little more," Levinson pointed out.

The FBI was going to put me in a straight-jacket, I figured.

"Wait a minute," Richards said. "You're not saying that it's magic or something paranormal? You're not saying this is really Sammic we're dealing with?"

"The ghosts are real," I replied. "We know that for a fact. How hard is it to think Sammic hasn't possessed his successive grandsons? I mean, look at the dates of death and the birthdates of those grandsons. That can't be coincidence twice in a row."

"Or maybe it's part of what set him off," Levinson replied. "Crazy coincidences that he sees a pattern in. That's a symptom of schizophrenia. He has no children, so he comes here to end the line from his great-great grandmother, like you were saying, too. The copycat nature of the beheading makes sense in that regard."

"I suppose," I allowed. I'd always felt there was something wrong with the man. Being off his rocker and carrying out killings for his long dead great-great grandfather was definitely more earthly than the possession theory. In his demented mind, he may have blamed the witches for the end of his bloodline. It didn't have to make sense to a sane mind. It didn't have to resemble even half a reason to us normal people. It only had to matter to him.

"This is good work, India," Gus said to me. "I'm impressed you found this. Don't let that imagination of yours get the better of you. Go on back to the house and treat yourself to a good night's sleep. I'm sure it will be clearer in the morning."

"What will be clearer in the morning?" asked Alice Duvall, wandering into the conversation.

Richards told her what I'd found out and her eyes popped wide.

"Dear God!" she exclaimed. "He was right there in front of us the whole time? How did he pull it off? You have got someone watching him, haven't you?"

The three of us went mute and blank faced. For all our focus on the how and why, we'd not given the obvious a single thought.

"Excuse me while I go call the FBI," Levinson said and headed out to his car.

"Let's get home," Richards suggested and Mrs. Duvall nodded her agreement.

"Come along with us," she told me.

"I want to hear what the FBI says," I said.

"I'll call Gus, when we get home," Richards said. "Right now, let's head home together. No driving alone at night for you. Okay?"

I wanted to argue, but he was right. There was safety in numbers and Levinson couldn't escort me later.

He had his own family to drive home. I relented and followed them back to their mansion where Richards waited with the garage door open for me to make the quicker dash into it than to the kitchen door. All was quiet in the black, wet forest.

Robert called Levinson immediately, as promised, as the garage door closed, only to find out he'd had to leave messages for both agents. Gus had also tried the campus police in Ames, but they had been uncooperative and the city cops had wanted to hear from the FBI first. There was nothing more we could do that night, they assured me. I still felt we should have been doing something. If not patrolling the woods, then trying to convince the police in Ames to watch Willis. I was going to have to content myself with feeling relieved that Francine and the others knew who to watch out for, and the wheels were at least in motion. No matter what I said, they didn't seem to feel the same urgency.

Agnes had some hot cocoa ready for us on our return, along with some fresh oatmeal raisin cookies. It was a tradition that had started when Robert had been a child, although back then, it had been his mother making the cookies by way of bribing him to go to the weekday service. Once he had come of age, another change had occurred in the tradition. Frangelica liqeuer had come to be added to the hot cocoa. It was decadent. They were turning me into a fat lush.

We were in the library in a semi-circle in front of the fire. A third chair had been added to the setup, replacing the desk chair I'd been using. We were all sinking wearily into microfiber plushness, with the alcohol, cold weather, and long days taking their toll.

Alice Duvall did not go for seconds tonight.

"I'm all in," she declared with a yawn. "I need a good night's sleep tonight. I'm on the decorating committee for the costume ball tomorrow. I do wish you'd reconsider and come with us, India, instead of the Wiccans. Nothing against them. I'd just rather you were with us."

"Thank you, Mrs. Duvall," I told her. "I want to join the other women because it will be part of saying goodbye to Melissa."

Mrs. Duvall's look of not completely getting the relationship was clear, but she nodded and said she understood anyway, before rising and heading off to bed with a rub of my shoulders.

"Well, I'm not on the decorating committee," Robert declared and poured himself another hot cocoa and Frangelica. He motioned to top mine off, but I waved him back. He grabbed another cookie and chomped half of it away in one bite. He ate them hungrily and happily like the child they always brought him back to being. He was so neat when he ate anything other than these cookies; it gave me a small smile.

For a moment, the thought of sleeping with him went through my mind. And it was gone a second later. The alcohol, the fatigue, the worry about Willis, and the fact that knowing tomorrow we would be making our final farewells to Melissa had me missing her as much as ever; they were adding up to making me feel needy. I pushed it back. I had a question for him anyway; why he wouldn't have wanted me to warn the witches.

"I really wish you'd stay out of it," he told me, beating me to the punch and killing any mood that had been starting.

I knew what he meant and my ire was raised. "Out of what?"

"The investigation. Leave it to the professionals."

"They didn't find the connection. I did."

"They can take it from there, India." He sounded exasperated. "I don't want you anywhere near them anymore. I'm afraid for your safety."

"I know, but you needn't be. It won't just be Francine and me tomorrow, you know. They started gathering a week ago. It would be a lot safer if you'd listen to me about finding Willis tonight."

"We've called everyone we can call," he replied. "I

know the women have been gathering. I'm afraid of what could happen if they get any more stirred up."

"Nothing will happen, Robert. They're peaceful people, not the lynch mob type."

"Neither are we," he commented, confusing me.

"Sorry?"

"I mean, I don't want to be judgmental, but I'm not entirely as convinced as you are that they'll stay peaceful. Think about it, they're being pushed into a corner, so to speak. Who knows how they might react?"

"You're worrying too much."

"I worry about you. I don't want anything to happen to you."

He was inclined on the arms of my chair, his face a little more than a foot from mine. I could see in his eyes that he really did care, even if he was being stupid. When he leaned in, I let him kiss me. It was caring, not hungry. For one more split second, the thought of sleeping with him returned, but I pushed the thought back again.

Part of me was still trying to take me back to where I had been, to familiar territory as it were, to return me to solid emotional ground. That part of me had never cared whether a relationship had been healthy or not. It wanted me to be with Robert, my usual type of mate, as though the world would revert back to normal with me. My instincts were saying "no." As they always had. I no longer ignored them.

After briefly holding our foreheads together, I pushed him back, but kept my hand on his shoulder. "I'm sorry, Robert. I still need some time"

"We have time," he told me lowly. "Please promise me you'll leave the investigation to the professionals. If you don't want to go to the party with us, then at least stay here. Promise me you won't put yourself in harm's way."

"I won't be in harm's way, Robert," I told him. "I can promise you that much."

"You didn't think you were when those hounds showed up," he pointed out. "Those women are all in harm's way. You can't help but put yourself in harm's way just by being with them."

I was already edgy. His insistence was making me angry. "I'll be all right, Robert," I replied a little testily and gave him a gentle push as I started to rise. "I'm tired. I need to get some sleep."

He moved aside to let me rise with an exasperated look on his face. He knew he had started to piss me off and was smart enough to shut up, or just too tired himself to keep arguing. I headed to bed wondering what in the hell I was thinking, giving him encouragement by telling him I needed more time. I didn't need any time. I was leaving soon and forgetting them when the book was done. I don't know why I'd bothered to be gentle or let him kiss me for that matter. Yeah, I was regaining control over my mind and emotions, all right. Hardly.

I shed the Phyllis clothes and crawled into bed in my usual shorts and sleeveless T. I wasn't sleeping in the Phyllis PJs anymore. I felt like I had started acting like someone else and needed to get my act back together. Only how does one go back to being herself when you were no longer sure who that was?

Chapter 19
Samhain

I didn't dream that night, unless you count constant visions of Willis laughing at me for the fool I was. Now, I understood why he'd never said anything about me screaming that night when Samuel Duvall attacked me. He had told Duvall to attack me. I didn't need to join the witches to be in danger. I only needed to be anywhere at all in Willow Creek.

I was rubbing my eyes and drinking strong coffee at the kitchen table when Richards came in, dressed casually, the next morning. He would be working at home that day. He plopped into a chair as Agnes poured him a mug of super steaming coffee.

"I heard from Gus," he told me. "The FBI found the connection to be significant, but when they'd sent someone to question him, Willis wasn't there. Apparently, he hasn't been home for a couple of days."

"You waited until now to tell me?" I was pissed.

I'd told them they needed to move last night.

"You said you needed sleep," he replied. "We figure he has to be in the area somewhere, so Gus has got everyone calling the hotels and checking campsites and anything we can think of. He's enlisted all of the Sheriffs in the neighboring counties. An alert is out for Willis' car, too."

"You should have started this last night," I told him.

He ignored my words. "I told Gus you'd keep a low profile. That you'd stay in the house so he doesn't have to worry about watching out for you, as well."

"I planned on working until it's time to head over," I told him. I was still upset, but I couldn't argue the logic in giving Levinson one less thing to worry about. He wouldn't need to, but I knew he would. Robert waiting until I woke up to tell me something important, because of what I'd said before angered me. No sense of what my priorities would be. Typical. "It's not like I'm going very far."

"What are you supposed to do for them anyway?" He wondered.

"Nothing," I answered. "Not being a witch I don't have anything to do other than to prepare emotionally to honor my beloved dead, which includes my parents and other relatives, not just Melissa."

"That's what Halloween means to them?"

"It's called Samhain," I pointed out. "It's for that and to welcome the end of the growing season so the earth can rest and renew for the next one. It's also the end of the Celtic year, like the end of the Celtic day is when the sun goes down. The year and the day both begin with the world starting to rest, refreshing itself."

"Why is it like that?" It seemed weird to him, having grown up tied to a clock.

"It was an agrarian society, based on when you could work the fields. The day ended when it was too dark to do so and the year ended when the growing season was over," I explained, which were all things Melissa had taught me in telling about her study of all religions. "You needn't worry about tonight. I basically intend to keep working until after dark, then go meet them."

"That's good," he said. "I'll be working from home. Halloween is a big deal here. We close the offices and warehouses early so parents can safely take the kids trick or treating and then to a pot-luck dinner at the Community Center. It's an annual thing for them. The entire town celebrates Halloween, not just us at the Country Club. It's too bad the old mansion is in such bad shape, though. I've been saying it would have made a great haunted house, maybe draw some people in from out of town, and make some money for the city."

"I thought the same thing on first seeing it," I told him.

He smiled as he rose from the chair. "Brilliant minds, eh," he said. "Anyway, it's off to work for me. I've got some calls to make." He headed for his office as I finished the simple breakfast of toast, jam, and fruit. I told Agnes I was worried about breaking my bathroom scale when I got back, so she'd fixed me a lighter breakfast and promised a healthier lunch for me, as well. You probably could have wrung the cholesterol from me at that point.

Despite feeling on edge, the day went by fairly quickly and simply, everyone's anticipation for the night growing. Agnes was not cooking because dinner would be at the various events. For me, it would be back at Francine's after the prayers and rites on Coven Ridge. I hadn't mentioned it to Richards, but I expected to stay the night there in Melissa's room.

Alice Duvall, dressed as Queen Elizabeth, headed out first late in the afternoon as dusk fell to oversee the final decorating of the club. Her costume was perfect as one would have expected and she was affecting the royal attitude with humor.

"*We* still hope to see you there," she told me almost off-handedly just before leaving.

A while later, after night had taken over outside, Agnes came in to show off her Little Bo Peep costume to me with a huge, impish grin. It was definitely no child's costume!

"Wow, do you look dishy or what," I told her. "Are you trying to kill that cowboy of yours?"

"Hah," she laughed sarcastically. "If there was one. Maybe I'll knock a few off their horses. If not, there's always this." She brandished the hooked shepherd's staff.

"I don't think you'll need that," I told her and she laughed again.

"Have a blessed evening, Indy," she told me. "Yes, I do know a little of the Wiccan ways. I'll see you later."

Richards, in absolutely perfect vampire get-up, came in as she was reaching the door. His eyes widened and eyebrows went up at the sight of Agnes in her outfit.

"Oh my! Perhaps I should have dressed as a sheep," he remarked. "You look marvelous!"

She just waved a hand at him with a laugh and went out. Maybe she wasn't attracted to him, but she was clearly pleased with the compliment.

"I've come for your blood," he said in a terrible accent and exaggerating going after my neck with his cape flared out.

I laughed and pushed him back. My unease had ebbed and I was feeling more relaxed. I couldn't have known this would be our last light moment ever. Not that I would have changed what was about to come.

"No, you haven't, you cad," I told him. "You've come to try talking me into that lady pirate costume you were showing me earlier."

"You have to admit, you'd be the envy of all in that outfit."

"If I didn't die of embarrassment." It was hotter than Agnes' had been, if I'd had the right body for it. "I'm not changing my mind. You know why."

"I do, but I just want you to be safe."

"I'll be in a protective circle surrounded by a lot of capable women," I tried to assure him once again.

"I wouldn't bet my life on that," he said. "I really don't want you to either."

"The protections work. I've seen it."

"Those things are still out there. Those wolves or hounds."

"Then let's call Gus and have him assign a couple of Deputies to guard the witches. He should be doing that anyway."

"He is and they'll be in danger, too," he answered. Then, his face took on a serious note that startled and alarmed me. "It won't work, India. You can't go out there tonight."

"Why?" I demanded. A light came on in the back of my mind. "What will happen?"

"I don't know," he told me, but it was obvious he was lying.

And then, it became crystal clear that he'd been lying all along just as my instincts had been telling me from the start.

"You haven't told me everything, have you?" I asked.

He stood tense and irresolute, unprepared to answer me, and turned away.

"You know what's going on, don't you?" I prompted.

He answered me with more silence and not facing me.

"Tell me, Robert."

He wouldn't, or couldn't, and forced me to play my trump card without even thinking about it first. "If you want me to trust you and someday love you, then you've got to be honest with me. Tell me the truth."

The obvious conflict and frustration in him boiled over. He shook his fists at the sky and screamed. He half staggered away from me to the middle of the room and shuddered with anxious aggravation.

"What!" I yelled at him. We were alone in the house at that point. There was no one to hear our argument.

"Why can't you just listen to me?" he pleaded in exasperation, grabbing his head. "You're driving me crazy!"

"Willis is really Sammic, isn't he?" I said.

He dropped his arms to his side and sighed. "Yes," he confirmed simply with a tone of giving in.

"You knew? You knew all along?"

"Yes."

"Yet, you did nothing?" I was beyond astonished. "You didn't even warn me. When someone I loved was murdered, you didn't even say a word."

"I never thought you'd be targeted."

I was shaking with anger. It was all I could do to keep from going into a rage and doing to him what Willis had done to Melissa. I had to know how he knew, so I kept it together and calmly posed the question. "Tell me, Robert. How do you know who he really is? How did you know about the possession?"

His answer chilled me to my core. "He told me."

My throat went dry and I trembled from my center out. For a moment, I couldn't even think. For a man that professed to have feelings for me to also have concealed the truth about a madman wanting to kill me was simply astounding. I couldn't fathom it. I wanted to beat him silly with the first thing I could lay my hands on, but I took a deep breath and plowed on for the reason.

"I need an explanation." How could he have betrayed me like this?

He sighed and sat down in front of the cold fireplace. He never faced me once as he told me the story.

"There was no prosperity spell," he told me. "There was no deal between Sammic, Samuel Duvall and the others. The arrangement was that the Duvalls would try and convict all of the members of the Coven for the murders of Bernadette Sammic and her mother, as though it had been some sort of ritual sacrifice they'd all been in on. They would all have been hung back in the day."

"They're not like that. How could they have expected that to work?"

"We're talking a century ago," he answered. "People didn't know any better then. My ancestors were to finish what Sammic had started. Even if people would have believed it, a trial for witchcraft was an embarrassingly antiquated concept and they had no stomach for mass murder.

"They fell back on harassment, slowly driving the witches away instead. Because they didn't put the Coven to death, Sammic put a curse on them, interrupting their reincarnation and binding their souls to the old mansion in punishment. Had any of us ever finished the job, he would have lifted it. None of us could go through with that. Samuel Duvall probably hadn't ever intended to go through with it."

"But why?" I questioned. "Why make a bargain in which you got nothing in return?"

"Samuel Duvall hadn't wanted the embarrassment of a sensational trial involving witches and warlocks," Robert answered. "Business was starting to boom here and they were afraid that kind of notoriety would have ruined the town. Allowing Sammic to escape spared Samuel and Willow Creek from that shame."

I couldn't respond. Sammic had needed to offer nothing to the town's leaders. Samuel Duvall and the rest had acted out of their own greed and fear.

At my silence, Robert continued, "We went on hoping we'd eventually find a way to remove the curse. We tried a lot of different things, including my hiring you."

"Why has he come back?"

"When Willis didn't have any children and knew his line was ending, he came back to finish the job himself," Robert told me. "Just like you thought."

"Robert," I sighed. Who was he? What kind of man did this?

"I hadn't known a thing until Willis came to me the week you started the job," he carried on explaining. "Willis hadn't known you were going to be at the mansion or researching our history. He was afraid you'd find out about him, which you did, and he was leery of killing a visitor. He didn't want to attract attention."

"What did he do?"

"He contacted me and promised he would lift the curse on all of us, including me and any future generations of mine, if I made sure you didn't get in the way."

"What?" I couldn't believe it. "You knew it was him all this time? You knew and did nothing?"

"I didn't expect you to become friends with them," he said, standing and looking at me with an expression asking for understanding. "I didn't imagine you would give them much thought. Then, you became friends with Ferrier and Willis felt he had to take action. He kept trying things to scare you away. Samuel Duvall, releasing them all from the cellar, then the hounds. We had no idea you'd become more than just friends with Melissa."

"You let him kill her," I breathed out. I was numb and trembling from head to toe in shock. "How could you have done that?"

What kind of man was this in front of me?

He turned away from me again and returned his stare to the cold fireplace. There had been an answer in his eyes, but he hadn't wanted to say it.

"Robert?" There was so much pain in my voice, while I was too astonished yet to begin crying. I felt the horror and the rage and the despair I'd felt on finding Melissa dead pressing on me again, wanting to take over.

"It was either them or my own soul, and that of my father and grandfather and uncles and all," he told me. "Which would you have chosen?"

I was disgusted. "I can't believe you agreed to abet murder."

"I told you I was desperate," he returned half-angrily. "I told myself it was partly their fault anyway for not having controlled Sammic a hundred years ago. I wouldn't have been in that position if they'd handled it correctly."

"That's ridiculous," I told him. "You can't blame these women for something their ancestors did. He was uncontrollable anyway."

"He still is," Robert replied and turned back to me. He leaned on one of the arm chairs and faced me over the table. "I didn't know what to do. It was either them or my own family. Which would you have chosen? You've seen what he can do. There were no options!"

I did see his dilemma, but my heart was with the witches. There was more to this than what he'd already confessed.

"He's planning to attack them on Coven Ridge, isn't he?" I guessed. "That's why you're so adamant about my not going up there."

He hung his head. There was no denying he'd known about it for some time. "He told me not to take any action to keep the gathering from occurring tonight. Everything he's done to date has been meant to draw them all to that spot in solidarity so he could finish them off."

"You *can't* let that happen," I told him.

"In exchange for my soul not being damned, I agreed to look the other way," he told me. "You know what will happen to me if I go up there."

"Your own God will damn you for it," I pointed out. "Whether you wield the sword or not, you're still party to murder, to Melissa's murder."

He raised his eyes to me, torn and terrified, but he couldn't find a reply or the will to move.

Tears finally found the corners of my eyes. "Robert, you let him kill someone I loved."

I think then he finally saw the pain that realization was causing me; that he had caused me. He hung his head again and let out a deep sigh of resignation as his conscience finally resurfaced. "I guess you're right. We brought this on ourselves. I never expected you to get involved with the Wiccans. With Melissa. And sleeping with me left me really conflicted, especially as my feelings for you have grown."

"Then be on my side. Don't let this happen."

He finally nodded and told me to keep in mind what it meant for his soul. I followed him to his office, where he called Levinson and told him that Willis was insane and had called him telling him not to let his little lady, meaning India, go anywhere near Coven Ridge, if he wanted to keep her safe. How the lie came so easily to him was astonishing. He was so good at finding the reasonable words.

I heard Levinson's voice from where I stood beside the desk. "Why would he warn us? That doesn't make sense."

"He's nuts; he doesn't have to make much sense," Robert replied. "Maybe he doesn't want to hurt anyone that isn't a descendant of Bernadette Sammic. Who knows? The fact is the women are in danger and you need to get out there right away."

"I'm on my way," I heard Levinson say and felt terror that another person I had come to like and respect was about to be in harm's way.

"Let's go," I told Robert. "What?" He blinked at me.

"Gus is farther away." I told him. "We can warn them sooner."

"I'll go," he said. "You stay here, where it's safe. He promised not to do anything to anyone in the house."

"I'm going," I said.

"Please, India," he pleaded. "Please stay here. Please stay safe. I just hope you're right that making up for past sins will get a higher power to forgive and release us from the curse."

"There is *no way* I'm not going," I told him as adamantly as he was trying to keep me from going.

He sighed and relented, as he unclasped and dropped the cape over his chair. "Okay. But run if I say so."

"Fine," I said, having no intention of running away and led the way in a fast stride toward the garage.

Although, I never got there. In the kitchen, his hands clamped onto my upper arms from behind and he literally flung me into the pantry with strength I didn't know he possessed. As I stumbled to keep on my feet, I heard a lock snap shut on the door.

"Robert! No!"

"I'll be back to let you out when I return with Francine and the others," he yelled to me. "But I'll be damned a second time over if I'm going to let you get hurt."

I yelled and pounded on the door, but knew he'd left without me. I heard and felt the vibrations of the garage door opening and closing behind him. I started looking for a way out. There was no window as it backed up to the garage. The hinges were on the outside of the door and the lock was keyed on the inside. Why the hell do you put a lock on a pantry door anyway?

I pushed on the door to find it solid. I kicked at the frame testing it and knowing my legs were strong from running. Yet, it was too solid for that even. I would have hurt myself before doing any damage to that door. It was built like one for Fort Knox.

I didn't know how to pick a lock, but it appeared to be the only option I had. I started looking for something to try using when I heard Richards coming into the kitchen. He could not have gotten there and back already. The bastard had changed his mind.

My anger boiled over and I smacked the door with both fists and yelled at the top of my lungs, "Robert Richards, you let me out of here, you bastard!"

"Indy?" called Agnes' voice in startled and confused reply. The lock snapped open and I stumbled out for hurrying to escape. "How did you get locked in there?"

"Richards did it. Why the hell does anyone lock a pantry door anyway?"

"It used to be for the liquor," she explained. "Why did he lock you up?"

"To keep me from going with him to the witches," I told her, hurrying for the back door and my car. "Thank God, you came back."

"I put my silly shepherd's staff down to dig out my keys and then forgot it of all things. The costume was wrong without it," she answered. "I'm stunned he really doesn't want you to be with the Wiccans so much."

I replied from the back door without thinking of any consequences. She liked me, but her loyalty was to Richards. "Willis is coming to kill them all and he knew it."

"What?"

"No time to explain. I have to get up there."

I whipped open the door to see the hell hounds ten feet away at Agnes' truck. With a growl, they launched at me as I spun around inside and slammed the door with my back against it. The hounds hit it with enough force to push me away from the wood. Fortunately, it was just as, if not more, solid than the pantry door. I snapped the lock shut on it. They hit it again and it creaked ominously. Sturdy or not, it wasn't going to hold.

A terrified and panting Agnes stood in the center of the kitchen, holding that huge butcher's knife, the one she'd said was like cooking with a sword.

"Sword!" I shouted and ran for the office with Agnes on my heels. It stood as it had all these weeks, point down in the wax hands of the Chinese figure in the unnaturally quiet room. I grabbed it so quickly, I broke the wax man's hands off, then bolted back for the kitchen, with Agnes and her anlance-sized knife still a step behind me.

The dogs were breaking down the back door. They'd splintered a panel and chewed away a gaping hole. Ben and Jerry were to either side and barking and growling in vain to scare them off. The first hound was clambering in as I drew back and cleaved its head in half, and then stabbed the second as it climbed over the fallen one in front of it, gnashing teeth at the hilt.

As I stepped away, dripping blood from the sword onto the tile floor, I saw two very normal wolves lying dead before me. Some magic had made them more than what they had been. I felt a sickening in my stomach and sadness at having killed them. Most of all, I held an anger at Willis for causing this and everything else that had happened.

Sword in hand, I was determined to go finish things myself. However, as hounds, the wolves had chewed away my tires and Agnes'. Both vehicles were going nowhere.

"Barricade yourself inside with the boys," I told her and took off at a dead run for the path Melissa had told me about, the one they once used for processions. Only it was no ceremonial procession going up it tonight as the thunder rumbled and rain threatened despite the forecast.

On Coven Ridge Francine and the others had set up the portable altar and despite the wind got a small bonfire going. Francine wondered where I was and was beginning to feel the start of worry. She looked toward the line of cars, in which mine should already have been, and debated not drawing the circle until I arrived. With the weather threatening, there wasn't much time to be spent waiting. She drew the circle and they began to gather around it, when she saw the headlights rolling up the hill and presumed it was me.

Richards, in his vampire costume, surprised them as he came into the light of the fire. The second set of lights coming up they again presumed were mine, but it was the Sheriff. Presumptions changed to that of being thrown off the land, and for all her even temper, Francine Brindley felt her hackles rising.

"You've got to leave," Richards told them and in their anger they missed the desperate urgency in his voice.

"How dare you, Robert Richards," Francine said indignantly. "Of all the years to accost us."

"No. No," he cut her off hurriedly. "I mean, you have to come with me. Willis is on his way here to finish you all off."

"What are you talking about? All of us together? That's insane."

"He isn't sane."

"How do you know this?"

"Never mind how," he returned. "I just know and you all need to hurry down to my house where you'll be safe."

"What?"

"He's right," Levinson assured them. "We came here to protect you."

"Where's India?" Francine wondered. She wanted to hear it from me. At about that point I was killing the hounds at the kitchen door.

"At my house," Richards said, not mentioning the locked door he thought I was still behind. "I'll explain everything there."

"Let me explain for you," said a deep voice in the

darkness.

They turned to find low, slinking eyes glowing red in the firelight, creeping in from three sides, pinning them to the cliff behind them. Growling, the hounds slipped from the tree line, an entire pack hemming them toward the hundred foot drop to the rocky shore.

Willis, smiling with a gleaming sword in hand, strolled from the darkness and into the light. He was at ease, almost at peace with the world and the scene before him. After a hundred years, and three personalities, he was finally going to satisfy his anger. Gray images like the suggestions of shapes of men, the Duvall males were fanned out in the darkness behind him.

"Stop right there!" Levinson ordered and drew his revolver. A hound grabbed his wrist and dragged his hand down to the ground, grinding the barrel in the muddy earth. The would-be hero of my imagined novel ended there. Willis leapt in and the sword swept down, adding Levinson's head to his collection.

The horrified Deputy drew, but Willis was imbued with unnatural speed that night and the man's hand and pistol went sailing, harmlessly to Willis, to the edge of the circle. With a scream of pain and despair, the Deputy fell back and scrambled away on his back to escape a killing blow.

Willis had spun in a different direction and Eleanor, Francine's sister that I had not met, was caught flat footed and joined the fallen, her body landing near Levinson's and her gaping head hitting the ground with a sickening thud.

The women, shielding the wounded Deputy, scurried back into a group near the edge, but within the circle. The hounds could have gotten into it had they wanted. It wasn't strong enough or meant to have kept any such things out. But the beasts were only meant to keep the women from escaping.

It was then that Richards found his courage and got between Willis and the score of women.

"Stop this, Sammic," he yelled. "You can't do this. You can't get away with killing the police. You can't keep holding us to a deal our ancestors broke over a century ago." He glanced at those ancestors with a trembling fear; gaped as he spied his father among them.

"You don't hold authority over me," Willis replied, moving inches closer to the huddled women.

Richards stayed in front of him. "Listen Sammic. You have to let it go, let me and my ancestors go," he told the crazed man. "What does it matter anymore? Father, tell him. It's already over. We're all dying out anyway."

"Your line hasn't died out yet," Willis replied calmly and motioned for one of the hounds to attack.

It bounded in and Richards' courage broke as quickly as he'd gained it. He ran instinctively away to his left, where another changed his direction again. Maybe he'd lost his sense of where he was and thought he'd turned toward the path I was then charging up. We'll never know, but the trees he dashed toward in his panic were the ones on the edge of the cliff. He simply ran off the edge and out into space, screaming like a child a hundred feet down to the river's edge.

"Now it has," growled Willis as the hounds fell in line with the others. They had all moved closer, tightening the circle on the women. The shocked Deputy stood among them, being comforted and treated by them even as they faced their own deaths.

"Your time has come. None of you will be seeing the sunrise tomorrow," he told them with a chillingly calm malice. Lightning and thunder flared and rolled in the distance and the wind kicked up the leaves. "It has been a long time coming, but I will fulfill the promise I made to destroy you all."

He scarcely motioned again and two hounds bolted into the group of women, bowling them aside like pins. From the pile, they grabbed Carla by the ankles and dragged her face down away as her sisters screamed and frantically tried to pull her back. But the other hounds pounced, beating them away. Carla was dragged to Willis' feet.

He grabbed her by the collar and lifted her up to his hips as he struck in one fluid motion. Her head rolled over toward the women, whose tears of horror and grief became uncontrollable. They fell back into a tighter pack, huddling Francine to the center. Sammic clearly meant to start with the last of his old wife's direct descendants.

But Francine calmly parted them to face Willis. He stood as though expecting her to step forward to meet her doom. There was no escaping it anymore.

"Come forward, Willis," she said, seeming to surprise him. "Step up and let us free you of Sammic."

"You dare take me for a fool?"

"It's not too late to free you of your grandfather's evil spirit," Francine told him. "Let us help you."

He just laughed hard and derisively at them. "It is definitely way too late. What would I do with such an old body if you did free me now, anyway? He will die, when I die. But you die tonight."

Hounds pushed into the women, snapping at them as they tried to push away. Scratching and biting at the women that grabbed them, the beasts would not be stopped. They nudged Francine forward from behind and pulled her by her dress. It was impossible to halt them. None of their protections worked against these creatures.

Francine bravely faced Willis as he reached out with his left hand to caress her fine face. There was a near regretful look in his eyes, an appreciation of the beauty he was about to destroy.

"The female side of the blood line was always favored with fair looks," he noted. "In a moment, that will be gone and I will be the last of the direct descendants, as I should have been the last all those ages ago, if not for the weakness of the Duvalls. They have paid for their lies and failure, down to the last heir." He glanced at the cliff where Robert had gone over.

Grasping her chin, he turned Francine's face left

and then right, admiring the beauty of his ancient wife's line. He drew the sword back deliberately, holding it up alongside him as though he needed to aim the stroke perfectly.

"And now it is time to end this," he said as I came out of the dark into the flickering light, the wind in the trees and leaves having covered the sound of my foot falls.

Hearing those words. Seeing the scene before me. I was filled with a cold dread. Only anger and a bitter need for revenge filled me more. Melissa's killer stood with a bloody sword, already killing again. Rage overwhelmed me as I came in without breaking stride and recklessly through Samuel Duvall.

His raised sword shielded the right side of his neck. I'm left handed. I swing from the left. I pivoted and twisted and put my entire body into the strike.

Then, the world went black at the sudden thud into my gut. The hounds had seen me at the last minute and crashed into me as I tried to attack.

I went flying one way. The sword went another. I hit the ground so hard my lungs were shocked empty and my eyesight and hearing were gone. For a second, there was no breath in my body. I couldn't even smell the forest.

I was dead.

The hounds would have me; searing teeth and flesh tearing claws were coming for me. My mind's eyes saw and already felt it all. Chunks of muscle bitten from my legs. Teeth crushing my wrist. Arms pulled from their sockets. Eyes clawed out. Throat rent. There was no way to escape them, but I still scrambled back to get away as clarity came to me. I took in a breath. I didn't understand it. I was not being torn apart. Nothing had touched me.

The scene came to me slowly as my vision cleared and my mind was able to take it in.

At first I saw a lone, gray wolf a few feet from me. He was looking at me motionlessly. I swear I saw a look of remorse on his face. To my right stood another regretful-looking wolf. I felt nothing but sorry for them. The fear had left me.

At the edge of the firelight, where I expected to find Willis, only Francine stood, looking down. At my feet, Willis' gaping head stared at me in surprise and seemed to be trying to speak. That artfully made sword, I thought. I hadn't missed. I had simply not felt the impact that came from the razor-sharp, finely-made blade. His body had stumbled past Francine and flopped forward, his blood running into the edge of the fire and setting off a dark, foul smoke as it crackled and burned.

In that moment, I didn't know what to feel and so, I felt it all. Relief at the end of it. Satisfaction at avenging Melissa. And, oddly, remorseful that I had killed. The sword lay glinting in the firelight near Willis' body. If I had been closer to it, I might have kicked it into the fire.

Shedding their supernatural forms, the freed wolves trotted back into the forest, empty of Duvall men, and disappeared into the night. Francine would tell me years later that the wolves often came by her gardens, keeping the rabbits at bay, as though they had been forever changed by that night and felt a kinship with, and debt owed to the Coven.

She was the first to me, making sure I was okay before crushing me in a tearful embrace.

Chapter 20
The Clearing

What more could I say about what happened that October?

We figured a lot more out over the next few days, while I stayed with Francine. How the hounds disappeared made sense now, if it was a temporary transformation by Willis. In retrospect, we felt foolish for not realizing that Richards was connected to it, given how his house had seemed to be a safe place.

It also finally came to us what Samuel Duvall had meant by not wanting to let me ruin them for all time. He had meant if I had stopped Willis from completing his revenge, then they would never have been freed from the curse. They had wanted to stop me before I learned who Willis was and stopped him.

I was never charged, of course, as it was self-defense and the defense of others. The Deputy had seen it all, although seeing apparitions and the bit about the hounds turning back into wolves left his testimony questionable. They simply wrote that off to shock. No one believed that Sammic had possessed Willis. There was no denying he was a descendant, and that he had been insane and killing people. However, possession wasn't even put in the reports. The FBI called it some kind of psychosis, but I'd have to look up the report to remember what it was called.

A section of the old mansion's roof had finally given away that Halloween night and the porch collapsed the next morning. No one was allowed in it anymore. I returned the key to Mayor Baker at City Hall. The ghosts were no longer being sensed at the old mansion, though. Sammic's death had apparently broken his curse. So, Samuel Duvall had been wrong again and Richards had gotten everything he had wanted except the chance to enjoy life without knowledge of his imminent doom. In a way, I saw that as a lesson for me, too; the one Melissa had been trying to teach me, to just enjoy what I had without worrying about a destiny I couldn't avoid. I wasn't ready to take that cavalier of an attitude.

Not just yet.

Maybe I didn't need to stress or obsess, like Richards and I had before. From then on, I chose the attitude that I was still going to be making the moves I felt were right and then work with what Fate gave me.

To make peace with her family's past, Alice Duvall secretly changed her will when she sold out and moved away. The only property she held on to was the beach house where she was going to live and eventually die in as had her daughter, Richards' mother. She was finished with Willow Creek and Missouri in general.

She swore me to secrecy and I agreed not to tell. Alice Duvall bequeathed the remains of her estate, whatever it would be when she passed, to Francine Brindley and the other witches equally in compensation for what her family had done to them, even if only to clear or appease her own soul. She had no more direct heirs left to give it to anyway and she had neither pet charities nor the desire to see any of it go to undeserving relatives. It was going to be mostly cash and liquid investments. The business was the first thing she sold, followed closely by that huge house.

While it may seem that I was breaking my promise by even mentioning it, the sad truth was that Alice Duvall had not lasted much longer after leaving Willow Creek. Heartbreak, many people felt, and disappointment at the collapse of her family and their legacy.

Francine Brindley was a bit irritated that I never

told her about Mrs. Duvall's new will, but she understood and eventually laughed over it. The estate had still been somewhat sizeable and they were still debating the best ways to use their individual shares. Suddenly coming into money was not undermining their non-materialistic ways, other than all buying good, new cars, and fixing up their homes and appliances. It was all utilitarian spending. For them, having money was actually a dilemma, which I found amusing.

I shared in it, too, indirectly. While a query for a book comparing all religions was deemed interesting by my regular publisher, the project is languishing as they seek out the perfect religious expert for me to partner with on it. In the meantime, the witches were using their newfound wealth to fund another of my ideas; a sensitive and truthful history of witchcraft in Missouri, which I have been working on with Francine.

I also ended up with the Phyllis collection at Mrs. Duvall's insistence. It was as though she hadn't wanted anything to go to people she didn't know. I had figured to donate it, but oddly, having it here as a constant reminder of what I went through helps to keep me grounded. It keeps the lessons fresh.

I never finished the Duvall family history. Alice Duvall paid me the balance of the contract to leave it undone and forgotten. With Richards dead before having children, their line had ended. There would be no more direct heirs of the men that struck the deal with Sammic, just as there would be no more direct heirs of Sammic himself with Melissa gone. There would be no one else who would care to know what happened.

I don't mean to give the impression that I'm a whole lot better off. I'm not really. Not that much. Financial troubles might still find me next year anyway, depending on how things continue to go. I'm holding my own now, though. I no longer feel like I'm fighting with life to make it work.

I'm just living life.

I still miss Melissa, but I feel I'm preserving her memory by featuring some of her words and teachings in our history of witchcraft.

Romantically, I'm with Tim, the guy with his own organic coffee shop. Despite his desire to own his own business, he isn't an alpha male type. It was more that he wanted to do something good and found a way to do it, and it wasn't eating up all of his time. We always have plenty of time for leisure after our work is done. Being with him feels right. It's been two years and we're still going strong.

Agnes struck out on her own, with a generous loan from Alice Duvall, to start her restaurant in Kansas City. She met her cowboy, happily and finally, along the way as he was doing the same thing. Together they are making a name for themselves with their country style restaurant. I was not first in line, though. Their families were in front me with all four of her sisters. They were a hoot!

Also, as much as Arthur had followed me around, it was Aubrey that had jumped into my car the day I left Willow Creek. He had sat down on the passenger seat and looked at me as if to say, "Let's go." He had no trouble adapting to city life and being mostly indoors. Of course, I give him the life of Riley. I have that little piece of Melissa with me still.

Melissa had wanted me to relax and adapt to what life was giving me. You must make some effort to build a life, but you will have wasted it, if you do not enjoy it and celebrate it for the gift that it is. I had always known that. Yet, it had taken Melissa and Willow Creek for me to learn how to walk that walk. Those were the lessons that were staying fresh.

I hope you understand what I mean. But whether you do or don't, blessed be.

The middle child of seven, growing up in Chicago in the 60's and 70's, Frank was there for the Beatles' debut, the Space Race, the Cold War, Vietnam and the first moon landing. He started writing at the age of twelve as a hobby and way of escaping the world. The nuns in his parochial grammar school always admonished him for daydreaming.

Over the years he's been a market researcher, a computer consultant, a computer store manager, an industrial tool salesman, a stay at home Dad, a Hospice business manager, a real estate attorney and a data analyst; all of which he calls his previous lives. But he never stopped writing.

As an author, he writes stories as they come to him. When asked where his ideas come from, his answer is, "Your guess is as good as mine."

Currently, he lives in Des Plaines, Illinois with his daughter and their six cats. He enjoys tending his indoor jungle, baking cheesecakes to die for, entertaining, and paranormal investigating

Correspondence may be directed to PO Box 191, Des Plaines, Illinois 60016-0191.

Made in the USA
Lexington, KY
29 June 2015